SHE SMELLS OF TURMERIC

SHE SMELLS OF TURMERIC

Natasha Sondakh

NEW DEGREE PRESS

SHE SMELLS OF TURMERIC

ISBN

978-1-63676-811-3   *Paperback*

978-1-63730-231-6   *Kindle Ebook*

978-1-63730-255-2   *Digital Ebook*

To Mom & Dad, who have raised me in the values written in these pages.

CONTENTS

*Throughout the coming ages we will be
the visible display of the infinite, limitless
riches of His grace and kindness, which
was showered upon us in Jesus Christ.*[1]

—EPHESIANS 2:7

1   Eph 2:7

Ottoman

i.
the flag slashes me with an
antique tongue, white and blue
speckled blood stars
shed for white lovers
dressed in gold leaves
leaving a trace of iron fallacies
on my broken
consciousness
forgetting

ii.
all the walls in my mind are haunted
by a voice from this flag bleeding for a
name to be recognized by those who call out
for mercy
　　　for mercy
for a grace that does not arrive on time
for colored people to regret their moralities
corrupted by a faded chastity

iii.
i ache for affirmation that seeks
to provide for a country that leaves me
bleeding dry into my *kebaya*
leaving behind a suppressed legacy:
　　　an antique ottoman
forever sitting in my living room
weight amplified by iron, by rust
by belonging to a sinister flag
that coated itself in gold

FOREWORD

———

Mom fed me *rawon* until I told her that I hated it. The Indonesian soup from Surabaya, Mom's hometown, featured beef simmering in a hot black broth, darkened by the *keluwak* nut. The soup was delicious, but its color was unappetizing for eight-year-old me, who would much rather have bright red spaghetti and golden pork schnitzels.

"You used to like *rawon*, Tish," Mom said.

"No," I lied, crossing my arms. "I don't like *rawon*. It looks like poop."

"But it's delicious."

"But I don't want it."

I only tasted *rawon* again six years later, when I turned fourteen. I learned then that the dark *keluwak* nut was what amplified the turmeric, candlenut, coriander, and other spices in the broth to make *rawon* one of the most unique and flavorful soups in the world.

As I grew older, my perspectives on Indonesia changed. I grew to prefer Indonesian food to Western food, craving *rawon* over pasta. I grew patient with Jakarta's dreadful traffic. I started to like the dirty and rickety structures that dotted the city, acknowledging that they preserved some sort of authenticity that would always remind me of home.

Indonesia is an idiosyncratic archipelago teeming with 16,056 islands, 2,500 languages, and 1,340 tribes.[1] She is home to 268 million people and over 350,000 wildlife species.[2] But in spite of her greatness, I wasn't proud of being Indonesian for most of my childhood.

I live in Jakarta, Indonesia's capital city, which is so physically dirty and polluted that as a child with asthma I hardly got to enjoy the outdoors. I wasn't allowed to walk alone outside of my gated house because my parents were concerned about my safety. Drinking tap water would guarantee a week's worth of vomiting. To put it simply, my life wasn't as cool as those characters portrayed on Disney Channel. As I often visited my birthplace in Los Angeles, I was reminded that the country of my heritage was always going to feel less: less clean, less friendly, less perfect.

I learned that Indonesia was harsh on my childhood because she wanted me to be brave, strong, and independent.

I spent the summer after I turned fifteen in New York City. An intoxicated homeless man followed me into the subway because of my "Chinese ass." A couple hours later, a White boy asked *what* (yes, "what," not "where") Indonesia was, and why *it* brought me all the way to New York City. It was the first time in my life that I felt self-conscious about how I represented myself, my country, and my heritage to the world.

---

1   Badan Pusat Statistik, *Statistik Indonesia* (Jakarta, Indonesia: Badan Pusat Statistik, 2020); Akhsan Na'im and Hendry Syaputra, *Hasil Sensus Penduduk 2010* (Jakarta, Indonesia: Badan Pusat Statistik, 2010).

2   Badan Pusat Statistik, *Statistik Indonesia*; Hayyan Setiawan, "Keanekaragaman Hewan Berdasarkan Jenisnya di Indonesia," *Ilmu Hutan* (blog).

But that summer was also the summer I met Katrine Øgaard Jensen, an award-winning Danish translator, who introduced me to the beauty of language, translation, and world literature. She encouraged me to bring Indonesian literature to the world map and taught me how to love my country so that other people can too.

When I came back to Jakarta, I started translating Indonesian literature. Although it was something that I didn't end up pursuing long-term, translating gave me an insight into the emotions behind languages, how different nuances of the Indonesian language differed from its English counterpart, and how these differences alluded to the intricacies of Indonesian culture. By translating Indonesian prose and plunging into the culture, I began to internalize how beautiful my country really is.

I wrote this book as a love letter and tribute to Indonesia. This book is a journey of self-exploration and is here for you to understand and dissect who we are and where we come from. As a Chinese-Indonesian woman with Dutch roots and an American education, my life is a melting pot of various cultures. This means that, sometimes, my American mind will nag at my Chinese upbringing, clash with my Indonesian way of thinking, and connect with my Dutch subconscious.

But this also meant that, sometimes, I felt alienated by Indonesia. By any country, to be more precise.

This alienation is a symptom of being a "third-culture kid." I attended an international high school in Jakarta, so the concept of a third-culture kid wasn't too foreign, but I had always associated it with kids who were constantly on the move and grew up abroad, not kids who felt out of place. These kids were just called "outcasts."

I guess I was one of them.

Like many of my peers, I struggled with the notion of being "perfect" and "Indonesian," as if these two concepts went hand-in-hand. I wanted to understand why I was so intrigued by them, whether these independent variables became gradually dependent on one another, and whether this equation was simply a facet of my imagination, a byproduct of upbringing and life's melancholies. But I was drawn to it because it was so toxic. Relating the two together meant that because I was Indonesian, I had to be perfect.

I had to be perfect because people would comment if I had gained a couple kilograms on vacation, would tell me not to wear jean shorts in sixth-grade because I "look like a slut," or would tell me that the medal I won for my individual performance in a debate competition "wasn't good enough" to carry the team through to finals (the only medal my team received was mine, and yes, my teammate's mom really did say this to me).

Indonesians have a phrase for it. *Jaga image*, or *jaim* for short. Indonesia's social networks are so interconnected that it could be dangerous for someone to tarnish their reputation, as it may impact job offers, future partnerships, or even marriage prospects. Oftentimes, we hid parts of ourselves that would've made us human and masked our faces in thick, complex layers to exhibit an identity beyond that which we had identified with because of the looming fear that other people would judge us for our real selves.

As I was shaped into this equation by the cultural cookie-cutter, "perfect" plus "Indonesian" ended up becoming equal to a very bad case of impostor syndrome.

Impostor syndrome is the feeling that you're not good enough, or that you don't deserve anything that you have achieved in your life. In other words, impostor syndrome is the fear of being imperfect or seeming that way. There was an illusionary idea of plastic perfection that many Indonesians felt that they had to uphold, including me.

I adorned myself with accolades instead of jewels, trying my hardest to prove that I was "perfect" and belonged to the greats. Stephen Hawking was "perfect." Jacinda Ardern was "perfect." My high school class valedictorian was "perfect." I was not. When I started attending college in the United States, I saw that everyone on campus was also "perfect." One of my roommates worked on a prototype to send to Mars. A friend graduated magna cum laude and was hired by a prestigious investment bank at age twenty. Another friend self-taught himself to code a program that could value stocks from scratch. They were all "perfect."

I was not.

Feeling like I wasn't "perfect" enough dawned on me so much that I began to question my own self-worth, and whether I was doing enough to be enough for the world. The pressure came with sleepless nights, anxiety attacks, and destructive thoughts. I was no longer happy for my friends. I was no longer happy with myself.

Eventually, I gathered the courage to confide in some friends. They told me that they, too, suffered from sleepless nights. One had an alarming alcohol dependency. One was on antidepressants. One suffered from such deep-seated anxiety that actually made them more productive in their academics. While some were fortunate enough to escape in healthier ways, the pressure to be "perfect" imposed itself upon all of us. Other friends at different universities across the world felt the exact same way.

And slowly, as I had more conversations with more people from varying backgrounds, the universe felt slightly smaller, and just a little cozier. I realized that the "perfection" we all strove for created very broken people. I realized that the "perfection" I observed didn't reflect the brokenness. I also learned that impostor syndrome is a universal concept. Feeling lost, alone, and imperfect are, too.

This book invites you to explore all the answers to the questions I've been pondering the last few years of my life. Although this book is a work of fiction, Cecilia's character is molded based on these feelings and reflections about perfection. She feels herself being confined and constricted into different silos of her identity (her familial, social, professional, Indonesian, and American identities) that she has to uphold and maintain. These different identities challenge Cecilia's notions of self-awareness, belonging, and self-worth as she navigates what it means to be Indonesian and what it means to be human.

There is a philosophy in my father's hometown of Manado, in North Sulawesi: *torang samua basudara*, which means "we are all a family." I dedicate this book to you who are searching for a place to belong to. Whoever you are, wherever you come from, I hope you will find a home and a family within these pages.

I

The Woman at the Ice Cream Parlor

is a nameless face
sipping coffee in sweatpants.

Why is a woman like her
as beautiful as Shakespeare's sonnets
drinking coffee at an ice cream parlor,
you ask. I say

that she enjoys how the windows refract

the moon's twilight
that she only eats ice-cream
with a cup of coffee

that her sweetened lips desire
more than just a caffeine high

But her face is engulfed
in rice paper and pores
dotted by acne, which
represent keyholes of a heart that
lock repressed memories
that you could read through
her tortured brown eyes.

Do you realize that she
reeks of decayed coffee leaves,
the kind that had been sitting around
in a jar for too long.

Does she not remind you
of fresh love letters
from a boy with crumpled lips
who speaks silver sentences.

1

Dad died on Christmas Eve. The fluorescent light above his lifeless body was blinding against the EKG's monotonous screech. My world moved in a slowness that amplified the bleach undertones in the air. I stared as the doctors stepped back from the crash cart and hung their heads to say little prayers. Nurses in Santa hats peeked in from outside Dad's hospital room, their eyes brimming with pity. People died all the time, but it was cruel for them to die on Christmas.

Mom wailed while the doctors tried to restrain her. It was difficult. She broke free, clawed her way to Dad's bed, and pounded her fists at the man who betrayed his promise of forever. His stillness shredded her insides. I fisted my hands, digging my fingernails into my palms until they drew blood. Dad's silence was torture. I refused to cry in front of strangers, but Dad's peaceful state was heartbreaking. I shattered to the ground and shrieked into the dirty floors, refusing to look at the doctors who pulled a cloth over his head and wheeled him into the morgue.

Cancer stripped away a life that was just short of forty-seven years.

A week before his death, when the sunlight was warm and the EKG was melodic, Dad was healthy, or rather, he seemed to be. After a treacherous brain surgery that withered his body weight and drained the color from his face, Dad was still smiling.

The doctors told us he was recovering well. We visited him when he was out of the ICU and brought his favorite things: his Kindle, his iPad to watch Netflix, and his favorite bathrobe, monogrammed in glorious gold threads. Dad's hospital room was chilly in the early morning. I hugged my cold arms, but Dad asked me to join him on his narrow hospital bed. Mom helped me up to make sure that I wouldn't trample on his tubes. He wanted us to browse the internet to see what white dress I should wear to graduation next year to make sure that I "wouldn't pick out one that was short enough that the boys could see my underwear."

"I'm twenty-one," I said, playfully nudging him. "I'm also turning twenty-two in January."

"No, you're not," Dad smirked. "In my eyes, you're always three years old."

"Dad…" I rolled my eyes a little.

"Do you remember when we sneaked out in the middle of the night to get ice cream?"

"Yes, I do."

"Yeah, and we snuck past Mom who was snoring like a gorilla."

"Hey!" Mom said, looking up from her phone. "I don't snore!"

"Honey, I've lived with you for, what, twenty-five years now? Ask CeCe. You snore."

"It's true, Mom," I said.

Dad patted my head.

"You want to know what you sound like?" Dad said.

Dad proceeded to imitate Mom's snoring. His nostrils flared as he breathed out a loud, harsh sound. The fluids he was connected to, though, refused to let him finish.

"James," Mom said, rushing to his side as he decided to cough. She grabbed his hand and squeezed.

"I'm okay, Kari," Dad said. "I'm okay, I promise."

Little did I know that those would be Dad's last words.

Mom and I helped Dad set up Netflix on his iPad. We watched *Narcos* with him until he fell asleep. Then we went home, hoping to return the following afternoon after Mom's work.

But when the doctor called us that night and told us that Dad was unconscious, we dropped everything and rushed back to the hospital. I saw him connected to even more tubes this time, one shoved down his trachea, yet he was undisturbed by our tears. Dad's face was so serene. It was undoubtedly the most peace he had felt in years. I didn't want to accept that, though. The fact was that Dad had slipped into a coma in front of our eyes and we decided to leave him.

The doctors said that this moment of lucidity was common among patients who had undergone major surgeries, that his coma wasn't caused by us leaving him, but Mom and I were too wracked with guilt to listen. They had warned us about the risks of emergency brain surgery. They had told us what it meant when his benign tumor had metastasized into a cancerous one. They had told us that he only had three months left if we left his malignant brain tumor alone, that surgery, albeit risky, was the best option for him.

I knew then that he wouldn't live to see my college graduation. But I wasn't ready to say goodbye.

We buried Dad at the turn of the new year. Mom told me to take care of myself while she handled all the funeral arrangements. My paternal grandparents flew in from Indonesia to attend the funeral. I wondered why they hadn't come for the surgery. I wondered why they had never visited at all.

A light Californian rain greeted us as we lowered Dad six feet underground. I wailed into Mom's arms as I tossed a handful of dirt over his casket. I was numb throughout the next couple of days. I couldn't eat. I struggled to get out of bed. I stopped seeing friends. I lost so much weight that I couldn't recognize myself. Life wasn't the same without Dad. It never could be.

Dad's loss was a weight that trailed behind me like a shadow. His ghost lingered in my bedroom, my dreams, and as a permanent scent on my clothes. I broke down whenever I sat next to his favorite couch. I struggled through the second semester of junior year. I refused to enter his empty home office, and Mom refused to put his things away.

Mom told me that Dad would want me to live a normal life, that he couldn't rest peacefully if he saw me like this. But no matter how hard I tried, I felt like I would never recover from the gaping hole that Dad had left in my heart.

+

I graduated cum laude with a bachelor of arts in economics from the University of Southern California. Dad had left us for a year, which meant that Mom and I had received grief counseling for at least nine months at that point. It was probably the only way we managed to make it through the toughest year of our lives.

I wore a white dress that went past my knees. It was the least I could do to honor Dad's second wish, since I couldn't honor his first, taking a photo with my USC diploma as a family. I spotted Mom in the ocean of heads, waving as her face lit up and wilted simultaneously. I knew, then, that she was thinking of Dad. I was too.

As I waved goodbye to the friends and professors that I would probably never see again, Mom ran towards me, hugging me so tightly that she started tearing up. When Mom cried, I did too.

"I am so proud of you, CeCe," she said.

"Thank you, Mommy," I said.

"Dad's proud of you too. You know that, right?"

"I do."

Dad's favorite BMW cruised down the 110 freeway to take us from downtown LA to Pasadena for lunch. My best friend Macy met us at Boiling Point with her mom Jennifer. We decided to meet up once more before she left for Seattle the next day.

Macy bounced towards me as I alighted from the car. She looked different today. Her auburn hair was curled and tucked neatly behind her ears. Her green eyes complemented the multiple graduation cords on her neck, each symbolizing academic honors of the highest degree.

"Wow, Valedictorian," I exclaimed, pointing at her neck. "Microsoft made the right choice hiring you."

"Don't," Macy said. "I can't believe I'm going to be working on Monday. I feel so incredibly old."

"You're an adult, Macy dear," Jennifer said, squeezing her. "Own it."

She was so much smarter than I was, but she never bragged about it. When we were assigned as roommates in freshman year, Macy always had people over to help them out with their homework. Her genuine kindness was what sparked our friendship. If Macy wasn't tutoring her friends, she was cramming for her classes.

We entered the quaint restaurant that specialized in pan-Asian hot pot soups, decorated with brick and wood. By the time we were seated, a line had started to snake around the block.

The dishes were served on a bowl with a flame underneath to keep hot. In the past, Macy and I would drive up to Pasadena from campus to celebrate the end of midterm or finals season. In a way, eating at Boiling Point one last time before we parted ways felt poetic.

"This tastes so good," Jennifer said.

"Right? Thank God CeCe introduced me to Boiling Point," Macy continued, chowing down on her Angus Beef Hot Pot. "They have this in Seattle too, you know?"

"They do? Why didn't you tell me?"

"Well, mother, you said you didn't like Asian food."

A wide-eyed Jennifer slurped up a couple strands of enoki mushroom, smiling sheepishly.

"Well," Jennifer shrugged. "I like sushi, but that's about it."

"Have you considered trying Indonesian food, Jennifer?" Mom asked.

"Oh my gosh, Mom, you have to try Indonesian food." Macy said.

"What's that like? Is it like sushi?"

"They have the best fried rice, Mom. Also this dish, I'm totally going to butcher its name...*suh-tay uh-yeam*?"

"Oh! *Sate ayam!*" Mom said. Her face always lit up whenever people talked about Indonesia.

"Yes, *sate ayam*. It's delicious." Macy said.

I chewed on my fingernails when Mom proceeded to explain that *sate ayam* was barbecued chicken skewers with peanut sauce. The whole conversation made me shrink. While I enjoyed *rendang* and *sate ayam*, I was anything but

Indonesian. I looked Chinese, lived in America, and only spoke English. I felt guilty calling myself Indonesian when I knew nothing about the country.

The last time I went to Indonesia was when I was five, for my Makco Dora Ai-Ling Chen's funeral. Mom's grandma. I didn't know that Makco meant great-grandmother until quite recently; I had always thought that she was a distant relative, perhaps my grandma's cousin. Makco lived to a hundred and three but still looked like she was eighty.

Jennifer made it a commitment to find an Indonesian restaurant in Seattle. She was excited about the prospect of exploring new cultures. Macy apologized for her mom's lack of knowledge about Asian cultures, but Mom and I were already used to people not knowing about Indonesia at that point, especially after living in America for so long.

After we paid for our respective meals, Macy walked out with me.

"CeCe," she said. "I want to give you something before I leave."

Macy handed me a silver bracelet. It was engraved with the words *Cecilia Poetry & Macy Dearborn*.

"I know it's a little pricey, but I wanted to show you how much you mean to me," Macy said.

"Macy..."

Enveloping the bracelet in my palms, I felt tears blossom in my eyes. I couldn't believe how much she must have saved up for this.

"Just mail my gift to Seattle," Macy said. "Trust yourself, CeCe. Trust that whatever you do, wherever you end up, you'll be just fine."

"Says you, Microsoft, to my unemployed ass."

"What do you mean?"

"I'm still waiting to hear back from jobs, Mace. I'd take anything at this point. I'd even clean for Microsoft if they would offer me a job."

Macy took my hands. Her green eyes pierced into mine. "CeCe, look at it this way. You have the whole world at your fingertips. You can literally do whatever you want now! Unlike me, you don't have to worry so much about earning an income. I'd love to write a novel or bake cupcakes all day, but I have to support myself."

"Maybe I *should* write a novel or bake cupcakes all day." I chuckled.

"You can though!" Macy smiled. "Not everyone is as lucky as you, having a constant stream of capital from relatives you barely know."

"You know how complicated our relationship is with my grandparents, especially after Dad died."

"And I live with my grandparents, who are pretty much useless. I am that constant stream of income for my family, especially after Max and my mom split. I would never say this, but thank goodness for big tech."

"And your big brain."

"Sure, yeah. That only helps a little though," Macy rolled her eyes. "Cut yourself some slack, babe. Your dad passed away during recruitment season. The fact that you still tried to recruit for jobs last summer clearly shows your insane grit."

Macy came in for a hug.

"It's hard to recruit as a senior when all the good firms are only recruiting full-time from their summer intern pool," I said.

"Well, yeah," Macy said. "I know that. But what I'm trying to say is, don't be pressured to do what everyone else is doing. Life moves at different speeds for every person. And you have a luxury to do life how *you* want to, babe. You, of all people, have your shit together. Trust me, C. You'll be fine."

My eyes started to blur from the tears. I never had a friend as wise and kind as Macy.

Mom and I bid our goodbyes to Macy and Jennifer and hopped into the car. I knew that Macy's new job in Seattle would prevent her from seeing me as often as we both would've liked. I wondered how, in my joblessness, I could find another friend like her.

Fragments of orange sunlight spilled onto the surface of my graduation gown as we drove back to Beverly Hills. As I beamed at my glowing toga, I pondered on Macy's words. I hadn't heard back from any of the thirty-something jobs that I'd applied to. I grew anxious at the thought that I was going to be jobless.

Maybe I should apply for a teaching job in Westwood so I have something to do in the meantime.

As we exited the freeway, Mom's phone rang. It was Oma Shaan, my paternal grandmother in Indonesia. Mom and I looked at each other; she never called us. She hadn't checked up on us since we dropped her and Opa Robby off at LAX after Dad's funeral.

The only other time I had seen Oma Shaan was when I was five, when my family went to Jakarta for Makco's funeral. In the same way that I didn't remember much of Jakarta, I didn't remember much of my grandparents, either. They never visited us. They never called, until they started sending money a few years ago for Dad's startup. Even that felt odd. Dad would always brush off the conversation when Mom tried to ask about it.

"Hello, Mama?" Mom said.

"Karina?" Oma said, her Indonesian accent permeating through the dashboard.

"Yes, Ma," Mom said. "Cecilia is here too."

"Hi, Oma Shaan," I said.

"Oh, hello Nonik," Oma said. "Congrats, ya, on your graduation."

"Thank you, Oma."

"Mm," she said. "I wanted to say something to you both."

"Sure, Ma," Mom said. "What's up?"

"Karina, I'm not your friend," Oma said. "Please don't use that kind of 'what's up' language with me."

Mom and I looked at each other. Mom had always had a strained relationship with Oma Shaan. Oma never approved of Dad's marriage with her, which was partly why my parents refused to go back to Indonesia.

"Nonik, Opa Robby wants you to come to Indonesia once you're done settling your school stuff," she said. "Can you come here at the end of the month?"

The end of the month? I looked at mom, my anxious eyes meeting hers. Going to Indonesia wasn't actively on my mind, let alone packing up and moving thousands of miles away from Mom.

The silence stretched until it became awkward to answer.

"What? What's wrong with that?" Oma said.

"Ma," Mom said. "It's too soon. CeCe just graduated. She still wants to explore her opportunities here."

"What is Cecilia going to do there anyway? Do you have a job, Nonik?" Oma said, her tone rising.

"No, Oma," I said. "I don't."

"See?" Oma said. "If you don't have a job, then why do you want to stay there? Maybe it's better if you come home."

Home is where Mom and Dad are. Home is where I grew up. Home is here, in LA.

Mom and I kept quiet.

"I'm giving you until tonight to give me an answer. If you're still going to insist on answering 'no,' then go talk to Opa yourself, okay?"

"Okay, Ma," Mom said.

Oma Shaan hung up.

The rest of the car ride was silent. I rested my head on the window, staring out at the dark clouds while Dua Lipa played on KIIS FM. I had no idea what was going to happen to me for the rest of my life, but going to Indonesia had never crossed my mind.

We pulled over to a curb near our apartment on Sunset Boulevard.

"CeCe," Mom said, taking my hands.

I looked away.

"Your oma did bring this up to me before today," she said.

"What?" I said. "Why didn't you tell me?"

"They told me not to," Mom said. "Look, honey, your grandparents are already in their seventies. They want to connect with you before they get even older."

"I know."

"I think they regret not spending time with Dad before he died. And now they want to make up for lost time with you."

"But Mom, I barely know them, I—"

"And, you know, they did help us pay for Dad's chemo and startup losses. You know how hard it's been for us lately."

In the last six months before Dad's passing, my parents fought into the night over unpaid debts and piling medical bills. It took a while for Mom to convince Dad to ask for Oma and Opa's help, but for some reason, Dad would always refuse.

"I'll get a job, Mom. I was thinking earlier that I could get a teaching job at Westwood and work nights bussing tables, and then—"

"Sweetie," Mom said, stroking my forehead. "You know I can't let you do that. I can't let you live a life like I did. Not when you have this amazing opportunity to explore your heritage."

I looked down at the rim of my white dress, stained with Dad's words and the promise I made to him years ago about eventually visiting Indonesia again.

"I miss him, Mom."

"I know. I know that this is a hard decision. But I also know that doing this would have made Dad really happy."

"I guess."

"Even though he had a strained relationship with them, Dad really wanted you to get to know your grandparents and, you know, reconnect with his side of the family," Mom said. "You know how much he talked about his childhood in Indonesia. Although Dad might not have meant literally moving there, you know, maybe it might be nice."

The remainder of Mom's words faded into the engine's buzz. We arrived home in time to eat an awkward dinner, refusing to acknowledge the huge elephant that Oma had dropped into the room. I helped Mom with the dishes, then she left to vacuum the living room.

I couldn't fall asleep that night. The only exposure I had to Indonesian culture was Mom's food and some of my parents' Indonesian friends, whom I didn't even connect all that well with. While the prospect of moving to a whole new country was both nerve-wracking and exciting, I couldn't help but realize that the distance from home would make me feel so alone.

I thought about Dad. I thought about his flat heartbeat, his casket underground, and his smell that still lingered in our house. I thought about how much he talked about Oma and Opa even though they rarely called.

Most of all, I thought about how he missed Indonesia. He would constantly rave about "beautiful Indonesia." Mom would refer to Indonesia as Dad's first wife while she was his second. He talked about his adventures in Indonesia as a boy, following Opa Robby to his home in Manado, where he would dive into the sparkling ocean, inviting the diverse array of fish to devour his breadcrumbs. He had munched on cuttlefish and pastries from street vendors in Pontianak; hiked up Mount Ijen with his high school classmates, where he saw the blue fire, remnants of burning sulfur; and walked alongside Komodo dragons on the island of Flores. He would constantly talk about how he would find excuses to go on Opa's yacht and zip away to the Thousand Islands off Jakarta, where he would explore quiet islands, go jet-skiing, and swim alongside tiny fish and monitor lizards.

Dad's adventures in Indonesia had always attracted me, especially since our initial intention for going back there as a family was to visit the places he had raved about. But because he feared Oma and Opa, it never happened. And now, that perfect family vacation wasn't even possible anymore.

I only knew Indonesia through Dad's eyes. But maybe it was time for me to explore the country on my own. Perhaps I could go there, live with my grandparents, get to know them a little better, and see for myself what Dad had talked about for years. Maybe I hadn't heard back from opportunities here for a reason. Maybe getting a job there won't be so bad.

"Mom," I said, bursting out of my bedroom.

"Yes, dear?" Mom looked up from the couch, pausing an episode of her Korean drama show.

"Do you have a spare suitcase I can use?"

"Yeah...Why?"

"I'm moving to Jakarta."

2

Macy had called me earlier today. She was elated when I told her that I had decided to move to Jakarta. I was worried about the fourteen-hour time difference that could make it difficult to keep in touch, but she assured me that she'd always make time to call or text.

I tossed an old t-shirt from high school into Mom's red suitcase. Dad raved about the sweltering heat and humidity that dominated Indonesia, so I stuffed the suitcase with my favorite sundresses and summer clothing. Oma booked my flight from LA to Jakarta for a week from today, so Mom and I decided to spend my last week in LA packing and taking care of last-minute housekeeping items. I felt guilty leaving Mom behind to take care of things by herself.

Just as I rummaged through my closet to dig up some jeans to bring to Jakarta, Mom's phone rang.

"CeCe," Mom called out from the kitchen. "Can you get that?"

"Okay," I said, searching the living room for Mom's phone.

Her phone was buried in between the cushions of Dad's favorite couch. Mom had been sleeping there for the past few days while a contractor repainted her room, so the couch was cluttered with blankets, pillows, and Mom's notebooks. She wanted to paint over the beige walls because it was a boring color, but deep down I knew that she repainted her bedroom so it wouldn't remind her too much of Dad. Mom's pride would never let her admit that, though.

When I dug up her phone, the caller ID read Shaan de Jong. It was Oma Shaan. I put her on speakerphone while I tidied up the rest of Mom's things.

"Hello?" I said.

"Karina?" Oma said. "Why did you take so long to answer the phone?"

"It's Cecilia, Oma." I said.

"Oh. Hello, Nonik," Oma said. "Where is your mom?"

"She's cooking."

Oma clicked her tongue.

"*Aiya*, you girls are there alone," she said. "Why don't you get some help? Hire a maid?"

"It's alright, Oma. We manage pretty well on our own."

"Ah, you Americans," Oma said. "You're so stubborn."

I fluffed the throw blanket and folded it in half.

"Anyway, Nonik," Oma interrupted. "You need to get a job."

"A *what*?"

"Yes. Opa wants you to get a job. Preferably before you come here next Wednesday."

I slumped onto the newly made couch.

Oh my god. A job.

Since I had decided to move to Jakarta two weeks ago, I was so focused on packing and spending my last days with Mom that I'd completely forgotten about my career plans.

My heart pounded like rumbling thunder. Sweat beaded on my palms. *Where do I start? How do I start? Do Indonesian companies list jobs on LinkedIn? Are companies even recruiting for full-time jobs at the end of May?* I was overthinking so much that I forgot to speak. I shuffled in my seat, fixing my eyes on Mom as she gracefully tossed mushrooms in her pan.

"Nonik? Hello? Nonik, are you there?" Oma asked.

"Yes, yes," I said, sitting back down on the couch. "Sorry, Oma, I'm here."

"Why are you so quiet? You're going to talk about how you don't want to work, right?"

"No, I—"

"Don't worry, Nonik. Anyway, you have to. It'll look bad if Opa Robby's granddaughter isn't working."

"No, Oma, I do want to work. I just—"

"Good. Then find one, okay?"

"Oma, I don't even have an Indonesian passport. It'll be really hard for me to get an entry-level job as a foreigner."

"Don't worry about that. With Opa's connections you'll get an Indonesian passport before you get here on Wednesday."

"No, Oma," I said. My voice was crisp but hoarse. "I don't need Opa's help. I can manage on my own."

What did Opa Robby do for a living to be able to get a passport so easily?

Passport or no passport, I couldn't let Mom feel obligated by my grandparents' help.

"See!" Oma started to raise her voice. "You're so stubborn, just like your mother. Why can't you just accept Opa's help?"

"It's not that I don't want to, I just—"

"Fine. Just get a job before you get here. Your start date should be the Monday after you arrive."

"That's so soon, Oma!" I exclaimed.

"Just get it done, okay? Make Oma and Opa proud. Bye bye."

Oma hung up the phone, leaving me with a billion questions and nowhere to start.

Too anxious to eat lunch, I pushed the mushrooms around my plate while I updated Mom on my phone call with Oma.

"Oma Shaan does everything out of love," Mom said. "I know she can be a lot sometimes, but try to make her happy. She loves you a lot."

Mom was like that. She was so gentle that many people took advantage of her kindness, including Oma and Opa.

Together, after washing the dishes, Mom and I whipped out LinkedIn on my laptop to start my job search. From positions in human resources, quality assurance, and purchasing, LinkedIn had it all. But I wasn't interested. I had always wanted to work in a startup after Dad started his. He told me about the insane learning curve and the excitement that came from being an entrepreneur of some sort. I tried applying at startups in LA and the Bay Area, but I hadn't heard back from any of them. Any startup would do at this point.

"Here! Look at this." Mom pointed at the screen. "Tokopedia is hiring!"

"What?"

"Tokopedia," Mom said. "It's an Indonesian e-commerce marketplace. My friends buy stuff from there all the time."

"Oh, wow," I said. "I'll apply."

We found a couple job openings in Jakarta's start-up scene. They all sounded interesting. In addition to Tokopedia, there was Gojek, Halodoc, OVO, Traveloka, and Ruangguru. I had no idea what these companies were, but Mom said that they were all successful startups based in Indonesia.

I applied. I sent in my resumé and cover letter through their career portals, anxious when I checked the box indicating that I required visa sponsorship to work in Indonesia.

In between chores and packing, Mom and I would go to Urth Caffé on Melrose. Macy always commented that I was very cliché for liking that cafe so much. But I knew that nothing in Jakarta could match their Rumi Latté, a gorgeous blend of turmeric, cinnamon, and oat milk. Dad, who was lactose intolerant like me, always complained about Indonesia not having enough dairy-free options.

As my departure date inched closer, our trips to Urth Caffé became a daily occurrence. Mom and I enjoyed people watching while sipping on our hot lattes.

"Did you get anything yet?" Mom asked one day.

I scrolled through my inbox, which remained empty.

"Nope."

My heart raced as Oma's dreaded deadline neared with every passing minute.

"It's okay, my CeCe," Mom said, reaching over our drinks to stroke my hair. "It doesn't mean you're not qualified."

I looked down at my fingers. That's what Mom had been saying ever since I got rejected from jobs in LA. But she was my mom. She was supposed to say things like that.

"It's actually unfair that Oma is making you do this so last minute," Mom said. "Companies are hard on foreigners in the entry-level because they are obligated to pay you higher. So don't feel too bad about not getting anything, especially after just two days."

I knew that. But it didn't change the fact that I still didn't have a job.

The next morning, I woke up to yet another empty inbox. I walked out of my bedroom, wiping the sleep out of my eyes when Mom came to me with a cup of coffee in her hand.

"Morning, sweetie," she said, handing me the dairy-free, creamed coffee.

"Morning. Is the contractor still coming today?"

"I called Opa Robby."

Mom looked hopeful, but I couldn't anticipate any great news coming out of a conversation with my grandparents.

"Mom, I told you not to ask for help from—"

"Here."

Mom grabbed a crumpled piece of paper from her pocket and pressed it in my hands.

"Opa Robby gave us a list of twenty potential companies to look into," Mom said. "They're all early-stage startups, and he thinks you'll like at least one of them."

Did Opa Robby know me enough to know what I'd like?

"Oh, and CeCe, Opa said that if you have trouble applying, you could just work at his office."

I gasped, spilling coffee on the table by Dad's couch. Mom rushed to the kitchen to grab some paper towels. She scurried back and blotted them on the table.

"I'm sorry." I helped Mom clean up the spillage. "I'm sorry, Mom, but I can't work there. Working with Opa just goes against everything that you and Dad worked for."

"It's just a back-up plan in case things don't work out, honey," Mom said, wiping the table down. Luckily nothing spilled onto the white couch.

I couldn't let Oma Shaan and Opa Robby strengthen their grip over my family.

"I don't need a back-up plan, Mom," I said.

"I know you don't. But it's there in case you need it."

I whipped open my laptop and started whizzing through Google to look up all the companies Mom listed. Bombarded with a cacophony of colored pixels, my vision spun. The startups ranged from healthcare and media to tech and mining, which were all interesting industries, but nothing that was inherently *me*.

The last company on the list was the only one with a very Indonesian sounding name. Kopi Sedap. I had no idea what it meant, but I had already run out of options.

Kopi Sedap introduced itself through an HD picture of coffee beans. It was a clean, minimalist website, with black and white hues and a signature emerald tint that popped in their logo. Kopi Sedap had ten locations across Jakarta and was a subsidiary of an Indonesian conglomerate company, Macan Group. Their motto was to "Brew Authentic and Traditional Indonesian Coffee."

I could get behind that.

Kopi Sedap didn't have an official career portal or a listed HR contact online, so I sent my resumé and cover letter to the email that Opa listed next to the company name.

As a reward for finally picking a job site, Mom treated me to a drink at Urth Caffé. The queue that day was longer than usual, but at that point, the cafe's staff already became familiar with what we liked.

"Cecilia, right?" the barista asked when I made it to the front of the line. "The usual? A Rumi Latté with extra cinnamon?"

"Yes ma'am," I said.

We couldn't get a seat in the cafe this time, so Mom and I decided to enjoy our lattes in the car. I chose a longer route home to admire the city.

"I'm going to miss LA," I said.

"I'm sure Jakarta will be just as nice," Mom said.

"I hope so."

From the palm trees to the jammed highways and glorious sunsets, I'd never enjoyed LA in its full beauty. The buzzing metropolis was always full of life and culture. The international cuisines, art districts, and healthy outdoor spaces made for a great childhood. Living in Jakarta didn't seem like it would be anything too different, but I was nervous for the changes that could arise from leaving the home that I'd known for my whole life.

"Actually, CeCe, is it okay if we get In-N-Out for dinner?" Mom asked.

"Of course," I said. "You don't want to cook?"

"Not today. I feel tired after dealing with the contractor."

I glanced at Mom. Her hair was frizzy, bags sagged under her eyes, and her complexion was paler than usual. To put it simply, Mom was exhausted. And I knew that she was going to feel even more tired after I left.

Maybe Oma was right to suggest that we get a part-time housekeeper to help around the house.

We took a further detour to stop by the In-N-Out on Sherman Oaks to get our favorites—two Double-Doubles, fries, and a chocolate milkshake. Mom lit up instantly as she sank her teeth into the burger.

Another thing I was going to miss about LA was how many drive-through restaurants there were.

"How do you feel about Kopi Sedap?" Mom asked, mid-chew.

"I mean," I said, driving out onto the streets. "It's not my first choice, but it's better than everything else Opa listed. Plus, I haven't heard anything from the startups you suggested."

"Yeah. I'm sorry Oma threw this on you so last minute. Let's just see how things go."

"I don't know, Mom. I'm not hopeful at this point."

"You never know, CeCe," Mom said, sipping on the milkshake we shared. "Check your email tonight. Don't give up hope yet."

Upon returning home, I showered and did a little more packing. I also checked my email before going to bed. Kopi Sedap had invited me to a phone interview the next day. I rushed out of my room. Mom was lying on her couch. "Mom!" I cried. "They invited me to an interview!" "That's amazing, honey," Mom said. "Do you need to prepare?" "I think it'll be fine. How hard can it be?"

Mom brought me some chamomile tea and essential oils to make sure that I slept well that night since I had to be up at 6:00 a.m. for the interview.

+

"Hello?" I croaked into the phone.

I hadn't had my morning coffee yet.

"Hello, Cecilia?" the voice said. "This is David from Kopi Sedap. How are you today?"

"Yes, it's me."

"Yes, I know. How are you?"

Sweat drenched my palms.

"Oh, yes, I'm good, and you?"

"I'm fine, thank you. So Cecilia, before we begin the formal interview, I'll tell you a little bit about myself and the company. Does that sound good to you?"

"Yeah, totally."

"Perfect. My name is David Kwok. I am the founder and CEO of Kopi Sedap."

I'm interviewing with the CEO?

"I did my undergrad at Babson College, my master's at Stanford, and worked at McKinsey in SF. And then I came back to Jakarta to be near my family. I founded Kopi Sedap on the premise that Indonesia has a large demand and market for coffee, but a lack of infrastructure to deliver affordable, high-quality coffee to the masses."

"That's cool," I said.

"Alright, that's all about me. Now tell me about yourself."

I froze. My tongue tied itself into a knot. Letters that once formed words were now tangled in gibberish. I took a deep breath to stop myself from embarrassment. By the time I collected myself and gathered the courage to answer, twenty seconds had passed.

"Hello? Cecilia?"

I jolted.

"Yes! Yes, I…Sorry, the WiFi cut out."

It hadn't. I'm sure David knew that too.

"Sure. Please continue."

The sweat collected underneath my arms and started dripping. While invisible to David, I felt very self-conscious.

"Yeah, um, so I just graduated from the University of Southern California with a degree in economics. What else…on campus I was an opinion columnist at the Daily Trojan. I was part of some clubs here and there. I applied to Kopi Sedap because I'm really interested in coffee and people."

"Can you not speak Bahasa Indonesia?"

"What?"

"You didn't pronounce Kopi Sedap properly. It's *koh-pee suh-dahp*, not *co-pee say-dahp*."

"Oh, sorry, um, I was …I was born and raised in California, so I can't speak Indo."

"I see."

I swallowed my tongue listening to David typing on his computer.

"Mm," David cleared his throat. "Tell me why you want to move to Indonesia."

"I, um, my grandparents are there," I said. "And, oh yeah, my dad, he died a while ago."

"My condolences."

"Thanks. He was a great guy. He taught me a lot of things, like how to ride my bike and how to cook his signature scrambled eggs. I miss him."

"Okay, so—"

"But yeah, he, well, he and my mom, um, are from Indonesia."

"I see," David trailed off. He exhaled into the phone. "So why do you want to work at Kopi Sedap?"

"Um...um...I guess I've always been interested in coffee," I answered.

Oh god.

"Have you looked at our website or spoken to anyone else in the firm?"

"Yes! Yes, I, um, saw the really big coffee bean picture on your website. I loved that, I mean, I really love coffee... and, you know, this would be my first full-time job, so I'd love to get my hands dirty in a startup since you get a lot of experience in one, and I just think that brewing authentic Indonesian coffee is great in general; it's just that I don't have much experience in the industry, you know? But, of course, I'll contribute anything I can; my perspective as an American could greatly benefit your organization, I think."

I exhaled. *That did not go well.*

"Okay. Where do you see yourself fitting in in our organization?" David asked.

"What ...um, what do you mean?"

"I mean, you wrote in your cover letter that you're, let's see here, 'interested to gain work experience in any field.' We do have an opening to work under our Chief Marketing Officer. Is that something you might be interested in?"

"Yes," I cleared my throat. "Yeah, I could do marketing. I could do anything you want me to, really. If you take a look at my resumé, I took a few marketing classes at USC, and I also did a marketing pitch for a boutique near campus as part of a club project."

"Did you win the pitch?"

"Sorry?"

"I mean, did the boutique end up choosing you to help with their marketing?"

"No."

My upper body shivered as I listened to the deafening sound of David typing on his keyboard.

"Alright, Miss Cecilia," David said. "Thank you for your time. You'll hear back from us within the week."

"That's it?"

"Yes. Thank you."

"Oh, okay," I chuckled nervously, wiping away a bead of sweat. "Thank you, David."

David hung up. *That definitely didn't go well.*

I checked the call log. What felt like an hour turned out to only be a ten minute-phone call. Feeling defeated, I curled into my bedsheets to drown in my shame.

The following day, against all odds, Kopi Sedap offered me a position as their Growth Strategist. My jaw dropped as I scanned the email. They said I was passionate, driven, and was the right fit for the company's culture. The interview hadn't gone as badly as I thought it did after all.

I scratched my head. *They liked me?*

"Oh my god! You got it, CeCe!" Mom squealed, holding my shoulders. "I thought you said the interview went badly?"

"I guess not," I said.

Mom hugged me. "I knew you could do it, honey," she said. "Let me go grab some champagne to celebrate."

I swirled the champagne in its flute with a plastic grin plastered on my face. Traumatic memories of the interview with David flashed in front of my eyes. The sweat, the nerves, and the stumbling words all culminated into an acceptance letter? Kopi Sedap was on its way to become the next Starbucks. And they chose me to be a part of their story.

I clinked the champagne flute with Mom's, sipping it and feeling the heat from the alcohol fill my body and expel the negativity. Nothing made sense, but it didn't matter because the fact was that I got the job. I was definitely underestimating myself. My resumé stood out more than I had anticipated. David liked me. He liked well-rounded people who were willing to jump at the opportunity to get their hands dirty. That's what I presented, and that's what he hired. I hadn't entered Indonesia yet, but it was already treating me well.

In Macy's words, *I was going to be fine.*

3

We arrived at LAX a little late. Traffic on the 101 had plagued our journey. Anxious travelers wheeled their children and luggage into the international departures terminal, trying to handle all ten pieces by themselves to avoid those ridiculous SmartCart fees. Mom stopped our car at the curb where I attempted to do the same.

A man rushed over when he saw me visibly stumble with my luggage. He carried my boxes all the way to the check-in counter while Mom parked the car. I gave him a ten dollar bill for being so kind, but I never got his name.

Mom ran over to the check-in counter from the parking lot, her cheeks flushed with exhaustion. When I locked eyes with her, I knew that we didn't have much time to say goodbye.

"Mom..." I said, coming in for a hug. Tears blurred my vision.

Mom kissed my forehead.

"Take care, okay?" Mom said, her voice shaky from the tears.

"I will, Mommy."

Tears started pouring down my cheeks. When Mom cried, I cried too.

"I love you, CeCe. You'll always be my princess."

"Love you," I said. "Take care."

As I walked away from her, I could feel myself leaving a trail of memories with every step. *Frolicking in the park as a little girl. Bumping into Ariana Grande at Disneyland. Driving by Antelope Valley's poppy field. Getting drunk at Korean karaoke bars with Macy and my USC friends.* I shed my scales to make room for new skin, but in the process, I felt cold and naked.

I boarded the plane that I trusted to carry me 8,000 miles across the Pacific Ocean. The city I grew up in shrunk and twinkled as the plane ascended, soaring above the hills and roads I called home. More memories floated down like feathers into the city. *Eating Indonesian food in Westwood with Mom, scootering around Santa Monica with Dad, running away after cops were called to a frat party, having my first kiss by the Hollywood sign.* As the plane faded into the clouds, each memory went along with it.

Reminiscing on the past twenty-three years of my life in LA made me start craving more. I craved the In-N-Out burgers I would eat after a night out. I craved Mom's delicious Shakshouka egg. I craved Dad. I craved it all.

And it was among the flood of happy memories, the tears I drenched myself in, and the plane's hum cocooning my ears that I lulled myself to sleep.

+

Jakarta welcomed me with torrential rain. I stared outside the plane's window as we taxied towards the terminal, watching each droplet slide down the window and magnify my view of Soekarno-Hatta International Airport.

Music blasted in my AirPods as I disembarked from the plane. The terminal was long and spacious. My body was sticky in the humidity. I was disoriented. I went with the crowd, following the trail of feet and wheels that guided me to wherever I was going.

Oma had called me whilst I was in transit in Tokyo. She told me to look out for a man called Mr. Sugeng, or Pak Sugeng, as one would say in Indonesian, at the airport, who worked for Opa's company. She told me that he would be dressed in the black Mandala Group uniform and holding up a sign with my name on it. Pak Sugeng was going to "help me out at the airport," Oma had said.

I wasn't quite sure what she meant.

After the long, ten-minute walk halfway across the terminal, I saw a man dressed in black from head to toe with the Mandala Group logo embroidered on his chest. He was about my height, perhaps even a little shorter, with a hunched back and slightly grayed hair. It was Pak Sugeng.

I walked towards him. He held up a piece of paper with my name on it, except it wasn't a name that I used anymore.

"You... Non Cecilia Putri Wongso?" Pak Sugeng asked with a strong accent.

My brain stuttered. I hadn't had anyone call me by my last name in years. It felt so familiar, yet so oddly foreign. I hesitated to respond to Pak Sugeng because Cecilia Putri Wongso wasn't me. I was Cecilia Poetry. That's who I was and who I'd always be.

I hadn't heard my true last name since the fourth grade when Larry Bergman called me "Ding Dong Wing Wong" after smelling the *sate ayam* that Mom had packed for me.

Every Asian-American friend of mine had experienced a version of this sob story, but because I had the option to romanticize my middle name from "Putri" to "Poetry," the "Putri Wongso" wound cut a lot deeper.

"Yes, hello," I extended my hand half-heartedly. "Please, Pak Sugeng, call me Cecilia. Cecilia Poetry."

"Good afternoon, Non Cecilia," Pak Sugeng said, looking at his iPad. "Is you the *cucu* of Bapak Robby, yes?"

"The what?"

"The *cucu*..." Pak Sugeng faltered. "The, um, child child of Bapak Robby."

"Grandchild?" I said.

"*Iya, betul!*" Pak Sugeng grinned. "Sorry, Bu. My English no good."

Around Pak Sugeng's eyes were laughter lines. I supposed that he was often happy in his natural habitat, but at that moment he was clearly very nervous to be speaking in a foreign language. I almost felt guilty for it.

"It's alright," I said.

"Can you give passport?" Pak Sugeng said. He drew a square in the air with his fingers.

"Huh? Why?"

"For immigration. So can go fast."

"Why?"

"Uh," Pak Sugeng hesitated. "So is fast, Non. Uh ... I and Bapak Robby always like that."

I dug into my purse for my passport. *Is this what Oma meant by Pak Sugeng helping me at the airport?* I didn't see anyone else surrendering their passports at this section of the airport.

I must be naïve to give my passport to a stranger.

"Thank you," Pak Sugeng took my passport with a small bow. "I take your bag?"

So I gave him my luggage and purse too. He wheeled it next to me as he spoke into his phone in Indonesian. He could be plotting my murder for all I knew.

But because Oma told me to trust him, I should be okay. Right?

As I surrendered my belongings to Pak Sugeng, I felt a tap on my shoulder. I turned around, but I didn't know who she was.

"Excuse me," a lady said, clicking her heels together.

The lady wore a tight dress with the Gucci logo on it, complemented by a purse made of crocodile-skin. She had her red-brown hair sprayed into the most obnoxious hairstyle I had ever seen. She wore tall stiletto heels and looked like she belonged at a luncheon instead of in an airport.

"Can I help you?" I asked, trying to figure out if I knew this lady from somewhere.

"I was just wondering," she pointed at the sign that Pak Sugeng was holding. "Your name is Wongso? Are you in any way related to Robby Wongso?"

"You know my grandfather?"

The lady's eyes lit up, cherry lips curling into a precarious grin.

"Robby Wongso is your grandfather?" she gasped. "Am I speaking to the future heir of Mandala Group?"

What in the world is this random lady talking about?

"Um," I said as she batted her eyes at me.

"Non," Pak Sugeng said. "Let's go."

"I'm going to go," I said, walking away with Pak Sugeng and my luggage.

The lady tried to run after us, but Pak Sugeng's glare intimidated her enough that she stayed put. I saw her pull out her phone and speak enthusiastically, staring at me as if I was her next meal.

"What was that?" I asked Pak Sugeng.

"Is normal with Pak Robby."

Being harassed by random strangers at the airport is normal?

I hadn't even set foot in Jakarta. If Opa Robby's name was going to stain me like this, I didn't want to be a Wongso after all.

Pak Sugeng helped me escape the airport. I didn't even have to collect my bags at the baggage carousel. He told me that he'd do it and proceeded to escort me towards a sleek black Mercedes Benz S-Class at the terminal's parking lot.

The driver stepped out of the car. He was dressed in the same uniform as Pak Sugeng. Pak Sugeng handed me my bags and said something to him in Indonesian, to which the man nodded and bowed in response.

"This Pak Sutikno," Pak Sugeng said, pointing at the man. "He take you to house."

"Hi," I waved. "Nice to meet you."

"Hello, Non," Pak Sutikno puffed his chest and smiled, opening the car door and gesturing for me to step inside. "Good afternoon."

I stepped into the car, a little flustered that Pak Sutikno sat on the right side.

Right. People drive on the opposite side in Indonesia.

Rolling down the window, I muttered a quick "thank you" to Pak Sugeng. He smiled, perhaps grateful that he didn't have to speak any more English to a stranger.

We left. I took a deep breath.

I'm here.

Jakarta was a blur behind the car's rain-washed window. The cars stood still in a single file, approaching a toll road. This was when I really got to observe Jakarta in all of its glory.

The rain's deafening pitter-patter muffled the outside world, darkened by the car's tinted windows. I watched as faded yellows, greens, and grey highlighted the buildings and roads, illuminating the mangroves growing near the airport and the people that populated the roadsides. Rain also forced cars to crowd around like ants, trying to push against one another. I thought the LA freeways were congested, but Jakarta traffic was a whole other story.

The humidity and jet-lag made my eyelids heavy. The journey on the freeway was stagnant for a while, with cars moving only a couple inches with each passing minute. Pak Sutikno said that traffic was always bad in the rain. He clicked his tongue, muttered something under his breath, and swerved two lanes to the left to enter the road shoulder.

Pak Sutikno stomped on the gas. I was pretty sure that we were going about eighty miles per hour, but all I could do was clench my teeth and hold onto my seat. If Pak Sutikno and any of the other drivers had driven like this in LA, he would've received multiple traffic violations by now, perhaps even had his driver's license revoked.

Eventually, as the skies started to clear up, the roads did too. I rolled down the window slightly, enough to catch a whiff of Jakarta's air. It smelled like sewer water and gas, a smell that was visibly urban, but uniquely Jakarta.

I'm here.

Although it had just rained, there were now no clouds visible to the human eye. A soft blue coated the sky, but it wasn't a blue that I knew. It was a lazy blue, a color that had tried its best to be blue but had simply fallen short of it, resorting to a soft hue layered with shades of ash.

The roads were slightly less congested than the highways, but there was far less green than there was near the airport.

Jakarta was the definition of a concrete jungle. With high-rises, cracked sidewalks, and motorbikes, the urban metropolis was thriving.

But it was also peculiar.

Cats ate leftover rice on the street near a stall. Some people walked up to cars at the red light trying to sell flowers and toys. Others skipped the antics and simply begged for money. A family of three clung onto one another on a single motorbike without helmets on.

After what seemed like a very long hour, Pak Sutikno pulled into a neighborhood. The roads were small, big enough for only one car, but two lanes managed to fit. Pak Sutikno squeezed past a van, our side mirrors scraping the bushes and trees that lined the walls. At the corner of the residential street sat a humble structure, built with bamboo walls and an aluminum slab for a roof. People gathered there, feeding their bellies while heartily chatting and laughing with the old woman who stood behind a pot.

"Is that a restaurant?" I asked.

"That is *warung*," Pak Sutikno said.

"*Warung*?"

"Yes. Small shop. They sell food also. Very yummy," he said, grinning.

While I fixed my eyes on the *warung*, Pak Sutikno turned into a black iron gate sitting between tall white pillars. I marveled at the gate's twisted black rods and gold carvings, fashioned to look antique. Pak Sutikno gestured to a man, dressed in police uniform, who sat in the guard house with a cigarette in between his fingers. The security guard rushed to open the gate and we pulled into the driveway.

Where were we?

"Okay, Non," Pak Sutikno sighed, stopping the car.

"Okay what?" I asked.

Pak Sutikno stepped out of the driver's seat and opened my door. My jaw dropped down to the car seat.

The house's cream and gold exterior resembled that of the Palace of Versailles. A fountain spewed water in three different directions into the stone mouths of fish and mermaids. Outlining the fountain and building's perimeter were lush green shrubs decorated with jasmine. Tall, plumeria trees covered the lobby, shading incoming cars from Jakarta's rain and heat.

"Nonik!"

Oma Shaan walked out in a red silk robe. She looked at least twenty years younger than she was, with the exception of the graying hair that perched above her collarbones. Her round, brown eyes, greatly resembling Dad's, lit up as they met mine.

I'm here.

"Hi, Oma Shaan," I said, managing a smile while my eyes continued to wander. "It's nice seeing you again."

"Ah, my darling," Oma said. "Give me a kiss."

I leaned in for a hug, but before I touched her, she jerked back.

"Ew, you're smelly!" Oma exclaimed. "Go take a shower first, and let's catch up later, ya?"

"Alright," I giggled.

"How was your trip?" Oma said.

"Good," I said. "Very long, but good."

"I can tell," she said, pinching her nose. "Come inside, my dear. Have you had lunch yet? Our cook prepared some *sop buntut* for you."

Oma has a personal cook?

"What's that?" I asked.

"Oh it's, um, oxtail soup. Your opa's favorite."

Oxtail? Ew.

"Thank you, Oma, but I've eaten on the plane," I lied.

My stomach grumbled, but I could probably survive on the KitKat bar I saved from the flight.

"Okay, dear."

"I'm going to go to my room, Oma, if that's alright," I said.

I walked to the trunk of the car to grab my luggage.

"No need," Oma said, grabbing my arm. "Let Sutikno do it. That's what he's here for."

"It's okay, my bags aren't that heavy," I said.

"Don't worry," Oma said. "You should rest your arms after that long flight. Anyway, he's paid to do this. Let him do his job."

Watching Pak Sutikno push my bags into the house made me feel uncomfortable. Mom and Dad raised me to be independent. They made sure that I could book doctor's appointments, replace light bulbs, and take care of insurance plans. I refused to be curbed. I was twenty-three and healthy. If I was able to take care of myself, I was more than capable of carrying my own bags.

Oma Shaan placed her cold hand on the small of my back, inviting me inside the house. In spite of my discomfort, I followed her, allowing my pungent body to bathe in the house's warm, serene glow.

4

"House" was an inaccurate word to describe my grandparents' home. I would describe it more like a palace in the middle of the city. Iridescent hues ascended from the heavens, highlighting the exquisite marble flooring and artisan wood structures that stood upon fine, hand-woven carpets.

I can't believe I walked into a palace with leggings, oily hair, and body odor.

"Do you like it?" Oma Shaan said. She must have caught me staring at the banister's intricate carvings. "I flew in a carver from Italy. And these statues I got them …ah, from where ya…if not from a Sotheby's auction, probably a private gallery. But they're all original pieces."

"This is a really beautiful home, Oma," I said.

I wandered into the living room. Paintings of mountains, koi fish, and porcelain people decorated the walls. Their eyes pierced my soul. Photographs of children, probably cousins I didn't remember, were delicately framed and placed atop a grand piano. Behind the piano hung a huge family photo.

Oma and Opa, ten years younger, sat on a velvet couch in the middle while their children and grandchildren huddled around them. I spotted my Uncle Richard and Aunt Isabella with their families huddling so densely that there was no space for Dad, Mom, and me.

"It's your home now, too, Nonik," Oma said from a couple feet away.

It really didn't feel that way, but I smiled regardless.

"Do you want to see your room? You can rest there until dinner."

As I was about to go upstairs, I heard a loud bark. A small dog, peppered with soft gray fur, ran towards me and pounced at my shins. It wore a red collar on its neck with a silver bone-shaped pendant. I squealed in glee. Mom was allergic to dogs, so we never had one. I gazed into its beady eyes and showered it with rubs and pets.

"I think he likes you," Oma said.

"What's his name?" I asked, showering the dog with kisses.

"Leader," Oma said. "He's a miniature schnauzer. We just got him about a year ago."

Macy kept a white miniature schnauzer, Tintin, in Seattle. I saw him in LA when I went over for Thanksgiving dinner a few times. Seeing Leader reminded me of Macy.

"He's so cute," I giggled as Leader cuddled up next to me.

I snapped a photo of him to send to Macy.

"You're just like your dad," Oma said, patting my head. "He loved dogs too."

Leader followed Oma Shaan and me to one of the spare guest rooms on the second floor, where my luggage was already waiting.

"Here's your room, Nonik," Oma said. "Do you like it?"

The guest bedroom had the same classic feel as the rest of the house, with wood and earthy tones that crawled up the high ceiling. In addition to a bed big enough for two, the room was equipped with its own bathroom, desk, and a mini fridge. A painting of a very pale ballerina hung close to the wardrobe. She wore a sad tutu and soiled ballet slippers. She posed confidently, her feet en pointe, her arms curved to an elegant C. Most importantly, her eyes were fixed on the grass, so I didn't have to worry about her judging my every move.

"It's really cozy," I said. "I like it a lot. Thank you."

"I'll leave you to rest," Oma said. "See you at dinner."

Oma smiled and stepped out, leaving me alone with the ballerina and my belongings.

I took a deep breath and lay on the floor. I let my body loosen. Since I arrived, I'd been calculating the number of ways that I could fall onto or break something, or exhibit any sort of behavior that would risk me getting kicked out onto the streets.

I hopped into the shower, washing all the stink and dirt off of my skin, reminiscing about the pictures in the living room. Mom mentioned that Opa and Oma weren't too fond of Dad because of how he neglected them and moved to LA for her. Meanwhile, Uncle Richard and Aunt Isabella's spouses doted on Opa and Oma so that their children could receive greater inheritances from them. She explained how this blatant contrast greatly jeopardized my grandparents' relationship with our family.

"But money isn't everything, sweetie," Mom would say. "Love was how Dad and I met even though money would have kept us apart. I raised you to learn how to be grateful with less, so you won't have to covet for more."

Then she would smile, pat my head, and tell me that she loved me.

I stepped out of the shower, dried my hair, and brought these thoughts to an afternoon nap. A text from Macy popped up as I snuggled under the covers.

*Sorry for replying late C, big coding project due
at work. Would wish you a safe flight but I think
you've already arrived! How's Jakarta?*—15:40

As my fingers crafted a bittersweet reply, I dozed off until dinnertime.

+

Three knocks woke me up from my two-hour slumber. In that time, the once-blue sky outside my window had already darkened into a quiet gloom, complemented with rumbling thunder and rain falling in staccatos.

"Come in," I said, rubbing the sleep from my eyes.

It was Oma Shaan and Opa Robby.

"Hello, hello!" Opa Robby said from the door. "It's so good to see you in Jakarta, Nonik."

Opa Robby came in wearing a straw fedora hat, a white polo, and bright blue shorts. He had a tall, lean build with very smooth skin for an elderly man, with the exception of clear laughter lines around his eyes. It was hard to believe that Opa was seventy-five and turning seventy-six soon.

"Hi, Opa Robby," I said. "I missed you too."

"Sorry it took me this long to come see you," Opa Robby said. "I just got back from playing golf with my friends. But it looks like you've had a good rest after your flight, is that right?"

"I did," I said. "Thank you for asking. And for lending me your home to stay in."

"But this *is* your home, Nonik," Opa said.

If it really was, you would have pictures of my family.

"Nonik, since you're already awake, can we have a chat?" Oma Shaan asked.

"Sure, Oma. Is everything okay?"

"We wanted to ask you about what you wrote on your job forms," Opa said.

Oma and Opa sat at the foot of my bed, far enough that I had my own space, but close enough that I felt a little suffocated.

My muscles tensed up. *What could I possibly have done wrong with my job forms?* I scrummaged my brain for any mistakes I might have made on the forms—writing the wrong home address, writing my now-expired USC email address instead of my personal one, forgetting to sign the documents. But what came out of Oma's mouth was beyond what I could have imagined.

"I noticed you wrote 'Cecilia Poetry' instead of your real name on the forms. Did you do that on purpose?"

"Oma," I said. My lower lip trembled. "'Cecilia Poetry' *is* my real name."

I thought of the lady at the airport earlier today.

"No, it's not," Oma said. Her eyebrows twisted into a sarcastic angle. "Your real name is 'Cecilia Putri Wongso.'"

"I stopped using my last name a long time ago."

Oma lifted a hand to her pearls.

"Are you ashamed of this family?"

"I never said that."

"If you're that ashamed, then why did you come here, Nonik?"

Oma fisted her trembling hands. Her chestnut eyes contorted into an intimidating, witch-like glare. Opa Robby patted her back.

"Is there a reason why you don't use our last name, Nonik?" Opa said.

"With all due respect, Opa, I just—" I glanced at Oma, who was glaring at me.

"Robby, this is exactly why I never approved of James moving to LA for that woman," Oma interrupted. She pointed at me. "He was going to raise kids like *this*. Luckily they only had one."

"Oma!" I shouted, jerking up from the bed.

"Hey!" Oma Shaan yelled. She stood up and pointed at me. "*Kamu kurang ajar ya!*"

I knew little Indonesian, but enough to understand what Oma said. I had learned "rude" in my parents' language before ever learning "love."

I got out of bed and curled up in the corner with the ballerina. My brain flooded with words and stories I could use to fight back against Oma Shaan—when Mom cried because Oma and Opa refused to speak to her about her parents, when Uncle Richard refused to see Dad because Oma and Opa forbade him to, and when the whole family but ours was invited to my Aunt Isabella's daughter's christening.

Of course I was angry at them. I had been angry for years.

But I knew that taking any action would mean that I was going to sleep on the streets in a foreign country. At a loss for words, I retreated to a slump, with everything I wanted to scream out instead collecting itself in streams of tears.

"Stop it, Shaan," Opa Robby growled in between his teeth. "That's enough."

"How?" Oma said. "How, Robby, when I lose both my son and my granddaughter because of one selfish woman? And now look at how Cecilia turned out! She's ashamed of our family!"

Silence brimmed in the room. I used hard blinks to prevent myself from uttering anything else that might further anger Oma.

At this point I decided to stare at the darkness outside my window. I could still make out the silhouette of a large tree branch that swayed dangerously to the heavy rain's pitter-patter. I went through so many emotions in a span of ten minutes that at that point I felt like an elongated rubber band that had exceeded its capacity to stretch any further.

"Nonik," Oma Shaan started again. "I just want to understand how you can reduce yourself to a poem. Your name is 'Putri Wongso.' Do you know what that means?"

I shook my head, eyes fixed on the hem of Oma's long skirt.

"Putri means princess, you know? As Putri Wongso you are the princess of Robby Wongso. Do you know how many people would die to be your opa's grandchild? It's the highest honor you could ever have in society, and yet you decide to lower yourself to words on a piece of paper?"

The lady at the airport popped in my head again. Was that why she approached me? Because she was jealous about me being a Wongso?

But what did that even mean?

Oma Shaan couldn't stretch me any further. She should give up. I wouldn't break. I couldn't break.

"Okay, Oma," I said, rubbing my eyes. "If it really means that much to you, I'll start using Wongso from now on."

"Good," Oma said. She looked away, avoiding eye contact with me.

"Was there a reason why you didn't?" Opa Robby asked.

"Didn't what?" I said.

"Well," Opa Robby said. "Why did you ever take Wongso out of your name? Was there a reason for it?"

"I mean, legally, my name is still Cecilia Poetry Wongso."

"It's 'Putri,'" Oma Shaan interjected. "Stop with that 'Poetry' nonsense."

I fisted my hands so I didn't have to scream.

"But why did you take 'Wongso' out in the first place?" Opa Robby asked.

"I mean," I said. "When I was in elementary school, my classmates kept calling me 'Ding Dong Wing Wong' because I was the only kid with a weird last name. So I took it out and just never used it since. That's really it."

"*Aiya* Nonik," Oma Shaan said. "'Wongso' is a common name in Indonesia, so you don't have to worry about that here."

"I know," I said. "It's just that I stopped using Wongso when I was in, what, fourth grade? So I just never considered using it again. That's it, Oma; it was never because I'm ashamed of this family."

"Well, if you really cared about this family, you would've kept the name, you selfish girl."

"Enough, Shaan," Opa Robby said in a stern voice.

Oma Shaan lowered her weapons and retreated. She looked everywhere but at me and fiddled with a loose string on her skirt. The silence pushed me to notice the rain's tropical echo spiraling with the air conditioner's roar, in a lullaby that would have sent me back into a deep slumber.

"Like Oma said, Nonik, you don't have to worry about being made fun of here," Opa said, breaking the silence. "People will respect you if you're a Wongso. I've made sure of it. And if they don't, tell me and I'll deal with them myself. Okay?"

"Okay, Opa," I said. Opa Robby was always so sweet.

"Okay, good girl," Opa said, patting my head. "Come downstairs for dinner after you get dressed. We're eating *mie goreng* from Bakmi GM. You'll love it."

"Alright, Opa."

We had a very quiet dinner. I slurped on my *mie goreng*, thoughts bursting with all the ways that argument could have gone further south, if I had said, for example, "I hate the Wongsos," or even gone further to say, "Fuck this family." Thank goodness Mom and Dad taught me self-control. I was so close to losing the only safety net I had within 8,769 miles, which would not only result in losing the roof over my head but also Mom's and my primary source of income.

There was too much at stake to cause a fuss with my grandparents. If that meant waving my white flag in defeat, that was what I was going to do.

What a way to start my new life in Jakarta.

"I'm sorry, Oma," I said.

Oma Shaan refused to look at me. She clinked her fork on the plate but barely touched her noodles.

"Oma," I said, a little louder this time.

"What?" Oma scowled.

"I'm so sorry, Oma," I repeated.

"Good," Oma said, stuffing a forkful of noodles into her mouth.

"Thank you, Nonik," Opa said.

Opa proceeded to ask me about so many things. The flight from LA, graduation, what my first impressions were of Jakarta. He was such a gentle giant. Oma started to let her guard down. She stayed for the conversation and chimed in at times.

Soon after Opa and Oma had their fruit platter for dessert, I excused myself from the table and went back into my room.

I brushed my teeth and slipped into an oversized t-shirt, lying in bed while I gazed outside the window. The big tree that blocked my view stood blissfully still. The clouds rolled back to reveal a blank night sky with a single star that shone over the city, illuminating vignettes of skyscrapers that tried to but couldn't match the star's brilliance.

The night made me think of Peter Pan, how he somehow convinced three innocent kids into an adventure full of magic, danger, and beauty. In a way, Jakarta was my Neverland and Dad was my Peter Pan. I hoped that Jakarta was going to turn out the same way as it did in Peter Pan's legend, even if things were off to a rough start.

It was ridiculous that, as a twenty-three-year-old I felt like I was six again. That was the last time my parents ever yelled at me. I distinctly remember Dad chasing me around the house because I refused to do my multiplication tables. I was a good kid, and arguably a good person, too, but to my grandparents "good" wasn't "good enough."

My iPhone chimed. I rolled over to grab my phone on the bedside table. It was a text from Mom.

Miss u baby. How are u?—20:40

I lay in bed, staring at the uniquely carved cream ceiling. I wondered how I was going to survive in this peculiar place if the people I lived with were going to be cold and manipulative. Anxiety crept up on me as I thought of the days that waited ahead. But I had to be strong. I had to be strong for Mom. If I got up to any funny business, Oma and Opa could stop sending Mom money.

I crafted a text to Mom, a tear sliding down the side of my face.

It rained today but I avoided the storm. I'm doing better than ever, Mom.—20:42

5

My bed sheets began to feel stale. I had been sleeping for so long, which meant that it was finally morning, finally time for me to soak up the Indonesian sunlight, so I opened the curtains to reveal—

Darkness. It was only 3:30 a.m.

Groaning, I buried my head in my pillow. What felt like a lifetime of sleep turned out to only be five hours. I tossed and turned some more, but I gradually realized that my body wasn't going to let me sleep any longer. Jakarta was fourteen hours ahead of LA. I would have been having lunch with Mom or my friends at Nobu, not staring into pitch darkness in Oma and Opa's guest room.

Jet-lag is pathetic.

I texted Macy, hoping that she was on her lunch break. While waiting for her reply, I feasted my bloodshot eyes on hours of Netflix. Before I knew it, the sun emerged from behind the buildings. It was finally 6:00 a.m.

A beautiful sunrise dawned upon Jakarta. I walked out onto my balcony to witness chirping birds, the fresh smell of dew and humidity, and pastel yellow streaks in the sky. The same pale light shone through layers of mist and mystery, as well as illuminating the hibiscus and jasmine in the backyard.

At dawn, the city felt like a forest with steel trees. Wisps of smog and mist crowded the empty horizon, weaving its way between buildings and inviting taupe doves to fly amongst their warmth. But instead of singing crickets, I heard roaring cars, motorbikes, and food sellers crawling on the street.

I took a deep breath, inhaling all that Jakarta offered, and imagined the adventures that awaited me. The fog that dawned on the city gave it its enticing peculiarity. It was like the city was inviting me to play but didn't give me any toys, allowing me the freedom to explore it in my own way.

As I counted the cars that whizzed past our neighborhood, my stomach started to grumble. A sharp pain pierced my belly, twisting it from the inside out. I had a choice between munching on another KitKat bar I found from yesterday's flight or heading downstairs for a hot breakfast.

Wincing, I pulled a robe over my pajamas. An eeriness lingered as I walked down the dark, cold, and lonely halls of this huge house. The pillars caved in. All the paintings on the wall held colder stares. I gripped onto the banister, its bumps making the carvings come alive. Shivering, I scurried into the brightly lit kitchen like a scared mouse.

But I wasn't alone.

The two maids glared at me like I was a ghost. One was mopping, and the other was standing by the stove. Both of them dipped their heads a little, chanting *"Pagi* Nonik" all together, as if rehearsed. I must have caught them off guard.

Mom told me that in Asian households, the wet kitchen was where all the heavy cooking took place. It wasn't as pretty as the main kitchen that all the guests see, which was probably why I found the maids hanging out there.

"Hello," I said, pursing my lips together awkwardly.

The women smiled.

"What are your names?" I said. "Or, actually, what should I call you guys? Sorry, I'm new to Indonesia, so I'm not too sure what the customs are."

"I am Ani," the woman who was mopping said. "This is Bu Ratih. She cook."

"Nice to meet you, Mbak Ani," I said. "And you too, Bu Ratih."

I remembered that Oma tried to hire an Indonesian maid to help Mom and me in LA. Mom called her Mbak, so I did too, although I wasn't too sure what the word meant.

"She...She no English," Mbak Ani said.

She tapped her fingers awkwardly as Bu Ratih watched. Mbak Ani was young, petite, and probably in her early twenties. She had long curly hair that bounced off her collarbones and large doe eyes that sparkled under the fluorescent light. A tattered apron draped over her frail body. Bu Ratih, on the other hand, was much older, with wrinkles that wrapped around her eyes. Her fingers were yellow and calloused. When she turned away from me, her sleeve rolled up to reveal boils on her wrist, perhaps recovering scald wounds from cooking.

"Non," Mbak Ani enthusiastically broke the silence. "You want eat? Bu Ratih cook for you."

"Yes please," I said. "What do you have?"

"Have everything. It depends, Non want eat what."

Having choices for breakfast made my brain shut down. Mom always prepared food in advance for me. She would get upset if I refused to eat her mediocre cooking. The endless possibilities here were dangerous for a hungry woman like me.

"Can you make a cheese omelet, Bu Ratih?"

"Omelet…omelet…" Mbak Ani trailed off, looking into the fridge. She and Bu Ratih had a little back-and-forth before she said, "Yes!"

I checked my phone to see no texts from Macy, so I propped myself down on a plastic stool by the kitchen aisle. Mbak Ani served me a glass of water. I said "thank you" but all she did was give me a very genuine, shy smile.

Mbak Ani paid close attention to Bu Ratih as she whipped the eggs. I watched her too. Her cooking skills were mesmerizing.

"Nonik," Mbak Ani said. "Can wait in dining room. Later I bring you omelet."

"Is it okay if I eat here?" I asked.

"Ibu Shaan…Ibu later angry."

"Don't worry. Oma can't get mad at me. I'm not doing anything wrong."

Her eyes flustered. She forced a smile and then said, "Okay, Non."

I leaned towards the table and focused on Bu Ratih, who effortlessly whisked eggs in a bowl. She then poured the whipped eggs on a sizzling pan, added the cheese, and let the mixture sit for a few minutes. When the omelet was done, Bu Ratih served it to me on a white porcelain plate. She lingered behind me eagerly to see if I liked it.

I took a bite. Cheese oozed out of the silky egg and scalded my tongue.

"Ouch!" I jumped back. The eggs spilled out of my mouth and onto the floor.

Bu Ratih stared at her eggs with a gaping mouth. Mbak Ani, as if on cue, rushed to pick up the hot egg from the floor with a paper towel.

"I'm so sorry!" I said, "Here, let me clean it up."

"Is okay, Nonik," Mbak Ani said. "We clean for you."

"No, I insist," I said, wrestling the paper towel out of Mbak Ani's hands.

I picked up the partially-chewed egg from the floor. At the corner of my eye, Mbak Ani and Bu Ratih shuffled in hesitation, wringing their hands. They cast nervous glances at the door, perhaps wondering if they were going to be in trouble. But why would they? I was helping them, after all.

"I'm sorry, Bu Ratih," I said, tossing the paper towel into the bin. "Your omelet is really good. I just, it was just way too hot earlier. Thank you."

I took a bite. The melted cheese, combined with the silky egg texture, exploded on my tongue.

Bu Ratih said something back, and Mbak Ani translated it to, "You're welcome, Nonik."

"How do you say delicious in Indonesian?"

"Um…" Mbak Ani looked up. "*Enak.* Delicious. *Enak.*"

"Well, Bu Ratih, your omelet is very *enak.*"

Mbak Ani grinned. Bu Ratih laughed. They seemed a lot more relaxed than they were when I first walked in. Perhaps they were nervous about meeting new people. But I wasn't going to be new for much longer, so I should get to know the people I live with.

"So, are you all from Jakarta?"

"No, I from Tegal. Far from Jakarta," Mbak Ani said. "Bu Ratih from Pekalongan."

"Cool," I nodded, even though I didn't recognize these places. "So how did you learn English so well?"

"I study from school until eighteen years old," Mbak Ani said. "Then come Jakarta for work."

"Oh, wow."

"I want my *adik-adik* to study. I work, send money, they study."

"*Adik-adik*?"

"Uh...how to say, um, small sister small brother."

Are public schools not free here?

"Your *adik-adik* will get a great education because of your hard work, Mbak Ani," I said, putting my hand over hers.

Just as I bit into the last piece of my omelet and Bu Ratih finished washing the dishes, Oma Shaan burst into the kitchen. Leader followed closely behind her.

"Good morning!" Oma announced.

She commanded the room in the same robe that she wore to welcome me. Her red lipstick complemented her outfit. I wondered why Oma, or anyone, really, would wear red lipstick to eat breakfast in their own home.

Oma whipped around and stared at me.

"What are you doing?" Oma said.

"I just finished eating breakfast," I said.

"That's not what I asked."

"Well, you asked what I was doing, and I'm telling you that I just ate breakfast."

Both women trembled. Mbak Ani's eyes darted to the floor. Bu Ratih clenched her teeth, jaw taught. A shiver traveled up my chest, although I wasn't too sure why.

"Were you talking to someone?"

"Yeah, I was talking to Mbak Ani."

Oma wore a smile that curled up to her eyes, smirking just enough to show her cold beauty.

"Let the maids do their work, Nonik," Oma said. "They're doing what they paid to do."

I kept quiet.

"Can I talk to you?" Oma asked, furrowing her brow.

"Okay," I mumbled.

Oma grabbed my arm and walked me out of the kitchen, rather briskly for a seventy-year-old woman. She sat me down on a velvet dining room chair.

"What are you doing there?" Oma whispered angrily. "You're not supposed to hang around them."

"I just thought I should make friends with the people I live with," I said.

"They're not your friends! And this isn't a bed and breakfast. This is a house. Our house."

"But—"

"They live here because it's cheaper for us. And them. So don't spoil them with the attention."

I fisted my hands, anger boiling within.

"Oma Shaan, with all due respect, I wasn't trying to disturb Mbak Ani and Bu Ratih. And they served me breakfast. I just didn't want eat alone."

"Cecilia," Oma Shaan said. She held my face in her palms. "You don't understand yet, so let me tell you. These maids are not your friends. They're here to work and serve us. If you spoil them and treat them like your friends, they won't respect us anymore. And then they'll do all kinds of things to hurt us."

"I don't think that's how it works."

Oma cleared her throat.

"One of my friends treated her maid like a queen. Paid her hospital bills, sent her kid to school, and everything. And then that bitch stole my friend's money and bought a car. A Kijang! Can you believe it? These maids earn nothing compared to the price of a car. Let alone a Kijang. Easy money for her! Look at this house. There are so many things for them to steal. You want that to happen to us?"

I shook my head.

"They're not like us, Nonik. They are here to get paid. So let them do their jobs."

They're not like us.

They're not like us because life didn't hand them the same cards that it did us. They're not like us because of brutal global inequity. But just because they're different, other people don't get a pass to treat them like they are less.

Dad's voice echoed in my head. He was the one who taught me to be kind to everyone I met and strike up meaningful conversations with them. Mom practiced it; he lived it. After all, that's how he was able to meet Mom, a middle-class woman who waited tables at her parents' restaurant.

No wonder Oma disapproved of her so much.

"Okay," I said.

My mouth was sour from the lie. Things were already tense between Oma and me, and I didn't want to upset her again, especially after I saw how heated she became during our argument yesterday. And I especially didn't want her to disrespect Mbak Ani and Bu Ratih even more.

I felt a little guilty for not fighting back, but I didn't know what good that would do. Mom told me that respect for others couldn't be demanded out of people. As I looked away from Oma, I saw Mbak Ani peek out from behind the kitchen door. Though, instead of looking like she wanted to scream and pounce at Oma, she smiled. It was probably the first time that someone in the house had finally stood up for her.

Warmth embraced my heart. Despite Oma's wrath, I had found my first friend in this foreign land.

6

I was up and wide-eyed by 6:30 a.m. Jet-lag was helping me morph from an owl to a rooster. Jakarta allowed me to love its mornings, even though I only watched from my window. An orange glow, radiating from the early sun, teased the day through a slit in the curtains.

Maybe today felt a bit more special because it was my first day at Kopi Sedap.

My first full-time job. I had dreamt about this day since I was little. Back then I wanted to be many things when I grew up. Once, my dream job was a veterinarian after our vet healed our golden retriever Daisy. Later, at thirteen, I wanted to be an architect after visiting Chicago. Architecture continued on as my dream until Dad quit his job at JPMorgan to start his own company, which motivated me to study economics and get a job in Silicon Valley's startup space. The last thing I had expected was to work at a seed-stage coffee company thousands of miles away from home.

I took some time to breathe in the stuffy morning air before blasting a podcast on my speakers and shuffling into the shower. While I towel-dried my hair, I stared into the closet. I wasn't sure what companies in Indonesia expected their employees to wear, so I picked out a checkered blazer that Mom got for me, a plain white t-shirt to wear underneath, and threw on some dark colored jeans. I then slipped into black Tory Burch flats to complement the outfit. Dad got me the flats for my twenty-first birthday, the last birthday we ever celebrated together, and told me that I looked beautiful in them. So I thought I'd take him to work with me.

Finally, I smeared on some eyebrow gel, mascara, and lip gloss, then rushed down to the kitchen.

Bu Ratih had prepared scrambled eggs and yogurt for my breakfast. Mbak Ani brought the dish into the dining room where I sat, then left after staying for a quick "good morning." It was 8:00 a.m., late enough in the day for Oma Shaan to walk in at any second.

As I gobbled my yogurt down while replying to Mom's and Macy's texts from last night, Oma Shaan walked into the dining room.

"Good morning, Nonik," she said, the same red robe draped over her slender frame.

"Morning," I said.

"Are you excited for—" Oma paused. "What are you wearing?"

"This?" I tugged at my blazer's lapel.

"Oh, no no no," Oma shook her head. "Don't wear that."

"Why not?"

"Nonik please ... it's too ... it doesn't even match. Can you change into something more ... appropriate?"

"But this is all I have."

"*Aiya*, so how...ah," Oma paused. "Wait here. I'll be back."

Oma rushed upstairs, her signature robe following her swift movements. She returned with a navy blue suit and a white, collared shirt.

"Try this, Nonik," Oma said. "You look like you're my size."

I went to the powder room near the dining table and pulled Oma's suit over my body, surprised to see how perfectly the clothes fit, and amazed when I realized how well she dressed.

I walked out of the bathroom and did a little twirl.

"Wow!" Oma exclaimed. "Beautiful, Nonik!"

"Thank you, Oma." I said, beaming from ear to ear.

Oma Shaan walked me out of the door and gave me a hug.

"Good luck at work!" Oma Shaan said. "Tell me if your boss gives you trouble."

"I'll be fine, Oma," I chuckled.

I climbed into the car, where Pak Sutikno was waiting, and we drove off. Oma was acting a little too nice for my liking, but I indulged in it.

We arrived ten minutes later. I looked at my watch: 8:47 a.m.

Thirteen minutes early. Perfect.

David had emailed me yesterday to tell me to be at the office building before 9:00 a.m., and someone from the office would pick me up. But now nobody lingered in the lobby. Security came up and asked if I had an appointment, to which I answered that I did, even though it didn't feel like I did.

But finally, at 9:30 a.m., a man exited the elevator and walked towards me. He wore a light blue shirt, tucked messily into baggy trousers. In his hand were two ID tags attached to lanyards that he twirled dangerously in the air like batons.

"Cecilia?" the man asked.

"Yeah…" I said. "And you are?"

"David. Hello!" David reached out to shake my hand. He seemed a lot friendlier in person than he was over the phone. "It's nice to finally meet you. I've heard so much about you."

"From who?" I chuckled.

"Just…some friends."

David and I stuffed ourselves into a crowded elevator. While passing minutes in the elevator, my mind buzzed with all the things I imagined myself doing, like helping Indonesia's economy, engaging in life-changing projects, and meeting colleagues that would turn into lifelong friends. Today was the day that my life was going to change.

I took a deep breath.

The door opened to the thirtieth floor, leading into a hallway with modern glass doors and beautiful wood flooring.

"This is us," David said, walking me into the office unit.

I scanned the room. Kopi Sedap looked like an adult playground. It had couches, bean bags, and a ping-pong table. Desks were placed in groups of four with monitors and cables tangled with one another, similar to how my middle school computer lab had been arranged. The HD photograph of coffee beans from the company website was framed on the wall. A whiff of artificial freshness grazed my olfactory senses as I walked into the office, greeted by a tall, lanky man in a tacky blue suit.

"This is Raynard Kurniawan, our Chief Marketing Officer," David said. "You'll report to him."

"It's Ray," Raynard said. "Just Ray. And your name is?"

As Putri Wongso you are the princess of Robby Wongso. Oma's voice echoed in my head. *Do you know how many people would die to be your opa's grandchild?*

But perhaps it was wise for me to stick to the name that had aided me throughout my life, especially after what happened at the airport. I didn't want what happened there to happen at work, too. I didn't want to be branded as a Wongso, whatever that meant.

"Cecilia," I said, shaking Ray's hand. "Cecilia Poetry."

I felt a little guilty for breaking my promise to Oma, but she wouldn't know.

Ray puffed out his chest, rolled up his sleeve, and extended his arm to me.

"Welcome, Cecilia Poetry," Ray said. "It's nice to see a new face around here."

The first thing I noticed about Ray was his jaw. He had a crisp jawline that could cut a person in half, complemented by sharp, dark eyes that drew me in. Ray seemed like the dangerously cunning but persuasive type, the perfect marketing persona.

"Alright," David said. "If all is good, Cecilia, I'm going to hand you over to Ray so he can get you onboarded and all that nice stuff. Does that sound good?"

"Yeah, for sure," I said. "Thanks, David."

"Come with me, Cecilia. You'll have a great time if I take you around."

Ray winked. I laughed.

When we left David, Ray said something to me in Indonesian.

"Cecilia," he started, before muttering strings of letters that I couldn't decipher.

"Oh, I don't—"

"Are you not Indonesian?" Ray was slightly taken aback.

"I'm technically American, but ethnically I'm Indonesian."

"Oh, I see. Sorry about that. David didn't tell me that you couldn't speak Indo."

I soaked in the embarrassment and blushed. I had never been bothered that I couldn't speak the language of my parents' country. I felt a tinge of guilt for not paying attention to Mom's lessons a couple weeks ago. Perhaps it was time that I started learning Bahasa Indonesia.

Ray took me to meet everyone else in the office. I met Amelia and Yanti, the Chief Operations Officer and Chief Financial Officer of the enterprise. Kopi Sedap had a small team. Everyone here but me had chief positions. Ray talked to me about Kopi Sedap's history: how David was able to start the company from scratch a year ago, grow it, attract angel investors, and how the company prided itself on being a subsidiary of Macan Group, which was a conglomerate holding group that provided Kopi Sedap with a strong support system and a hefty network.

Ray brought me to an empty cubicle, big enough for a circular meeting table fit for four, where the Chief Technology Officer waited with two laptops.

"Cecilia, this is Kai Pribadi," Ray said. "We all call him KP."

"Hi, KP," I said.

KP smiled. "Nice to meet you, Cecilia."

"KP will get you started with all the tech-related things that you need. I'll leave you two to it. My desk is right behind this door, so just wave once you're done, okay?"

"Okay, Ray. Thanks so much."

Ray left, leaving me in an airtight room with translucent glass panes and a very attractive young man.

"I heard you just moved here," KP said. "How do you like Jakarta so far?"

"It's great here, KP. Very different from LA."

"Ah please...please, Cecilia, um, call me Kai. I hate it when people call me KP."

"Oh, alright then," I giggled. "Kai does sound a lot better than KP anyway."

Kai's eyes crinkled with his careful smile, revealing an intensity and a gentleness that melted me in my skin.

He fixed me up with a laptop, an email address, ID card, and gave me some branded office merchandise. In addition to overseeing the development of Kopi Sedap's app, Kai was also responsible for onboarding newcomers. I was his first one.

When we finished, Kai opened the door to Ray waiting on the couch nearby. Ray took me to an empty desk where David was sitting. The two of us sat in the empty chairs near him.

"How's everything so far, Cecilia?" David asked. "Good?"

"Yeah," I said.

"Good, good," David said. "So I wanted to give you your first task because your role as a Growth Strategist is so important to this company, especially while we're working in these early stages. You're going to be working with Raynard a lot in terms of scaling this company."

"One hundred percent," Ray said. "You should know that you need to make connections in Jakarta first, especially if you want to succeed in marketing and growth."

"That's very true," David said. "And that's why Raynard's network is my prized possession."

Ray grinned, revealing two dimples sitting at the corner of his lips.

"Raynard and I have decided to start growing your network here by leveraging the connections we already kind of have in the office," David said.

He handed me a stack of about five hundred name cards.

"Okay, first we're going to teach you how to network in Indonesia," David said. "To do that, you have to email all of these people. Some are potential investors, some are people we can potentially collaborate with. I want you to introduce yourself, the company, and tell them why they should be interested in us. This is your long-term project. Work together with Ray to figure out the best way to attract potential investors and partners. And when you're done, put all of these names into an Excel sheet, and track their responses as you go. You'll most likely hear back from ten to thirty percent of these people, which is a good percentage to aim for. Is that okay?"

"Yes," I said. "I'll get started right away."

"Good! I love your spirit," David said, patting my back. "I'll leave you to it. Raynard, check in on Cecilia throughout the day and be available to her if she has questions."

"Yes, Pak David," Ray said.

I slaved away at the laptop, crunching the first out of five hundred emails. Ray picked out familiar names from the cards and taught me how to craft an email to excite a response, so I started there.

Ray said that Indonesians had a very particular way of email-writing that was slightly different from how it was in America. Adding fluff and formalities to emails here would yield a higher response rate; going straight to the point was going to land your email in the trash. To make things worse, Ray said that writing in Indonesian was preferable. He had to comb through his contact cards and assign me to those people who could understand a decent amount of English.

I dragged my fingers across the keyboard. It was a frustrating challenge that required me to switch my writing style all together, so I knew going in that I was already at a disadvantage. I definitely wasn't in my comfort zone, but Ray made me feel welcome and comfortable.

After drafting and sending my fifteenth email, around two hours later, Ray invited me to go to lunch. We walked towards the elevator, where we bumped into Kai.

"What's up, KP," Ray said. He gave Kai a fist bump.

"Hi, Ray," Kai said. "Hi, Cecilia."

Kai tinkered with a leather necklace on his neck. He shuffled a little awkwardly in Ray's shadow.

"Are you going down for lunch?" Ray asked.

"Well, it's 12:30 p.m., so yes," Kai said. "Are you?"

"I was just going to take Cecilia to Pacific Place for Thai," Ray said. "Want to join us?"

"Sure," Kai smiled.

The Kopi Sedap office was located at the *Bursa Efek Jakarta*, Jakarta's Stock Exchange. The BEJ was right across from Pacific Place Mall. The two buildings were connected by a tunnel equipped with small shops like food stalls, a barber shop, an eyelash extension bar, and even a karaoke bar. The tunnel could be a mall in itself.

We walked up the escalator and into the mall. The mall was vibrant, decorated with luxury shops and restaurants that decked the six floors. I followed the men into Busaba, a Thai restaurant that sat in the middle of the mall, with no walls or kitchen present in sight.

Ray picked a table that was in the corner of the restaurant and placed our orders. I sat facing the open mall so I could people-watch like I used to in LA. Mothers chased after their toddlers. Young people in work attire rushed into the mall, cups of coffee in their hands. A group of uniformed students walked in a single file with their chaperoning teacher.

As I lost myself in the buzz of Jakarta's social scene, the waiter served us the restaurant's signature Thai iced teas.

"So what brings you here, Cecilia?" Ray asked. "You said you're Indonesian but grew up in America? What's that like?"

"My parents are from Jakarta," I said. "Well, to be more accurate, my dad grew up here and in Manado, and my mom grew up in Pontianak, I think? But they met here and got married in LA. And my grandparents still live here."

"That's so cool," Ray said.

"Yeah, thanks," I gushed. Ray was so good with his words. "So yeah, my dad passed away recently, and—"

"I'm so sorry to hear that," Ray said, his fingers meeting my wrist.

"Thanks, it's alright," I said.

I pulled my wrist away from Ray. He was nice, but his touch wasn't very comfortable.

"Anyway, yeah, I decided to come here to honor Dad's heritage and explore my Indonesian roots, I guess. And spend time with my grandparents."

Kai nodded, sipping on his Thai iced tea.

"America's nice, though, right?" Ray said. "I went to Berkeley for college and had a great time."

"How was that?" I asked. "Berkeley was my dream school, but I didn't make it in."

"It was good overall," Ray said. "Can't go wrong being in the Bay Area. I had a lot of fun in college, lots of drinking and partying. I genuinely don't know how I graduated."

I chuckled. Ray was fun to be around.

"KP, you went to Cornell, right?" Ray said. "How was that?"

"It was okay," Kai said. "I liked London better than Ithaca though."

"You lived in London?" I asked.

"Yeah, I did my master's there," Kai said.

"Ah, you're too humble, KP." Ray said, putting his arm around Kai. "This guy is a genius, Cecilia. He went to Imperial for his master's in, what was that, machine learning? And didn't you graduate summa cum laude from both schools?"

"No, no," Kai said, gushing. "Imperial doesn't use the Latin honors system. And I only graduated magna cum laude from Cornell."

"And that's how my buddy here became Chief Technology Officer at only twenty-five. Pak David recruited him straight out of graduate school. Can you believe that, Cecilia? You're among the greats here at Kopi Sedap," Ray said.

Kai smiled sheepishly. He was very humble for someone so accomplished.

We spent the rest of our lunch talking about Ray's personal life. He told us about his recent ex-girlfriend and how this other girl was chasing after him. Kai gave him some realistic advice. I got lost in the conversation since Ray threw in so many names, so I ended up quietly munching on the delicious green curry on the table.

It was about 2:30 p.m. by the time Ray, Kai, and I returned to the office. David was nowhere to be found. Kai disappeared behind a desktop. I continued to work on my sixteenth email while Ray called some of the investors hidden in the pile of name cards. He spoke in Indonesian, so I couldn't understand what he was saying, but he was laughing and smiling on the call. I was sure that the investors were all enchanted by him. It was difficult not to be.

By the time I crafted my thirtieth email, Ray came up to me.

"By the way," he said. "Do you have any plans on Wednesday night?"

"No, I don't," I said. "Why?"

"Do you want to join KP and me for dinner? I believe my friend's sister will be there. She's really nice. I think you might get along with her."

"Yeah, sure," I said, beaming. "Thanks for thinking of me. I'll be there."

"Amazing!"

Ray touched my shoulder. I gently moved my arm away. I wasn't sure if doing so was polite in Indonesia, but to me, being rude was better than being uncomfortable.

"Oh, and also, if you want to leave for the day, you can," Ray said.

"But it's only 4:30 p.m.," I glanced at the wall clock behind Ray. "Doesn't work end at 5:00?"

"Ah, it's close enough. Anyway, Pak David is out for a meeting with our coffee bean supplier, Amelia, and Yanti. Even if he did, it's your first day, so I'm sure he'd let you take it easy. You're still jet lagged right?"

"Yeah, a little bit."

"Go home, Cecilia. Get some rest. You did great today."

"Okay, thanks. See you tomorrow."

I packed my bags and left the office to Kai and Ray. Pak Sutikno picked me up at the lobby and drove me home.

Leader greeted me when I arrived home. He wagged his little tail and jumped on my shins. I squeezed his little body, cradling him in my arms. If Leader wasn't with Oma, it must mean that Oma wasn't home.

"Oma, Opa," I called out. "I'm home."

True enough, Mbak Ani came rushing over from the kitchen.

"Hello, Non," she said. "Ibu Shaan go out. Pak Robby also."

"Oh, okay," I said. "I'll be upstairs, then."

"Non," Mbak Ani said. "No eat?"

"No thank you, Mbak Ani. I'll just eat dinner later."

"Okay."

I brought Leader with me to my room. Gold sunlight spilled onto the bed and illuminated a box, neatly tied and placed onto my bed. A hand-written note slipped underneath the bow.

Nonik—

These are some suits for your work. Please try them on and see if you like them.

Love, Oma Shaan

From pinstripe to white and a classic black suit, the box had it all. All the clothes were somehow tailored to fit me perfectly. I couldn't help but smile. Oma was so thoughtful. It might have been the first time that she showed her kindness. Maybe I had to warm up to her to see her soft side.

I smiled at the mirror, pressing the pinstripe suit against my body.

II

Fawn

She runs:

as April hallucinates
in snowflakes the ballad of night
and day merge in the horizon

Titanium glares into doe eyes
piercing mist with a bitter cold;
Little rockets soaring

Creating a loose bruise
on her breast that travels from plum
to sunset crimson

A heart—now battle-bled,
sinking between lungs
throbbing through platelet stitches

in the ache of a faded sun
She is lucid in darkness,
covered in rain kisses as
her thighs carry her through

the bullet; the black;
the bright

7

I closed my laptop lid on the cheery Wednesday evening and went to the office bathroom. I snuggled into a sleeveless, black top from Urban Outfitters and some light blue skinny jeans. I told Oma and Opa that I was going out for dinner with my colleagues. They seemed ecstatic but told me not to come home too late.

"You look nice," Ray commented as I walked out of the office bathroom.

"Thanks," I said. My cheeks flushed a little.

Ray, Kai, and I made our way down the building's elevator and out to the lobby, where Ray's Bentley and driver were waiting. I sat behind with Kai while Ray hopped into the front seat. His driver stomped on the gas.

"KP," Ray said. "Do you know Bryan Halim?"

"Who?" Kai said.

"The guy who's dating the CEO of Pronto, the property rental agency."

"Wait, Bryan's gay?"

"Bro, no!" Ray laughed. "The CEO is a girl!"

"Oh!" Kai chuckled. "I'm sorry. I shouldn't have assumed."

"I forgot her name, but I think she went to Babson with my friend's older brother."

Ray and Kai proceeded to talk about this Bryan guy and the girl he was dating. They threw in names that I didn't recognize. The conversation trailed off in my mind as they started to interweave Indonesian words and phrases in their sentences, so I stopped pretending to listen and tuned them out altogether.

Jakarta looked vibrant at night. Bright lights twinkled into constellations that illuminated the roads. I gazed at raindrops that glazed the car window like freckles, watching as cars and trees passed us by. I let my thoughts wander. I thought about Dad. I wondered where he fit in this vibrant city, but knowing him and his outgoing personality, he probably felt at home amongst the hustle and bustle.

The car stopped about ten minutes later at the lobby of the Four Seasons Hotel. The grandiose hotel sparkled. Glass walls teased a high ceiling, a graceful chandelier, and carpeted grand stairs. Stone and water combined to form beautiful structures that graced the arrival lobby. I wondered how they were able to make the place authentically modern with a classic Indonesian touch.

We got out of the car. Ray and Kai walked ahead. They were still talking about Bryan, so I intentionally walked closely behind them to the hotel lobby. The scent of fresh flowers swept over my olfactory senses. A waterfall-looking chandelier brightened up the guests and geometric marble floors. I let my eyes marvel at the tiny details. The intricate wall carvings, vibrant Indonesian paintings, and modern glass sculptures sparkled brilliantly. I smiled at the friendly staff who greeted me.

"C'mon," Ray said, gesturing for me to come over.

I quickened my pace and followed them into an elevator, sparkling in gold and white, that took us all the way to the twentieth floor. When the elevator doors opened, my eyes were welcomed with bold crimson hues. It was a red that was dark enough to taste like fine wine but fell short of its mysteriousness. The scent of freshly-baked bread traveled from the kitchen into the dining area. My stomach grumbled, but I was too mesmerized by all the luxury to care.

"Mike," Ray called out. "Hey!"

Ray walked towards Mike, taller, fitter, and more well-dressed than all of us were, who was sitting by a table with two girls. One girl wore a tight yellow dress, while the other wore a cropped top with high-waisted leather pants. They were wearing heels, and I was very underdressed.

The people at the table stood and approached Ray and Kai, exchanging greetings and hugs.

"Is this the new girl at the office?" Mike said.

"Yeah," Ray said, gesturing to me. "This is Cecilia Poetry, she just moved here from LA."

"Poetry?" Mike said. "That's such a cool name. Really rolls off the tongue."

Thankfully you won't hear my real last name, then.

"Thanks," I said.

"I'm Mike," he continued. "This is my sister Faith and her best friend Grace."

"Hi, everyone," I said.

"Hi, Cecilia," Grace said.

"Hello, Cecilia," Faith echoed. "It's nice to meet you."

Faith and Grace were both absolutely gorgeous. Grace had flawless caramel skin that glistened crisply under the dim light. She wore sharp eyeliner that emphasized her dark doe eyes. Long dark hair beautifully framed her jaw. The yellow dress she was wearing accentuated her breasts and tiny waist. I concluded that Grace was the type of girl who looked casually hot in a dress and professionally sexy in a suit. Not many girls I knew could pull that off.

Faith, on the other hand, had long ebony hair that she hid in a braid and thick eyebrows that complemented her brown eyes. I especially adored her cherry red lips that highlighted her cheekbones when she smiled. Any person would be crazy not to fall in love with her.

A server led us to our table, a round one at the back end of the restaurant, near a window that opened to a balcony overlooking the Jakarta skyline. I purposely sat on a chair that faced the window to admire the night. Kai sat next to me. Faith and Grace sat across me.

"So, Cecilia," Grace said. "You just moved to Jakarta?"

"Yeah, I did. I got here a week ago."

"How do you like it so far?"

"It's pretty great," I said. "I'm adjusting to a lot."

"Have you had diarrhea yet?" Grace asked.

The sip of sparkling water I just took slid down my throat. I almost choked.

"Grace!" Faith's eyes widened.

"What?" Grace said. "I'm serious. Have you, Cecilia?"

"No." I chuckled. "Am I supposed to?"

"Well," Grace said. She leaned in closer. "A friend came here for an internship, and literally within the first day of arriving, she got diarrhea. And yet, she was Singaporean, dude. I'd think they'd be used to street food there so their stomach could take Indo food."

"Okay, well," Faith said. "Singapore's street food is way cleaner than what we have here. You probably took her to some dirty *warung* and spoiled her diet."

"No, I swear!" Grace said. "It was clean! I took her to the *sate* stand in Menteng."

"Yeah, but—"

"Yes, honestly, I fucked up. I knew that the *sate ayam* we ate smelled fishy, but I kept quiet."

It was hard not to smile around Faith and Grace. I glanced at the rest of the people at the table. Ray and Kai were on their phones. Mike was pointing at the menu to order food from the waiter. I admired his sparse eyebrows and high cheekbones, similar to Faith's. Their family must have inherited great genes.

"CeCe—actually, can I call you that? CeCe?" Faith asked.

"Yeah, definitely!" I said. "Everyone calls me CeCe back home."

Faith smiled. "Thanks. Saying Ce-ci-li-a is going to get hard down the line. We shorten everything in Jakarta. We're super lazy."

I laughed. Kai put his phone down and joined the conversation.

"Where did you move from, CeCe?" Faith asked.

"LA," I said. "I was born and raised there, but my parents are technically from Manado and Pontianak."

"Oh, wow, that's nice," Faith smiled.

"Yeah," I said.

"Can you speak Indo?" Kai said.

"No," I said. "I'm slowly learning, though."

"Here, I'll teach you a word," Grace said. "*Jayus.*"

"What does that mean?" I said.

"It means someone who tries to be funny but isn't. Specimen A: Ray. He's *the* definition of *jayus.*"

Faith and Kai giggled. I glanced at Ray, who was talking to a white man in a suit. A moment later, Ray introduced the rest of us to him. Nico, the Four Seasons General Manager. I've never been greeted by a hotel manager before. The occasion seemed more typical to everyone else at the dinner.

"If any of you need me, Ray has my number," he said. "Your dad was here with some government people the other day, but I had to take care of a wedding, so I couldn't see him."

Ray guffawed.

"Send your mom and dad my regards," Nico said.

"I will, Nico," Ray said. "Thank you."

Ray's dad is close to the hotel manager? And he meets government people, too?

When Nico left, Ray smirked, cleared his throat, and leaned against the table.

"Did you guys hear about the Bryan drama?" Ray started.

"Bryan who?" Mike asked. "Humanto? Jessica's brother?"

"No," Ray said. "No, Bryan Humanto is chill. I'm talking about Bryan Halim. The guy with the shit ton of Rolexes."

"He's the guy who got expelled from high school like ten years ago, Koko Mike," Faith said. "Remember? The drug dealer? All the moms went crazy when it happened."

A high school drug dealer? My high school experience was so tame compared to this. My friends and I went to see movies, studied, and sometimes went on road-trips together along the Pacific Coast Highway. It was a great time. We would get high sometimes, but marijuana was legal in California so we wouldn't get in trouble for smoking a little weed. Mom told me that doing or dealing drugs in Indonesia was just as good as a prison sentence. I don't know how true that was, but if it was, then this Bryan guy should have received more than just an expulsion.

I slurped on my glass of sparkling water, listening intently to the conversation. I gazed at waiters balancing plates upon plates on their forearms, scurrying from table to table and into the kitchen. The dynamic of the staff was so flawless that it almost looked staged.

"Oh…*that* Bryan," Mike nodded. "I remember him now. I think he's around my age. What about him?"

"KP and I were just talking about him," Ray said. "Apparently he's dating the CEO of Pronto Group."

"Wait, Christie?" Grace jumped in. "As in, Christine Basuki?"

Does everyone know each other around here?

"Yes!" Ray said. "I completely forgot that the Basuki family owns Pronto. So I'm guessing this Christie is the company's heiress?"

"She's the founder's daughter and currently serves as the CEO," Grace said. "What's your point?"

"You won't believe this," Ray said. "Christie is cheating on Bryan with a married man."

"No way," Faith shook her head. "I know who you're talking about. Kenneth Prasetyo, right?"

"Yes," Ray confirmed. "Wait, you know him?"

"Actually, I think I know Kenny," Kai said. "He's my cousin's husband's friend."

"What!" Ray exclaimed, holding his head in disbelief.

"What are you guys talking about?" Faith asked. "Christie just met Kenny for a business dinner in Hotel Mulia. Totally platonic. But you know how Indos can be. Someone took a photo of them and it spread."

"Goddamn it, Ray," Mike shook his head. Kai laughed.

"That just means I need wine, you guys," Ray said, plastering a cheeky smile on his face.

Grace looked agitated. She shifted in her seat and turned to Faith.

"Dude," Grace whispered, nudging her. "Are you sure Christie—"

"She, um," Faith said. "She told me to shut down all the rumors. And knowing Ray, he'd tell everyone if he knew."

"Okay. Because I'm pretty sure I saw a man come up the elevator when I was leaving her apartment a couple nights ago."

"I'm not surprised. Jon's dad is close to Kenny and he said that he's been overly busy...but I don't want to get into it. Are you sure you saw Kenny?"

"If I think I know what Bryan looks like, then yes. This guy looked way older. Like in his late forties at least."

"Oh my god."

"Don't say anything," Grace said. "You too, CeCe."

I nodded. It was nice to be trusted with secrets, even if I didn't know who they were about.

Just then, the waiter served us our dinner. He brought steaks, pastas, and fish that blanketed the whole table. There was enough food to feed ten. But I was ravenous after sending emails all day, so I could probably eat a lot more than usual. Kai cut up and placed some medium-rare steak on my plate, which I gobbled up almost instantly.

"So what do you guys do for a living?" I asked, mid-chew.

"I run my own business," Grace said.

"Oh cool, what kind?"

"I own and manage a luxury dog salon." Grace twirled pasta on her fork. "It's called Oscar & Vinny's, named after my two huskies."

"That's adorable," I said.

"Thanks!" Grace said. "We started off pretty rough because the market's so niche, but I think we have a good footing now. Honestly, I just feel really lucky that my parents let me become an entrepreneur and do something I actually like. Not everyone has that privilege."

"I feel that," Kai said. "My parents wanted me to work in the family business. It was hard for them to accept that I wanted to be a software engineer."

"At least you chose a 'viable' career path," Faith said. "I really wanted to paint and sell my art for a living, but my mom wouldn't let me. It 'doesn't make enough money,' according to her."

I pulled a lock of hair over my cheek to hide behind it. I felt a little embarrassed that I never had this problem, that my parents were supportive in everything I wanted to do. They let me major in anything I wanted to in college, even as I jumped around from Architecture to Pre-Law and ended up settling for Economics. Mom and Dad constantly preached individuality and encouraged me to follow my dreams and make my own path in life. They always wanted me to be uniquely *me*.

"Faith, honey, you're a UI/UX designer at Gojek," Grace said. "That's the thing about art. Even though you're not painting, you can still do something that plays into your interests. The world may not be kind to painters, but it still needs designers."

"That's true," Kai said, cutting up his piece of fish fillet. "Art is such a gift. I wished I had learned it when I was younger. It would help my career a lot if I was more art-savvy."

"Don't worry," Grace said. "You're a software engineer! You're fine."

You're going to be fine, CeCe. The same words echoed in my head in Macy's voice. But it hit differently this time. These people, who were also around my age group, had achieved far more incredible accomplishments than myself and my LA friends.

"Thanks," Faith blushed. "But you know, I don't know how my brother does it. He works in PwC's Deals Advisory department. *Bor-ing.* But I guess there are a lot of people out there like Koko Mike and my boyfriend Jonathan who really, truly enjoy being corporate slaves."

"Jon works at BCG, by the way," Grace said. "He just got promoted, right?"

"Yeah, he did," Faith said.

"Wow, congratulations," I said. "And the friend you mentioned earlier, Christie, was it? She's a CEO?"

"Yeah," Grace said. "She just inherited the company from her dad last year, at twenty-nine. Isn't that wild?"

So the first two friends I've made in Jakarta, and their friend, led successful lives. And I guessed that, since they were friends with Ray, they were also pretty well off. Rich, gorgeous, and intelligent. What more could they want? More importantly, how the hell could I ever fit into this world?

"What about you, CeCe?" Faith asked. "What do you do?"

"Oh…I just graduated last month," I said. "And now I'm working at Kopi Sedap."

"Ah, so that's how you know Ray," Grace said. "Where did you graduate from?"

"I went to USC," I said.

"No way!" Faith said, jumping up from her seat. "Me too! I just graduated last year. How did we not meet each other? You didn't join ASIS, did you?"

"What's that?" I asked.

"The Association of Indonesian Students," Faith said.

I felt my fingers sweat. The fork that held my steak felt slippery.

"No, I didn't," I cleared my throat. My voice became small. "I didn't feel like I deserved to be part of it."

"Aw, why not?" Faith asked. She tilted her head.

"I don't know," I gulped. "I just never saw myself as Indonesian, that's all."

"Well, I hope that changes soon," Faith said, smiling as she ate her first spoonful of food.

Faith and Grace were great people to be around. They tried their best to include me in conversations, including those that were in Indonesian, even though a part of me couldn't help but feel like I wasn't meant to be here.

Never in my life did I ever want to be Indonesian as much as I did at that moment.

I watched everyone gobble up the feast before our eyes, slurping up the pasta and fish and tomato salad that graced the table. Faith, however, barely touched her plate.

"Are you not going to eat, Faith?" I asked nonchalantly, while stuffing myself with another spoonful of pasta.

Grace shot me a look that I couldn't decipher.

"It's okay. I'm good," Faith said. "Thanks, CeCe."

Just as Kai and Mike scooped up the last bits of fish and pasta onto their plates, Ray asked for the bill.

"Ray, please, let me take it," Mike said. "I was the one who invited you guys today."

"Don't be silly!" Ray said. "When else can I take you out? It's fine. Let me pay!"

"No, you guys," Kai said. "Don't do that. I got my bonus from David this month. I'll take it."

"Faith!" Mike hollered. "Get the waiter! Give him my card!"

"Okay guys," Ray said. "While you figure it out, I'm going to go to the bathroom."

I stayed silent and watched as the five friends waved their hands around, fighting to pay for dinner. *Wouldn't people be happy to get a free meal?*

"I don't mind paying for my portion of the dinner," I said.

"CeCe!" Faith giggled. "You're our guest today. We'll treat you."

"This happens all the time when I go out with them," Grace said to me. "I don't remember the last time we actually split the bill."

"Mike insists on paying because Ray always ends up treating us," Faith said, waving her hands at the waiter.

"But I feel bad," I said.

"It's okay," Faith said. "We can do this again another time, just us girls, and you can treat us then."

That was a relief. The bill would've dragged my pockets. I didn't have enough cash on me to pay for even a sixth of the entire dinner. When the waiter finally arrived, he arrived empty-handed and said that the bill was already paid for. And then Ray appeared from behind him and stuck his tongue out at the rest of us.

"You didn't think I actually had to pee, right?" he said, smiling cheekily.

"Ray!" Mike exclaimed. He got up and playfully punched him. "Thank you for dinner, brother."

"Thank you, Ray," everyone echoed.

We all got up to leave the table. After quickly dumping my phone and wallet into my work bag, I briskly walked towards Ray.

"Hey, Ray," I said. "Thanks for dinner. You really didn't have to do that."

"No worries, CeCe," Ray said.

"How do I pay you back?"

"What! Don't be silly. I got you. If you want to, you should just repay me by going out for drinks sometime."

"Sure," I said. "Let's do that."

Ray's hands grazed the small of my back. I twitched. The ghost of his touch lingered on my spine. I followed him closely behind, watching his broad shoulders shrink in the maroon corridor. Ray was charming.

"CeCe! Wait up!"

Grace sprinted towards me. Her yellow dress flowed behind her like waves. Faith pranced closely behind.

"Come, let me get your number," she said, whipping out her phone. "What's your WhatsApp?"

"You guys use WhatsApp here? Not iMessage?"

"Nah," Grace said. "Not everyone here has an iPhone. You should start getting used to WhatsApp if you want to survive here."

I punched my phone number into Grace and Faith's phone. I felt like I was transported back into freshman year at USC, exchanging phone numbers and social media handles after community events.

"Cool! Let's grab lunch or dinner soon," Grace said. "I'd love to introduce you to more people in Jakarta."

"For sure. Thanks for inviting me." I blushed.

"Actually, are you free next Thursday night?" Faith said.

"I should be."

"Come join us for dinner at Cengkeh Bunda then. We're having Indonesian food with a friend. I'll WhatsApp you the details once they're more ironed out."

"That sounds great," I grinned.

I was stumbling out of happy nerves.

"See you, CeCe. It was great to meet you," Grace said.

I walked in between the girls as we strolled into the elevator that Kai held open for us. The doors closed.

"Do you need a ride home, Cecilia?" Kai whispered.

"Um—"

I checked my phone for Pak Sutikno's text to tell me that he arrived at the lobby. It had been delivered thirty minutes ago.

"I'm okay," I said, my cheeks flushed. "My driver's here."

"Oh," Kai said. "Okay then. Maybe next time."

I blushed, silently hoping that Kai would stick by his word, that the friends I made today were going to last for a long time.

8

It was 5:00 p.m. when I wrapped up my fifth official day at Kopi Sedap. I told Pak Sutikno not to pick me up from the office as I planned to walk home. The building's air conditioner was broken, so my office space was humid beyond comprehension. I stripped out of my dress pants, sweaty legs sticking onto the fabric, and slipped into fresh clothes.

Equipped with my bra and leggings, my usual fit for weekly walks with Dad back in LA, I stepped out of the office building. At this time the sun morphed into a warm orange as darkness started taking charge. I watched as motorcycles and cars weaved in and out between one another, red and white lights waltzing as the city let out a solemn exhale. Dad always started each walk with stretches. As I put my arms over my head, I could hear him next to me.

"CeCe, you've got to *really* stretch your arms, okay?" Dad would say as the sun beamed on his face. "You have to take stretching seriously if you don't want to end up with a bad back like me."

I grinned as I put my arms over my head. When the lights came on and people in office attire stared at me, Dad disappeared, and the world didn't hesitate to engulf me in loneliness again. But I couldn't be defeated. I had a new life in Jakarta. This life could have been Dad's, but it was mine now, so I had to start living if I wanted to survive. Macy had said I was going to be fine. I held onto her words as I punched the house address into Google Maps, took a deep breath, and headed wherever I was told to go.

The humidity entangled itself in my hair to form large droplets of perspiration that trickled down along my spine. It was Jakarta in June but felt like LA in August. The two cities struck a chilling contrast. LA's sun sizzled on my skin; Jakarta's boiled. LA's landscape was lush and posh; Jakarta's was solemn and grey. LA's breeze was eerie and exciting; Jakarta's was lukewarm and lonely.

My eyes glittered as they wandered around. Jakarta's nights felt like a different world. The glow of fluorescent lights inside Pacific Place Mall refracted upon its sleek exterior while streetlights twinkled like bokeh on a stranger's glasses. At one point, I looked up and saw a myriad of brilliant neon colors dancing on the exterior of Pacific Century Place. I was absolutely mesmerized.

Google Maps eventually took me past William's, a quaint restaurant that sat halfway between the main road and residential road. The block housed Gojek drivers squatting by the restaurant's entrance, wearing green and black blazers, waiting to pick up and deliver their customers' food. They exhaled cackling words that I presumed were Indonesian.

As I started my hike up Senopati, I witnessed distant heads bobbing behind windows, eating and laughing with elaborate gestures. Many parts of Jakarta didn't have sidewalks so I hiked on the main road, keeping to the right as much as I could to stay among the restaurants. Motorcycles and cars fought for one lane on the road. A cyclist with no helmet strove up the incline, putting all of his energy into the trek. I could smell the pungent body odor as he biked past me, swaying left and right to maintain his balance and momentum.

People swarmed the streets and restaurants like bees. Senopati was crawling with bars, lounges, and hip eateries that made SCBD the most popular destination for young adults, even on a Thursday night. I couldn't tell their ages apart as Indonesians looked so young compared to their Western counterparts, but I was quite sure that I saw high schoolers walk up to restaurants in Gucci tops, Chanel bags, and Louboutin heels.

I knew traffic was bad here, but walking in the midst of it was a whole other story. I bumped into trees, jaywalkers, and other people who were mingling on the side of the road, sipping what looked like black tea in a plastic bag. Some men stood in the middle of the already-crowded road to help drivers park their cars for tips. Pak Sutikno had called them *tukang parkir*, which, from mere phonetics, probably referred to an advanced parking assistant in human form.

Google Maps now said that it would be a ten-minute walk for me to get home. I arrived at a foreign-looking neighborhood that had very minimal lighting, just a tiny light bulb that illuminated each house's gate. It was difficult to see anything past a couple feet. I switched on the flashlight on my phone to scan the vicinity, but all I found in my way were neglected plastic cups, browned leaves, and the occasional stray cat scurrying away behind the dumpsters.

As the roads darkened, so did my spirit. The humidity transformed from warm to eerie. The haze grew suffocating. I puffed my chest and took a deep breath only to cough and choke on oppressive pollutants. I could feel my congested lungs physically reject the air and begged for mercy. LA was the only place I'd grown my roots into, but now I was here, in the middle of a polluted city, with a tropical humidity that engulfed my entire being and dust particles that suffocated my respiratory system.

My eyes darted up to see a black sky. In LA, the night was dotted with stars that congregated in constellations. Jakarta's sky was an empty canvas stained with minute dirt particles that lingered in the heavy air. My contact lenses dried up and blurred my vision. I couldn't stop blinking. I rubbed my eyes, quickly but gently, to quench the dryness and to make sure that I didn't have to pop my lenses back in with dirty fingers. I yawned, cracked my neck, and started walking again.

I turned into a corner that felt just as dark, but a little more ominous. Google Maps said seven more minutes if I decided to jog. I couldn't breathe properly in this weather. My lungs couldn't keep up with the pollution.

Amidst the quiet night and the scrunching of my shoes against dry leaves, I saw Dad again. He was jogging this time, a little faster than I was, but it was he who lit the way. He gestured, inviting me to keep up with him.

"Your legs are longer than mine, Dad," I would say while panting and out of breath.

"That's not an excuse, honey!" Dad would call out as he dashed even further, disappearing into the darkness.

I smiled as the distant memory replayed like an old film. Dad felt close in Jakarta. I wondered why the city brought back memories that I never shared with him. When I reminded myself that he had been dead for a year, a single tear rolled down my face.

As I paused to adjust my sports bra, I heard a whistle. I glanced over and saw an old man, presumably in his late fifties, smoking a cigarette while staring at something below my eyes. It didn't take a genius to figure out he was looking at my breasts. He smiled to reveal a missing front tooth and droopy eyes. He said something in Indonesian that made me shiver, even though I didn't understand him.

Swallowing my fear and anxiety, I started jogging again. I couldn't breathe properly, but that didn't stop me. Adrenaline pumped through my arteries, forcing my heart to beat faster than it did throughout the entire evening. The man proceeded to get up, walk towards me, and reach into his pockets. Alarms went off in my head. He could pull out anything: a gun, a knife, or even a taser.

I dashed into the darkness, pouncing at any chance to take the faster route, which meant trudging through patches of grass, stepping on unknown matter, and trusting my instinct to guide my journey. I neglected Google Maps and let my feet take me where they wanted to. My heart skipped so fast that it echoed throughout my arteries.

After five minutes of running, I cocked my head back to see if the man was still following me. Fortunately, I had lost him amidst the chaos. I stopped running. I wiped the sweat that curtained my forehead, held my knees, and tried to catch my breath. My knees felt sticky, though I wasn't sure what from. I didn't care at that point. I was just glad that I was safe. I was glad that I was alive.

When I looked up to wipe the sweat that curtained my forehead, I saw a familiar yellow light illuminate the darkness.

It was the *warung* at the corner of my street.

How lucky I am to have run the right way home.

I exerted every last droplet of energy to jog the last block over to the house, banging on the tall black gate to get Pak Sutikno's attention.

"Nonik!" Pak Sutikno cried.

Pak Sutikno frantically ran out of the gate, rushing to unlock them. At this point, I really regretted asking him to stay behind.

"Hello, Pak Sutikno," I said in-between breaths.

He proceeded to spit some worried-sounding Indonesian words at me that ended with "okay?"

"Okay," I replied.

The house's lights highlighted the dirt and pollution that stuck to my limbs. My work bag was soaked in sweat and anxiety. My legs were covered in ash, dirt, and unidentified gray matter. It smelled like cat poop, but I refused to accept that. I flicked off the tiny yellow leaves that stuck to my skin and wiped my shoes against the welcome rug.

When I entered the house, looking and smelling like trash, Oma Shaan happened to pass by. Her jaw dropped.

"Nonik!" Oma gasped. "Why do you look like that?"

"Hi, Oma," I muttered.

I really regretted going for a jog now.

"Did you just come home from work?" she asked, pointing at my bag.

"I did, Oma," I said. "I wanted to go for a walk."

"What? A walk? You went for a walk by yourself after dark in your underwear?"

I squeezed my thighs.

"And you didn't ask Pak Sutikno to come with you?"

"I thought—"

"Are you crazy, Nonik?" Oma yelled. "Are you asking for trouble? Your body will be seen by those *tukang*! You want to give them a free show? You want them to rape you?"

"No one asks to be raped," I said.

My mind darted to the man with one front tooth. I shuddered.

Getting raped was most definitely a long shot.

But, as I pondered Oma's words more, the man really could have pulled out a weapon, immobilized me, and very well have raped me in the middle of the darkness. Getting raped wasn't much of a long shot after all.

"You think you're so smart, Nonik?" Oma scoffed. "What if something bad happens? You could get hit by a car; you know that? Have you seen how reckless these drivers are?"

Oma's words slowly sunk in. Over the past hour, I had been walking on the side of the road, alongside cars, motorcycles, and people. There was no designated sidewalk for pedestrians. I couldn't believe I braved through all of that without weighing the risks.

"I realize that now," I said.

"Good," Oma said. "If you want to run, we have a perfectly good treadmill in the gym downstairs."

"But it's different, Oma."

I hated treadmills. I hated the concept of tiring myself by moving a grand total of zero inches.

"Sorry, Oma." I hung my head.

"Now go shower," Oma said. "I'll call the security to make sure no one followed you here."

"Okay," I hung my head, proceeding to walk to the stairs.

"And take off your shoes, please?" Oma said, pointing at the trail of mud that I had left behind in the few steps taken. "Can you make that a habit in this house?"

Oma Shaan rushed to the home telephone and dialed the security guards. I went upstairs and curled into a ball in my bathroom, feeling grateful that I was safe but anxious about Oma's wrath. I had to be careful next time.

As I slumped on the floor, scrolling on my phone, I saw a missed call then text from Mom that had come in earlier that day.

I know you're busy but call me when you're free sweetie. I miss you—15:40

I felt a knot in my stomach. I missed Mom so much, but what could I say when she asked how I was? *Sorry for the late reply, Mom, I almost died today* or *Hi, Mom, I'm doing great, besides the fact that I can't do anything in Jakarta without Oma's permission.*

I stared at the mirror, seeing all the dirt that had rubbed across my body and clothes. I ran my fingers across my face, smelled the cat poop that made its way to my shins, and broke into tears.

9

Macy's Instagram stories featured her eating at fancy restaurants, getting manicures with her new friends, and partying with boys. My eyes fixated on the glaring "Read" underneath my texts to her. I knew she was busy, but I didn't think she'd be busy enough to ignore me.

I looked up from my phone to see a now-familiar Jakarta cityscape. The ominous darkness still scared me, but the blank skies had started to grow on me. At least I was safe in the car with Pak Sutikno. I leaned against the car's rain-washed windows and listened to the humming vehicles that whizzed past us.

Eventually, Pak Sutikno stopped the car, got out, and opened my door.

"Thank you," I said as I exited the Mercedes Benz.

Fearful of being underdressed, I wore the brand new stilettos that Oma had bought for me. I clicked my heels against the stone steps that led up to the restaurant. My stomach fluttered. Faith and Grace had invited me to dinner with one of their friends. I couldn't help but feel excited about somehow finding a place in this strange, new world.

I swung my yellow Prada bag across my body as I pushed the heavy glass doors. I stepped into the restaurant, but before I could take in the elegant restaurant, my heels slipped on some liquid on the floor. I grabbed onto a potted plant to ease my balance, but—

Thud. I fell. I was sure that I pulled a muscle. I squeaked. Thankfully the plant stayed intact.

"Ibu!" a woman said, rushing to my aid.

She added something in Indonesian. My body felt even more sore now that I couldn't understand her.

"Hi, sorry," I said, tucking a lock of hair behind my ear. "I don't speak Indonesian."

"Oh, um," she said. "Are you okay?"

Thank goodness the lady could speak English. I realized then, through her uniform and professional demeanor, that she was a waitress.

"Yes, yes, I'm fine," I said, my ankle throbbing. "Thanks, Mbak."

"We just mopped the floors, so they're slippery, *aduh*, I should've put a sign up. Sorry, Ibu. We'll make it up to you."

"Oh no, it's alright, really." I didn't know why I felt guilty. "Don't worry about it."

"It's okay, Ibu, we'll get you something on the house. Do you have a reservation?"

"Yes, it should be under Gracelyn Michelle for four."

"Okay. You're the second person to arrive. I'll show you to your table."

I got up, my head throbbing now too, and followed the waitress into the restaurant. Wood carvings of rice *padi* fields and Indonesian *wayang* puppets graced the walls. Glass chandeliers dangled above the mahogany tables like frozen butterflies. Two men dressed in *batik* played the *gamelan* at the center of the restaurant. Cengkeh Bunda was the fanciest Indonesian restaurant, according to Grace, which was why she invited me to check it out.

The waitress escorted me to a table, where a lady sat, hiding her face behind a menu.

"Hello there," I said.

"Hi," the lady said, lowering her menu.

I was taken aback by the woman's features. She looked like an Asian Audrey Hepburn. Her crisp jawline, sunken cheeks, and carefully manicured eyebrows were nothing short of perfection. Her hair was twisted into an elegant bun, secured tightly with a dazzling headpiece. Not a single hair was out of place.

"Are you Grace's friend?" she asked.

"Yes, hi, I'm Cecilia Poetry," I said, reaching out my hand. "And you are?"

"Christine," she said, shaking my hand. "But call me Christie."

Christie, as in, the girl who's allegedly cheating on that Bryan guy?

"Nice to meet you, Christie," I said.

Christie's lips twisted into a smile that highlighted her cheekbones. She was gorgeous.

"Take a seat," Christie said. "Guess how old I am."

"What?"

"I ask everyone this when I first meet them. I'm just curious to see how old people think I am."

"Um, twenty-five?"

She definitely looked much older, but I rounded down in case she got offended.

"Close! I'm thirty, actually," Christie giggled, outlining her jaw with her fingers. "I'm flattered that you think I'm so young. Want to know the secret?"

"Um…"

"I use this ginseng extract serum on my face every night," Christie showed me a photo of the serum on her phone. "You can only get it from Japan. It tightens your skin so much that I'm still only going to look thirty in thirty years."

"Oh, wow."

"If you want, I can get some for you. You look like you're already showing some lines. Or I could also introduce you to my plastic surgeon in Hong Kong. He can tighten your face up really nicely."

"Thanks, Christie, but I don't need any of that."

I raised my eyebrow sarcastically and forced a smile. *You don't know everyone's story, so you have to be polite, darling,* Mom's voice echoed in my head. I fiddled with the peach-colored napkin on the table, hoping that Christie would get that I wasn't interested in her skincare routine.

"Oh, girl, everyone needs a nice face lift. After all, nobody's perfect."

Christie squinted at my face, looking as if she was analyzing a bacterial sample.

"You can totally get some work done on your nose, you know, make it more arched like mine. But I totally understand if looking beautiful isn't your priority."

I scoffed.

"I think I look fine," I growled.

"No one's saying you don't," Christie said. "It's good to see that you have some sort of self-confidence, but the reality is that no one is as pretty as they think."

"Excuse me?"

"Well, I guess it's a good thing if you don't prioritize beauty. Beauty is expensive. Luckily my father can afford my expensive lifestyle. After all, I am running his company. He better do something to pay me back for it."

This girl is so fucking self-centered.

"Hey, CeCe, Christie, you made it!"

Faith and Grace had finally arrived. But they didn't look like they did at last week's dinner. Instead of youthful outfits, they wore dull, patterned clothes and had slapped on a heavy layer of makeup. Faith wore a bold red lip while Grace wore dark eyeshadow. I'd met them once, but it didn't take a genius to guess that they were dressing older to impress Christie.

"Hi, my loves," Christie said, getting up to give them cheek kisses.

"You've met CeCe already?" Grace asked.

"Yeah," I said. "We had a lovely chat about Christie's skin."

"I suggested my plastic surgeon to her," Christie said. "Don't you think she can get some work done on her face?"

My eyes twitched. I looked to the family of four eating peacefully next to our table in an attempt to calm myself down.

"Have you guys ordered?" Faith asked.

"Yeah, I ordered what I liked last time, plus the *gulai ikan* that Grace mentioned in our chat yesterday," Christie said.

"You didn't order the *bubur ayam* that I wanted?" Faith said.

"I didn't feel like it," Christie said. "That's okay, right? I'm watching my weight. You should, too, especially if you don't want to end up fat like you were a few years ago."

Faith plastered on a sheepish smile, trying to look unbothered by Christie's comments, but distress brewed in her eyes.

Faith and Grace sat down. I focused hard on the men playing the *gamelan*, trying not to stare at Faith's red lips that made her complexion too pale. She looked a little ill, but it was probably because her thick foundation was a shade lighter than it was supposed to be.

"I want to update you guys on something," Faith announced.

"What is it, darling?" Christie asked.

Faith showed us her hand, her ring finger adorned with a large, pear-shaped diamond.

"Oh my god!" I squealed. "Congratulations, Faith!"

"It happened at dinner a couple nights ago, on our two-year anniversary, actually," Faith said, admiring her ring. "And here are the 'save the date' cards for the engagement party in October. It's in four months, but we want to take things slow. Plus, it never hurts to party twice, right?"

"*Someone* finally had the balls to pop the question," Grace said, hugging Faith as she handed us the invitations.

"Remind me what he does again?" Christie said.

Can't Christie just be happy for Faith? Does it matter what her fiancé does for a living?

"He works at BCG," Faith said.

"I know, but isn't his dad super rich or something?" Christie asked.

"Om Anto?"

"Right, Anto Budiono," Christie said, looking at her nails. "Their company basically has a monopoly on cacao and palm oil in Indonesia, right? Wow, you're so lucky, Faith, marrying into a billionaire's family. Congrats."

Faith and Grace giggled, but I couldn't. Christie was being so rude. I couldn't believe she could get away with her materialistic comments. I clenched my jaw and stared into the restaurant, gazing at the symbiosis of waiters that scurried around to each note played on the *gamelan*.

Shortly after I buzzed out of the conversation, the restaurant manager came over and delicately placed a plate of fried spring rolls on our table.

"This is on the house," the manager said to me. "Apologies again, Ibu."

"Thank you," I said.

I leaned over and smelled the dish. Oil sparkled against the crisp surface of the rolls that smelled like flour and fried vegetables. I reached out to grab a piece.

"What happened?" Grace asked.

My fingers paused in mid-air, inches away from the spring rolls.

"I slipped at the lobby," I said. "They were mopping the floor and forgot to put a warning sign up. And I'm wearing new heels. So, *voilà*."

Christie howled in laughter.

"I can't believe you fell in the middle of the restaurant," Christie exclaimed. "It must've been *so* embarrassing."

My cheeks flushed. *Faith and Grace were friends with her?*

"It was," I growled.

"Anyways, let's dig in," Grace said, perhaps sensing the tension. "I've tried this before, and it's really good. Thanks for getting it for free, CeCe."

"Of course," I said, darting a side-eye to Christie.

Because everyone else used forks to pick up their rolls, I did, too. Oil and flavors oozed into my mouth as I bit into the spring roll. It tasted unhealthy, but I indulged in it anyway.

"How's work, Chris?" Grace said, cutting up the spring rolls.

"Good," Christie said, stabbing a piece with her fork. "I just fired this bitch of a secretary."

"Why? What happened?" Faith asked.

"I asked her to get me white curtains, but that idiot got me beige ones," Christie said. "Isn't that fucked up? How can someone not know the difference between white and beige? I was so mad."

"I don't think that's worth firing her over, though," I said, munching on my spring rolls.

"Well," Christie said. "You don't know the start of it. She started growing pimples all over her cheeks. I can't stare at her ugly face all day. She can come work for me again when she has better skin."

Faith and Grace laughed. I fisted my palms so as to not throw myself at her. Luckily, before I could, the rest of the food came. The waitress served us black fried rice with shrimp crackers, yellow soup called *soto ayam*, chicken curry, as well as other local dishes that I didn't recognize. The platter of food smelled like lemongrass and turmeric.

"It's really good, CeCe," Grace said. "I think you'll like it."

"Let's eat," Faith said. "Help yourselves."

Faith scooped a spoonful of fried rice onto Christie's plate. When she took a bite, her face contorted into a sour expression.

"Ew!" Christie said. "It tastes so bland."

"I agree," Faith said mid-bite. "Let's ask for some *sambal*. That might spice up the flavor."

"You're right." Christie said. "Mbak!"

A waitress with three plates balanced on her forearm came running over.

"Yes, Ibu?" the waitress asked.

"Do you have *sambal*?" Christie asked.

"Sorry, Ibu. We ran out."

Like a five-year-old child, Christie banged the table and got up. Faith, Grace, and I stared at her, hoping that she wouldn't cause a scene, but neighboring tables were already starting to look.

Christie squinted at the waitress' name tag.

"Tell me Mbak...Dewi," she said. "How can an Indonesian restaurant run out of *sambal*?"

"Sorry, Ibu. Sorry," the waitress said. She looked like she was on the verge of tears.

"I spend my blood-earned money on your disgusting food, and you tell me that you don't have the one thing that can make it taste good? *Anjing kamu*. I'll tell the owner, Ibu Tini, about you. *Awas*."

"Sorry, Ibu." It was all she could say.

The poor waitress looked like she was about to cry. I so badly wanted to comfort her, but I knew that that would just make things even more awkward. She bowed and scurried away like a scared little mouse, back into the staff's hole, hidden from cats like Christie.

Christie, on the other hand, looked unbothered by the fiasco. She sat back down and continued to eat nonchalantly while scrolling through her phone. Faith and Grace also continued to scoop up food into their plates as if nothing had happened. How could they keep quiet amidst all of this? I couldn't stay quiet. I had to defend the waitress for Mbak Ani's sake. People didn't deserve to be bullied by the Christies of the world.

"Wasn't that a little harsh, Christie?" I prompted. "It's not her fault that the restaurant ran out of *sambal*."

"If *these* people are paid to serve us and fail to do so, they should be reprimanded. Fired, even. I know the owner of this place and if I breathe a word of this to her, that idiot will be gone in a matter of seconds."

"What do you mean, *these* people? What are you trying to refer to?"

Faith shot me a look. Grace shoved a bunch of rice into her mouth so she couldn't physically respond to the ongoing situation.

I felt my heart thumping against my chest. I wasn't the confrontational type, so having to confront Christie made me nervous.

"Look, I know you're new here, but these locals are the bane of the Indonesian society. They're lazy, incompetent, and stupid. That's why they're waiters and workers. They're not like us. They can never be like us."

There it was again. *They're not like us.*

"Being of a different social status doesn't give you license to treat people like shit."

"It does if I pay them for doing things that benefit me," Christie said, chewing on the chicken curry.

Anger bred, churned, and bubbled to the surface like magma, ready to erupt. I looked at Faith slurping on her tofu and chewed on my own.

"Do you realize that the reason why you have food on the table, why you have a house, and why you can run your dad's company is these so-called 'lazy, incompetent, and stupid' people who work their butts off to give it to you?"

"Okay, smarty pants." Christie sneered. "Quit telling me what to do. You're younger than me. Remember that."

"And the reason why people are waiters and workers isn't because they're lazy or incompetent," I continued. "It's just because these people lack opportunities to grow and be empowered. You can't say—"

"Guys," Grace interrupted. "Let's not talk about that here. We're at a Michelin-star restaurant. It's inappropriate."

So, Christie's classism, elitism, and racism are appropriate, but debating real issues at a sophisticated restaurant isn't?

"Yeah," Faith said. "Let's just enjoy the rest of the food before it gets cold."

"For sure," Christie said. "Sorry, guys. I just get so disgusted by poor people."

I chewed on my chicken curry to keep my mouth shut, staring into the heart of Cengkeh Bunda. It was a glorious space. Light crystallized into rainbows against the refraction of the chandelier's glass details, illuminating the main actors on stage. One waiter was taking orders. Another was balancing dirty plates on their arms. And a third waiter was cleaning iced tea that was spilled on a table. It was 7:30 p.m. by that time. The restaurant had started to buzz with more people chatting away on their elegant Thursday evening.

"How's Bryan?" Grace said, breaking the silence.

"He's good," Christie said. "I mean, yeah, he's okay."

"That's nice."

"Has Faith told you, Grace?"

"Told me what?"

"You know...Kenny," Christie nudged Grace's elbow.

Faith kicked Grace under the table and gave her a look. I tried my best not to eavesdrop, but the conversation was too interesting to not see it unfold further.

"You really want to talk about that here?" Faith whispered.

"I mean," Christie giggled. "He's pretty cute."

Dating a married man is one thing, but bragging about your scandalous affair to your friends is only something people like Christie can pull off.

"What happened to Bryan?" Grace said.

"Bryan's fine with it," Christie said.

"Are you sure?" Faith said, sipping her iced tea.

"Well, he'd better be if he still wants me," Christie said.

"Who else knows?" Grace said.

"I'm pretty sure a lot of people know. It's not like I hide my personal life."

The magma within me erupted.

"Isn't he married?" I blurted out.

I never confronted anyone. I never started fights. But Christie embodied everything that I hated about the human race. I didn't care if she hated me.

"What?" Christie said.

Faith and Grace looked at me, their faces drained of color.

"This Kenny guy," I said. "Does his wife not know?"

"Does that matter? He's literally begging for my attention."

"Do you not care that you're breaking up a family?"

"He's the sinner, not me."

I stabbed the chicken with my fork.

"You're a sinner too," I exclaimed. "Innocent women don't go after other women's husbands."

Christie scoffed.

"What do you know about dating? Do you like someone?"

"What, no," I said.

"A little birdy told me that you were after the Kurniawan family," Christie said.

"Who?"

"Oh, don't play dumb, Cecilia. Raynard Kurniawan. Isn't he why you started working at Kopi Sedap?"

"Ray?"

"Didn't you get the job at Kopi Sedap just to go out with him?"

I couldn't let her words asphyxiate me.

"Are you being serious right now?" I scoffed.

"Oh, did that not happen?" Christie said nonchalantly, cutting up her chicken. "I don't know, you seemed like the type to do that, pretty new girl and all."

I gripped onto the napkin resting on my thighs and squeezed it in my hands. Grace's eyes scrambled around, frantically looking for a distraction.

"Dessert?" Grace called out.

"Yes!" Faith said.

"Is anyone down for *es cendol*?" Grace said. "The one here is really good."

"What's that?" I asked.

"It's a dessert made of beads of green jelly-like flour, coconut milk, and brown sugar. It's really good. If you like brown sugar, then you'd really like this."

"Okay, I'll try it."

I stayed quiet for the rest of the dinner, shutting down from Christie and her egocentric tongue. Not once did she ask about Faith, or Grace, or me. I couldn't understand why Faith and Grace wanted to stay her friend, or why they acted so differently around her. I bit my tongue whenever Christie said something that triggered my anger.

As the three ladies laughed around me, I opened my phone. Still no text from Macy.

Macy, call me? I met a bitch today and got some juicy stuff for ya!—19:50

Macy texted back almost immediately.

C! Sorry babe it's been a hectic week. Yes, I promise to call you once I finish my morning jog.—19:51

I glanced at my phone every minute to see if Macy called, or if she ever would. In the meantime, I ate my *es cendol* quietly while Faith and Grace gazed at Christie like she was a celebrity. She was undeniably a beautiful woman, even though she had horrible values.

When they finished their meals, Christie paid the bill with her exclusive, special edition credit card. She said it was her least favorite of the five that she owned, but because it was red and had her horse zodiac on it, she thought it was a lucky card when buying meals for her friends. While Faith clapped and Grace laughed, I rolled my eyes.

Christie was the most pathetic person I've ever met.

By the time I thanked Christie for the meal, it was almost 8:30 p.m. Macy hadn't called. I said my goodbyes and briskly hopped back into the Mercedes, where Pak Sutikno drove me away from the chaos that was Christie.

I was never going to get invited to anything with Faith and Grace ever again.

I called Macy with no luck. It was past 9:00 p.m. at this point, but she still hadn't answered. Perhaps she had gone to breakfast with her coworkers. I was glad that she was thriving in her new life, even though my night went horribly.

Just as I was about to doze off to the car's hum, I got a text from Faith.

CeCe, my mom's cooking at my apartment next Friday night. Christie can't make it, so it'll just be me and Grace, and maybe my sister Clarissa. Come join us!—21:07

Accepting that Macy was thriving in her new life, I decided that the only way forward was to thrive in mine. I accepted Faith's invitation, locked my phone, then closed my eyes, praying that my friendship with Macy would survive the long distance.

10

It was a serene Friday evening when the elevator doors opened up to the entrance of Faith's apartment unit. On empty bellies, Faith, Grace, and I exited the elevator. Faith's unit was twenty floors atop the Eaglewood tower at the Pakubuwono Residences.

A small table stood in front of the elevator, decorated with purple orchids and photo frames. I spotted Faith in her maroon USC graduation gown and a photo of young Mike in a ski suit. In another photo, Faith, Grace, and their families posed in Christmas sweaters at a Japanese ski resort.

"Where was this?" I asked, pointing at the picture.

"Oh gosh, that was at least six years ago," Faith said. "Our families went to Niseko together over Christmas break in high school. Grace's sister Georgia is close to my younger siblings, Clarissa and Jason, so our families always look forward to trips together."

Faith and Grace were a lot closer than I had thought. My trips with Macy always stayed within California, but even then, the trips were never very long.

Before I proceeded to open the front door, Faith shoved her body in front of me.

"Shoes!" Faith said, pointing at my Adidas sneakers.

I looked down at Faith's naked feet, and behind me at Grace who was removing her right shoe. I remembered Hanna Wang, a Taiwanese engineer from freshman year, who always forced us to take off our shoes before entering her dorm room. My parents stopped enforcing that rule when I was ten, but I guess that's how it was in Indonesia as well.

"I'm sorry," I said. I took off my shoes and set them aside next to Grace's.

Faith smiled, slipped her key into the keyhole, and pushed the door open.

"Ma, I'm home!" Faith called out, dropping her keys in a little basket by the door. "Grace and Cecilia are here."

"Hi, Tante Lam," Grace said.

"Hello," I chimed in.

We headed towards the kitchen, where Faith's mom was standing over a pot. It was a small and simple kitchen with dirty pots and plates stacked atop one another in the deep sink. Jars of spices were organized neatly into a tower that graced the sides of the white marble aisle.

"Hello, Cecilia," she reached out her greasy hands to shake mine. "I'm Lam Ing. It's nice to meet you."

Lam Ing's dark hair perched perfectly on her shoulders, tracing her sharp jaw and highlighting her black doe eyes. She wore a plain white t-shirt and jeans that accentuated her slender frame. I would never have guessed that she was Faith's mom; she could definitely pass as Faith's sister.

"Hi, Lam Ing," I said.

"Call me Tante Lam, please, my dear."

Oh no.

"I'm sorry, Tante Lam," I said.

"CeCe is from LA, Ma," Faith said. I could tell that she was also embarrassed of me.

"I see," Tante Lam lit up. "Well in Indonesia you call older women *tante* and older men *oom*."

Tante Lam patted me on the back. Faith and Grace looked at me. They seemed relieved. Tante Lam was a lot more accommodating after knowing that I was foreign to Indonesian customs.

The Salim family's modern apartment was adorned with cream and walnut wood accents. Chandeliers hovered above the dining table and living area. Large family portraits hung on the walls. Below one was a fishbowl with a single googly-eyed goldfish. An empty dog cage, fit for a dog as small as Leader, sat next to the L-shaped couch in the living room.

"Where's Kingsley? Why isn't he in his cage?" Faith asked, peering into the corner.

"Clarissa took him to her friend's house," Tante Lam said.

"What about Ko Mike and Jason?"

"*Aiya*, who knows? Out somewhere," Tante Lam rolled her eyes. "You kids always disappear on Friday nights. Can you feed the fish please?"

After Faith sprinkled pellets into the fishbowl, she and Grace hovered over Tante Lam's shoulder as she swiftly tossed greens on a sizzling wok. The garlic aroma floated through the room, spotlighting Tante Lam and her wok as the other items blurred into the background.

The maid took a large, red crab out of the warmer and placed it in the middle of the dining table. Steam ascended from the plate, hovering above the oil, garlic, and ham that the crab was braised in. My mouth watered as I envisioned the harmony of bacon and garlic melting on my tongue.

Tante Lam transferred the greens from the wok to a serving plate. She brought the dish to the table, right next to the crab so the aromas blended nicely together.

"This is Mama's signature dish," Faith said. "She never makes this unless it's for special occasions."

"I think the last time we had it was on your birthday two years ago," Grace said.

"You're right," Faith exclaimed.

"This crab is the best thing I make," Tante Lam said, pointing at the crab. "My friends always pre-order this dish from me."

Everyone, except Tante Lam, chose their seats and sat down. I sat at the empty seat that was clearly designated for me.

"Let me walk you through the meal," Tante Lam said, straightening her back. She pointed at the dishes that laid on the table, waiting to be devoured. "This crab is inspired by Surabaya's famous Beatus restaurant sauteed with garlic and ham. But I put my own twists to it."

"She's the only one in Jakarta who can replicate the original," Faith said.

"*Aiya*, Jie, don't say that *lah*. I'm not trying to replicate it. I'm making my own version of the crab."

Watching Faith and Tante Lam made me miss Mom dearly. She had decided to take up a side job selling handmade quilts on Etsy after I left. I asked her why, since it wasn't like she needed extra cash, but she told me that she wanted to keep herself busy in her loneliness after work. Mom's sister, my Aunt Krista, had been accompanying her at home on the weekends and helping out with her new side hustle. Though she was tired, I was glad that she was keeping herself busy.

"It's good, Tante," Grace said. "You got it right!"

"You girls are too kind," Tante Lam pointed at the vegetables. "This is *kangkung belacan*, which is...*aduh* Jie, how do I explain this?"

"*Belacan* is some kind of spicy seafood sauce," Faith said. "But *kangkung* is *kangkung*. Is there an English word for it?"

Grace opened Google Translate.

"*Kangkung* means water spinach," she announced.

"Got it," I said, having no idea what water spinach was.

"Come, let me serve you, Cecilia," Tante Lam said.

I handed my plate to Tante Lam as she scooped crab claws, garlic, and bacon onto my plate. Everyone cracked their crab shells. I cracked the claw, dug up its flesh with my fingers, and took a bite. The symbiosis of savory flavors exploded in my mouth. Who knew that garlic and bacon would be perfect condiments to crab?

"*Enak*?" Tante Lam asked.

"Yes, *enak*," I said, remembering the Indonesian word that Bu Ratih taught me. "It tastes really good, Tante."

Tante Lam started telling me about how she started cooking after divorcing Faith's dad. A housewife with no college degree, four young kids to take care of, and a very stingy divorce settlement had left her at a crossroads, not knowing how she could support her family in the long run. Faith and Grace ignored her and continued ravaging the crab and water spinach.

A classic rags-to-riches tale.

"My mother warned me about that idiot," Tante Lam said. "I should've listened."

When Tante Lam and her ex-husband were still married, Faith's paternal grandma left them with a maid, Mbak Tri, who taught her all of the family recipes. From the best way to dice garlic to cooking the perfect fish, Tante Lam learned everything from her.

Cooking started off as a hobby, making meals and cakes for her kids and close friends. But as her savings depleted and her children grew up, Tante Lam realized that she could capitalize on her talents and start cooking professionally, especially with her connections to powerful people in Jakarta.

"That's how our families know each other," Faith said, indicating to Grace, her plate piling up with crab shells.

"Yeah," Tante Lam said. "You know, we went on trips together. It wasn't until I met Grace's grandpa that I could finally afford to send my kids to college abroad."

I sat at the edge of my seat, fingers deep in my crab claw.

"My friend is married to Grace's uncle, who introduced my food to his dad, so Grace's grandpa, Pak Awi Kusuma, owner and president director of Kusuma Group, which owns BTI TV," Tante Lam said.

She pinched some crab meat with her fingers, ate it, and chased it with a piece of garlic.

"Pak Awi offered me my own cooking show called *Dapur Mama Lam*, Mama Lam's Kitchen, and I used the funds from there to start my own private dining business," Tante Lam said mid-chew. "That's also when Pak Awi introduced me to his son Hendra and his wife Stella. What a happy coincidence for their kids to be similar in age with mine."

"That was, what?" Faith said, looking up momentarily. "Oh gosh, almost twenty years ago?"

"Wow, yes," Grace nodded. "Time flies."

"And our families just clicked. Stella is like my older sister and the kids, well, they get along so well as you can see."

Tante Lam pointed at the photo hanging over the piano. I hadn't gotten a proper look at it before, but I realized now that it was a family photo of Faith and Grace's families. The women dressed up in white dresses while the men wore luxurious tuxes. I spotted Yves Saint Laurent shoes peeking out from underneath Grace's dress. They really were a family.

I bit the crab awkwardly, feeling a little queasy. My insecurities sent me down a dangerous spiral. *I'm not good enough. I'm never going to fit in.*

I'm not supposed to be here.

My eyes darted at the hanging portrait. What were the chances that the first two girls I got along with in Jakarta were so close that they belonged to this perfect little family?

But I couldn't belong to another family. Mine was dysfunctional enough.

"Who does Mike hang out with?" I pointed at Mike, tucked away in the corner of the photo.

"He mostly hangs out with me and Grace since we're the ones closest in age with him," Faith said.

"That's not the only reason why," Tante Lam winked at Grace.

Mike likes Grace?

"Tante!" Grace exclaimed, dropping her crab. "You know that's a lie."

"*Aduh* Gracie," Tante Lam said. "It's so obvious that he's liked you for a long time."

"He's just a brother to me," Grace said. "And that will never change."

"Sis," Faith said. "You've got to be blind if you don't see it. Mike is super into you."

"I kind of see it, too," I said, just to join the conversation.

"See, Gracie?" Tante Lam said. "Even the new girl agrees."

Tante Lam's words struck me. I was the "new girl" now, the underdog, the naïve one, the girl who had to try even harder to fit in. I felt my solitary walls cave in. The bright room felt gloomy and suffocating. I felt an urge to leave, but I couldn't bring myself to after Tante Lam's story.

Imagine having the life you do because of another person.

I watched as Tante Lam's skinny fingers scratched the crab, wondering how calloused they must be for her to arrive at where she is today. She undoubtedly got what she wanted because of her incredible talent, but she owed everything else to Grace's grandfather: her wealth, her career, and even her children's education.

No wonder she was so kind to Grace.

Dad told me that he left Asia to avoid this kind of proximity politics, the pressure of having to rely on your network of friends and colleagues to succeed. I couldn't imagine all the fake smiles that were exchanged just so that people could get what they wanted. For all I knew, Tante Lam could be faking her niceness to Grace and her family. It didn't seem that way, but it very well could be.

How could I fit into a world where I was the "new girl" who knew nobody?

I shivered at the thought but worrying was no use. My new life in Jakarta was barely beginning. The best I could do was look pretty, play the game, and win. And I absolutely had to win. I had to win for Dad. For Mom. I had to win to prove to Oma and Opa that my parents raised me well.

"Dessert?" Faith said as she put down her crab shell. "We have some *es podeng* in the fridge."

In spite of my discomfort, I knew that I probably had to rely on people like Faith and Grace to make it in Jakarta. I took a deep breath, dampened my frustrations, and exhaled a strong, confident "yes."

11

Faith called and asked me to come over to her apartment later. She told me that she had planned to have drinks with Grace, who had to cancel at the last minute, but she wanted me to come over to "get to know me better." Although I hated the idea of being someone's second choice, Tante Lam had gently scared me into making friends in Jakarta. Without much hesitation, I accepted Faith's invitation.

Since Indonesian schools open the academic year in July, the 5:00 p.m. Monday traffic to Faith's apartment was harsh. Pak Sutikno drove at only twenty miles per hour while I leaned my head against the window at the backseat, scrolling through my Instagram feed. Macy had just posted a new photo of her at a bar. I gave the post a quick like and locked my phone.

I rubbed the inner corner of my eye. Macy still hadn't texted or called me back since she promised to three days ago. Since she had clearly moved on from her college friends, it was probably best that I did, too.

Maybe it's a good thing that I was hanging out with Faith today.

As Pak Sutikno dropped me off at the Pakubuwono Residences, Faith picked me up at the lobby. We meandered through people and lush green shrubs illuminated by an evening glow.

"Thanks for coming, CeCe," Faith said. "I didn't want to waste the soju that Mike got for me."

"Of course," I said, plastering a smile.

Tante Lam hollered from the pantry as Faith and I shuffled into the apartment.

"Hi, Cecilia!" she waved. "I have some *nastar* in the oven. Do you want some?"

I shot Tante Lam a puzzled look, but she was too busy to notice.

"*Nastar* is pineapple tart," Faith whispered to me.

I nodded and grinned.

"Sure, Ma," Faith said.

"Also, Jie, do you know where your sister is?"

"I think she took Kingsley to her friend's house."

"Again?" Tante Lam said. "She never spends time at home anymore."

"Clarissa's a college freshman, Ma," Faith said. "Just wait. She'll want to be home every day once she starts work in four years."

Tante Lam chuckled.

"We'll be in my room, Ma," Faith said, grabbing my hand.

"Okay, *sayang*. Have fun."

I gave a half bow to Tante Lam and followed Faith into the bedroom. Her room was girly but minimalist. White and cream tones were splashed across the interior, with the apartment's signature walnut wood floors. Two twin beds stood adjacent to each other. I'd always liked contemporary architecture, and the Salims did it well, creating a modern space that was both stunning and cozy.

"Your room is so neat," I exclaimed, fingers grazing her pale pink bed sheets.

"Well, it's not just *my* room," she said. "Mama wanted Clarissa and I to be close, so she made us share a room."

Faith opened her closet to reveal a wine cooler. Bottles of soju were stacked up against one another.

"Which one do you want? I have grape-, peach-, and apple-flavored soju," Faith said.

"Ooh," I licked my lips. Drinking soju reminded me of my karaoke days in LA's Koreatown. "Grape sounds great."

"Good choice," Faith said, tossing me a bottle.

We plopped down on the fluffy microfiber rug in between the two beds. It was the same rug that I eyed at Bed Bath & Beyond but never got because it was a dust-trapper, hence too tedious for me to vacuum.

I couldn't stop running my hands through the rug's fibers.

"Feels nice, huh?" Faith took a sip from her soju.

"Yeah, wow," I said. "I never bought this because it's a bitch to clean."

"It really is," Faith said. "I feel bad saying this, but I feel so lucky that we have Mbak Tri here to vacuum everything up. Otherwise, I can't be bothered to clean it myself. Speaking of which…"

Faith got up, dug through her bedside table, and tossed me a coaster. I eyed the rest of the room. Everything from the alignment of the beds to the arrangement of stationery on the two desks were so neat. Even the power cords were securely bound with colorful pipe cleaners.

"Sorry," she said, sensing my judgment. "Clarissa would kill me if we stained the rug."

"It's alright," I said, placing my coaster next to my legs. "Are you two close?"

"I'm closer to Koko Mike, just because we're closer in age. Clarissa is five years younger than me, so she just finished her freshman year at Boston U."

"I see."

"What about you? Do you have any siblings?"

"No, it's just me," I said.

"What about cousins?"

"I'm not close to anyone else in my family," I almost felt embarrassed to admit that. "It was just me, my mom, and my dad growing up."

"That's nice," Faith said. "My parents got divorced when I was a kid, and I haven't met my dad since. At least your family unit is complete."

No, it isn't, I wanted to say. My family was never going to be complete again. I pinched the skin between my thumb and index finger, trying to make it hurt enough that I wouldn't start sobbing in front of Faith.

"Can't you find him?" I said, steering the conversation elsewhere. "Your dad?"

"I guess I could, but he was kind of an asshole to Mama, especially during the divorce. So we kids felt that it was best not to find him and potentially stir up more trouble."

"And your mom doesn't want to remarry?"

"Nah. She hasn't dated since the divorce," Faith said. "She's pretty much married to her kitchen show. Mama's a power-house of a woman, and I look up to her a lot. And I'm happy the way things are. It just sucks that my siblings and I never grew up with a father figure."

Just then, Tante Lam barged in with a tray of *nastar*, fresh out of the oven. The scent of butter radiated from the pastries and flooded the room. They smelled like the pineapple tarts that Mom's friend used to bring us from Taipei, but these *nastar* were shaped in little circles, unlike the Taiwanese ones that were large and boxy.

"Here you go," Tante Lam said. "Faith, don't eat too much, okay? This is for Cecilia."

Faith's face soured as Tante Lam left. I took a bite. The tart taste of pineapple, combined with the crumbly, cookie-like texture exploded on my tongue. It was delicious, but Faith wasn't having any.

"Faith," I said with my mouth full. "Have some."

Faith chugged down her drink with furrowed eyebrows. She got up and dashed to her closet.

"CeCe," Faith called out from her closet.

"What's up?" I said, taking another *nastar* from the plate.

"Since we're friends now, I'm going to tell you something really personal."

She waddled out of the closet. Under the light, Faith's once-pale face now blushed like a ripe tomato.

"You okay?" I asked. "Do you want some water?"

Faith held up a top at least three times her size. It was a yellow button-down top adorned with white daisies. The shopping tag was still attached on it, although the Forever 21 logo had already faded.

She would sink in the shirt if she were to wear it now.

"This shirt…" She slurred her words. "This used to be too small for me."

I gasped, but immediately regretted my reaction.

"I'm sorry, I didn't mean to—" I started. But Faith laughed it off.

"It's okay! It's not anything to be ashamed about. But I used to be eighty kilos, once upon a time," Faith said.

"Sorry, I don't understand kilos."

"That's a hundred and seventy-five pounds, kiddo."

I watched as Faith propped down on the rug and opened her second bottle of grape soju.

"I intended to return this shirt, which is why I kept the tag even though it was the only shirt that fit me for two months."

"Why did you keep it, though?" I said, letting my eyes scan her body that was at least forty pounds lighter.

"It's a reminder of my strength," Faith said, twirling the shirt in her hands. "I went through a lot, CeCe. I think people misjudge fat people for being careless with their bodies or being pigs, whatever. But the truth is I decided to eat because I wanted to push boys away."

Faith? Pushing boys away?

"I was raped by my ex-boyfriend when I was fifteen."

I stared into Faith's dark brown eyes, now reflecting shadows of the demons that must have haunted her for years.

"Don't look at me like that," Faith said.

"Like what?"

"Like you pity me," Faith took a sip from her soju. "I don't want you to feel bad for me. I didn't do anything wrong, so I have nothing to be ashamed about."

"Sorry," I said, leaning against the foot of Clarissa's bed. "I hope you're okay with everything. I mean you look, um, happy now."

"I was always a chubby kid," Faith said, pinching the lower part of her stomach. "Mama called it baby fat, but at the same time she would always tell me to stop eating junk food even when I didn't. And when her girlfriends came over for wine or a potluck, they would always pinch my cheeks and comment that I looked fatter."

Faith's story brought me back to fourth grade, when the boys in my class would always bully this fat kid, Donald, who was fat enough that his chin was nonexistent. They called him Donald Duck and mocked him for having "man boobs" that jiggled when he tried to run in gym class. I couldn't imagine what it must've been like for Faith, when her bullies were not classmates but her mom's friends.

"What did your mom say to them?" I asked.

"She had good intentions, but she'd tell them that I couldn't stop eating unnecessary junk food when I wasn't, look straight at me, then ignore me for the rest of the night."

"I'm so sorry," I said.

"That wasn't really the worst of it, though," Faith said. "I didn't really care about what people said, you know, I was perfectly happy with my body as a kid. And when I grew older, I started doing sports and I shed away all my 'baby fat.' Mama was so happy, but her happiness was cut short."

Faith shifted in her seat. She took another gulp from her half-empty soju bottle. Her chest was turning red. I wanted to stop her, but it didn't feel right for me to stop Faith from telling her story.

"You know how I told you that I'm closer to Koko Mike than any of my other siblings?"

I nodded.

"Well, he mixed with a pretty bad crowd in high school. And when I started high school, he was still a senior, so he introduced me to his guy friends. They would come over a lot and I'd vibe well with them, and not long after my first semester I fell for one of his friends, Antoine Baudelaire, the son of the French ambassador at the time. Antoine was really sweet and charming at first, but then he became really manipulative and, ugh, just a lot of red flags. Grace hated him."

"That's not good."

"Then one day, when we were watching Netflix at his place, he came onto me, carried me into his bedroom, and raped me in broad daylight."

I slumped against the bed. Faith was so naïve to have trusted a guy so much until he broke her in a matter of minutes.

But she was only fifteen. How cruel this world was to have shattered her at fifteen.

"Oh my gosh, Faith," I said. "I'm so sorry."

"I told you not to pity me."

"Sorry, um," I cleared my throat. "Did you tell Mike?"

"No, I couldn't, I just," Faith took a deep breath. "I couldn't make him lose his friends. Ko Mike was really close to Antoine, and it was their senior year. I couldn't bear to ruin it."

"You know you wouldn't have ruined it, right?" I said.

"I know that now," Faith said. "I told Ko Mike after his first year at Berkeley, and he cut all ties with Antoine. That's also why Ko Mike became so close to Ray, who was his roommate at the time. Ray helped him deal with the whole thing. It was really hard on him, but I don't regret anything. We grew a lot closer, too."

I popped another *nastar* in my mouth, allowing the taste of pineapple to numb me from all of Faith's troubles. I watched as Faith took another gulp from her soju, taking a small sip myself so she wouldn't feel too lonely.

"I hope you got help," I said.

"I did in college," Faith said. "Grace was the one who forced me to. But by the time I did, I was already stuffing myself with fats and sweets and carbs. My body slowly swelled. I went back to my childhood and used food to escape from my trauma. I didn't want boys to touch me. I didn't want anyone to. And food was the only way I knew how to escape."

Faith shrank into her body. Her arm was slung around her waist as her fingers tugged at the loose microfiber strands in the carpet. I wanted to hug her, but it probably wasn't what she wanted now. I took a drink instead. She did, too.

"What changed, then?" I asked.

"Obviously, because I'd reverted back to my pig-out days, whenever I came back to Jakarta for the holidays, Mama and her friends would always comment on how fat I'd gotten. She'd make me fear every bite by telling me stuff like 'do you really want to eat that piece of bread, Jie?' or 'if you don't want to diet, you could get a liposuction. I'll accompany you to Korea to get it done.'"

"That's so fucked up," I said.

I felt my body temperature start to rise, although, I wasn't sure if it was from anger or the alcohol.

"Well, at one point this guy, Oom Erwin, was interested in Mama, so he came over a lot. He also happened to be a gym junkie. He joined a local fitness club that met in GBK at 6:00 a.m., you know, that sort of person. And he encouraged me to work out, cut my carbs, stuff like that."

"It worked though, right?"

"I mean," Faith sighed. "When someone tells you that you're ugly over and over again, you tend to believe it. And after getting raped, I was convinced that I was worthless for a good couple of years. It took a long time for me to start trusting boys again. Obviously, no one in college wanted to date the fat girl."

"I'm sure that's not—"

"It's true," Faith interrupted me. "I'm a living testimony. My friends, including Grace, got boyfriends and party invitations while I was stuck in my dorm, staring at packs of Indomie. It hurt, CeCe. I know I'm not supposed to measure my worth on such superficial things, but when it's absolutely crushed by so much trauma, you tend to measure yourself against the world's standard of worthiness."

"I'm so sorry."

"Don't be sorry, CeCe. It's not your fault."

I'd never been severely overweight, but USC's sorority girls looked like Barbie dolls: tiny waists, full busts, and huge blue eyes. I, on the other hand, had fat bulging out from the strangest places. But Faith was gorgeous. She had soft ebony hair that curled into her chin, warm brown eyes, and cherry lips that arched into a cupid's bow. She was the last person I ever expected to have gone through such a toxic relationship with herself.

"Anyway, Oom Erwin encouraged me to count calories, which I did, but it got to the point where I went from cutting carbs to cutting meals. I lost so much weight that I finally heard Mama calling me beautiful again. But I constantly felt tired. I'd always feel like fainting throughout the day."

I took another sip from the soju. When I looked up from the glass bottle, my vision vignetted. My heart pounded through my veins. I looked at Faith with sad eyes and felt a strong urge to hug her, even though she probably didn't want me to.

"There's a happy ending to all of this," Faith said, perhaps noticing my distress.

"Who? Grace?" I asked.

"Well, yes, and Jonathan, my fiancé."

"Aw," I said. "Cheers to that."

Faith shifted closer to me and clinked her bottle with mine.

"I met Jonathan two years ago, at this young entrepreneurs' gathering," Faith said, swirling her drink. "He was miraculously able to convince me to go out with him, because at the time I still refused to date. But I'm so glad I pushed through and said yes."

"That's so sweet."

"Jon was the first guy I dated who, you know, understood how to treat women well. I told him about my struggles with self-worth, boys, and food. He would always tell me that he loved me for who I was, not what I looked like, and constantly assured me that Mama felt that way too, but she just never told me."

"Words are really powerful," I said, wiping a stray crumb from the corner of my lip.

"For sure," Faith said. "I make it a point to always check up on my friends and compliment them. Like, you never know what people want to hear. I know Mama loves me, but if she had said just once that she loved me in spite of my obesity, I think things might have been different."

Dad had said things like that to me all the time. He always made a point to tell Mom and I that he loved us every day, because he wished that Oma and Opa did that to him. He always wanted us to feel loved.

I traced the water droplets that condensed on the surface of the green soju bottle.

"I'm glad you found someone like Jonathan," I said. "He sounds like a really special person."

"Yeah," Faith said, grinning. "He's a great guy. He and Grace helped me get back on my feet, too, by helping me get off the calorie tracker and start eating three meals a day. They also found a personal trainer who trained me to be healthy, not skinny."

Faith held the flower shirt in her hands and pressed it against her tiny body. She sank behind the curtain of fabric.

"I'm still on the way to healing and fully accepting myself, but that's why this shirt means a lot to me."

"I'm so glad to hear that," I said.

"Yeah," Faith said. "I don't tell a lot of people that story. I'm glad you're really supportive."

"Cheers to that," I said, holding up a piece of *nastar.*

Faith grabbed the last piece of *nastar*, pushed it against mine, and popped it into her mouth along with a sip of soju. I did the same. The soju tasted sweet with the tart pineapple. I felt a little bad for misjudging Faith. I was glad that Grace didn't show up, glad that I'd had the chance to get to know Faith better because now I knew that the "good girl" was a lot more broken than the "new girl."

As I pondered on these thoughts, Faith's slightly blood-shot eyes smiled at mine. I caught a glimpse of the glittering stretch marks etched on her inner thigh, battle scars that I now knew were a sign of pain, passion, and triumph.

12

The water fountain mumbled through the car's windows as Pak Sutikno drove the Mercedes into the tall black gates that surrounded Opa's house. Jakarta's sky looked more grey than black, perhaps due to the gradient of pollution that painted the atmosphere. I felt uneasy leaving Faith passed out drunk in her bedroom, but Tante Lam had asked me to leave at 10:30 p.m. so she could take care of her.

I stepped out of the car and shuffled towards the front door. My tongue still tasted the essence of soju on my lips from that evening. It was a good thing that I was slightly intoxicated. Alcohol made me sleepy, anyway.

Pak Sutikno followed behind me to open the front door. I muttered a quick "good night" to him and watched him park the Mercedes in the garage.

Leader waited inside the door. He jumped around in circles and pounced on my shins, begging to be cradled. I picked him up and nuzzled him into my denim jacket, squeezing him so tight that I heard him exhale a slight whimper.

But if Leader is out, that means Oma is still awake.

I glanced at my watch. 11:00 p.m. Oma would usually be in her bedroom by 10:00 p.m. sharp, where she and Opa would watch some TV. What was she doing up? Why did she stay awake for this long? Did something bad happen?

Or worse—did I do something wrong?

If Oma was still awake at this hour, she must be cranky, which meant that I had to hurry to my room to avoid her nagging.

I feel like a kid again.

A bead of sweat made its way down my scalp and onto my neck. I put Leader down, slung my purse over my shoulder, and tiptoed up the stairs. My fingernails slowly made their way to my teeth. I put one foot in front of the other, avoiding the creaky steps while my head pounded from the alcohol, when my phone decided to chime.

"Who's that?"

Shit.

I cocked my head to the direction of the voice. Oma and Opa sat on the living room couch, holding hands, and squinting into the distance. Their vision had blurred with age.

"Hi, Oma. Hi, Opa," I said. "It's me."

"Ah, Nonik. You're home," Opa said. "You were very quiet when you walked in. Or maybe it's these cancel-sound head-phones. Is that what they're called, Shaan?"

"Come join us, dear," Oma said, pointing at the empty cushion next to her.

As I approached the living room, I noticed brightly colored headphones dangling around their necks. Then I remembered Mbak Ani telling me that the TV speakers in the living room weren't working.

No wonder I couldn't hear them.

A bare-faced Oma Shaan was lounging on the couch in a silk, leopard-print nightgown, its edges embroidered with delicate gold lace. I remember Oma telling me that Opa's sister made it for her before she passed away, which was why she grew so attached to it. Opa sat comfortably on his leather armchair in cotton shorts and a baggy singlet. He munched on this Papuan fruit that had a forgettable name, and occasionally reached over to sip on his glass of Hibiki.

I plopped down on the sofa beside Oma. As soon as I sat down, Mbak Ani rushed over to serve me a glass of water. I smiled at her, but she was probably too tired to notice. She had to be up in six hours, anyway.

"Have you watched this?" Opa asked, pointing at the silent TV. "It's about Qin Shi Huang, the first emperor of the Qin dynasty. It's very good. You must watch it."

"I told you, Opa," I said, squirming at the slain corpses on screen. "I don't like those kinds of shows. They're so... violent. And gory."

"But you learn a lot," Opa said. "Battle is all about strategy."

"*Aiya*, Nonik, just sit here awhile," Oma said, extending her arm out to hug me. "We haven't seen you all day. Come sit and accompany your old Oma and Opa."

"Okay."

Fifteen minutes was bearable. I took a sip from my glass of water and felt my body slowly sober up.

Opa Robby watched TV without subtitles, so all I could see were swordsmen dying on a maroon-stained battlefield. I was more interested in Oma, though, who neglected the TV to knit a cute hat for Leader. Oma Shaan held an elegance that I could not begin to describe. Her skin, untouched by time, sparkled under the fluorescent light. She had a short and pointy nose that met in the crevice of her plump lips. Mom said that Oma got lip implants when I was little. Though she hadn't been sure, the photos in the living room were definitely living proof.

Oma's eyes spoke of a kindness that I used to see in Dad, one that twinkled in his pupils until he died. Dad's eyes were his best feature after all. He always tried to make me feel loved, even when I was at my lowest. "The joy of my life," he'd call me, before proceeding to shower my forehead with kisses. No one could ever show me the same kind of love he did.

Opa Robby, on the other hand, gave Dad his big forehead. Opa told me that a big forehead meant a big brain, which made sense since Dad spent most of his career working at JPMorgan. Dad always told me that leaving his stable job there to pursue a startup idea was a stupid decision, but that he believed in living spontaneously. I was a little bit stubborn like him, which was probably why I was watching a Chinese drama in my grandparents' living room instead of devouring buckets of Panda Express with Mom.

And yet, in spite of their physical similarities, Dad loathed my grandparents, and they had stopped caring about him.

"So, Nonik," Oma said, eyes focused on her yarn. "Where did you go? Why did you come back so late?"

"I was at, um, Faith's place," I answered.

My head was pounding. I was itching to leave.

"Who's that?" Opa said.

"Um—"

"Who's her dad? Or her mom?" Oma said.

"Her Mom is Tante Lam."

"Lam...Lam..." Opa pondered.

"Oh!" Oma exclaimed, putting her knit down. "Lam Ing Ng, Ling Ling's daughter. The one who cooks, right, Nonik?"

"Yeah," I said.

"Ah," Oma said, sitting at the edge of her seat. "So you must've met Awi Kusuma's granddaughter too, hm? Ling Ling told me that Lam Ing's daughter is very close to her. What's her name again? Gabriella, was it?"

"Grace?"

"Yes, Gracelyn! She's a nice girl, that one. Quite pretty, too, like her grandma. And her younger sister is…"

"I think it's Georgia," I said.

"Oh yea, G and G," Oma said.

How is my world so interconnected with my grandparents'?

"You know Grace?" I asked.

"You should invite Awi's granddaughter here sometime," Opa continued. "I saw her when Tante Stella just gave birth. I didn't think she was your age. I forgot that you are already, what, twenty?"

"I'm twenty-three, Opa," I said, looking down at my feet.

"Right, right," Opa said. "Invite Gracelyn over sometime, Nonik. She's a good friend for you to have. Comes from a good family. Next time you meet Gracelyn, tell her to send my regards to her grandfather."

"Okay."

I rubbed my bloodshot eyes, letting tears glaze the outer layer of my pupils. A yawn signaled for me to go to bed.

"Um, Oma and Opa," I cleared my throat. "I'm going to go to bed now."

"Stay a bit longer, *lah*, Nonik," Oma shot me a longing gaze. "I want to hear more about your day."

Like vines, tension crept its way up to my shoulders. Remains from the alcohol pounded against my head. I looked up at the clock that read 11:30 p.m.

Boy am I tired. I also have work tomorrow.

"Oma," I said, getting up from the couch. "With all due respect, I'm twenty-three years old."

"And so?"

Heat engulfed my body, so much so that even my fingertips started to sweat. I felt the alcohol take over my tongue.

In a split second, without hesitation, I blurted out, "And so, I didn't come to Indonesia to be babied by you."

Oma stood up and slammed the table, knocking over the last drops of Opa's Hibiki and shattering the glass. The kindness in her eyes was replaced by a tiger-like ferocity.

"Cecilia!" Oma yelled. "*Kamu kurang ajar ya!* I am your grandmother. Do you understand that?"

"I'm just tired," I said.

"You want to talk back to me?"

"Oma."

"You stay in *my* house, eat *my* food, and use *my* things, and this is how you repay me? You never spend time with us. You said that you wanted to come to Indonesia, and we helped you, and now what, huh? You leave in the morning and come home at night, not caring about your old grandparents?"

"No, I—"

Opa jerked up from his armchair. Some pieces of his fruit cascaded to the floor, next to the shattered whisky glass. I shivered.

"Hey!" Opa yelled, lowering his headphones. "What's going on?"

"Ask Cecilia," Oma said, pointing at me. "This is what happens if you leave her to be raised with Karina. So selfish. Doesn't even care about her grandparents."

"That's not true and you know that."

"You ungrateful child," Oma cried.

"Shaan." Opa cleared his throat. "Stop that."

I cowered under Oma's wrath. I had to concede. I couldn't keep fighting her any longer, even if it meant sacrificing a little bit of sleep.

"Opa," I said. "It's late and I just want to sleep. Is that too much to ask?"

"Oh, and wanting to spend time with my granddaughter is too much, is it? That's what you're trying to say, right, Nonik?"

"Shaan." Opa cleared his throat. "Stop that. Let the girl go to bed."

"She's been gone the whole day, Robby," Oma said, then stared at me. "The least she could do is spend time with the people who have given her food and a home."

"Oma," I said.

"Don't raise your voice at me," Oma bellowed.

Oma hurled the half-knitted hat to the ground. Leader whimpered at her feet. Oma's kind eyes faded away into a wrath that exploded out onto her wrinkles. I hid my shivers by fixating my eyes on the elegant piano behind Oma and tried not to blow up.

"Nonik," Opa said. "I think what Oma is trying to say is that she wants you to spend more time with us."

"I want to," I sighed. "But I'm tired, Opa. I had a long day today and will have a long day at work tomorrow."

"You haven't spent any time with us since you got here. You've been out with your friends, working, and we just want to have a chance to get to know our granddaughter."

"What else did you expect, Opa?" I cried. "Do you expect me to just sit around and not have a life?"

"Don't talk back to your opa like that," Oma snapped.

Opa fixed his sad gaze at me, his eyebrows turned slightly downwards. He had warm eyes, but they weren't Dad's.

"Nonik, how about this. Let's have brunch this Sunday," Opa said.

"Sunday...July 7?" Oma asked. "I thought you didn't want to do anything for your birthday."

"I know, Shaan, but it'll be nice for Nonik to get to know the rest of the family. You remember Uncle Richard and Auntie Isabella, right? Your dad's siblings?"

How can I not remember them? You've indoctrinated me with their faces by plastering them all around this house.

"Yes, I do." I would have said anything at this point to get myself to bed.

"You better show up," Oma growled. "It's your Opa Robby's seventy-sixth birthday."

Oma Shaan refused to look anywhere but at a slumbering Leader, whom she petted with her feet. I started to cower in the biting cold that she had radiated. If I didn't warm up to her, I might start to freeze.

"Okay, Oma," I said, biting my tongue.

Conceding didn't feel half as bad as I thought it would.

"Good girl," Opa said. Oma said nothing.

After a couple minutes of silence, a king's coronation on TV, and Oma falling asleep on the couch, I managed to excuse myself to my room. I hadn't expected my grandparents to be so controlling. I had been a legal adult for two years now. Shouldn't that have earned me some measure of freedom?

I walked into my room and leaned against the door. Streams of tears dripped onto my cheeks as I hugged my arms. I missed LA. I missed the warmth of the dry sun that sizzled the tips of my skin. I missed the ability to drive aimlessly without a destination.

I looked towards the ballerina that watched over me, a woman trapped in a painting for eternity. I wondered how she survived. I wondered how I would, too. But all I could do now was bathe, sleep, and hope for a new day.

III

Ophelia

She gathered rose petals from the river
to repair self-inflicted cracks,
for she had lost herself to calamity.

Her ceaseless portrait cherished in the broth
nails thrusting into broken skin like
screeching twigs combing through her dry bones.

As petals floated above water,
she hummed a sacred lullaby
to commemorate awful sorrows.

Capsized dress; her hourglass
hopeful for a life anew. Milky tears
christened the river, revealing

a self in wisps of rotten soot.
    a self-coated in grey cells, yellow eyes
        a self that petals cannot recognize.

13

Opa Robby turned seventy-six today. As promised, I cleared up the day for family festivities over brunch that Oma Shaan had organized at Taste Paradise, a posh Chinese restaurant in her favorite mall, Plaza Indonesia.

It was finally time to meet the extended family.

Oma prepared a baby blue *cheongsam* in my closet that was sealed in a garment bag. I zipped into the dress that hugged my insides. If I tried to squat, the dress would tear.

"You look beautiful," Oma said nonetheless, disregarding the fact that I couldn't move.

She wore a bright red *cheongsam*, intricately embroidered with sequins and beads that formed a tiger on her stomach. A silk scarf draped over her shoulders, and she carried a Hermès handbag made of crocodile skin.

"Thank you, Oma," I said, envying the elegance that made her look at least twenty years younger.

Oma left the room so I could put some last-minute touches on my makeup. I was sweating a little. After the recent argument, I was a little nervous to spend an entire day with my grandparents.

But a promise was a promise, and it was too late to back out now. I sucked in my stomach, puffed out my chest, and walked downstairs. Leader met us at the bottom of the stairs with Opa, who was wearing a golden *changshan*. He glowed like fine wine under the sun.

"Happy birthday, Opa," I said.

"How do I look, Nonik?" Opa said, doing a little twirl on his heel. "I look like your brother, right?"

"*Aiya*, old man," Oma chuckled, playfully shoving his shoulder. "You are seventy-six already. Seventy-six, not twenty-six."

I crawled into the back seat of Opa's white Lexus before Pak Sutikno helped my grandparents in. Pak Sutikno drove us to Plaza Indonesia, one of the biggest malls in the city. It was Oma's favorite place in Jakarta. She would always go for tea in the afternoons if she wasn't attending Mandala shareholder meetings.

"You like dim sum, right, Nonik?" Oma said.

"Yes! I love dim sum," I said. "We used to eat at Din Tai Fung in Santa Monica all the time."

"You can't compare American and Asian dim sum," Oma said. "Even if it's Din Tai Fung."

"You'll like Taste Paradise then," Opa said.

When we arrived in Plaza Indonesia, we climbed up several escalators to the giant Chinese restaurant, where the server led us in between people to a private room. A decadent chandelier hung from the high ceilings over a brown table that could sit at least fifteen. The tableware was a classic black and silver color, like it was made for the royals that Opa had watched on TV. I sat facing a painting of cherry blossoms, delicately painted on a cream wall panel.

"Ah," Oma sighed as she sat down next to me. "It's a nice place, right, Nonik?"

"Yeah," I said, pulling my *cheongsam* down as it hiked up my thighs.

"My children are late," Oma sighed, glancing at her watch. "As usual."

I found myself periodically glancing at the door. My heart skipped and pounded simultaneously. What would Aunt Isabella and Uncle Richard be like? Dad talked about them sometimes. He had been close to Uncle Richard since they were only two years apart, so they spent a lot of time in high school playing on the varsity golf team and going clubbing together. Aunt Isabella had been so caring and wise, and would always do her best to help Dad with his girl problems, at least until he moved to LA.

But I hadn't met them since I was five. I hoped they were nice. I hoped they would like me.

I hoped they would talk about Dad.

Fifteen minutes later, a server opened the door. A woman walked in with a brilliant red lip to complement her sparkly, sequined *cheongsam* that accentuated her thin figure. She looked like the female version of Dad, a strong jaw, wide eyes, and very prominent eye bags. Her hair looked like Oma's, thick and frizzy.

Aunt Isabella.

"Hi, Ma, Pa," Aunt Isabella said. "Sorry we're late. Rosa was being very fussy this morning."

Shortly after, a man followed closely behind. He was a short man with a square figure and glasses, carrying a fat bag with blue and yellow trucks. He looked like a balder version of the man in the photographs with Aunt Isabella and her family, displayed so prominently on Oma's grand piano.

He must be Uncle Johan, Aunt Isabella's husband.

"Hello," Uncle Johan said.

"Bella, Johan." Oma shook her head. "You are late."

"I know, I'm sorry, Ma. Good to see you guys," Aunt Isabella said, walking towards Opa to hug him. "Happy birthday, Pa."

"Happy birthday Papa," Uncle Johan echoed. "We brought you something."

Aunt Isabella and Uncle Johan walked up to us and placed a Richard Mille box next to Opa.

"*Aiya*," Opa said, hugging them. "You didn't have to get me anything."

"You'll like this, Pa," Aunt Isabella said. "It's the latest edition."

A little girl, dressed in a pink *cheongsam* with embroidered flowers, ran in between Uncle Johan's legs. She sucked her thumb while staring at us with round, beady eyes that could grow to resemble Aunt Isabella's. Thick and dark like Oma's, her untamed head of hair bobbed at the jaw.

"Mommy, mommy!" she said, tugging at Aunt Isabella's hand.

"Say hi to Oma and Opa, Rosa," Aunt Isabella directed.

"Hi, Oma and Opa," Rosa said, her voice retreating to a mumble.

"Hello, Xiao Meimei," Opa said.

"And say hi to...is that James's daughter, Ma?"

I stood up, pulled my *cheongsam* down to hide my stomach folds, and smiled.

"Um, hi, Aunt Isabella," I said, a little nervous. "I'm Cecilia."

"Cecilia! Yes!" she said. "Wow, you're so grown up. The last time I saw you, you were about Rosa's age. How old are you now?"

"I'm twenty-three," I answered.

"Oh my goodness, I met you eighteen years ago? Time flies," Aunt Isabella said. She turned her head towards Oma and Opa. "Cecilia looks so much like James."

I beamed. I'd inherited Dad's signature bushy eyebrows and brown, almond-shaped eyes. In a way, if they squinted hard enough, some of my LA friends might say that I looked like Aunt Isabella.

"Really?" Oma said, scanning my face. "I don't really see it. She looks more like her mother."

Mom gifted me her sharp chin and pointy nose. I brushed my index finger against my nose. Everyone back home said that Mom's features were my best qualities. But the fact that those words came from Oma meant that they were intended to be insulting.

I looked down to my hands and picked at my cuticles.

"Where's Richie, Bella?" Opa said.

"He should be here soon," Aunt Isabella said, settling down next to Oma. "Ko Richie had to buy something from ACE Hardware for Matius' school project."

"All of you are always late." Oma clicked her tongue.

As Aunt Isabella settled down with her family, the door opened.

"I'm here," a man announced, walking into the restaurant. "Happy birthday, Papa."

"Finally, Richie," Opa exclaimed.

Uncle Richard.

He waddled in wearing a salmon-colored top, buttoned all the way up and tucked into black pants, held up by a belt that choked his balloon-shaped belly. Uncle Richard was exactly as Dad described—tall, muscular, and nerdy, all at once.

Uncle Richard's wife, Aunt Felicia, trickled in behind him, holding a ten-year-old boy by the hand while carrying a chic Dior purse. Her neck was adorned with diamonds that were big enough to pay for my college tuition.

"Mommy," the boy said, pulling Aunt Felicia's arm. "Can I play with your iPad now?"

"Matius," Aunt Felicia said. "I told you, no."

"But why?" Matius whined.

A teenage girl walked in. A dragon etched itself on the end of her yellow *cheongsam*. She was scrawny like Aunt Felicia, had a square face like Uncle Richard, and was perhaps a little too young to be wearing makeup as heavy as she did. She chewed on some gum and had glued her eyes to her latest iPhone, bedazzled with a marble print casing.

"Matius," the girl said. "Stop it."

What a snob.

"What?" Matius stuck his tongue out at her. "You're so bossy, Jie Elisa."

"Elisa, spit out your gum, please," Aunt Felicia said. "It's rude to be chewing gum during meals."

"It's almost finished, Mommy." Elisa crossed her arms.

"Don't talk to your mother like that," Uncle Richard said, stroking Elisa's head. "Have you both said hi to Oma and Opa?"

"Hi, Oma, hi, Opa," Matius and Elisa said.

"And…" Matius shot me a puzzling look and pointed a finger at me. "I don't know who that is, Daddy."

"Oh, hello," Uncle Richard said to me. "You must be James's daughter, right? Celine?"

All eyes in the room darted towards me as if I was a museum specimen. In spite of the tight *cheongsam* that suffocated my insides, I felt totally naked.

"It's Cecilia," I said, standing up again. "Nice to meet you, Uncle Richard. Dad told me a lot about you."

"Good things, I hope?" Uncle Richard laughed. "I miss him. He was my best friend."

"Mine too," I said, but he had stopped listening at that point.

Aunt Isabella and Uncle Richard's families settled down. Elisa, Uncle Richard's oldest, sat next to me. Matius took Aunt Felicia's iPad and blasted his YouTube video on maximum volume.

Shortly after, a nanny ran into the private dining room. She was wearing white and blue uniform with a giant bag slung on their shoulders. She gave Oma and Opa a little smile, sat next to Rosa, and whipped out packed meals for her to eat.

I'd heard from Mom that, in this part of the world, it was common for families to hire nannies. I knew that raising kids was difficult, but was it difficult enough for moms to not do it themselves? Mom didn't want help when she raised me. Maybe that's why we grew so close. I wondered how Rosa would grow up now that Aunt Isabella left her with a nanny.

"You had to bring a *suster* to Papa's birthday lunch, Bella?" Oma said, visibly cross.

"I'm sorry, Oma," Aunt Isabella said. "Johan insisted because Rosa has been very clingy to Sus Mira."

"Did you leave Rosa with the *suster* again?" Oma asked.

"I told you, Ma," Aunt Isabella exclaimed. "I don't have a choice nowadays. I have back-to-back meetings in the middle of Mandala's restructuring, and with Johan securing a big client at his private equity firm, I kind of don't have a choice."

"Yes, you do. You're a woman, Bella. You have to take care of your kids. It's your job."

"Well, Ma, Papa needs a lot of help after the PR scandal last year. You know how bad things have gotten. We have to build our reputation from the ground up."

A Mandala Group PR scandal?

"It's still no excuse to ignore your kids," Oma scoffed. "They'll turn out very disrespectful."

Oma shot me a look that pierced my heart. Was she trying to imply that I was disrespectful because my parents had ignored me, when all they did was give me a beautiful life? I wanted to kick and scream and storm out, but I kept everything buried in my heart. After all, I was hungry. I could use some food.

Soon enough, servers entered balancing dumpling steamers on their arms and placed them on our table's lazy Susan. An assortment of dishes blanketed the table. The piquant aroma of chives, garlic, and truffles made my mouth water. As I reached my chopsticks out to snatch a vegetable dumpling, Rosa's nanny walked over to us from across the table, with Rosa holding her hand.

"Show Oma, Rosa," Sus Mira said, in her best English. "Show Oma what you draw."

Rosa pushed a piece of paper to Oma. Incomprehensible crayon scratches filled the page.

"Wow, Meimei," Oma said, holding Rosa's drawing up to her face to squint at it. "It looks so nice. What is it, *sayang*?"

I turned a little sour as I chewed on the delicious dumpling. Dad called me *sayang* all the time, but I'd never heard it come out of Oma's mouth.

How silly I am to expect Oma to love me like Dad did.

Rosa pointed at Oma as her lips curled into a smile. Her beady eyes looked into Oma's, filled with hopefulness, and then in a shy fit she curled into Sus Mira.

"She's so cute, Bella," Uncle Richard said. "Looks like you when you were younger."

"Did you hear that, honey?" Aunt Isabella nudged Uncle Johan. "I was a cute baby. Cute like Rosa, Ko Richie said."

"Well." Uncle Johan rolled his eyes.

"Johan says I looked like a rat as a baby," Aunt Isabella said. "I did not!"

"Okay, okay," Uncle Johan sat at the edge of his seat. "To be fair, there was one photo of Isabella with her nostrils all flared up. And there she looked a little bit like a rat. But that's it! That's all I was referring to!"

"Richie also looked a little bit rat-ish when he was a boy," Aunt Felicia said.

"Now you guys are too much," Opa exclaimed. "If both my kids looked like rats, are you saying that I do, too, hm? Johan? Feli?"

The room erupted in laughter. Even Matius stopped watching his YouTube video to engage in the conversation. I'd never seen my grandparents this happy before. Being around Uncle Richard, Aunt Isabella, and their families put smiles on their faces. I couldn't help but think that perhaps being around Dad would have, too.

But that wasn't the case. I'd lived with them for almost two months now, and they were never this happy around just me. I scraped my fork against the plate, trying to tune out the joy that I didn't feel. The food was served, but I still wasn't too amused.

"Jie Cecilia," Elisa said, tapping my arm.

I almost jumped out of my skin.

"Hi," I stuttered. "Elisa, right?"

"Actually, it's Elisabeth," Elisa said, holding her nose high. "Elisabeth Juliani Wongso. But you can call me Elisa."

At least Oma would be proud that Elisa loves her last name.

"Got it," I said, trying not to cause a scene.

"How come I've never seen you before?" Elisa said.

"I just moved here from LA."

"LA? You mean, like, Rodeo Drive?"

Elisa's eyes lit up. She picked up some noodles in her chopsticks and stuffed them into her tiny mouth.

"Not Rodeo Drive exactly, but yes," I said. "Your dad used to come visit us when I was younger, probably around Rosa's age."

"Oh. I've always wanted to go, but we never got the chance to. Mommy likes going to London because my Yi-yi Lily and her family are there."

"I'm guessing Yi-yi Lily is your mom's sister?"

"Yes," Elisa said, tossing her hair. "She married a British guy."

Elisa was so mature for her age. She was the type of girl that wanted to appear wiser, smarter, more respectable to the family, similar to myself when I was younger.

With someone to talk to, maybe this brunch won't be so bad after all.

"Do you like London?" I asked, picking up a *xiaolongbao* with my chopsticks.

"It's really gloomy, but sometimes we visit other countries in Europe. And the shopping in London is really nice."

"I'd bet."

Oh, how I longed to go to London one day.

"Here, Jie Cecilia, I got this bracelet from London. Daddy bought it for me."

My eyes glued themselves onto the bracelet, a quaint, silver cuff studded with colorful rocks. *What a cute kid's bracelet,* I thought, until I noticed that Elisa was wearing Cartier.

Oh my god. That meant that the rocks and gold on her wrist must be real.

A rock-studded white gold Cartier cuff. On a thirteen-year-old. My wrist looked so naked now without the rocks.

Dad bought me simple things when I was thirteen. The only expensive thing he bought me was a $1,000 Gucci jacket that was too small for Mom, which I wore until I was about sixteen. I never complained. Anything that my parents got for me was like my treasure. Elisa, on the other hand, was wearing $10,000 on her wrist. I had never felt more insecure in my life.

"It's really pretty," I said, hiding my wrist under the table.

I'd crawl under the table if I could, too.

"Nonik," Oma said, resting her hand on my thigh. "Why don't you eat some more?"

"Yes, Oma," I said, looking at my half-eaten *xiaolongbao*.

"Here, Nonik," Oma scooped up some rice and lobster to dump it on my plate. "You have to eat. Elisa, *sayang*, eat please."

There goes Oma with her "sayang" again.

"Yes, Oma," Elisa said.

"Good girl. Pass me your plate. I'll take some for you," Oma said.

"No need, I can do it myself," Elisa said.

I pinched my wrist. *Was I really going to be intimidated by a thirteen-year-old?*

I maneuvered the conversation to familiar ground.

"Have you been to America, Elisa?" I said.

"I've been to New York. I've always wanted to go to LA, though. Do you watch *New Girl*? The one with Zooey Deschanel?"

I chuckled. "You watch *New Girl*?"

Isn't she too young to be watching New Girl?

"Does LA look like that?" Elisa said.

"Um," I said, racking my brain to remember how *New Girl* depicted my home. "I don't really remember. But LA is so big, so there are tons of places to explore. You have the beaches in Santa Monica, amazing barbecue in K-Town, red carpet events in Hollywood—"

"Are there a lot of hot guys there?"

"What?" I spat out.

Elisa gazed at me with her sly brown eyes.

"You heard me," she said.

"Um…"

What was I supposed to say?

"My boyfriend is such a sleaze," Elisa said. "He's a really bad kisser. And he's really stupid. He got downgraded from advanced math to, like, stupid math."

I wanted to hide in a hole so badly.

"What's your boyfriend like?" Elisa asked.

"I don't have one," I said.

"No way," Elisa said. "How old are you again?"

Elisa sounded like Oma. I wanted to squeeze the rice out of her snobby mouth.

"Twenty-three," I answered.

"And you're not dating anyone?" Elisa shrugged. "You should get Oma to help introduce you to some boys."

"You know, I really prefer that you didn't involve—"

"Oma," Elisa called out.

"Yes, *sayang*?" Oma said.

"I believe Jie Cecilia needs you to look for a boyfriend for her."

Elisa batted her eyes at Oma, who looked more interested in me than she ever had before.

"Ah," Oma said, putting down her chopsticks. "You're right, Elisa. Cecilia is twenty-three, but she hasn't dated anyone yet, have you?"

"It's okay, dating isn't really on my radar right now," I said, sweat sliding down my hairline.

"Oh no," Oma said. "I'm sure my friends have some single grandsons your age."

I thought of a million ways to squeeze the life out of Elisa, but this argument wasn't worth my energy. I scooped up some rice from my plate and popped it into my mouth, tugging at my *cheongsam* to make room for my bulging belly.

But in spite of my anxiety, Elisa and Oma returned to eating as if nothing had happened.

"Cecilia," Aunt Isabella called out from the opposite side of the room. "When did you come to Jakarta?"

I swallowed my rice.

"Um," I said. "About a month-and-a-half ago? I came at the end of May."

"Wow, time flies." Opa smiled

"End of May," Aunt Isabella echoed. "So, you moved here right after graduating university, I'm assuming?"

"Yes."

"Where did you study?"

"I went to USC."

"Oh, nice. Ko Richie went to UCLA. I went to the University of Hong Kong until my parents *finally* let me go to the United States for grad school. And then I went to Penn."

Are all the Wongso women snobs?

"Wow, that's really cool, Aunt Isabella."

"She's always been the smart one," Uncle Richard said. "After this she's going to start bragging about how she graduated summa cum laude from Wharton."

Aunt Isabella rolled her eyes.

"What have you been doing here?" Aunt Isabella continued. "Do you have a job?"

"I'm working at Kopi Sedap as a Growth Strategist," I said.

"Kopi Sedap?" Aunt Isabella said. "Who's the CEO, um, David Kwok? That's Oom Jeff's son, right, Pa?"

"Correct," Opa said.

"That's nice," Aunt Isabella said. "But why not chase a career in finance?"

"Um…I don't know. I've just never been a math person."

"Everyone is a math person," Aunt Isabella preached. "I studied political science in Hong Kong, but I pivoted to finance after working at Morgan Stanley. I learned so much there. It's a tough environment, but it has a great learning curve."

I nodded along. Some of my USC friends were working in big banks and hedge funds, but working behind a desktop and slaving away at Excel spreadsheets was never really my cup of tea.

"But, I have to admit, it was a lot easier to get into banks back then than it is nowadays," Aunt Isabella continued. "All the top kids nowadays want to be bankers, consultants, or start their own ventures. You know Tati, right, Pa? Her daughter just got a full-time offer at Barclays."

"Oh, wow," Opa said. "In New York?"

"Yeah," Aunt Isabella said. "That girl is a genius. She's on the Dean's List at NYU Stern."

I nodded along.

"Cecilia, you know, the raw truth is that startups fail, so if you're thinking about career growth opportunities, you should work at a bank."

"But I wouldn't like it," I said, fully knowing that it was rude to talk back at older relatives, especially those whom I barely knew.

"What is a growth strategist anyway? It sounds made up," Aunt Isabella said. "Do people get confused?"

"It's under the marketing team."

"Oh," Aunt Isabella cackled. "You don't learn a lot in marketing. I did it in high school. It's mostly just common sense."

Is Aunt Isabella trying to liken my full-time job to a high school extracurricular?

"Not really." I felt my face heat up.

"Trust me. Go for finance. Your dad will thank you later."

"My dad?" I cried.

Memories of Dad flooded into my head. I followed in his footsteps to work at a startup, even though he started off as a private banker. Would he approve of my profession? Would he have been proud of me?

"Oh, sorry," Aunt Isabella said. "I'm so sorry, Pa, Ma, I meant to say 'grandpa.'"

But she didn't apologize to me.

I shrunk into my shell like a broken puppy. I wanted to leave, cry, or crawl under the table to disappear. No one seemed to care that Aunt Isabella had forgotten about her own dead brother.

Except Oma.

Oma held my thigh and squeezed it, even though the *cheongsam* was already squeezing it hard enough. She didn't look at me. Her wrinkled fingertips stroked my knees. Oma Shaan was the last person I had expected to comfort me at a time like this, but I still didn't want to reject it. At Oma's touch, I felt my eyes glaze, but I couldn't afford to ruin Opa Robby's big day.

Just when Oma lifted her hand from my leg, the serving staff burst in through the door. They erupted into a "happy birthday" chorus while two waiters wheeled a towering chocolate cake with a figurine of Opa Robby. The rest of the family joined in, but their smiles couldn't outshine Opa's. Even at seventy-six, Opa was a kid on his birthday.

"Come, everyone," Oma said. "Let's take a photo."

Oma and Opa made their way to the cake. Uncle Richard and Aunt Isabella helped make them comfortable. Everyone gathered around Oma and Opa. Uncle Richard's family stood to their right, while Aunt Isabella's family stood to their left.

And I was left stranded, awkwardly centered behind the cake, keeping my arms to my side like a lost soldier without direction. I plastered on a Cheshire cat-like smile and let the many phone camera flashes sting my eyes.

I excused myself to the bathroom after the photo-taking session. When I found that no one followed me, I ran the other direction and zipped out of the restaurant. I wished I could zip out of my *cheongsam*, too.

I walked as far away from the restaurant as I possibly could, looking at shop display windows and taking my mind off the whole ordeal.

Maybe pacing around the mall could soothe my nausea after devouring so much bullshit at brunch.

How naïve I was to think that Dad's siblings were nice. They were rude, spoiled, and arrogant. No wonder Dad got out so quickly. I would have, too. My grandparents didn't even think to defend me from Aunt Isabella's rude comments. And they were the only people I trusted in that room.

But Oma took the time to comfort me. Without words, Oma managed to make me feel safe and loved.

"CeCe?" A familiar voice called out from behind me.

I turned around. It was Kai.

"Kai," I exclaimed, sucking in my stomach as I walked over towards him. "Hey. What a pleasant surprise."

"I know," he said. "I didn't think I'd bump into anyone at Plaza Indo, but I guess everyone comes here on the weekends."

"What are you doing here?"

I've never been so excited to see a friend. Kai wore a simple outfit with sneakers, standing awkwardly opposite my uptight *cheongsam* and Prada heels.

"My parents are accompanying my little brother shopping for a suit," Kai said, touching his hair. "What about you?"

"Oh, um, it's my grandpa's birthday today, so we had lunch as a family."

"That's nice," Kai said. "Happy birthday to your grandpa."

"Thanks."

Kai's eyes scanned the vicinity, presumably to look for my family members.

"My family's still at the restaurant," I said, before he asked any questions. "I just had to leave for a bit."

"Is everything okay?"

"It's just, you know, typical family things," I said. "You know how rough family can get sometimes."

"Yeah, I get it." Kai smiled, his empathetic eyes meeting mine.

I pulled down my *cheongsam* to hide my food belly.

"CeCe, you know, you can always talk to me if things get rough," he said. "Moving to a new country is really tough, so I hope you know that you have me if you need to talk to someone."

"Thank you, Kai," I smiled, tucking a lock of hair behind my ear. "That means a lot."

Kai's phone rang.

"It's my mom. I have to go, but—"

"Oh, okay," I said. "I should go back too."

"But should we..." Kai stuttered.

"What?"

"Should we have lunch?" Kai said. "Sometime next week, maybe?"

My eyes lit up.

"Sure," I grinned.

"Okay," Kai said. "I'll text you. Bye, CeCe. See you at work tomorrow."

"Bye."

Joy streaked through me like a comet. I never thought of Kai as a close friend, but it was nice to know that people like him, whom I barely knew, had my back.

I skipped back to the restaurant, feeling invincible. When I walked in, heads turned. I strode into the dining room like a peacock.

"Hey, Jie Cecilia, where were you?" Elisa asked.

"We saved you some cake, Nonik," Oma said.

"Thank you, Oma," I said, as I pulled the plate of cake closer to me, ready to wolf it down.

14

The morning light illuminated the Kopi Sedap office through its tall glass walls. I walked in five minutes late to an empty office. I liked being the first to arrive at work since I had the satisfaction of ripping off yesterday's date from the pull-apart calendar that we all shared. Once the calendar read July 19, I settled down at my favorite spot by the window, opened my laptop, stretched my arms, and started working.

My colleagues started trickling in at 9:30. By then, I had already sent another two emails to different investors.

"Morning, CeCe," Kai greeted when he walked in.

"Morning," I said.

"I brought you your favorite."

"My what?"

Kai placed a cold brew from Starbucks on my table.

"I remember you telling me that you only drank cold brew because of your lactose intolerance."

"Oh my gosh, Kai, thank you," I squealed, grabbing the cup and taking a sip. The caffeine split my eyelids wide open.

"Of course." Kai smiled. "See you at lunch."

"Lunch?"

"Aren't we having lunch together today? At the ramen place?"

"Right." I grinned sheepishly. "I completely forgot."

"See you later," Kai said.

I watched his broad shoulders as he walked into his cubicle. I went back to my laptop, updating the Excel sheet I used to keep track of the 246 people I'd emailed out of the 500 that I was assigned. It was laborious work that yielded very minimal results. I hadn't received a single email back since I started in the beginning of June.

Until today.

Hi Ibu Cecilia,

Can I see your financial statements?
Thanks.

Rizki Gozali
Chief Investment Officer
Lyma Ventures Indonesia

I felt like I had just won a million bucks.

"Ray," I called out. "Ray!"

Ray cocked his head from his desk nearby.

"We got a response," I said. "It's from the venture capital firm you were eyeing."

"Oh wow! This is great news," Ray exclaimed. "Great job, Cecilia. Can you reply to them please? And try to set up a call?"

"Yes, I'll go do that."

I started typing furiously on the keyboard, beyond excited by this new opportunity.

But I wasn't sure what to say.

During my summer internship a year prior, I didn't send out an internal document because I assumed that it was confidential. And I didn't tell anyone about it. As a result, things got very complicated. The company lost the deal, and I got fired after, for good reason, but I distinctly remembered my boss scolding me. He told me never to hide important documents like that again.

I definitely learned my lesson, so I was going to implement it.

Dear Mr. Gozali,

Thank you for your interest in Kopi Sedap. Attached are our financial statements. They're updated to the end of March this year. Please browse at your convenience.

And if you are free, I'd like to schedule a call with you, our Chief Marketing Officer, and myself to iron out further details. Are you free sometime this week? How about 2:00 p.m. on Thursday?

Thank you and take care,
Cecilia Poetry
Kopi Sedap Marketing Team

I copied Ray in the email and sent it. I squealed.

"Cecilia," Ray called me short after.

"Yes?" I walked over to his desk. "Was the email good? It was good, right?"

"Cecilia." Ray's voice was stern. He pressed his temple. "This is not good."

"What do you mean?"

"If an investor asks for any internal documents, they have to sign an NDA before they can view them."

"Since when? Shouldn't all documents be public? Especially for an investor?"

"Cecilia." Ray refused to look at me. "We can't anyhow send documents to people outside our organization without ensuring their confidentiality."

"Oh." I hung my head.

"Shit, CeCe," Ray said, holding his face in his hands. "Now we run the risk of having all of our numbers exposed."

My fingers trembled. *What have I done?*

"Hello, Raynard and Cecilia," David chimed in. "Is something going on?"

"Pak David," Ray stood up. "Um, Cecilia was just updating me on progress. Lyma is interested to invest."

"Oh, that's great!" David said. "So why do you look so stressed?"

"Um, I—" Ray started.

"It was me." I stepped in. "Lyma asked for our financial statements, and I sent the documents to them without obtaining an NDA."

"You did *what*?" David shouted.

"I'm sorry, David," I said. "I'm so sorry."

"Ray, come with me," David growled.

David brought Ray to the little room where Kai had onboarded me. Muffled yelling and table-banging permeated through the walls. I paced around my desk, holding my fingers to stop them from shaking so much.

The two men exited the little room.

"Fix this," David said.

"Yes, Pak," Ray said.

Ray looked like he had just been beat up. He was heart-wrenchingly pale and emotionless. I ran towards him, grabbing his arm.

"Ray, I'm so sorry," I said. "I'll take full responsibility. Please."

"It's okay; you're still learning," Ray assured. "Let's just focus on fixing the problem. Don't beat yourself up too much."

"Okay."

"Go get your laptop and sit here. And let's figure it out together."

I grabbed my laptop and rushed over to Ray's side.

"What do you think, CeCe?" Ray asked. "How should we move forward?"

"Um, I think we should apologize," I said. "And send the NDA."

"Well, it's a little late to send the NDA now that Rizki already has our data."

"What if we apologize?" I asked. "I made a mistake. I'm sure Rizki will understand. Mistakes like this happen all the time, right?"

"Not really."

"But—"

"And we can't afford a bad reputation as a startup. Apologizing is not an option."

We stared at the laptop screens and then at each other. I scrolled through my Excel file again, hoping that any names could spark inspiration. Ray rummaged around in his head for a good tactic to use to keep this investor interested but came to the conclusion that we could only repair this relationship if someone at the firm already knew Rizki Gozali.

"I'll look through my contacts again," Ray said. "Pak David doesn't have any connections with Lyma, but maybe I might've crossed paths with Rizki somehow."

"Okay," I said. "Is there anything I can do in the meantime?"

"Um, you can...I don't know. Just send more emails, I guess."

"Oh. Okay."

I hung my head and grabbed my laptop, preparing to head back to my desk. Ray rested his chin on his palms and let out a long sigh. I felt horrible. It was all my fault.

Amelia came up to us with documents in her hand.

"Ray, do you need the NDA for our financial statements? David told me to give them to you."

Ray cocked his head towards Amelia.

"Have you not been paying attention to what's happening?" Ray bellowed.

"Oh, I was just—"

"Hey, we don't get to *need* the NDA because the email with our files has already been sent!" Ray screamed. "Do you understand? Can't you ask what's going on first before assuming things?"

"Sorry, Ray," Amelia said, retreating back to her desk.

"Jeez, these people," Ray mumbled under his breath. "How did she even get this job?"

Shivering, my muscles tensed up. Those words were definitely meant for me.

"Ray," I said, nudging him. "I'm sorry."

Ray looked up and smiled, as if he hadn't blown up a second ago.

"Don't apologize," he said.

"But Ray," I insisted. "Amelia didn't do anything wrong; she was just doing her job."

"You were too," Ray said. He twirled a pen on his fingers. "It's fine. Mistakes happen."

"But—"

"Why don't you go and get lunch, CeCe? Take a break."

"Are you not going to eat?"

"I'm going to find a way out of this first."

"I'll help," I said, knowing that Kai would understand if I had to reschedule.

"No, really, go to lunch," Ray said. "I work better alone on these kinds of things. I'll let you know when I need help, okay?"

I glanced at the clock. It was 11:45 a.m. I guessed it was close enough to lunchtime.

I walked up to Kai and nudged him, urging him to get lunch.

"Right now?" he asked.

"Yes, please," I said. "I'm really stressed."

"Okay," he said, getting up and closing his laptop.

We left our office building and walked to Pacific Place Mall. Sunlight bled through the glass roof. The day was gloriously bright, hot, and humid, which wasn't odd for a day in the middle of July. Even with the air conditioner, I had sweat under my armpits.

I loved the LA heat. But Jakarta's humidity was getting ridiculous.

Kai and I went to his favorite ramen place and settled down at a tiny table for two. The place was jam-packed with people. If we had left the office any later, we would've had to wait.

Kai took a sip from his green tea.

"So," Kai said. "Any progress on the project you're working on?"

I covered my face and groaned.

"What, why?" Kai asked. "Did something bad happen?"

I poured out my anxieties to him. Kai leaned in, his eyebrows reacting to my words. I focused on the mole on his chest, next to his shirt collar, to stop myself from crying.

"It's all my fault, Kai," I said. "I'm such a failure. I shouldn't have assumed things based on a mistake I made a year ago."

"I'm sure it's not that bad, CeCe," Kai said.

"Kai, I got one response in two months," I said. "One! Out of the hundreds of emails that I've sent! And still, somehow, I was able to screw that up. Do you know how many more will come? The response rate has been 0.4 percent. What do you think are the chances that a response like *this* will come again?"

"Okay, okay," Kai giggled. "I think I get it."

"Why are you laughing?" I said, a little annoyed. "It's not funny!"

"I'm sorry. It's just, I don't know, you're pretty funny when you're stressed."

"Kai!" I exclaimed.

"CeCe," Kai said. "You'll be fine. Ray is smart. He knows a lot of people, too. I'm sure that you'll get somewhere with all of this, even if you have a 0.4 percent response rate right now."

"I guess."

Without noticing, I was gazing in between Kai's unbuttoned shirt collar again. His pale skin was speckled with light freckles and a scar, hidden behind the folds of his shirt.

"Are you looking at my scar?" Kai asked, interrupting my gaze.

"What, no…no."

"It's okay," Kai chuckled, peeling his shirt back. "It's a really dumb story. Want to hear it?"

"Sure."

"When I was five, I was accompanying my mom when she was cooking. I was sitting at her feet playing with some toy cars or something while she minced garlic. Then my dad came and hugged her from the back, which really shocked her, so she dropped the knife and it sliced my chest open."

"No way."

"I know," Kai said, stroking his scar. "It's so dumb, right? I feel extremely lucky that the knife didn't nick the carotid artery. Or literally anything else."

The server came and served us a bowl of ramen each.

"That's crazy. You got stitches and everything?"

"Yeah. There was definitely some supernatural force that somehow, I don't know. It's hard to explain. I don't know if you believe in these things, but if you think about it, right, if my mom had dropped the knife in a different angle, it probably would've stabbed my leg, or worse, my head."

"Wow, Kai," I said, munching on the ramen. "You're very lucky."

"Yeah, I know. My parents remind me of that incident a lot so I'll learn how to count my blessings. So it's kind of symbolic that I carry this scar around with me."

"In that case, we all need to be reminded of your scar, then."

"Exactly," Kai smiled, slurping on his ramen.

We talked and laughed until we returned to the office, where Kai and I parted. And as he left to his desk, I felt an ache in my stomach. I felt guilty for having momentarily forgotten about the email I left Ray to fix alone.

I walked to my desk and passed Ray's. His name cards were scattered all over the table and he was making a phone call, but his desktop was open to Lyma Ventures' website. When he hung up the phone, I approached him.

"Ray," I said.

"CeCe! We have great news," Ray said. He kicked back his chair.

"What is it?"

"Turns out I know Rizki. I made a call with him a couple months ago."

"Okay…" I still didn't understand how that was great news.

"Yeah!" Ray said. "I just called him and told him that one of our junior employees forgot to send over the NDA, and he was more than happy to sign it."

"Oh."

"So just take Rizki off your contact list. I'll be dealing with him from now on."

"Okay," I said. "Is there anything else I can do to help?"

"Just get back to writing more emails, I guess," Ray said.

"But—"

Ray's phone rang.

"It's Rizki," he said. "I expect twenty more emails sent out today, okay?"

I walked slowly to my desk. Outside my window, a plane soared high above the skyscrapers. From my limited perspective, the tiny plane looked like it was going to crash into the high-rises, but it ended up flying through them. I wondered how many times planes almost crashed into buildings but didn't, or how many times they didn't mean to crash but did. How many times a knife could've dropped and stabbed a little boy's head, or how many times it didn't drop at all. How many times sending a flawed email could've cost millions of dollars, and how many times that mistake could've been fixed by a fortunate connection.

Yet, in spite of the infinite possibilities, the plane didn't crash. The knife didn't stab little Kai's head. The email to Lyma ended up getting fixed, even if it wasn't by me. Maybe Kai was right to count his blessings. Maybe I should, too.

I took a deep breath, cracked my fingers, and crafted my next email.

15

Faith and Grace said they were going to meet me at Pison Coffee in Senopati at 4:00 p.m., but it was 4:17 p.m. and they still hadn't arrived.

A couple days ago, Grace had opened up my world to Instagram shopping—shopping from local merchants who put their catalogs on Instagram. While waiting for them to arrive, I spent those empty minutes tapping away at different profiles and clothing collections while sipping on a glass of water. My hungry fingers almost bought a shirt.

Maybe next time I should come late to be on time.

"Hey," Faith said, bursting through the door. "Have you been waiting long?"

"No, it's okay," I lied, getting up to hug her. "Where's Grace?"

"She's finishing up a work call. Have you ordered? You said you wanted to try their avocado coffee, right?"

"I haven't ordered. I was waiting for you guys."

"Oh my gosh, you should've gone ahead. Come, let's order. I'll buy today."

"Okay. Thanks, Faith."

Faith called on the server and ordered an affogato for herself, a long black for Grace, and an avocado coffee for me.

"I wonder where Christie is," Faith said, whipping out her phone.

"You invited Christie?"

"Actually, she was the one who asked us to invite you."

"What?"

Christie invited me?

My jaw dropped. Last I remembered she couldn't stand my so-called "straightforward" attacks against her classism. I still didn't understand why Faith and Grace loved her so much, since all Christie could talk about was her own beauty and promiscuity. I pictured her witch-like plastic face and grumbled at the idea of having to share another meal with her.

"I know you don't get along with her, CeCe, but she's actually kind and generous." Faith shrugged. "She's just pretty brash, that's all."

"She's more than brash, girl," I said. "She's racist, elitist, and—"

Before I could finish, the café's front door opened. A pale, sullen, and unkempt Grace walked through. Her hair looked like hay. Her eye bags were sagged down by multiple sleepless nights. She dropped her body next to Faith and let her limbs sag on the chair.

"Hey, guys," Grace said, sniffling.

"Are you okay?" I said.

As soon as Grace sat down next to Faith, Grace held her head back and cracked her neck. I cringed at the sound of crackling bones.

"God," Grace sighed. "You wouldn't believe the shit you have to go through as an entrepreneur."

"What happened?" I asked.

"It's going to sound so stupid if I say it out loud," Grace said.

The server came and served us our drinks. I held the avocado coffee in my hands, indulging in the creamy avocado and espresso flavor notes.

"Is Christie not coming?" Grace asked.

"I don't know," Faith said. "She's supposed to."

"Actually, it's good if she doesn't come. I don't feel comfortable talking to her about this."

I couldn't help but let slip a smile, knowing that I wasn't crazy for despising Christie as much as I did.

"What happened?" I asked, taking another sip from my drink.

"Two days ago, a client requested one of our exclusive treatments for her pug, but it turned out that the pug was allergic to an ingredient in the shampoo we used."

"Oh no," I said. "Did you know about the allergy?"

"No!" Grace held her head. "We have a section in our registration forms where every new client has to write down any existing medical conditions and allergies for their pet. Of course, right? That's standard for any spa or salon, even for humans. We checked the papers all the time before treatments, and it turned out that we were never informed about her dog's allergy."

"Could you use that to disprove the owner's disputes?" Faith asked.

"It's too late now," Grace said. "She posted on her Instagram, saying that Oscar & Vinny's poisoned her dog. Turns out she used to be one of the Miss Indonesia candidates, so her post got a lot of traction. And since it happened two days ago, we've lost 3,000 followers on our page, received gnarly threats, and lost sixty percent of our bookings for next week."

My jaw dropped. Grace hung her head, visibly upset.

"Oh my god," I said. "I'm so sorry, Grace. That's horrible."

"The damn pug only broke out in hives," Grace said, slamming her fist on the table. "He didn't even die! But somehow that bitch was able to convince her army of idiots that we fucking poisoned her dog."

Grace fanned her face as her eyes became glassy. I'd never seen her like this.

"I worked so hard, CeCe," Grace whimpered. "Everything I built was destroyed by a stupid pug. I can't. I will never recover from this PR nightmare."

"Gracie," Faith leaned on her shoulder. "I'm sorry."

"I don't know what to do, you guys," Grace said. Tears started to flow. "I can't quit now. I can't. My parents just invested in Oscar & Vinny's after so many years, and finally let me leave the family business. I can't let them down now."

"This happened at a firm I interned at in the US," Faith said, rubbing Grace's back. "Don't get too caught up on it, love. It'll blow over. Your clients will come back."

Grace refused to make eye contact with us. She quietly wrapped her fingers around her coffee mug.

"It's all about perception in Jakarta," Grace said. "People don't care about the truth. They don't check the facts. They gobble up whatever shit they want to believe in even if it's not true. The groomer who took care of the pug already left because he couldn't stand all the death threats, and it looks like others might follow."

"Have you done anything to try and mediate the conflict?" I asked.

"We issued a statement speaking our truth and got some of our influencer clients to defend us, but all it became is a social media war of the girl's 300,000 followers and ours. And I've tried to keep up the morale of my employees, but it looks like a lot of them just want to get out."

Grace buried her head in her arms.

"This is really it, you guys. My career is over."

"Don't give up," I said. "My grandpa hasn't been able to retire because his company suffered a pretty bad PR issue last year, and because of that whole thing, they had to restructure the entire company."

"Your grandpa handled a PR nightmare last year?" Faith raised an eyebrow. "You mean…"

"Actually," I said, remembering Opa's words. "He said that he knew you guys. Well, your parents. He's a good friend of your grandpa's, Grace. I'm sure he'd be willing to speak to you if you need some guidance on your business."

"Okay, CeCe," Grace said. "Thank you."

Faith put her arms around Grace and squeezed. For the first time since she arrived, Grace smiled. Faith and I tried to divert the conversation elsewhere, talking about Faith's engagement party plans as we cooled off with our drinks.

Gray skies dominated the once-cloudless arena, sending a torrential downpour our way. We sat with our coffee cups, admiring the rain that kissed the roof we took refuge under.

"Hey, lovelies," a familiar voice called out from the door.

It was such a distinct voice: perky, shallow, yet intimidating.

"Christie." Faith waved. "You didn't reply to my texts. I thought you weren't coming."

"Hi, everyone," Christie said. "Sorry, I was so busy with back-to-back meetings today that I just didn't have time to reply to texts. But you saved a seat for me, right?"

Grace stayed silent, but Christie looked over her. A waiter dragged a chair from an empty table and placed it next to me. Christie hung her purse on the back of her chair and looked at me.

"Ah, you made it, Cynthia," Christie said.

"It's Cecilia," I grumbled.

Would it be too rude of me if I just got up and left?

"Right, right. I still can't get over how much you look like Lisa."

"Who?"

"Kenny's wife, Analisa."

I furrowed my eyebrows. Faith cupped her mouth, but when she saw me frowning, she looked away.

"How's that going?" Grace asked, wiping her glossed eyes with her sleeve. "Are you still together?"

Is Christie not even going to ask if Grace is okay?

"Absolutely," Christie said, her eyes lighting up. "Sneaking around is far more exciting. It's true what they say, a forbidden rendezvous just tastes a lot sweeter."

Christie called over the waiter and ordered a soy matcha latte. I paused to look out the window, watching how people reacted in the rain, storming into shelters, stray cats licking water puddles by the street, and the traffic jamming up on Senopati. I wondered how Christie managed to keep her hair so neatly tucked in that signature bun of hers even with the horrid humidity. Not a single strand of hair was out of place.

"Cynthia," Christie called out as the waiter walked away from our table.

"Cecilia," I growled, again.

"I wanted to ask you something," she said. "By any chance are you...do you know someone by the name of Robby Wongso?"

This can't be happening.

"CeCe just moved. Why would she know him?" Faith said.

"Because she's his granddaughter."

"What? No," Grace said. "Her last name is Poetry. Cecilia Poetry, right? Not Cecilia Wongso. Unless..."

There was no way that they could've figured it out this easily. I'd tried so hard to hide it. I was doing so well.

Grace shot me a look, her eyes sparking with wonder. It seemed like she had completely forgotten about her work issues. Perhaps it was good that she was distracted, but not like this.

"Isn't 'Poetry' just a romanticized version of 'Putri'? It's Cecilia Putri Wongso," Christie said, batting her serpent-like lids at me. "Right?"

Christie's words set off my alarms. My walls went up. No words came out of my mouth. All that my lips could do was tremble.

I shouldn't have come here today. I shouldn't have caved into my fears of not having enough friends.

"Um." It was all I could say.

"So it's true," Christie insisted. "You're Robby Wongso's granddaughter."

"How...how did you know?" I stammered.

"My grandma knows Robby's wife, Shaan," Christie said. "Anyway, she mentioned that Robby's granddaughter just moved here from LA."

"It could just be a grand coincidence," Faith said. "A lot of people moved back to Jakarta from LA."

"You could say that, but my grandma heard that his granddaughter is working for Jeff Kwok. Well, his oldest son, David. Isn't he the guy who runs Kopi Sedap? I was like, no way, Cynthia doesn't act like she'd be Robby Wongso's grandkid, but what are the chances?"

I trembled silently in my seat as the three girls talked over one another, neglecting the fact that I was in the room at all.

"Who's Robby Wongso?" Faith whispered to Grace.

"You don't know who Robby Wongso is?" Christie exclaimed. "He's the blood and brains behind Mandala Group.

They own and operate The Mandala, a.k.a. the best five-star hotel chain in Southeast Asia, they own all the major newspapers here, and control the biggest coffee plantation in Indo."

My pupils dilated. *Opa has that much money?* I thought he just managed hotels.

"Wow," Faith said, looking at me.

"And this little lady is his granddaughter," Christie continued.

Christie plastered a smirk on her face. Faith and Grace looked at me like they did the expensive hair piece in Christie's hair. I could hear my heart thumping. My eyelids trembled. I felt like a naked statue in the Louvre, lusted after and admired by enthusiasts. I hugged my waist, fingers squeezing my upper thigh.

The last time this happened the kids at my elementary school just made fun of the name. But Wongso carried more weight now. It tied me to Opa and Mandala. That tie could never be severed. I could never be myself without being Opa's granddaughter first.

I shivered at the thought. To Christie, Faith, and Grace, I was never going to be *just* Cecilia Poetry again. Were they going to treat me differently now? Ask for bizarre favors? Pester me with questions about Opa and Mandala that I couldn't possibly answer?

Of course they will. You don't actually believe that people in Jakarta like you for you, right Cecilia?

You're not worthy of love, Cecilia.

They only love your family's money, Cecilia.

"Oh!" Grace said. "So when you said your grandpa and the restructuring thing earlier, you meant—"

"What restructuring thing?" Christie asked, sipping on her drink.

I gulped.

"Earlier, CeCe mentioned that her grandpa's company is going through restructuring after a PR nightmare." Faith shot me a look. "And I think it's connected to the story about The Mandala that went viral last year. You know, the one where two of the hotel staff got raped by a senior director?"

I looked out the window, focusing on the rain that descended onto the pavement. I wished I could take back what I had said. I wished I could run out and scream.

My worst nightmare is coming true.

"Holy crap," Grace said. "My dad told me about this when it happened last year. The scandal was so bad that you guys had to restructure the entire company?"

"The senior director sits on Mandala's board, dude," Faith said. "I heard from my grandma that there were other rape cases by other directors. And so the Wongso family had to fire most of their board members."

How do outsiders know more about Opa's company scandal than I did?

"How the hell did you guys talk about this without knowing that she was Robby Wongso's granddaughter?" Christie said.

"We were talking about Grace's PR nightmare at Oscar & Vinny's."

Grace darted her head at Faith. Faith cupped her mouth, perhaps just remembering Grace's request to not let Christie find out about her work issues.

"Shit, Grace, I'm so sorry," Faith said.

"What PR nightmare?" Christie asked, at the edge of her seat.

I strapped on my seatbelt for the rollercoaster that was about to unfold in front of me.

"Oh, it's nothing," Grace said, fidgeting in her seat.

I could tell that she was nervous, but I was mostly glad that the conversation wasn't about me anymore.

"It's just a small issue with one of our clients, that's all," Grace continued, looking down at her fingers.

"Are you talking about Mariana Citra's post on Instagram? The one about one of her pugs getting sick because of your dog salon?"

"You know about it?" Faith said.

"Of course," Christie said. "Mariana is one of my friends from...I think I met her at a bridal shower. She's *really* out to get you, Grace."

I rolled my eyes.

"Shouldn't you say something to Mariana, then?" I said. "Since you know her? And because you're Grace's friend?"

"Gracie, darling," Christie said, stirring her hot coffee. "How many times do I have to tell you to just quit your dog shit and just work for Kusuma Group? Your grandpa owns BTI TV and that huge tobacco company, Kusuma, for God's sake. Your last name itself is a household legend, yet you don't even use it."

Right. Even the Cengkeh Bunda reservation was under Gracelyn Michelle, not Gracelyn Michelle Kusuma.

Grace clenched her jaw. Perhaps Grace and I weren't too different after all.

"I know, Christie. You've said this to me every time we talk about Oscar & Vinny's," Grace said, wiping away a tear with her sleeve. "It's a small thing. I'll get over it."

It's not small, Grace. But she probably said that to look good in front of Christie.

"I have to go," Grace said, neglecting the last drops of her coffee.

She got up, slammed her chair into the table, and slung her purse over her shoulder.

"Grace," Faith said, holding her arm.

"I have dinner with my parents," Grace said, pulling away from Faith's grip. "It's nice seeing you guys."

Faith followed Grace out of the cafe and into the pouring rain. I watched Faith hugging Grace as she sobbed into her arms through the rain-stained window.

"This is all your fault, Cecilia," Christie said.

At least she got my name right this time.

"How, exactly, am I to blame for this?" I asked.

"If you had told us about your grandpa earlier, my friendship with Grace would still be fine."

I slammed my fists on the table.

"Listen, you bitch," I barked. "You got it all wrong. You think you're so wise and loved, but all you are is a cunning, manipulative, goddamn attention-seeker. That is why you seek pleasure in terrorizing younger women and creating this façade of glory around you when you have none. Don't you dare turn this around on me."

Christie looked at me in disbelief. She touched a loose lock of hair that fell from her bun amidst the commotion.

"And you," Christie scoffed. "You're a lying, privileged little brat who can't do anything but run to grandpa for help and money."

But her words didn't hurt me. I stood up, grabbed my purse, and prepared to leave.

"Yes, Christie, I *am* Robby Wongso's granddaughter," I chuckled. "My Opa Robby turned seventy-six two weeks ago and he's still working. He's still golfing. And he's the best Opa I've ever had."

I don't know how much I believe those words, but they should be enough to keep Christie from using Opa against me.

I fluffed up my hair and walked out the door. I let the rain soak me as I searched around for Faith and Grace, but I couldn't find them.

"Non Cecilia," Pak Sutikno called out. "Go home?"

"Yeah," I said.

Pak Sutikno escorted me to the Mercedes and prepared to drive me home. The drive would've been a short one, but the rain jammed up the roads.

In the midst of the traffic, I received a paragraph of text from Grace.

> *Hey girl. Sorry if Faith & I seemed super obnoxious when we found out about your grandpa. It totally wasn't right for us to react like that and for Christie to be the one to tell us about him. I totally know how you feel about wanting to keep your family's status hidden, so I'm here for you if you ever need to talk.—18:04*

I beamed. In spite of the circumstances, Jakarta felt a little more flawed, and a little less lonely.

16

It was on the evening of July 31, after we wrapped up our Kopi Sedap monthly check-in meeting, when Ray asked me out for drinks.

"CeCe, are you free on Friday?" Ray asked. "I believe that's August the second."

The end of the month was always the busiest time for me since I had to summarize my research into monthly reports, so it was pretty easy to neglect my social life. In fact, I hadn't met Faith and Grace since last week. Faith had been working on a big design project at Gojek while Grace appeared in the media almost every day to rebuild Oscar & Vinny's.

"I should be," I said, tossing my things into my work bag. "Why?"

"I wanted to check in with you and see how you've been doing in Kopi Sedap. Are you up for some drinks?"

"Drinks?" I didn't feel particularly comfortable drinking alone with a guy.

"Yeah," Ray said. "Didn't you want to pay me back for the dinner at Four Seasons?"

Right. I had completely forgotten about that promise two months ago.

"Of course," I smiled.

"Alright. I'll pick you up."

+

Ray stopped his Bentley in the lobby of a boutique hotel in the heart of Central Jakarta. To get there, he had to maneuver through roads that lacked streetlights while I sat comfortably in his car, admiring its leather interior. The traffic on the humid August night was the worst, with cars snaking past one another to congested intersections, but after almost an hour of wandering around, we finally made it to The Hermitage.

A young man in a suit rushed over to open Ray's car door and mine. Ray handed the man his car keys, and we walked into the hotel. It was only when he looked back and smiled that I finally noticed his twinkling eyes. I couldn't tell if his pupils reflected the yellow light from the hotel lobby or if they were naturally bright.

The hotel's interior was clean, cream in color with earthy accents etched in the corners. Classic furniture decorated the black and white floors. But what Ray wanted to show me at the hotel was their famous La Vue Rooftop Bar, which, according to him, exhibited the most glorious Jakarta skyline views. The lights from the buildings bloomed into a dynamic portrait of the city, parting the haze to allow the city's best colors to shine.

Jakarta was stunning.

The bar wasn't for the faint at heart. It sat on the topmost floor of the hotel, so Ray and I had to maneuver through elevators, tight spaces, and steep stairs to arrive at the dimly lit bar. But it wasn't until Ray chose a seat at the edge of the bar that the whole journey became worth it.

Jakarta's blank black sky meant that only light from the skyscrapers adorned the darkness. The breathtaking cityscape glittered like sequins, blurring against the night, while a melody of cars and motorbikes driving by hummed in my ears.

"Gorgeous, isn't it?" Ray asked as he handed me a menu.

I nodded.

I ordered a gin and tonic while Ray got a negroni. I couldn't take my eyes off the city.

"Thanks for taking me here," I said, sipping on my drink.

"I only take special people here." Ray smirked.

"I would too," I said, keeping my eyes on the darkness.

From the corner of my eye I caught Ray fixing his dress shirt's collar. He was gazing at me, but I wasn't sure how I felt about it. On one hand, I was a little flattered that he could look at me for that long. But even though Ray was a good friend, he was also my boss. I couldn't ruin our friendship.

"How are you liking Jakarta so far?" Ray asked, swirling the glass in his hands.

"I like it," I said, though I wasn't sure if I meant it.

Ray shifted a little closer to me. There was something strange about the night, but I dismissed my feelings. Ray was just trying to get to know me better. He wouldn't do anything to disrespect me.

"I mean you lived in LA. Jakarta must be so much worse than LA."

"LA has its pros and cons," I said, leaning away from him. "But it's always the people that make it better."

"You mean, people like me?"

I bit my lip.

"Well, I—"

"I'm just messing with you."

Ray nudged me. I forced a smile, staring ahead at the blinking city lights to distract myself from the discomfort. Silence brimmed in the air shortly after, complemented by a strong evening breeze.

I drank my gin while admiring the view. I'd always been mesmerized by lights. They held a certain beauty that felt artificial yet warm. Dad started taking Mom and me to Mulholland Drive to admire the city's lights when I was three. He would stop the car at a look-out point and open a bottle of Martinelli's to share with Mom. "Look at the lights," Dad would say to me before pinching my cheeks. Though Dad was gone, my love for long drives and cityscapes hadn't changed.

Ray's phone interrupted the silence. He adjusted his sleeve and reached into his pocket to pick it up. He was answering an email.

"Who are you emailing this late?" I glanced over to take a peek. "Another investor?"

Ray jumped in his seat.

"I'm sorry. I didn't mean to look," I fiddled with my fingers.

"It's okay," he said, his shoulders relaxed. "I've been exchanging emails with a luxury hotel brand."

I dug around in my brain. I didn't remember seeing any hospitality companies in Ray's contact cards.

"They want to invest in Kopi Sedap?" I scratched my head.

"No, it's for something else."

Ray continued to type furiously. He slouched his shoulders as his eyes fixated on the glowing screen, taking occasional breaks to drink.

Just as I took another sip from my drink, not having enough friends to receive notifications from, I saw three girls looking at us and whispering. All three wore dresses that I found too extravagant for a serene rooftop bar. The first girl, hair tied into a ponytail, pointed at us. Her friend, who was wearing a hijab, giggled and nodded along with the first. And a third girl who wore a bright pink headband was searching through her phone, as if trying to find something for them.

I continued to drink, but I couldn't help but wonder why the girls were staring at us the way they did. They acted exactly like I had when I met Ariana Grande in Disneyland a couple summers ago. But I was no Ariana Grande.

I looked at Ray. *What could he possibly be hiding?*

The girl in the headband gazed bug-eyed at Ray, who was still oblivious to what was going on. Her phone shone harshly against her chin. When Ray looked up and exchanged looks with her, she squealed and cupped her mouth. The other two girls tried to sneak quick glances and were giggling to themselves.

"Do you know them?" I asked.

Ray looked at the group of girls, who were huddled in a circle at this point.

"Nah," Ray shrugged.

"They keep looking at you," I whispered, trying to fish something out of him.

"Are you jealous or something?"

"What, no."

"I'm just messing with you, love," Ray said. "Just ignore them."

I couldn't just ignore them. The headband girl tried to take sneaky pictures of Ray while the other two were grinning at their phones.

Ray took his glass to clink it with mine. We drank, then called the waiter to order seconds. I looked at Ray, tilting my head, trying to decipher what the girls knew about him that I didn't.

"Is it that obvious that I'm hiding something?" He chuckled.

I felt my face burn up.

"I didn't say anything," I said, lifting a hand to my cheeks.

"You didn't have to."

Ray proceeded to open his Instagram app and switched from his personal profile to one with the username @awanfajar. The account had over 503,000 followers.

"Holy shit," I exclaimed.

The screen lit up with colors that felt exotic and sultry. As I scrolled through his feed, the Ray I knew transformed into a fearless, god-like creature. Professionally photographed pictures of Ray in foreign places, engulfed in high-contrast hues, blanketed his Instagram feed. He was clearly photoshopped from all angles, but the vibrant backdrops made up for the faux reality that he painted for his followers.

"This is you?"

"Yeah," Ray said, straightening his back. "'Awan' means cloud, but it's also part of my last name, 'Kurniawan.' And 'Fajar' is my middle name, which means dawn. So that's how I got to @awanfajar."

"That's so cool," I said. "So those girls know you as…"

"Yup," he said, tapping the screen. "Awan Fajar. That's me."

When the waiter served us our second round of drinks, I looked through Awan Fajar's posts. The most recent picture was an aerial shot, perhaps taken from a drone, of him laying on pink sand.

"You like that picture?" Ray asked.

I nodded.

"This was from my trip to Flores. I stayed at a hotel there that sponsored my trip. This, here, is the pink beach, and there are also these Komodo dragons…"

Flores. Komodo dragons.

Dad.

He had spoken about that place so much. The islands near the town of Flores that glistened against the ripe sunlight with colorful fish gliding underneath the surface. He spoke about the majestic Komodo dragons that roamed the Komodo and Rinca Islands, the beautiful Padar Island that had three turquoise bays with fairytale-like capped mountains, and the Kalong Island that thousands of bats flew around at sunset.

I had always thought that these places were a dream. But Awan Fajar made it real.

For a second I saw Dad as a little boy waddling along the pink beach, holding Opa Robby's hand, and looking ahead at the sun while the sea danced, washing against his little feet as the seashells tickled them. He was probably doing that in heaven now.

"What?" Ray asked, catching me in dreamland.

"I was just thinking about my dad. I miss him."

"I'm sure you do," Ray said, putting a hand on my shoulder.

His cold touch stung my body. I wanted to push him away, but my own icy shudder was oddly comforting compared to the grief.

"Cheers," I held up my second glass of gin.

"You want to cheers?" Ray chuckled. "To what?"

"I don't know. Magic. Memories. Everything in between."

I swallowed half of my second drink. I felt a looseness in my limbs.

Ray kept scrolling. I watched his thumb slide through the ocean of colors. Most of the posts were of him in iconic places: boating in Norwegian fjords, swimming in the iconic Marina Bay Sands infinity pool in Singapore, hiking up the Himalayas. And all of them had ten-, twenty-, thirty-thousand likes, with an average of a thousand comments on each post.

"So the company you emailed," I asked. "That was for this account?"

"Yeah. They want me to stay in one of their hotels so I can review it and upload pictures."

"That's awesome. You're an influencer!"

"I guess you could say that, yes."

Ray puffed his chest. I caught the three girls gazing again, this time intense enough that their eyes started to bulge out.

"Who else knows?" I asked. "I don't remember Faith or Grace ever mentioning @awanfajar."

"Oh, they know. I'm not sure if KP knows, but he probably does. It's not like I hide it."

"You know, a little off topic, but you should stop calling Kai 'KP.' He doesn't like it."

"That's just him trying to flirt with you, CeCe," Ray said. "We've been calling him KP for years, and he's never complained."

Ray took a sip of his Negroni, licked his lips, and grinned. I was too drunk to continue pestering him about Kai. Maybe he was right that Kai was just trying to flirt with me.

"Anyway, yeah," I said. "I would never have expected you, of all people, to be running such a famous Instagram account. How did you do it?"

"It was a cold and stormy night," he started.

"Seriously." I beamed, rolling my eyes.

Ray laughed. He rested his arm on the back of my chair.

"I don't know what to tell you, CeCe. The best answer I can give you is that I started posting, and people liked it, and slowly my follower base grew."

"And then?"

"What do you mean?"

"Your story doesn't sound finished."

Ray put his glass down and looked into my eyes. His eyes remained a light brown color, but the twinkle was gone.

"Well, I met this famous photographer when I was in Italy... wait, maybe it was Spain." Ray scratched his chin. "Oh, my bad, It was in Paris. Yeah, it was definitely in Paris, because I had just come back after a weekend at my friend's château."

I grew a little envious of Ray. He blurred all the European countries together because he had been to them all. He had this whole second life with the opportunity to travel around the world, whereas the only other time I had left the United States was when my family came to Indonesia all those years ago.

What a life to live.

"Anyway, the guy I met had an Instagram account with like, a couple hundred thousand followers? He approached me, said he liked my look, and offered to photograph me for free in exchange for me allowing him to post the pictures on his Instagram feed. With model credit, of course."

"So you took it?"

"Well duh." The stench of alcohol radiated from Ray's breath. "And that's how I developed a style and gained all these followers, pretty much. I mean, of course, I had someone else take photos after my account blew up, but hey, my pictures aren't bad, right?"

Around the time I heard the three girls leave, my head started to pound. With Ray's permission, I continued to scroll through his profile. Vicariously through his feed, my eyes hiked Machu Picchu, posed in a hanbok in Jeju Island, and passed out drunk at a beach party in Ibiza.

While I was reliving Ray's travel life, I stumbled across Ray, 120 weeks prior, holding a girl's hand at the edge of a cliff. She was gorgeous, a slim figure of a woman wearing a yellow floral dress that emphasized her large breasts and lean thighs. Her blue eyes hid behind her sunhat's shadow.

"Who's this?" I asked.

The pounding in my head grew louder.

"Her?" Ray scoffed. "She's just some chick I slept with a couple years ago."

"She looks a lot more than just a hookup," I said, observing Ray's hand curled around the woman's waist.

"Why do you keep asking about my love life?"

"You don't have to share if you don't want to."

It was then that I noticed that we had been talking about Ray the entire night. I felt a knot in my stomach. He definitely didn't ask me to get drinks to get to know me better. Something was wrong, but I couldn't figure out what it was because my head was hurting so badly.

"Well, I don't want to share because she's irrelevant now."

"Okay, that's totally fine. Sorry for prying."

"And, you know, she wasn't even that pretty anyway."

I pursed my lips and nodded. I gulped down the rest of my gin.

I always felt uneasy when guys spoke about girls that way, but Ray wasn't that kind of guy. He was a gentleman. Kind, daring, and a little cunning. I wondered, while I observed him on his phone with uneasy glances, whether I should intervene and say something.

No. It didn't work when I tried to get him to stop calling Kai 'KP.'

No. He was drunk. Frankly, I was too.

The anxious ache in my stomach grew into a hybrid of anxiety and nausea, evolving into a lightheadedness that made me too unbothered to speak up, but too tired to stay for the rest of the conversation.

"I see," I managed to blurt out, smiling half-heartedly.

"You know, I haven't dated anyone since that girl," Ray said, shifting his chair closer to me.

"I thought you told Kai and me at lunch the other day that you were seeing girls?"

"When?"

Did Ray forget who he dated?

"On my first day at Kopi Sedap. When you and Kai took me to Busaba."

"Oh right," Ray said, putting a hand on my knee. "But I'm not dating them, CeCe. They're just flings. I sleep with them, then, you know, if it's good, I stay. Otherwise, I dump 'em."

Ray's touch made my heart pound. The knot in my stomach tightened.

"I…"

Gin kept words from flowing out of my mouth. I felt Ray's arm creep up on my shoulders. He stared at me with his doe eyes, shifting a little closer.

Something was definitely wrong.

"Yes, love?" Ray asked.

His lips were inches away from mine. I felt his breath against my nose. My body trembled, but I was still rooted onto the chair.

I looked around to find an excuse to call someone, but I was out of luck since the bar and kitchen were downstairs. Ray and I were the only two people left on the rooftop. The city lights, far enough away that they were dim, grew into an ominous darkness.

Just as my lips shook, I felt Ray's lips start to touch mine. "Ray, I..." I jerked back. "I have to go."

"No," Ray said, putting his palm on my knee. "But CeCe, you wanted me, right? You wanted me this whole time."

"I'm sorry," I said, kicking his hand away. "I have to leave now. My grandma will be worried."

I found the strength to stand up and gather my things. I shouldn't have agreed to this.

"I'll take you home!" he said, reaching for my arm. "Don't leave now. It's only 10:00 p.m. And it's a Saturday tomorrow, anyway."

Oh my god. Work. I had forgotten all about work.

How could I face him at work on Monday? I had the weekend, but I couldn't hide from him forever, especially when the both of us had to spend these next few weeks preparing for a collaboration pitch.

You shouldn't have agreed to this. You're so reckless, Cecilia.

"Thanks for inviting me." I mumbled, yanking my arm away.

I rummaged through my bag to find three Rp100.000 bills and dropped them on the table to pay for our drinks. I couldn't let Ray have anything over me.

"Cecilia!" he shouted.

Ray tried to grab my arm again. I ran. My feet, squeezed into brand new Prada heels from Oma, carried my loose body downstairs. I almost tripped a couple times, but hearing Ray's footsteps chasing after me only motivated me to run faster. I managed to dash into the elevator just in time for Ray's drunkenness to lag him behind, pressing the close button repeatedly until my index finger went numb.

In the elevator, with shaky hands, I dialed Pak Sutikno. Thank goodness Oma Shaan asked him to tail Ray's car when we came. "He has to follow you for safety reasons, Nonik,"

Oma said. At first, I thought Oma was being ridiculous for having someone follow me at this age, but now I wanted to cry and hug her for making that decision.

I waited in a dark corner of the lobby in case Ray had decided to follow me down the elevator. The man that held Ray's car keys looked at me, puzzled. I tried to tell him that Ray was still upstairs, but my limited Indonesian prevented me.

Pak Sutikno pulled up to the lobby shortly after. I scurried into the car, slamming the door shut when I saw Ray rush out into the lobby.

"Cecilia!" he called out.

He marched towards our car. My heart started to pound. I fisted my hands, shivering from the sheer fear that something might have happened if I didn't run fast enough or decided to stay with Ray a little longer.

"Let's go, Pak Sutikno," I said.

Pak Sutikno stepped on the gas. I sat in the car, sobbing as I watched Ray run after us and shrink in the car's rearview mirror.

"Non," Pak Sutikno said, glancing over his shoulder. "Non okay?"

I held my arms and squeezed.

"Yes, um." A slight smile complemented my sad eyes. "*Terima kasih.*"

The rest of the car ride was silent. I hadn't seen this side of Ray before. But I refused to believe it. He was the guy that got me out of trouble at work. He was the friend that introduced me to Faith and Grace and had my back through adjusting to life in Jakarta. He might not have been a great boyfriend to those girls, but he was a good friend and boss to me. He couldn't hurt me.

What about today, Cecilia?

Maybe he just had too much to drink. Maybe I gave him misleading signals.

You know that's not true, Cecilia.

I met all my friends in Jakarta through Ray. I worked with him. I couldn't risk all the friendships that I had invested so much time in for the past few months over one drunken night.

Pulling out my phone, I wiped away my tears and texted him.

Sorry I had to leave. I forgot that my grandma wanted me to be home by 10:30 tonight. I'll see you on Monday!—22:28

I locked my phone, but the knot in my stomach was still there. Sighing, I stared out the window and let the city lights lull me to sleep.

17

Dark clouds reigned over the Sunday afternoon skies, spilling into torrential rain that resulted in people rushing for shelter. I had gone for a quick bike ride around the neighborhood to properly process the night out with Ray two days ago but ended up succumbing to rain. I trudged through the water with my bike, sweeping through curtains of heavy rain. My clothes were soaked down to my bra and underwear.

Pak Sutikno greeted me at the gate to let me into the house. I parked my bike in the garage and waddled through the front door.

Leader barked the minute I walked in. Oma Shaan's eyes darted at the door. When she saw me wring my hair that dripped with rainwater, her jaw fell.

"Oh my goodness, Nonik!" Oma gasped. "Where did you go?"

"I went biking," I said. "I told you I was going out for a bit."

"*Aduh*, don't you see how dark it is? Didn't you check the weather first?"

"I did, but the weather app didn't say that it was going to rain."

"*Aiya*," Oma said. "Still, you shouldn't go out when it's raining."

It wasn't raining when I left, though. And she knew that. Why was Oma intentionally blaming me for something she had initially approved of?

In spite of all of my thoughts, the only words that came out of my mouth were, "Okay, Oma." I didn't have the energy to fight Oma, especially not after what happened the night before Opa's birthday. I was still traumatized by her unreasonable wrath on that day.

Oma Shaan asked Mbak Ani to grab towels with the fear that I would "*masuk angin*," which referred to some sort of illness caused by the wind that might give me flu-like symptoms. It was a term that I still wasn't familiar with.

"Go upstairs and get changed, Nonik. And then come down to meet me. I want to talk to you."

"Okay, Oma."

I was growing weak with my grandma around. She was a reigning titan masked behind delicate silk garments. I was wary but terrified of her at the same time. How could someone be so cunningly manipulative but caring at the same time?

I showered, secured my wet hair in a towel, and slipped into sweatpants and a hoodie to head downstairs.

The rain echoed throughout the palatial home, bouncing off the walls' acoustics and into the people's ears. I met Oma in the living room, where she was snacking on peanuts that were boiled with turmeric. I hated that snack, but for some reason, it was Oma's favorite. Leader was sleeping soundly by her thighs while Opa Robby had his eyes glued on the TV that displayed the same Chinese Qin dynasty drama that he had been watching since last month. But this time, the TV's speakers were fixed, so the people on screen died with a lot more intensity.

"Ah, Nonik." Oma Shaan sat up. "Here you are. I want to talk to you about something."

"Okay, Oma." *There it was again.*

"I heard that you know Yusuf Kurniawan's grandson," Oma said.

"Yusuf Kurniawan?"

"Yes, um," Oma said. "What's that boy's name...Tommy's son?"

I only know one person with that last name. But no, it can't be.

"Ray?" I croaked.

"Yes! Yes, Raynard!" Oma squealed.

I had never seen her this happy about me knowing one of her friends' grandkids.

"Oh, you know Yusuf's grandson, Nonik?" Opa asked, pausing the blaring TV.

"How do you know Ray?" I asked back.

"You know that Opa Yusuf owns Semina right?" Oma said excitedly.

"What?"

"You don't know, Nonik?" Oma gasped. "Semina is the biggest textile manufacturer and distributor in Southeast Asia. They distribute to all the big retailers, you know. Very good family."

"I knew Yusuf very well. He was a really good guy," Opa said. "He passed away a couple years ago. Heart attack. So sad. James used to be best friends with his eldest, Tommy."

Dad knew Ray's dad? They were best friends?

"Raynard is Tommy's only son," Oma said. "The rest of Yusuf's grandchildren are still very young."

"*Wah*, small world, yeah?" Opa said.

"So tell me, Nonik, how do you know Raynard?" Oma said. "Is he handsome like his father?"

"Shaan," Opa Robby said. "I don't think Nonik's met Tommy. Have you?"

"No, I haven't."

I chewed on my nails. The conversation started to get very uncomfortable. I grabbed a handful of boiled turmeric peanuts from Oma's side table and started popping them into my mouth. I could manage Ray as a boss and friend, but anything beyond that was unacceptable.

My face soured at the peanuts' horribly bland and herb-like taste but hoped that my busy mouth could get me out of this miserable conversation.

"I'm sure Raynard is a nice boy, right?" Oma said. "His whole family is so nice. Yusuf used to help your opa a lot."

"Yeah," Opa said. "He was a good friend. We used to own a truck company, you see, and if we didn't know Yusuf, we wouldn't have survived. He was our first customer. What a good guy."

"What's Raynard like, Nonik?" Oma asked.

"He's…okay. He's my boss at work."

I munched on another bland peanut. *Should I have included the part where he tried to force himself on me a couple nights ago?*

"Wow!" Oma said. "Is he a good boss? He must be."

"Tommy was a good boss, just like Yusuf," Opa chimed in.

"He's okay, I guess."

Oma and Opa were in love with Ray. I remembered the dinner at the Four Seasons where the general manager told Ray that his dad was meeting government people, but I didn't think that Ray's family was rich and socially prominent enough for my grandparents to gush over them. Ray turned my grandparents into children drooling over lollipops from the window of a candy shop.

"Can I leave now, Oma?" I asked. "Please?"

Lightning struck. The atmosphere shifted. Sudden darkness fell. The table lamp cast deep shadows on the hollows of Oma Shaan's facial bones. I shivered.

"Why do you want to leave? Hm?" Oma said. "You just came back. Don't you remember you promised to spend time with me and your opa, Nonik?"

"I do want to, but I just—"

"I'm going to ask you a question, Nonik," Oma said.

Oh no.

"Who are your friends? Do you know who they are?" Oma asked.

"Huh?" I said. "I don't know, um, Faith, Grace, Kai—"

"No, no, no," Oma said. "*Who* are they? What have they contributed to your life?"

My mood shifted. I was no longer in the conversation for niceties. I wanted to scream.

"I don't know, Oma. I don't know *who* they are beyond nice people who I care about and who care about me."

"Okay, but do you know how these people can help you? Like in business, I mean."

"Oma, I...I don't befriend people because I want to exploit them," I crossed my arms.

"*Aiya*, Shaan, not all friendships have to be give-and-take," Opa interrupted. "You can give without asking for anything back."

Yes, Opa. Thank you for having my back.

"It's exactly give-and-take!" Oma raised her voice. "Nonik, you know there were many times in your opa and Oma's lives when we wouldn't have survived without knowing who we know."

"Yes, but that's not all a relationship is based on, Shaan," Opa countered.

"But you still should count what benefits you can take from the people you know. Right?" Oma said.

And suddenly, as the house amplified the rain's echo, my courage grew too.

"But why?" I added. "Is there something wrong with wanting to do things myself? To make my own path in life?"

I bit my lip, knowing that I had stumbled into dangerous territory.

"You Americans are so stubborn," Oma said. "If you're given food on the table, will you eat it? If your friend is the US president, would you not ask for a favor?"

"What Oma is trying to say, Nonik, is—"

"Stop it, Robby. The point is that Nonik has to understand what her use is to other people, and what other people's use is to her."

"Okay, Shaan." Opa got up and started rubbing Oma's back. "I think Nonik gets it."

I swallowed the courage and words I wanted to shout out. Opa looked at me with eyes that begged me to let it go. He knew that Oma's philosophy was flawed but chose to ignore it.

"Anyway, Nonik, do you have a photo of Raynard?" Opa asked.

She placed her hand on my leg and batted her eyes at me, as if unfazed by all the tension.

"Um..." I cleared my throat.

I stared at Leader, who was fast asleep, completely unbothered by the commotion. For a second, I envied him. I petted Leader with my feet, hoping to absorb some of his peace.

"Can you find it online?" Opa asked. "He's your boss, right? You must have a photo of him somewhere. Maybe the company website?"

With both Opa and Oma looking at me with hopeful eyes, I whipped out my phone and showed them Ray's influencer Instagram account. Oma and Opa took their reading glasses and zoomed into the colorful pictures on my phone. I enjoyed @awanfajar for the vibrant colors, but they enjoyed it for Ray.

"What a handsome young boy!" Oma exclaimed. "Looks like his grandfather. White skin, big eyes, and not too skinny... Even has Yusuf's big forehead, right Robby? Means he's smart. A good boy."

"Yes, yes," Opa said, still looking at Ray's photo. "Nonik, do you know how old Raynard is?"

"Twenty-nine."

"*Wah*, okay, okay. That's a good age," Oma said.

"A good age for what?" I asked.

"Nonik, how old are you again?" Oma said, sliding her reading glasses down the bridge of her nose.

"I'm twenty-three," I said.

Oma squealed in joy, twirling the pearl necklace that coiled around her neck.

"Six years difference only! That's great." Oma said.

"Nonik, maybe one day we can all have dinner," she continued. "Who knows, maybe you and Raynard can get along. His family is good to get to know."

This cannot be happening.

I hated Elisa. It had to be because of her that Oma Shaan was thinking about marrying me off to my narcissistic boss. I had to put a stop to it. And that meant not sticking to my formula of "Okay, Oma."

"No, no, stop," I said, crossing my arms. "I don't like him like that. I'm not going to date my boss."

"I don't see why not," Oma said.

"No, Oma, please," I said. Frustration started to cloud my vision. "Please. He's not a good guy."

"Of course he's a good guy! Look at his family. Look at his credentials. He's good for you."

"Your oma has a point," Opa said. "Maybe it wouldn't hurt to just give it a shot, Nonik."

"You don't understand," I said. "He only cares about himself! And he's a misogynistic asshole—"

Images of Ray chasing after me at the rooftop bar just a couple nights ago haunted me. The sound of raindrops slamming into trees complemented Oma Shaan's cackle. I shivered. I couldn't let Oma and Opa do this to me.

"That's every man, Cecilia," Oma stated. "Marriage isn't all about love. It's also about what you can contribute to your husband's family, and how they can contribute to yours."

"Marriage?" I gasped.

My skin turned pale.

"Okay, Shaan, I think that's enough," Opa said.

"What? It's true," Oma concluded.

Oma took some peanuts in her hand and went upstairs. Opa looked at me, genuinely concerned.

"Are you alright, Nonik?" Opa asked. "I'm sorry about your oma. She just feels pressured to find you a husband since you're almost of age."

"I can find a husband on my own terms, Opa," I said.

"I know that, but we're just trying to help."

"Then you chose the wrong person to pair me up with."

Opa tilted his head. Outside, the thunder clouds parted to make way for sunny, blue skies.

"Honestly, Ray…I can't date him. He's not a very good person."

"Did something happen between you and Raynard, Nonik?"

Blurry vignettes of the night flashed in front of my eyes. The stench of alcohol reeking from his breath, the texture of his chapped lips against my own, the city lights that morphed from warm to cold. I shivered.

I opened my mouth, but just as I had the courage to say something, Oma came back.

Maybe it's fate that I didn't tell Opa. I don't want to burden him anyway.

"You smell, Nonik," Oma said. "Didn't you wear this sweater yesterday? Go put on some fresh clothes. Boys don't like it when you have BO."

"Okay, Oma." I hung my head.

I got up from the couch and briskly scurried up the stairs, pouncing into my room and locking the door behind me.

I undressed and let my body breathe. I laid on the bathroom floor, my eyes glazed, thinking of how my grandparents could force me into big decisions that Mom and Dad definitely wouldn't have. I felt Oma's words cradle my neck just to choke me. Yet the only place I could run to was merely a couple doors away from where they were.

Tears flowed silently down my cheeks and dripped onto my chin. Who was I if not a byproduct of everyone telling me what to do? I was a disrespectful granddaughter, a selfish friend, and an incompetent employee. I trusted no one.

I stepped into the shower, thoughts flowing through my soul like the cold water that caressed my body. I embraced the icy loneliness that came with the country that my ancestors called home, but that which I knew as alien.

18

My long-sleeved shirt and pinstripe blazer didn't shield me enough from the air conditioner's roaring cold, probably because David turned down the thermostat again. The skies were grey. A thick haze hid the sun while clouds rumbled with thunder. I had to give a presentation, but it was clear that the world wasn't on my side.

I went over my slides for the billionth time that morning, sweeping through any mistakes or points that I might've missed. I even ignored an email that I had just received in my inbox. I didn't want to get Ray in trouble again for an email I wrote wrongly. I didn't want to feel guilty again.

This time, though, I was confident with my presentation. After sending out 447 emails, I finally had a lead on the project Ray and David gave me on day one. The Head of Corporate Partnerships at Artika Jaya, Indonesia's largest real estate developer, had responded to me, saying that they were interested in including Kopi Sedap as a tenant in fifteen of their malls for a discounted price.

I was confident that with Artika Jaya's rapid growth throughout Java and Bali, partnering with them would enable Kopi Sedap to soar. So I squeezed all the relevant information into a solid slide deck, decorated it with a nice theme, and stood in front of the entire Kopi Sedap team to present my pitch.

My body was shaking. I had never given a presentation to an entire team, especially when everyone was an executive except me. But I was confident in this partnership. I was ready.

Words flowed out of me like a river moving rapidly downstream. I gave the presentation my all. I had always felt like the black sheep of the team, being the youngest and least experienced employee. I eyeballed the room to see if people were engaged, or better, just as excited as I was. And when I felt an acceptable amount of agreement in the room (it was hard not to agree with this deal), I ended the presentation with a classic "thank you" slide and a very awkward bow.

"Well," Ray said, getting up from his chair. "I've been eyeing Artika Jaya for so long. I emailed them, called them, and had no luck, but it took you one email to get to them. I'm impressed, Cecilia!"

"Yeah," Amelia said, sipping on her latte. "I think the price they set makes sense for where we are right now, especially if they want to negotiate it further."

"It's definitely doable," Yanti added. "If it's a bulk deal, and if they're going to help us with it, then it'll make my job easier."

"I heard that Artika Jaya has a great tech platform," Kai said. "And if they're willing to let us use it, we're golden."

I grinned.

"So we're good?" I asked.

"I'm good with it," Kai said. Amelia and Yanti nodded.

"I think so," Ray said. "This is a solid deal. We'd really lose out if we don't take it. Pak David? What do you think?"

David sat quietly at the corner, taking a puff from his Juul. He squinted.

"The other real estate company. What was it called...ah, Wahana Salim. Did they get back to you?" David asked.

"Yeah, they did."

"Then no," he said.

The color drained from my face.

"Are you sure, Pak?" Ray asked. "If we say no to Artika Jaya, I doubt we can get a deal as good as this again."

"No," he said, eyes fixed on his phone as he walked back into his office.

My world slowed to a halt. Everything I had worked for in Kopi Sedap for the past two-and-a-half months had culminated into this moment. But with a single word, all my effort, confidence, and heart dissipated. I wondered why David said no. I wondered why he was so quick to do so.

Was this how Grace felt after experiencing the Oscar & Vinny's PR scare? Scared, alone, and ashamed?

Silence flooded the room. Along with it came embarrassment. I cupped my face, my heart beating faster by the second. Ray, Amelia, and Yanti returned to their desks, but Kai approached me.

"Hey," Kai said, hugging me. "You did great. I'm sorry it had to be like this."

"I don't understand," I said. "Artika Jaya gave us a really good deal!"

"I know. Why don't you talk things out with David? Try to make sense of his reasoning? Maybe you need to convince him a little more that you're on the right track."

"You're right," I said.

I marched over to David's office, determined to find my answer.

I knocked. "Come in," he said.

It was the first time I had set foot in David's office. There was something eerie about the space, but I couldn't pinpoint if it came from how clean or how chilly it was. Papers were stacked in a large cuboid on one corner of David's desk. Not a single sheet was out of place. His diploma frames were polished to the point that I could see my own reflection on them. He even had a couple plants that hung on the walls, but I was going to guess that they were fake.

"To what do I owe the pleasure, Cecilia?" David asked, gesturing for me to sit in one of the chairs opposite from him.

"I just wanted to ask," I said.

"Ask what?"

"Why...um...why Wahana Salim? Aren't they only two years old?"

"Yeah, they own Wahana Place in Pluit."

"Okay," I hesitated. I didn't want to say something wrong. "With all due respect, David, I don't think they're a good choice."

"Did they get back to you?"

"Yes, but—"

"Then let's just go with them."

"David, I don't think we should."

My hands started to shake. I felt intimidated by David, even though he had always treated me nicely.

"It'll be a much easier deal. The owner, Arjun Kapoor, is my very good friend."

"But Artika Jaya is a much better deal."

"Cecilia."

"I'm sorry, David," I raised my voice. "I've done extensive research on both companies. They got back to me last week. And I truly believe that Wahana Salim won't serve us well. They'll just waste our time. Could you please just hear me out?"

"You have one minute." David rolled his eyes.

I took a deep breath. I grabbed a piece of paper and a pen from his desk and started scribbling some sentences.

"Here are the three main reasons why we shouldn't partner with Wahana Salim," I said. "One, they are new and small. They only have three outlets across Indonesia, whereas Artika Jaya has twenty-six. Artika Jaya holds a large chunk of the real estate market here. Two, Wahana Salim's malls attract customers in the upper and wealthy classes, whereas Artika Jaya appeals more to the masses, a.k.a. our target market. Three, all three of Wahana Salim's malls already have major coffee outlets like Starbucks, Coffee Bean, and Kopi Kenangan, so we wouldn't be able to compete. Artika Jaya only has McDonald's as their 'coffee shop,' so we still have a good chance to integrate there with no problems."

I looked up from the paper to see David clicking his pen, chin resting on his palm.

I continued, "If Wahana Salim was the only contender in this race, then I'd say that it won't be a bad idea to partner with them. But since Artika Jaya also responded to us and gave us great prospects at an affordable price point, I believe that we should partner with them instead."

David tapped his fingernails on the desk. He raised his eyebrow and pushed up his glasses. He analyzed the chart I drew up and scanned a couple areas with his finger.

He threw the piece of paper back to me.

"No," he said.

"No?" I said. "But David, if we go with Wahana Salim—"

My words were interrupted by David's phone ringing.

"I have to take this, but let's just go with Wahana Salim, okay?" David said. "I feel bad for Arjun. His business isn't doing well."

He answered the phone. "Hello this is David...Parman, my man!...Fantastic...Hey, you'll be at the gathering tomorrow right?"

David shooed me from the room as he continued to laugh along with Parman, whoever he was, on the other line. Frustrated, I grabbed the piece of paper I was writing on and left his office.

I fisted my hands. I had to talk to someone. I went to Kai's desk, where both he and Ray were chatting.

"Hey, guys," I said, sitting at an empty chair next to them.

I tried not to make eye contact with Ray. Our relationship was still a little strange after the incident at The Hermitage three weeks ago. We managed to ignore the elephant in the room to make things convenient at work, but the looming awkwardness persisted.

"How did it go?" Kai said. "Did Pak David change his mind?"

"He insisted on Wahana Salim because his friend owns it. What the fuck, right? How is that a thing?"

"Wahana Salim..." Ray trailed off. "Arjun Kapoor? He knows Arjun?"

"Yeah," I said.

"Ah yes, I remember now," Ray said. "He mentioned that Arjun is a really good friend of his. They met in high school."

"Why would he do that?" Kai said. "Tank his company along with himself to save his friend."

"Exactly," I said.

"Are the repercussions that bad?" Kai said.

"Uh, yes," I leaned in for a whisper. "Wahana Salim is utter *shit*! It'll be the end of Kopi Sedap if we go down that route. You know that too, right Ray?"

Ray and Kai looked at each other. Ray rolled his chair a little closer to me but maintained a far enough distance that I still felt comfortable.

Maybe he really did learn something from that night.

"Look, CeCe," Ray whispered. "I'm going to give you some very important advice if you want to survive in Kopi Sedap."

"What?" I said.

"The boss is king," Ray said. "Whatever Pak David says is the final word. I know you worked hard on this, and I know how hard it must've been to even manage a response from a company as big as Artika Jaya. But if Pak David says no, it's a no."

"But Ray," Kai insisted. "It doesn't make sense. Artika Jaya is clearly the better choice, I mean, I don't know much, but my banker friends have told me that Wahana Salim is in a lot of debt. If that's true, then partnering with them will be destructive for us, too. There's no way Pak David doesn't know about all of this."

I smiled at Kai. It was nice to know that he had my back.

"I know; I agree with you," Ray said. "But it doesn't change the fact that Pak David has the final say. Once he makes up his mind, you can't change it."

I crossed my arms.

"Then what's the point of working here if David is just going to ignore my professional opinions and send the company into the deep end?" I said. "I can't watch him sink Kopi Sedap like this. He hired me for my expertise, right?"

"Just leave it alone," Ray said. "I know you're new to this, but please, don't make this worse."

"You can't keep brushing this off like it's nothing," Kai said. "CeCe's right to be angry. When Kopi Sedap loses everything, all of us will be out of our jobs. That includes you and me."

I hadn't even thought about that. But Kai was right. I couldn't watch David do this to me and my friends. How much of a failure would I be if my first full-time job went bankrupt?

I can't give Aunt Isabella the satisfaction of being right.

"I'm going to talk to David again later," I said. "I can't sit still and watch him burn everything to the ground. I have to fight for myself and all of you."

I stood up. Ray grabbed my arm.

"CeCe," Ray said. "Don't do that. You'll hurt yourself."

"What do you mean?"

"Cecilia," Ray said, more sternly this time. "Don't be stubborn. He can cut your pay or strip you totally of your job."

"Leave her alone," Kai said, yanking my arm out of Ray's grip. "She's doing what's best for all of us."

Kai gave me a smile and escorted me back to my desk.

"Thanks for defending me," I said, opening my laptop.

"Of course," he said. "I know this is a lot, but I appreciate you standing up for what's right."

I stared at the Excel file with the index of five hundred names. A lot of the firms I'd contacted, like the venture capital firms Lyma Ventures, Hayato Group, and Alpha-Omega Capital, were noted with "no reply yet" or "not interested." I even started highlighting promising contacts like Wahana Salim that were interested because there were so few of them.

But I wasn't sure what to add to the Artika Jaya contact on my notes. *Great deal but shitty boss? Not happening because of David's BFF?*

Frustrated, I exited Excel. I clicked around my empty desktop, wondering what I should do while waiting to fight David one more time, when I remembered that I had neglected an email just over an hour ago.

I read the subject line. It was a reply from a firm.

Dear Ms. Cecilia Poetry,

I hope this email finds you well. Thank you for having interest in our investment into Kopi Sedap, but if it is alright with you, I'd like to offer you a different opportunity.

Alpha-Omega Capital is an all-woman venture capital firm that specializes in investments in female-led startups across Southeast Asia. We've been looking for female professionals to join our firm as generalists, where you'll learn from investment experts, industry leaders, and join a strong network of professional women.

I had an opportunity to take a look at your LinkedIn page and see that you have a very impressive profile. I know you haven't been at Kopi Sedap for long, but are you interested in switching gears and working with us? You would be a very valuable asset in our team.

If you are interested or have questions, please don't hesitate to reach out. I'm looking forward to your reply.

Thanks!
Alicia Pujianto
Chief Executive Officer | Alpha-Omega Capital
Empowering Women

Suddenly, the gloominess outside my window felt bright. The first time I heard of Alpha-Omega Capital was when I did my research for this email. I was immediately in awe of their founder and CEO, Alicia. She came from a low-income background but was somehow able to lock in a full scholarship to USC's business school. It would be such an honor to learn from her.

But was I crazy to jump at a random opportunity to work at a random firm? A women-run venture capital firm in Indonesia felt too good to be true.

I quickly forwarded Alicia's email to my personal address and deleted it from my work inbox to avoid questions. I wanted to meditate on it before I jumped to conclusions. I couldn't just abandon Kopi Sedap after four months. What would I tell them? Would they understand?

"CeCe," Ray said, tapping my shoulder.

In my shock, I slammed my laptop shut.

"Yes?" I asked.

"Pak David is looking for you."

Burying my excitement, I put on a solemn face and geared up for battle.

I knocked on David's door. Pink drained from my flushed face.

"Come in," David said.

"Hi, David."

"You need to stop pursuing Artika Jaya."

I pulled the chair back and sat down, shifting my body weight towards his desk.

"David, please," I said. "You and I both know that Artika Jaya is the better option. They're bigger, have our market, and have less of our competitors. I understand that your friend is in trouble, but I don't think you understand the gravity of how badly this will turn out for Kopi Sedap if we go with Wahana Salim instead."

"Stop exaggerating." David chuckled.

"I'm not."

"Do you have something against Arjun?"

"What?"

"I know Arjun has done some horrible things, but I promise he's changed now. He built up this real estate empire, for God's sake. What else can he do to earn other people's respect?"

I knew well that it was impolite to talk back to people who were older than me. I had felt the repercussions of that at Opa's birthday last month. But I felt invincible with Kai's support. And I knew that I was doing something right.

"David, I know you want to help your friend, but Wahana Salim is having serious financial issues. Plus, we can't even compete with the other coffee outlets there. If we partner with their dying shopping malls, I can assure you that we will go bankrupt in a few months. I suggest you reevaluate what an 'empire' really means."

David slammed his fist on the table.

"What did you say?" he said.

"I was just—"

"Who hired you?" David said. "Huh? Tell me, who hired you?"

"You hired me for my professional opinion, so here it is. I don't want to work on a project that I know will burn this company down."

"Hey, princess," David said. "Do you think I, the founder of Kopi Sedap, who has secured billions of Rupiah in funding for this startup, do you really think that I would be stupid enough to burn this company down?"

With Alicia's email in my back pocket, I felt like I had nothing left to lose.

"Well, in my opinion, that's exactly what you're doing by deciding to partner with Wahana Salim."

"Oh, I see," David scoffed. "Fine, then. I'll do it myself since you're so useless."

I marched out of David's office, swinging the door shut behind me. Yanti, Amelia, Kai, and Ray stared. I had done what all of them had probably wanted to do since the beginning of their careers here. Maybe they were flabbergasted. Maybe they were in awe. I was both. I hadn't known that I was capable of such courage to say more than just "Okay."

Kai met me at my desk. He perked up when he saw me.

"Did you do it? Did you change his mind?" he asked.

I shook my head.

"I'm sorry," Kai said. "This is getting ridiculous. I can talk to Pak David and share my perspectives from the tech side if you want me to."

"No, it's alright. This should be between me and him. I appreciate the thought, but it's better if you don't get involved."

"I guess you're right," Kai sighed. "I'm going to investigate a little more about Wahana Salim, maybe ask more friends about them. And I'll let you know if I find anything."

"Thanks, Kai."

When Kai left, I opened my laptop. Again, I was confronted by the job offer from Alpha-Omega.

Artika Jaya wasn't my problem anymore. Wahana Salim wasn't my problem, either. I had nothing left in Kopi Sedap besides Kai, who I was sure would understand why I felt so out of place here, right?

But I couldn't just break my year-long contract with Kopi Sedap. I'd only been here for almost three months.

I guess I don't have to renew my contract. And it won't hurt to just talk to Alicia.

With tired fingers and a shattered ego, I started typing my reply.

IV

Black Dog

She had nowhere to go, no one
for company when a black dog
came. It sat on the opposite side of

the seesaw
which tipped over.

She recognized the mongrel. It
fed her father bourbon while he yanked her hair
She could only sit in silence,

Legs swinging,
mouth opened, closed
in mute motions,
her frail braids swaying

to the rhythm of her erratic breaths
Ibuprofen-stained, numbing stings from
wood splinters of the plank on her thighs

As her apathy grew, so did the black dog.
It weighed on the seesaw like a sky that
crumpled and engulfed her with a desperate
darkness that prompted her scream.

She struggled and stumbled
in her slumber as the black dog
barked. And her eyes rolled backwards with

her body
which tipped over.

19

Three weeks had passed since I debated leaving Kopi Sedap. Alicia and I had chatted on the phone once now, and she was a wonderful person, just like I had predicted. Work remained horrible. David hated me. Ray and I had bad work synergy. The only thing that kept me going was Kai, who would always eat lunch with me. I wasn't sure if Alpha-Omega was the right fit for me, so I told Alicia that I'd think about her job offer.

The overwhelming stress of staying in Kopi Sedap started to eat at me slowly. So when Grace called me to ask her to join Faith, Ray, and herself on her family yacht, I was ecstatic.

"Our boat just went through a round of maintenance in Singapore," she said. "And we just bought a jet-ski, so I thought it'd be fun to take y'all out for a trip to the Thousand Islands."

Dad had talked about the Thousand Islands, an hour outside Jakarta, referring to them as Jakarta's hidden gems. He told me he'd go every week on Opa Robby's yacht and race his friends on jet-skis. He told me about the schools of timid fish that island dwellers would catch and fry. I wondered if things had changed since he went thirty years ago. Opa told me that he sold the yacht shortly after Dad got married, even though Dad said that Opa liked to go fishing on that boat.

"Is Christie coming?" I asked.

"Honestly, I'd rather drown in the ocean than share a boat with her," Grace said. "I'm not speaking to that bitch after hearing what she said to the both of us at Pison."

"So you hate her now?" I chuckled. "Finally."

"I guess you could say that."

I lay on my bed, munching on potato chips.

"You're coming, right?"

"I'd love to go. Thanks for inviting me."

"Awesome," Grace exclaimed. "I'll tell the rest that you're on board."

She seemed chirpier than usual. It had been awhile since I caught up with Grace, and the last time I checked, she was still buried in work, picking up the pieces after the pug incident tried to destroy her months ago.

"How are you doing with the whole PR scandal?" I asked.

"We're doing much better, thanks for asking," Grace said. "We were able to convince seventy percent of our clients to stay with us. It was two whole months of calls and freebies, but we did it."

"I'm so proud of you," I said.

"Thanks, thanks," Grace said. "That's partly why I wanted to organize this trip. To celebrate successes, and you know, new beginnings."

I can't help but think that Grace is talking about me, too.

On that bright Saturday morning, we set sail on Grace's yacht at 8:00 a.m. We were in the middle of September, which meant that it was the true beginning of Jakarta's rainy season, but by some miracle our trip to the Thousand Islands was met with clear skies and a stunning sun. But unlike the original plan, the people who came along were Grace, Faith, and Kai, who came in place of Ray.

"It's a pity that Ray couldn't come with us," Grace said, looking out into the sapphire blue sea.

"I know," Faith said. "Ko Mike told me he's been pretty busy."

"Pak David is making him do this sales pitch to a potential real-estate partner," Kai said.

Without Ray around, I wouldn't have to cower in fear while bearing my semi-naked body to the world.

The four of us lay on a large sunbed at the yacht's stern, absorbing the ocean breeze and generous sunshine. I pulled my shirt off to reveal a pale body under a ruffled bathing suit. Grace wore a red triangle bikini, showing off her flat stomach. I touched my lower belly, bulging from the fried eggs Bu Ratih prepared for me this morning.

Pearly white clouds floated gracefully above the ocean, its reaches tinted with the sun's orange glow. Sprinkles of light reflected off the surface of the Java Sea. The yacht soared over crashing waves. My skin blended with the cream-colored sunbed. Oma loved it, but I missed my sun-kissed LA skin. I thought that I'd be tanner here than I was in LA, but there weren't many outdoor activities in Jakarta, at least, none that Oma allowed me to enjoy.

Grace played some music on a speaker as we soaked in the sunlight. I allowed the sun to caramelize my skin. The burn tingled. The breeze was unkind. It roared in my ears and tossed my hair around. Still, I was at peace. I forgot about Kopi Sedap and Ray and my frustrating grandparents.

Before we knew it, two hours had passed. The yacht slowed to a stop. Its engine hummed. Its turbines churned. The crew hurried up to the sides of the boat to lower anchor.

"So," Grace said, tossing us life vests. "We can't dock any closer because it's too shallow, so we have to swim to the island."

Grace pointed at a small island with a white beaches and bushes for trees.

"Unless…" Grace grinned.

"Unless?" Faith said.

"Does someone want to ride the jet-ski with me?"

"Me," Faith said. "I'm driving."

That meant that Kai and I had to swim.

I squinted through my sunglasses to see how far away the island was. It looked to be about a hundred and fifty feet. But it was a hundred and fifty feet across a navy abyss.

"I guess we're swimming, huh," Kai said, nudging me. "You ready?"

"No." I shivered from the thought of having to swim through that much ocean. "Are you?"

"You'll be fine. This is about, what, fifty meters? That's okay. We trained with fifty-meter laps at Cornell. Twenty-five meters, to-and-fro."

"You swam at Cornell?" I asked.

"Yeah," Kai said. "Not as an athlete, though, but I did some friendly matches here and there with my other swim club buddies. I swam varsity in high school."

"Show-off."

Kai smirked. We walked down to the boat's stern. He put his life vest on and made sure that mine was secure before stepping into the cold sea. Holding my hand, Kai helped me into the water. The deep blue sent chills up my body, but I kept my gaze on his comforting eyes.

With Kai beside me, and the life vest that carried my body, swimming across the sea felt less scary. We bobbed our heads above the water and watched as Faith and Grace sped across the ocean on the jet ski.

But eventually, we made it to the island. It was tiny, small enough to walk from end to end in fifteen minutes. A small family hung out in a rickety *warung*, halving freshly-harvested coconuts while their children played on makeshift swing sets. They were the only other people present. Lush trees encapsulated a majority of the island in a heart shape, leaving space for a sandy white beach. Surrounding it was a turquoise sea, home to small fish and two fishing boats in the horizon. It was a fresh sight after seeing the oil-stained, blackened sea off Jakarta's coasts.

"You aren't scared, right?" Kai asked, dusting sand off his knees.

"No," I smiled.

I'm okay because I have you, Kai.

The girls parked the jet-ski by the coast and snorkeled by the beach.

"How was the swim?" Grace said, emerging from the water.

She lifted her snorkel up to her forehead. The seawater had erased her mascara and eyeliner, but she looked beautiful nonetheless.

"Are there any fish?" Kai asked.

"Not really, just some small fry," Grace said. She ran her fingers through her wet hair. "But the water is super clear. And there are really cute crabs and seashells."

"Do you have extra snorkels?"

"No, these are Faith's and my own." Grace's eyes wandered. "Oh! You can try the jet-ski! The captain recommends that we go in pairs, but you guys can take turns driving the thing."

"Sweet," Kai said. "Thanks, Grace."

"Do you know how to drive it?"

"I drove a jet-ski once, so I should be able to."

"Just don't flip it or anything. And don't drive it too close to the shore."

"Got it."

Like a mermaid, Grace pulled her snorkel over her face and disappeared into the water, swimming up towards Faith. Two snorkels floated above the surface. Kai and I walked towards the jet-ski.

"You're going to drive it, right?" I asked.

Kai stopped and looked at me.

"Do you want to?" he asked.

"I...I don't know how."

Kai chuckled.

"It's okay; I got it," he grinned. "I can teach you later, and then we can trade places."

"Okay," I said.

Kai climbed onto the jet-ski and I hopped on behind him.

"Hold on," Kai said.

"To what?"

"Me," he said, wrapping my arms around his stomach.

He zoomed into the blue sky, accelerating as we moved further away from the island. We jumped over waves. We swerved and cut corners. I locked my fingers around his stomach, squeezing harder whenever I felt like I was going to fly off of the jet-ski.

"You okay?" he laughed.

"Can you go slower?" I cried, feeling the exhilarating wind tingle my body and face.

"You don't like roller coasters, do you?"

Kai touched my fingers, which were cold from wind and fear. My heart fluttered a little. I couldn't help it. He was sweet, thoughtful, and kind. Plus, I couldn't deny that I liked the attention.

"No, I don't." I pushed myself closer to him.

"Okay, okay," Kai said. "I'll go slower."

Kai decelerated. I looked at the back of his head more than I did the ocean. A braided leather necklace sat delicately around his neck. I observed each string of leather woven between one another. I ran my fingers along them.

"Stop," Kai said, twitching his neck. "It tickles."

"Sorry," I giggled.

"If you don't stop, I'll go faster."

"You can go faster," I said.

Kai pressed on the gas. We glided above the sparkling sea, enjoying the breeze and sunlight that cast rainbows on splatters of water. Fishing boats waved at us. Some other jet-skiers zoomed past.

I leaned the side of my head against Kai's shoulders and closed my eyes. The ocean sprayed my face, its fresh breeze tousling my dark hair. The air's salty taste tickled my tongue. Dad would've been so happy here. Who knew that I would be, too.

Closing my eyes, I grinned. *I could get used to this.*

+

We arrived back in Jakarta at 1:30 p.m. Faith brought us to eat lunch at her favorite noodle shop in North Jakarta, Bakmi Orpa. The restaurant was structured like a semi-food court, with tables that allowed for free seating. Two tables were fully packed with families that chatted heartily, so we sat at a corner near the door for some peace and quiet. Faith went up to the cashier to place our orders.

"Wasn't it amazing?" Grace said, tossing her wet hair to dry it. "I love going to the Thousand Islands. It's always so, I don't know, exhilarating."

I couldn't help but feel a little envious. What a life Grace led. Running Oscar & Vinny's on weekdays, boating on weekends.

"I had so much fun," I said. "Thanks for inviting me."

"Yeah, thank you, Grace," Kai said.

"We should do this more often," Grace said. "It's a nice break from work."

We ordered, and the waitress served us our bowls of noodles. As I was going in to take my first bite, I was interrupted by door chimes and the restaurant owner saying, "*Selamat siang.*"

A man and a woman walked in.

"*Selamat siang,*" the man replied.

Recognizing his voice, Faith's smile faded. Her eyebrows were slightly raised.

"Oh no," she said.

Faith lowered her head, staring at the ground. Grace and Kai followed. I cocked my head to get a quick glance at the people who had just walked in. I only saw the woman's back, curtained by locks of long, black hair over a simple summer dress. The man had an accented jaw and high cheekbones. He looked oddly familiar, but I couldn't figure out who he was.

"CeCe!" Faith snarled. "Don't look."

"What? Who's that?" I whispered.

The air in the room grew mysterious. Faith kept her head low until the man sat near the rowdy tables at the other corner of the restaurant. The server came to us and served our noodles.

"It can't be, right?" Faith asked.

"Girl, what the hell?" Grace said. "Who were those people?"

"That's Oom Tommy Kurniawan," Faith said. "Ray's dad."

I took another look at Oom Tommy. Opa Robby was right, he was good looking. Like Ray, he also had sharp, caring eyes. With the exception of his silvered hair, Oom Tommy could pass as Ray's older brother.

"I totally see the resemblance," I said. "His mom is gorgeous."

"That's not his mom," Faith said.

"What?"

Faith leaned into the table. All of us followed.

"That's Oom Tommy's mistress."

The table silenced, amplifying the clicking sound from the cash register behind us and loud chatter from the room across. I cupped my hand over my mouth.

The almighty Tommy Kurniawan was having an affair.

I shot a sneaky glance at Oom Tommy's mistress. The woman looked at least half his age, perhaps in her early thirties. She was the epitome of Indonesian beauty: bug eyes, a fair complexion, and cheeks that were oblong enough to pass as symptoms of an illness.

"Holy crap," Kai whispered, slurping on his noodles. "No way. He's that open about it?"

"Yeah," Grace said. "Ray's family is a bit...broken."

No wonder he never talks about his family. Ray, who thought of himself so highly, never talked about his well-to-do family. He could only talk about himself.

"Ko Mike told me about Ray's family," Faith said. "He had a really bad childhood. Poor guy. He's so strong."

"What happened?" I said.

"If I tell you guys, you can't tell anyone, okay? My brother told me all of this in confidence. And I told Grace because, well, she's my best friend."

Kai and I nodded. I slurped on my noodles, allowing their grease and flavor to seep into my tongue.

"You know that Oom Tommy runs Semina, right?" Faith said. "The biggest textile manufacturer in Indonesia? Semina pretty much had a monopoly on the cotton plantations here until about twenty years ago."

"Crazy, right? Their profits are still in the millions," Grace continued. "I heard Ray's grandpa used to go to Suharto's house on the weekends when he was still president."

"Shit," Kai exclaimed.

"Yeah," Faith said. "So you can imagine how much pressure there is on Ray's family to, like, look good in society. And yet their marriage is really falling apart. Ray told my brother that both his parents have affairs. This woman that Oom Tommy came with has been with him for, what, ten years now? And Tante Sally, Oom Tommy's wife, has had her affair for about half as long."

I stopped chewing my noodles, not knowing how to feel. I couldn't help but feel a little happy that Ray wasn't as perfect as he painted himself to be. But a larger part of me just pitied him for having a family that was so broken.

"Wait," Kai said.

He whipped out his phone and started typing furiously. He showed us a magazine spread of a glammed-up Oom Tommy and Tante Sally, who were posing like a young couple at a high school dance.

"My mom showed me this last week," Kai said. "They had a full spread on Tatler's latest issue. Are you sure that both of them are having affairs?"

"Yeah," Faith said.

"Shit," Kai sighed. "Thank god Ray didn't come today. It would've been so hard for him."

"That's what I was just thinking," Faith said.

"Why don't his parents just get a divorce?" I said. "Instead of staging appearances like this and causing Ray all of that pain."

"You know why," Grace said.

"Publicity?" I said.

"Yeah," Faith said. "It'll look bad for Semina if they both split up."

"What? Why?" I said. "Can't people differentiate between family and work life? Why the hell would a divorce affect Semina?"

Faith, Grace, and Kai looked at one another. Kai broke their gaze and raised the noodle bowl to his lips to drink the soup. Faith barely touched her noodles.

"It's like that over here," Grace explained. "Connections matter *a lot*. It can literally make or break you. Just look at Oscar & Vinny's as an example. We literally almost went bankrupt, but because we had a rich and influential client base, we managed to stay afloat."

"True," Faith said. "You heard my mom's story, right? She wouldn't be where she is today if she didn't have friends in powerful places. We started off as a middle-class family when my dad left."

"This society is so interconnected that, if you fuck up, the entire world will know. And then you can lose a lot of opportunities, including partnerships and potential deals."

I understood that connections were important, but wasn't it toxic for Ray to constantly pressure-cook himself to the point of losing his authenticity?

Is this also why Dad moved to LA, why he chose to be James Wongso and not Robby Wongso's youngest son? Because he wanted to get rid of the burden that comes with being a Wongso?

If this was true, then I was really stupid for deliberately walking into the trap that Dad so quickly got away from.

"How does Ray do it, then?" I asked. "Doesn't he get tired of pretending?"

"Well," Faith said. "His mental health is not great. Ko Mike has told him time and time again to see a therapist, but it's hard here. You can't really trust their confidentiality. And with Ray's family's social status, it's going to be detrimental if a therapist breathes a word of their sessions."

I stared at Oom Tommy and his mistress, who were holding hands. He looked happy, but at what cost?

"Jeez," Kai said. "Fuck this."

"I know," Faith sighed. "Poor Ray was neglected and abused in his childhood. When he had to enlist in the Singaporean army after high school, you know, since he's a Singaporean citizen, he was tortured by his lieutenants, too. But he told Ko Mike that he still preferred that to staying at home with his cold-hearted parents."

"They're only nice to him in front of other people," Grace said. "Or when they need to keep up appearances of a perfect little family. It *is* really screwed up. I feel so bad for him."

I slumped in my chair. A sharp pang of guilt pricked my heart. Ray searched for attention because he was so empty inside. I could see him crawling to his friends for help, screaming so loud even though no one could hear him.

Maybe he was going through a hard time. Maybe that's why he said all those horrible things to me with kind eyes.

I didn't think I could forgive him yet. Regardless, he deserved so much better.

"But if his family is so adamant on maintaining their reputation, what the hell is Oom Tommy doing here with his mistress?" Kai asked.

"I don't know," Faith said. "That's why I freaked out when they came in. I've never seen his mistress, but that sure as hell isn't Tante Sally."

My gut clenched. I thought of Dad again, the man who loved his wife so much that he left his family for her. He would never betray Mom, even if the world betrayed him time and time again.

Once we finished our lunch, we said goodbye and stepped into our cars. Since Kai's driver hadn't shown up at the restaurant, I offered to drop him home.

Kai and I squeezed awkwardly in the back seat, watching rickety shophouses and motorbikes outside the window flash by like a dynamic painting. I placed my hand on the glass, feeling the car's vibrations as we sped on the highway. The Jakarta I saw today was a little less sophisticated than it had been in my everyday travels.

"I've never been to this part of Jakarta before," I said, feeling my stomach grumble from the hearty noodles.

"You haven't?" Kai said.

"My grandma doesn't really like leaving SCBD. Well, except for Plaza Indonesia. She goes there almost every day."

Kai scratched his head and angled his body towards me.

"Let's have dinner then," he said.

"Dinner?"

"Yeah. Next Friday. I can show you around North Jakarta a little bit more, my old stomping grounds."

"I'm down for that."

Kai grinned. I blushed and turned my eyes to the windows, watching the roads lead us back home.

20

Humidity lingered in the serenity of the Jakarta wind. We drove toward the horizon that splits the earth from the sky, listening to Tulus on the radio as the sun retired behind skyscrapers. I gazed at the reflection of vehicle lights in the side mirror. My hair was perched on crater-like collarbones. My cheeks looked more angular than they used to be. I had definitely lost some weight since I arrived, but I wasn't sure if this was a good thing.

I sat in the front seat of Kai's C Class. Oma urgently had to use Pak Sutikno to go to the office, so he couldn't follow us. In a way I was glad that I was able to spend some time with Kai without having someone tail us, but a thought constantly bugged me.

What if what happened with Ray happens with Kai, too?

Kai isn't Ray, I told myself. He's a good person.

How do you know, Cecilia?

I didn't.

Ant-like cars cruised through the 5:30 p.m. traffic. The journey to North Jakarta was painfully long. Kai wanted to take me to a restaurant there that served really good sushi. I wore a peach dress with blue flowers that Dad had liked.

"How much longer?" I asked.

"Waze says," Kai paused, "twenty more minutes."

"Twenty minutes?" I groaned. "We've been on the highway for at least half an hour."

"Sorry," he muttered.

Kai's body physically tensed up. His biceps flexed as he tightened his grip on the wheel.

"It's okay," I smiled, looking at him. "I ate some fruit before this so I'm not hungry."

"Okay," he said. "That's good. It's 5:00 p.m. on a Friday, but I don't know, I didn't think today's traffic would be this bad."

"That's frustrating."

I paused. The traffic started to clear up a little bit more.

"You know what's funny?" I said. "I used to think LA traffic was bad. Everyone did. All my friends from the Midwest and East Coast thought the same."

"The thing that drives me crazy about Jakarta is the bad drivers. Look at this!" Kai honked, a little vein popping up on the side of his forehead. "This guy is literally driving halfway into the shoulder!"

We turned into a narrow street that housed four lanes of cars. Kai said that this was common in Jakarta because many vehicles parked on the roadside and thus didn't allow for other cars to pass by on their lane. A salad of trucks, rickshaws, food carts, motorbikes, cars, and people converged on the street.

The street felt different from what I was used to in SCBD, bleakly lit, but with harsh enough lighting to see its features. Rusted metal scraps slapped together to form a hut replaced skyscrapers. Tattered sheets of plastic replaced curtains. Rickety shophouses, worn out by time and a lack of funding, replaced towering, eight-story malls. Rusted steel held up by two skinny poles replaced roofs. Tangled power cables hung so low that an NBA player could get strangled in them.

People here wore torn clothes with yellow and black stains. They huddled outside by the streets either smoking cigarettes or digging into rice with their fingers. Some came up to stationary cars to beg for spare change.

Dirty, overcrowded, and underdeveloped wasn't the Jakarta I woke up to every morning.

"Kai," I asked. "Where are we?"

"We're close," Kai said. "The restaurant is just up ahead."

"No, Kai, I mean," I cleared my throat. "Why does everything look so ... different?"

"What do you mean?"

"Where are all the malls? The skyscrapers? The nice houses?"

With one hand on the wheel, Kai turned his head towards me.

"CeCe," he said. "The area we live and work in is the financial and entertainment hub. It's all a façade for capitalist monkeys. This is the other side of Jakarta. Cramped living spaces, dirty streets, and people struggling to eat."

My eyes glued on an old, skinny man pushing a fruit cart.

"I...I didn't know," I said.

"Yeah," Kai said. "This isn't even that bad. If you go deeper into the city, it gets worse. Some children drink out of browned river water. It's really sad."

"Do people know?"

"Of course. And still, some of our friends throw away millions of Rupiah on a lavish bottle of wine but refuse to spare Rp10.000 for a starving family."

"Who? Ray?"

"Well." Kai chuckled nervously. "I didn't want to say it, but yes."

"It's okay, I won't tell him."

"I don't know...It's fine if he wants to spend money on wine, but like, at least spare some money for a hungry kid. Rp10.000 is literally chump change for him."

After driving through this long road, we turned onto another one and pulled up to the restaurant. It was a beautiful place with white wooden walls, tatami mats, and a gorgeous stone-paved walkway that opened up to a mini bamboo water fountain. Servers wore traditional kimonos. Beautiful paintings decorated the walls. There was something about the Japanese aesthetic that felt so serene.

Kai chose a table at the corner, near the fountain. We placed our orders. Afterwards, the servers gave us complimentary green tea.

"You like the place? It's nice, isn't it?" Kai asked. "My parents used to take me here all the time when I was a kid."

"You drove for an hour just to come here for a meal?" I raised my eyebrow.

"I used to live around here," Kai said. "There's a neighborhood nearby and I lived there until my dad got promoted. The company gave us the apartment, and since it was also closer to school, we put up our house for rent and moved there."

"That's nice," I said.

I squeezed my sweaty palms. *Why am I so nervous?* I mustered up a smile as I sipped on my green tea. Kai looked at a painting on his left, which pulled his shirt enough to expose the scar on the right side of his chest. I couldn't help but stare at it, being reminded once again of my mistakes at Kopi Sedap.

Will Kai be upset if I decide to resign?

"It's sunburn," he said, breaking the silence.

"What?"

"Last week, when we went to the Thousand Islands. I got sunburnt then. That's what you're looking at, right? My absurd tan."

He pulled his necklace back to reveal a gnarly tan line.

"Oh god," I giggled. "It does look pretty bad."

"Yeah," he said. "It hurts when I shower. I should've put on more sunscreen."

Kai's necklace looked a little different under the dim lighting. Unkempt leather flakes hooked onto the necklace's edges. Sweat and time had stained the brown. The necklace, I suspected, evolved from a mundane accessory to a treasured family heirloom.

"Where did you get that necklace?" I asked.

"My grandpa gave it to me for good luck," he said. "It's some feng shui thing, apparently."

"You really believe in those things?" I chuckled.

"Nah. But I just follow along to make my grandparents happy."

"What?" I scoffed. "That's ridiculous. Even if you don't believe in it?"

"I guess, yeah," Kai said. "They're my grandparents, after all."

Kai wore a perplexed look on his face.

"Okay, but what if your grandparents ask you to do something ridiculous, like marry someone you hated because she came from a good family," I said, drawing from my own experiences. "Would you do it?"

Kai paused and fidgeted with his fingers.

"I don't know," he said. "My grandparents won't do that. They never force me to do things."

Perhaps that was the difference between Kai's grandparents and mine, then.

"But what if they were the forceful kind?" I thought about Oma. "What would you do then?"

"I mean, they're my grandparents, CeCe. They've lived longer. They know what's best for me. They wouldn't force me to marry someone I didn't love, but at the same time, I wouldn't disrespect them and elope in Vegas, if that's what you're asking."

I bit my lip.

"So you're saying that you need your grandparents' permission for anything in your life? Even when it comes to dating?"

Kai raised his eyebrow at me and smiled.

"Yeah," he said. "I'd actually feel pretty uncomfortable if I did something to upset them."

Was this what Indonesian culture was? Your family being the center of everything you do? Was that why Oma was butting into so many things that I did?

Was this why Dad was so adamant to pack up and leave everything behind for love?

"Is it not like that in your family?" Kai asked.

"Um—"

"Sorry. I didn't mean to pry. You don't have to answer if it's too personal."

"No, it's okay."

I tucked a stray hair behind my ear.

"My paternal grandparents disapproved of my mom. I always thought it was ridiculous that Dad let things get to his head, but now that you put it into perspective, I think I kind of get it."

"What happened between them?"

I parted my lips, but I couldn't say anything. Did I actually know what had happened between my family members? Mom said that Oma and Opa forbade our family from coming back to Indonesia after Makco's funeral. Dad said that he refused to come back because he hated Oma and Opa for what they did to Mom. And Oma said that Mom locked Dad up in LA like an evil witch and kept him from them forever.

Everyone pointed fingers at one another, but even though their stories had a common thread, none of them added up.

I couldn't believe it. *I don't actually know what happened between my parents and grandparents.*

"It's complicated," I said instead, drinking my green tea.

"Yeah," Kai said. "Family can be really complex sometimes. Does your dad talk about it often?"

"He died," I said, biting my lip. "Um, he's dead. He died last year. Brain tumor."

It was the first time I had said those words out loud in a really long time, and I missed him again.

"I'm sorry, CeCe," Kai said. "I lost my grandpa a year ago, too."

"Doesn't get easier, does it?" I said. "I still see Dad in my dreams. I haven't listened to jazz music in over a year because it reminds me too much of him."

"That's part of why I still wear this necklace. To preserve my grandfather's memory. Even though I don't believe in all the feng shui stuff."

I tugged at my dress. Not because I wanted to stop myself from crying, but because someone here *finally* understood the grief of losing a person they loved most.

The server arrived with our food balanced on her forearm. We ordered two rolls of sushi and a sashimi platter.

"Are you sure this is enough?" Kai asked.

"Yeah, definitely."

I didn't like eating a lot when I was out with guys for the first time. Maybe it was a self-conscious thing.

I studied the water fountain next to us while I munched on sushi. The piece of bamboo spouted out water into a smooth stone bowl, which overflowed to a bed of pebbles beneath it. It was such an interesting contraption. Simple, yet stunning. I wondered how people could create them.

"Wait, CeCe," Kai said, interrupting my train of thought. "Can I ask you something?"

"What is it?"

"Um," Kai chuckled. "Don't take this the wrong way. I just heard some things and was curious."

"Just say it."

"What's your last name?"

I gulped. Had Kai found out?

"Poetry," I said, biting into a large piece of tuna sashimi. "I'm the only person you've onboarded to Kopi Sedap. You should know this."

"I meant, um, your *real* last name," Kai said.

I stopped chewing on my sushi. My eyes darted to the ground as the palpitations in my chest grew louder and louder. With Kai batting his eyes at me, mouth agape, my insecurities arose again. I couldn't let him find out. Not today. Not like this.

But Faith knew that I was a Wongso. Grace knew, too. And yet, they didn't make fun of me. They didn't call me "Ding Dong Wing Wong." In fact, nothing had changed between us since that day. They still treated me like a great friend and embraced me for who I was.

"You know what?" Kai said. "Never mind. I feel like I'm pushing—"

"It's…Wongso."

A burden lifted from my chest. My ribcage felt a little lighter. This time, I could control whether or not Kai should know. He had my back. All I had to do now was hold my breath and hope that he would react the way I hoped he would.

"So your dad is…James Wongso?"

"You know my dad?"

"And your grandpa is Robby Wongso?"

I dropped my chopsticks on the porcelain plate.

"Yeah," I said.

Kai nodded. *So far so good.*

"I'm sorry, I just," Kai cleared his throat. "You mentioned that your dad passed away earlier, and I just kind of put the pieces together."

"Faith and Grace told you, didn't they?"

"What? They know?"

"Wait a minute. How do you know then? Who told you?"

It's starting to prove really difficult to keep secrets around here.

"My mom told me about how Robby Wongso's son passed away and that his granddaughter was moving to Indonesia. I figured it was you, but since your last name on your job forms is Poetry, I only just now put the pieces together."

So Faith and Grace didn't spill the beans. I couldn't help but beam. I guessed I had friends I could trust in Jakarta after all.

"Does…does that change anything?"

"No, of course not," Kai said, getting a little defensive. "I was just curious since, you know, I like you."

The words flowed so effortlessly out of his lips.

"What?" I beamed. My heart fluttered a little.

"I mean it," he continued, digging into his sushi. "I like you, CeCe. I like you a lot. And if you're open to it, I'd like us to date."

Who knew that the first time I'd find love would be thousands of miles away from home.

I grinned, tapping my plate with the chopsticks, struggling to string words together. Should I cave into my desires and say yes? Just stay friends? Walk away?

"Okay."

"Okay what?"

"I'll go out with you."

Kai lit up instantly. He grinned from ear to ear. I did, too.

We were planning to go to a bar for drinks after dinner, but since Kai drove today, we decided to call it a night after he paid for dinner.

I walked into Kai's car and strapped myself in. It was 9:30 p.m. by the time we set off for home, a journey that Kai anticipated another hour for. We drove through the streets, passing by the street with run-down homes and tangled power cables. Even at night, vendors and smokers hung around outside. Some of the *warung* and food carts had lines that snaked behind the block. Jakarta had amazing nightlife across its different locations.

Indonesian pop songs blasted through the car's speakers. I watched the trees and cars disappear behind us as we zoomed past them. I rolled down the side window, allowing the roaring wind to caress my face. The wind reminded me of drives along the 101 after trips to Koreatown in LA. Dad would always wind down the window. And when he did, I would always stick my head out like a golden retriever. There was something about the wind that made me feel so free.

Kai looked at me. I met his gaze as he tried to juggle looking at me and the road.

"What?" I asked.

He took my hand and laced it in his. I let my palms feel the texture of his palms.

"I'm happy you said yes," he said, stroking my thumb.

"I couldn't say no." I smiled.

I leaned against the edge of the seat while my arm extended over the gearshift, fingers entwined in Kai's. I watched the wind billow in his hair, unfolding each strand. I noticed features that I hadn't seen before. The shiny tip of his nose. The small mole on his chin. The way his eyelids curved into the center of his face, complemented with untamed eyebrows.

When Kai caught me staring, he blushed and squeezed my hand. I squeezed back. We did this throughout the entire car ride home, with the radio singing in the background.

The roads were clear that night because according to Kai, we were moving against traffic. We arrived at my house a half hour earlier than expected.

"We're here," Kai said.

"Do you want to come inside?" I said. "I think Bu Ratih just made some *pisang goreng*."

Kai's eyes wandered around the room before landing on mine.

"I…I'd prefer it if we take things slow," Kai said, squeezing my hand. "I hope that's okay."

I paused. I had never met a guy who "wanted to take things slow," but it made me like him even more. Kai was a nice contrast to Ray and the other boys I'd dated in college.

"I agree," I said. "Let's just park somewhere and talk then."

"Good idea."

Kai pulled into an empty residential street with a good view of the busy SCBD streets and rolled down the windows. I leaned against his shoulders, laughing as he recalled stories about his life. I realized then that I'd wanted Kai for a long time. I didn't need more. I didn't want more.

He wrapped his arms around me as I snuggled into him, feeling like the luckiest girl in his arms.

21

To alleviate all the pressure from engagement party-planning, Faith invited me to go clubbing at The Cove, the hottest club in Jakarta that just opened last month.

The only memory I had from the one night I went to a fancy club in Beverly Hills was my college friends and me dancing dangerously on top of tables. Afterwards, I woke up on Macy's bed. Since I was in a foreign country, with my grandparents and a job to come home to, I told myself to take it easy tonight.

I had forgotten how to dress up for a nightclub, especially on a humid October night. A skimpy short dress that Dad would never have approved of? A tight tube top with skinny jeans? Or a sparkly romper that showed off my cleavage?

I wore none of the above. I decided on a sleeved black top with a high enough neckline to hide my chest and paired it with blue skinny jeans and high heels.

At 10:30 p.m., Faith picked me up in her car and we drove off.

"Kai's meeting us there," I said.

"No problem at all," Faith said. "Ray and Ko Mike are, too."

"Ray's coming?"

"Yeah. Is that okay?"

I gulped. Having Ray there made me feel a little nervous, but as long as I stuck by Kai, I'd be fine.

"Of course," I said.

The Cove was embedded in a compound at the heart of Central Jakarta, neighboring a yoga studio and a Coffee Bean. Its entrance was incredibly photogenic, equipped with mirrors and turquoise strobe lights. We walked through a makeshift tunnel with blue glows that emulated the ocean, opening up to a haze of cigarette smoke and blaring electronic music.

Chilling blue hues splattered across the room, even though the music brought back warmth. Some huddled with one another to dance, while others gathered in small pockets of space to smoke and drink. I slung my Chanel purse over my body and hugged my shoulders for warmth and safety, fixating my eyes on the hem of Faith's top so I wouldn't lose her.

Grace squeezed my arm from behind.

"You okay, girl?" she asked.

"Yeah," I said. "I just haven't gone out in a while."

"It's okay. Nothing bad will happen tonight. We got you."

Ray, Kai, and Mike hollered at us from a table that we'd reserved. The three men were smoking cigarettes and held copper-colored drinks in their hands.

"We ordered vodka and some Moët," Kai shouted over the music. "Does anyone want anything else?"

"Can we get a mixer? Some Sprite and cranberry juice, maybe?" Grace shouted.

"Yes, let's get those. We'll get everything you guys want. On me!" Ray shouted, slobbering on his shirt.

Ray tried to get up, but he stumbled and rested his head on Mike's shoulder.

"How many drinks has he had?" Faith asked.

"I don't know. Maybe…seven vodka shots?" Mike said, throwing Ray onto the couch.

"Ko Mike!" Faith exclaimed, shoving Mike. "You were supposed to limit him. You know how rowdy Ray gets when he's drunk."

"Oops." Mike grinned.

Faith shook her head. Ray stared blankly into space. I tried to stand as far away from Ray as possible, so I shifted closer to Kai.

"Hey," he smiled.

"Hi," I smiled back.

"Do you want to drink?"

"Let's do it."

Kai poured me a shot of vodka. We clinked our glasses and swallowed our drinks.

A slow burn melted down my throat. My face soured. I bumped my head against Kai's and giggled as the alcohol's tingle warmed itself throughout my body.

A myriad of people gathered towards the middle of the club, girls in tight dresses that looked way too young to be drinking, sweaty men in semi-office wear who were handing out cigarettes, and Instagram personalities who huddled together for photos. I leaned on Kai. His body was warm, but his smile was warmer.

My cheeks flushed a bright fuchsia with each drink. I drank and drank until my mind buzzed into an indescribable joy. At that point I lost my body weight to the music that carried me from Kai's shoulder onto the dance floor.

The club was electric that night. Sparks of laughter and flashing lights ignited my soul. I let my limbs loose as I held hands with Faith, Grace, and Kai, twisting and turning and feeling so incredibly empowered by the alcohol that all my fears about Ray became trivial.

But everything changed when Kai broke off from the circle and squeezed into a quieter corner to take a call. Although I was still jumping around with Faith and Grace, I couldn't help but notice his distress. Kai spoke passionately on the phone, using gestures to indicate some sort of urgency.

My fun was ruined with a sentence upon his return.

"Hey, babe, I'm so sorry."

"What's wrong?"

"I want to stay longer, but my dad just called and asked me to come home."

I glanced at my watch. 12:50 a.m.

"But it's not even 1:00 a.m.," I said, a little dizzy. "Can't you stay a bit longer?"

"My mom suddenly spiked a fever," Kai said, holding my hands. "I have to go."

"Oh no. Is she okay?"

"I think so, but my dad wants me to come home and help him take care of her."

Kai turned to Grace and tapped her shoulder.

"Hey, I have to leave. My mom's sick," he said. "So please take care of CeCe for me."

"You got it," Grace put her arm around me.

I would be selfish if I decided to hold him back at that point.

"I hope your mom feels better," I said.

"Thank you, CeCe. Are you sure you're going to be okay here?"

"I'll be fine." I smiled. "Go take care of your mom. I'll text you when I get home."

"Okay. See you on Monday, yeah?"

Kai planted a kiss on my cheek and walked towards the door. I stared at the back of Kai's black shirt as he squeezed in between crowds. Sweat that couldn't be all mine crawled on my skin. I was sticky but sparkling.

And just like that, Kai left me tipsy, melted, and alone.

Afterward, the nightclub felt dull. The humidity among the crowd was unbearable. I wanted to leave. I had to. I squeezed through the walls of people to get to our table and grab my bag.

"CeCe," Grace said. "You're leaving already?"

"Yeah, sorry girl. I'm tired," I lied.

"Don't leave," she said, puffing a cigarette. I didn't even know that she smoked. "It's still so early."

"Sorry, Grace."

"I literally just ordered a bottle of Dom Perignon. At least stay for some champagne. Then I'll give you a ride home."

"You know what, yes," I said, putting my bag back down. "I'll stay until 1:30."

"Yay!" Grace exclaimed, hugging me as I sat down next to her.

Ray finally sobered up a bit after Grace and Mike fed him jugs of water. He was sitting up now, his phone's light illuminating his facial features. Veins meandered throughout the architecture of his pale face. I shivered.

But CeCe, you wanted me, right? His voice slurred in my ears. *You wanted me this whole time.*

I stayed with Grace at the opposite side of the table to avoid Ray even though I hated the musky smell of cigarettes.

When the champagne came, Grace poured us all a glass. Dom was heartier than I had expected, but anything was better than vodka. After wolfing down her drink, she pulled all of us back onto the dance floor. The champagne's buzz engulfed my being. I felt light again.

As I was throwing my fists in the air, jumping and twisting my hips, Ray walked up in front of me. I moved away, but he only inched closer. The strobe lights highlighted a green vein on his forehead. I shivered and stepped backwards, but we locked eyes.

There was a danger in him that set all my alarms off, but I couldn't shake him off when he grabbed my hand, leading me through a sea of bodies. Then he slammed my body against the wall.

"What are you doing?"

He placed his hands around my waist and planted a kiss on my face.

"What the fuck, man?" I jerked away, but he ended up pinning me to the wall.

"Cecilia." His alcohol-stained breath caressed my face.

He kissed me again, this time on my neck, this time harder.

"Stop it!" I yelled.

My lips trembled in between quickened breaths. I kicked and screamed but the music screamed louder. I tried to look above the bobbing heads of people dancing and spotted Faith, Grace, and Mike, who'd returned to our table from the dance floor to grab more drinks.

I thought they said they had my back.

I clawed my blunt fingernails into Ray's flesh, hoping that it would hurt him enough to let me go. Tears melted my mascara, but the more I sobbed, the more his champagne-stained tongue licked my skin.

Ray bashed my head backwards, slamming his hands against my neck and kept them there until I choked. My arms panicked. I pushed him back, but he pushed harder.

Groaning, I felt his stubby fingernails comb through the skin on my waist. Even though my mouth was open, I couldn't scream anymore.

Alcohol paralyzed me in a dark corner of The Cove. I let my limbs loose, clenched my eyes shut, and silently prayed that this tragedy would end.

I should've gone home with Kai.

In my prayers, I felt a body brush against me and pull Ray off.

"Hey!" a voice yelled. "Get off of her!"

A lightness swept over my limbs. I swam through the crowd, shoving people in my way until I could get myself as far away from him as I possibly could.

I stumbled into the girl's bathroom and locked myself in a stall. The sudden brightness stung my eyes. I kicked off my heels, stumbled on the floor, and clutched my waist, rocking myself to emotional safety. I didn't care that the tiles in the stall were slightly wet. I didn't care that I was probably sitting in pee or vomit.

My neck was throbbing. I was sure that it was bruised, but I didn't want to check. I covered the pain with my sweaty hair.

I should've gone home with Kai.

Tears blanketed my eyes. They were the only thing keeping me human in that furnace of numbness.

My waist pulsated. I ran my fingers against the scratch marks that felt wet with blood, rocking, counting sheep instead of throbs. I hoped that no one would come in, that no one would notice.

Help me, I thought. Yet no one heard me.

"CeCe!"

Someone knocked on all the bathroom stalls.

"Cecilia!"

It was Faith.

I unlocked the door and pushed it open with my foot. Faith rushed in, immediately locking the door behind her. She knelt on the floor. She didn't care that the tiles were wet, either.

"CeCe, are you okay?"

I couldn't speak.

"I'm so sorry this happened to you."

I traced a clump of fallen hair that spiraled by the drain.

"Can I hug you?"

I shook my head.

"Okay, I won't," she said, handing me a piece of tissue paper instead.

Humidity built up in the tiny bathroom stall. I could feel the sweat collect under my arms. But at that point my body was so drenched with a compound of fluids from my sweat and the ground that I couldn't tell them apart anymore.

I pressed the tissue against my bleeding waist. Lips parting, I focused my eyes on Faith's black top. My ears were ringing, but I could hear her breathing. I felt weightless. I was dissociated. Ray's grips and scratches replayed themselves on my body, which bruised and bled over and over again.

"I should've pushed him off." My voice shook. "I should've fought harder. I should've—"

"CeCe," Faith's eyes pierced mine. "I saw everything. I saw what Ray did to you. You have nothing to be ashamed of. *He* pushed you to a corner. *He* kissed you. *He* was so heavy that you couldn't do anything to resist him. Whatever happened was not your fault, okay?"

"But—"

"It wasn't your fault, CeCe. You have nothing to be ashamed of. And if you want to do something about Ray, I am on your side. I believe you, as a witness and your friend."

I took a deep breath.

"Say it, CeCe," Faith said, looking into my eyes. "It wasn't my fault."

It wasn't my fault?

"It wasn't my fault that Ray cornered me."

I didn't want him near me.

"It wasn't my fault that Ray started kissing me."

I didn't want him to kiss me.

"It wasn't my fault for not fighting Ray harder, because I couldn't."

I didn't want to fight.

My hands started trembling. Overwhelmed by numbness, another tear fell. As I allowed myself to feel, pain spilled out of my waist.

"But he's your friend," I said, allowing Faith to press tissue on the wound.

"I don't want to be friends with someone who hurts other people," Faith said. "Do you?"

"And he's my boss."

"Then quit."

"Quit?"

"CeCe, with your skills, you can definitely get another job with higher pay and better bosses."

I thought of Alicia's email, but I didn't say anything to Faith. Maybe Alpha-Omega was my way out after all.

"Hey," Faith said. "I've gone through what you have before, remember? It's not going to be easy. But trust me when I say that I will help you get through this every single step of the way, okay?"

When Faith stopped, tears receded from my eye sockets. Her eyebrows were furrowed. Her concern was beyond that of a mother's. We connected on a multitude of levels. Perhaps because like Ray had done with me, Antoine broke her in ways that couldn't be explained.

I stared at a speck of dirt on the stall's door. Faith stared at me. We remained this way until I could gather myself enough to utter the words "I want to go home" to her.

"Okay, okay," Faith said. "I'll ask Grace to get your bag. Do you have a driver?"

I nodded.

"Good. Do you want me to call him?"

I unlocked my phone, tapped on Pak Sutikno's contact, and pushed it to her. She dialed the number, spoke to him in Indonesian, and handed the phone back to me.

"He's coming. Let's wait at the entrance, yeah? Away from Ray. Away from this place."

Faith helped me up. She took sheets of tissue paper to wipe the wetness off of my skin. I cringed, but I held my breath.

She won't hurt you like Ray did, Cecilia.

"Can I hold your hand? So you won't get lost in the crowd?"

I nodded.

She held my wrist, gripping it so hard that I could feel my fingers throb, and led me through a meandering crowd of sweaty dancers. The blue hues at The Cove's tunnel entrance felt even colder, and this time, I shivered at its rigidness.

Faith ordered a bottle of water from the ladies at the front reception and gave it to me, making sure that I drank at least half the bottle. Shortly after, Grace came rushing over with my bag and Mike who happened to tag along.

"CeCe, are you okay?" Grace asked.

"Can I tell Grace?" Faith asked me. I nodded.

Faith went up to her and spoke on my behalf.

"Are you sure?" I heard Grace say as she cupped her mouth with her hands.

I stood on the sidelines, staring at a dirty coin on the ground while overhearing Faith's mumbling and Grace's gasps in response.

Pak Sutikno then pulled up with the car. I felt guilty that he had to take me home this late. I felt guilty that I dragged him into this whole mess. As I shamefully waddled into the car, Mike tugged on my shoulder.

"Hey, um," he said. "Ray was really drunk. He's going through a hard time personally. You understand, right?"

I clenched my jaw.

"I really hope you don't make a big deal out of this. Ray's a good guy. It's unlike him to do things like this."

Mike winked at me before I walked into my car. I embraced the darkness that engulfed me within the car's tinted windows, shielding me from men and strobe lights.

Yes, Mike, I understood. I understood that the prick of a boss who said that he was my friend decided to take advantage of me in a crowd of strange faces, and that by some miracle Faith saw everything and got me out before things could get worse.

Knowing that no one could see me, I leaned against the chilly window, allowing tears to silently spill down my face.

22

A cooing pigeon on the balcony woke me up at 10:00 a.m. the next day. I couldn't fall back asleep. I wished I could, not because I wanted to sleep again, but because I didn't want to wake up.

My curtains were closed, so morning in my bedroom looked like pitch-black midnight. I shuddered as the darkness replayed last night's events. I was drunk, but not drunk enough to forget.

His fingers that choked my neck. His tongue that planted slimy kisses all over my body. His fingernails that scratched blood from the sides of my waist.

My body ached again, wondering what I did to let him hurt me.

It's not your fault, CeCe. Faith's voice echoed. *Don't blame yourself.*

But it wasn't that easy.

I turned to my side, watching a single sliver of morning sun beam on the sleeved top and jeans still on the floor by the bathroom. The first thing I did when I got home the night before was strip out of those clothes to shower all of him off of me, but the harder I scrubbed, the more my skin broke and bled. Clean, cold water poured over me for about half an hour, but it didn't change the fact that I didn't feel clean and would probably never feel clean again.

The filthiness remained even as I slipped into clean clothes and tucked myself to bed. If it weren't for my drunken state, I wasn't sure that I would've fallen asleep, even though sleep wasn't the only thing I didn't have control over.

Now, rubbing the sleep out of my eyes, I brought myself to get up, open the curtains, and walk over to my vanity. As per Oma's request, Mbak Ani left some fresh coconut water in my room earlier this morning to help me recover from my hangover. The refreshing liquid slid down my throat, leaving behind an empty sense of longing that stained my lips.

As I sipped on my drink, a text from Kai came in.

Morning babe, I'm sorry I had to leave early last night. Did you have a good time? I hope Grace took care of you like I asked her to.—10:46

My stomach churned.

Can't wait to see you on Monday!—10:47

I told Kai that I was going to take leave from work due to "an incident that I will explain over call if you're free." And then I locked my phone and tossed it onto my bed.

I stared at the mirror on my vanity that revealed my physical state in clear daylight. Shaggy bed hair, bloodshot eyes, and skin on my neck that was now a deep purple. The bruises were the size of his thumbs. Touching them struck a bad chord in me. It hurt to move.

A concentrated ache throbbed near my stomach, right above my panties. I stood up, faced the tiny mirror on my vanity, and used my trembling fingers to lift up my shirt, revealing a waist that was abused by scratches and bruises. Yellows, blues, and reds smudged my pale Jakarta skin, like a paint palette that only colored foul canvasses. I took some iodine from the first-aid kit that Oma left in every room and smeared it on my waist, wincing at each sting that came with the healing. Oma told me that iodine could disinfect my wounds, but I doubted that it could disinfect my already-dirty body.

I plopped down on the chair again. I was everything and nothing at once. I was numb. I wanted to feel but couldn't. I shouldn't have let him take away my joy. I shouldn't have let him take away my pain. But I did. I did and that meant that I was never going to be the same person I was before that night, because now I was contaminated, tainted, forever unwashed.

I am everything and nothing at once.

For the first time since last night, tears started to trickle down, slowly at first, and then in a torrential downpour. I got up from my vanity and jumped back into bed, sobbing hard into my pillow and screaming at the world, wondering what I had done to make it hate me so much.

Suddenly, the door creaked open. Mbak Ani's head peeked through with a plate of mangoes.

"Non," she said. "Have *mangga* from Ibu Shaan."

Her tone changed as soon as she saw my wet face.

"Non!" Mbak Ani put the plate of freshly cut mangoes down on the bedside table and rushed to my side. "Non... Non okay?"

I sat up but stayed under my blanket, saying nothing.

"Non can tell Ani," she said. "Ani no say to Ibu Shaan."

I glanced at my phone. Kai hadn't replied yet. I had nothing to lose by telling another person, let alone one who didn't know any of my friends.

"Something happened last night," I said, using my sleeves to wipe away the dampness on my face.

"*Huh*, what happen?" Mbak Ani said.

"My boss...my boss hurt me."

"Hurt you?"

"He...assaulted me."

"What that mean, assault?"

I didn't know how else to describe what happened to Mbak Ani. It wasn't rape, it wasn't domestic abuse. But from the way she raised her eyebrows, Mbak Ani definitely understood me. She scanned my body for signs of trauma and fixated on my bruises.

"*Aduh*, Non," Mbak Ani said. "Is okay. Happen all the time."

"What?"

"Have to just...forget. Forget everything."

"How can I forget?"

Mbak Ani shifted closer to me. I jerked a little, but her touch was comforting.

"Non, Ani tell Non something," Mbak Ani said. "But Non cannot say to Bu Shaan."

"Okay," I sniffled.

"Ani never tell people," Mbak Ani said. "Last time Ani also..."

"Also what?" I said.

Mbak Ani took a deep breath.

"Ani from last time, from six years old, Ani have Uncle. Uncle kiss Ani's here," Mbak Ani said, pointing at her breasts. "Almost every day."

Mbak Ani went through something worse, yet she isn't complaining. You are, Cecilia.

"And then Uncle tell Ani is okay because this make Ani's Papa Mama happy. Ani scared, of course, so Ani told Mama. Mama say is okay, forget it, because later Papa will angry if Ani give Uncle trouble."

And here I was, sitting on the edge of my seat, hoping for a happy ending.

"So Ani just forget. Never tell people. Later Papa angry. If Papa angry, Ani lose Ani family."

I gulped.

"Every month Uncle come to house visit Ani's Papa Mama. So Ani move to Jakarta."

"Why didn't you report it to the police?"

"Police?" she scoffed. "Police don't care, Non. Police have other things to worry about. Ani don't tell anyone. No one care. No one listen."

Faith cared. Faith listened.

Mbak Ani smiled. I stared at clouds frolicking in the sky, picking at my cuticles. My tears subsided. I was numb again.

"Is okay, Non. Is fate. Have to go through this for Ani's family."

"But Mbak Ani, he hurt you. I'm sure your parents would help you instead of him."

"*Takdir*, Nonik. *Takdir*. It mean fate. Your life destiny. You just follow. Sometime life have bad thing like Uncle, but Ani don't want to sacrifice Papa Mama for Ani's *takdir*."

Fate? It was fate for him to hurt me?

No matter how much a part of me wanted to believe that, I refused to. It just didn't make sense. How could my fate be so tragic? Would my fate have changed if I had decided to leave with Kai? And if I had left with Kai, would fate have found a way for the incident to happen at another time?

"So you're saying that I should just keep quiet and not tell anyone about this to protect my family?" I asked.

"*Iya*," Mbak Ani said. "Protect Non boss also."

The last thing I wanted was to protect him. I wasn't sure why, but I loathed him. But Mom told me not to wish ill things on people, even if they were evil.

"What?" I said. "Why should I protect him?"

"Because Non have work. Non need work to help Ibu Shaan Pak Robby, right?"

"I mean—"

"Ani think like this, Non," Mbak Ani said. "If Ani have to suffer this, is okay. Ani will. Is *takdir*. Ani have to do it. So Non also go through for Non family. For Ibu Shaan, Bapak Robby, and Non's Papa Mama."

"My Papa is dead, Mbak Ani," I snarled.

Mbak Ani darted her eyes to the hem of the bedsheets. Awkwardness creeped into the atmosphere. I curled into my pillow like a broken puppy.

Kai still hadn't texted back. I wondered if I should tell him, or how I would. I wondered how he would react. Would he care? Would he care that it was Ray? Would he see me the same way?

Would he break up with me?

A hive of thoughts polluted my mind like a haze. I looked out at carefree clouds frolicking in the sky, wishing that I would be freed from the circumstances that had imprisoned me. Instead I was a rock tied to this life, this family, and this shame. And this fate too, apparently.

Suddenly, my phone vibrated. A text from Faith came in.

Are u ok? Do u need anything? Remember, I believe u CeCe. What happened wasn't your fault.—11:10

My eyes glassed over again. Suddenly all my thoughts aligned like constellations in a cosmos, germinating a single seed that Faith planted last night.

It wasn't my fault that he cornered me. It wasn't my fault that he started kissing me. It wasn't my fault for not fighting Ray harder, because I couldn't.

Faith's voice echoed through the walls. How rare it was for other people's words to become a diamond lighting your path to victory. A key that fit right into the gaping hole in your mind. The sword you needed to fight your battle.

For the first time since I arrived in Jakarta, someone had heard me. Someone saw me. Someone cared about me. And after months of obeying a predator who posed as a lamb, someone saw him for the wolf that he was. I thought I was delusional at the rooftop bar, but with Faith on my side, I didn't have to hide from him anymore.

"It wasn't my fault," I said.

"Huh?" Mbak Ani said.

"It wasn't my fault!" I shouted. "You're wrong, Mbak Ani. Faith saw everything. She saw him bruise me. She saw how hard I fought. She's my witness. I didn't do anything wrong, Mbak Ani. It wasn't my fate. He was a drunk asshole who took advantage of me."

"Nonik don't understand—"

"I was drunk! I never gave him consent. I'm sorry your uncle did that, but it wasn't your fault either Mbak Ani. It wasn't fate. You don't deserve things like this."

"Do it for your Mama Papa, Non."

"My Papa is dead, Mbak Ani!" I screamed again, slamming my pillow.

My words paralyzed Mbak Ani. The color left her face. I felt bad, but I wasn't about to be told what to do again, especially by someone whom I considered my ally.

"Mbak Ani, thank you for the mangoes," I said, gazing at the clouds again. "Please leave now."

Mbak Ani picked herself up from the carpet, dipped her head in a bow, and scurried out of my room, briskly shutting the door behind her.

I let out a breath. My eyes hurt, but the tears came again. I let them dampen my eyes, my cheeks, and my soul, so I could swim in a pool of guilt, shame, and pain. It was conflict after conflict, it always had been, but to fight with the one ally I had in this house turned out to be the worst stab to my gut.

I grabbed the plate of mangoes and started devouring each piece. Oma had been raving about these mangoes since yesterday, so they had to be good, right?

No.

They were unripe and unpleasant. I winced at the sour that stung my tongue with each bite. But I kept going. I kept eating until my stomach bloated into a balloon that burst through my skin.

That was just the way it had been in Jakarta. I swallowed so many voices until I forgot my own, reducing all my actions into other people's words. I would say, "Okay, Oma," and "Okay, David," and "Okay, Ray," until my own voice blended into the background like white noise.

I was tired. I was so tired. But I couldn't stand sitting still any longer.

I hopped off the bed to do some quick stretches to ease my bloating. As I let my thoughts wander, my phone buzzed. A text from Kai came in, asking me to call him as soon as I could.

I dialed Kai.

"Hello?" Kai's voice permeated through the phone.

"Hey," I said. "How's your mom?"

My voice was nasally after crying so much.

"She's okay," he said. "We brought her to the hospital last night and it turned out to be a stomach bug, so the doctors just prescribed some antibiotics and asked her to rest."

"That's a relief."

"Yeah. And CeCe, I'm sorry for not staying with you last night. I shouldn't have left you alone."

"It's okay," I said. I wasn't sure if it was, though.

"How was it? Did you have fun?"

I took a deep breath.

"Honestly, no."

"What happened?"

I gulped.

"Shit." Kai clicked his tongue. "I shouldn't have left you alone, CeCe. I'm sorry, I…I should've—"

"He…um…how do I say this…he assaulted me?"

My voice hesitated. I could hear Kai's body shift in the background.

"What? Who assaulted you?" Kai's voice was angry.

"Ray."

It was the first time I said his name out loud. I felt powerful, like I finally had a hold over him.

"Ray assaulted me. I couldn't feel anything. I couldn't stop it."

I sobbed, but saying the words out loud made me feel free. Color returned to my face as I embraced the pain.

"Oh my god."

"He was this different person, Kai. He literally pushed me against a wall and started touching me, and kissing me, and I…I can't." My words were barely comprehensible at this point. "I can't do it. I'm not strong enough to keep everything in. It's tearing me apart."

"I'm going to come over, okay?"

"And then Mike had the audacity to tell me not to make a big deal about it because Ray is having a hard time."

"I'm going to kill that asshole," Kai said. "Are you busy today? I'm going to come over and bring some food for you, alright? I could—"

"No, don't!" I cried. "Don't. I just…I want to be alone right now."

I clenched my teeth. I didn't want to be alone, but I knew that I couldn't be alone with a man, even if he was my own boyfriend.

"You can't expect me to just leave you alone when you're hurting like this, babe," Kai said. His voice trembled. Perhaps he hurt just as much as I did.

"I know, I know, I…I have to deal with this on my own."

Kai paused on the other end of the line. As I listened to his breaths, my heartbeat slowed. My fingers stopped trembling. I was able to lean back on my bed and enjoy the overflowing sadness that filled the numb emptiness.

"Okay," Kai said. "I'll send some food then. You like *gulai ikan*, right?"

"You don't have to send me anything."

"Of course I do," Kai said. "I'll drop it off at noon. You don't have to see me if you don't want to. But you should at least have something good to eat. Okay?"

"Thank you, Kai," I said.

What did I do to deserve a man who cares so much?

"And if you don't feel comfortable going to Faith's engagement party in two weeks, I'll stay home with you."

Oh no. I had forgotten about that.

"It's Faith," I said. "I have to go."

"She'll understand if you can't," Kai said.

"I know."

"But?"

"I can't miss her engagement party, Kai. I told her I'd go four months ago. I have to be there for her."

"Alright. But if you decide not to go, tell me, CeCe. We can have dinner together or something."

"Okay."

"I care about you a lot, CeCe."

"I know." I smiled. "Bye, Kai."

"Bye."

Kai hung up.

It was the first time in twelve hours that I could smile. While I was still battling the demons that told me I wasn't good enough, or that everything bad that happened was my fault, I was eternally grateful for these friends who turned into family.

23

The air conditioner's draft lifted the hem of my dress: a plain red one with short sleeves that dangled right above the knee. I loved it for its lace detailing at the neckline, but more so because Dad gave this dress to me on my first day of college.

I walked into a ballroom of sweet-smelling flowers and sequined people. Men were in suits and women adorned themselves in powder, jewels, and extravagant dresses. And here I was with minimal eyeliner, ballerina flats, and bare wrists. I dressed as one would for a friend's engagement party, but even the butlers serving food looked a million times more radiant than I did.

Did I read the invitation wrongly?

I whipped out the invitation that noted the "cocktail" dress code, blinking thrice to make sure that I wasn't dreaming the letters, but I couldn't be fooled by the simple serif font. In spite of this, people seemed ready to attend their own weddings. At first, I wished I had brought a cardigan to shield me from the blazing cold, but now being naked would be much less embarrassing than this.

While attempting to hide myself behind a pillar near the buffet section, I felt a tap on my shoulder. It was Grace, dressed in a radiant gown that showcased her long legs and tiny waist. Her hair was tied in an elegant bun, unlike mine, which was long and straight, how I always wore it.

"Hey girl, you good?" Grace said. "Why do you look like you're about to pee yourself?"

"Isn't the dress code 'cocktail?'" I asked.

"Yeah, it is," Grace said, scanning my dress. "Did you not read the invitation?"

"Of course I did. But everyone here looks like they're going to their own fucking wedding!"

"What do you mean? *This* is cocktail. Yours is what I'd wear to lunch."

"Are you kidding me?"

"It's okay." Grace searched through her bag. "Here. I brought a scarf in case it gets cold, but you can take it to dress your outfit up a bit."

She handed me a silk Hermès scarf, detailed with gorgeous horses and a lush landscape. The crinkles on the silk made the horses look more alive.

"Thank you, Grace, this is beautiful," I said, using the scarf to hug my shoulders.

"You look great," Grace said. "And, I know this is a bad time, but I wanted to ask if you're okay."

"What do you mean?"

"You know that Ray's coming, right?"

She stopped me in my tracks. I didn't know what to say, that I was better? That I knew it wasn't my fault even though I still felt disgusting? That I didn't know how the hell I was going to face Ray at work on Monday even though I had to?

"I'm actually quite surprised that you came today in spite of the whole…you know…" Grace said. "How have you been holding up?"

The past two weeks had been a rollercoaster of emotions. Days that I had to fake being sick to David so that I didn't have to go to work. Nights that I called Faith crying while she consoled and counseled me. I spent a lot of empty time eating and watching Netflix, trying to regain the strength that Ray had robbed from me.

"Never mind, I—"

"I'm okay," I sighed. "I took two weeks off of work and I'm feeling…much stronger."

"That's good to hear, sweetie," Grace said.

She looped my arm with hers and we strode towards Tante Lam to greet her. The ballroom was decadent, decorated with gold accents and pink flowers. Tables of ten were neatly arranged in rows throughout the room. A carpeted path led the way to the centerpiece of the ballroom, a photo wall decorated with flowers and a glass backdrop. Next to the photo wall was a harpist, elegantly perusing her fingers across the strings and enchanting guests into the beautiful love story of the newly engaged couple.

Opposite the photo backdrop was the buffet area where Tante Lam was speaking to some of her guests. She was sparkling in a white *kebaya* detailed with lace and pearl embroidery, her hair twisted into a complicated bun, pinned up by a golden hairpin.

"*Wah*," Tante Lam exclaimed. "You girls look so beautiful. Thank you for coming."

"Of course we came," Grace said. "The place looks great, Tante."

"Thanks, my dear," Tante Lam said. "It was a little difficult to decorate because Faith's one request was that she wanted peonies. So I'm glad you like it."

"Faith must be so happy." I beamed.

"Speaking of my daughter, have you seen her yet?" Tante Lam said.

Holding Jonathan's hand, Faith walked towards the photo wall. She wore a baby pink gown that glistened under the chandeliers. The happy couple posed in front of the peonies for the photographer who enthusiastically snapped every moment of it.

"She looks busy," I said, fixing my eyes on Faith.

I couldn't believe that, in the middle of wedding planning, an engagement party, and work, Faith still had made time to counsel me.

"She loves pictures, if you can't tell," Tante Lam said.

I grinned. Faith's family was so sweet.

"Enjoy the party, girls," Tante Lam said. "We have *nasi tumpeng, mie babat*, and…oh, you have to try the *babi guling*! I ordered it from a special *warung* in Bali. And for dessert, you guys should try the *kue putu*. I got those from Surabaya. Flown in specially by my sister. Please help yourselves, okay?"

"Yes, Tante," Grace said. "Thank you so much."

"Thank you, Tante," I said

"Of course. I'm going to take care of the cake and music, yea? You girls have fun. See you later."

"See you."

Grinning, Grace and I walked towards the table that we were assigned to on our invitations. Even the tables were beautifully decorated with framed sepia photographs of Jonathan and Faith, sequins that were sprinkled like confetti, and peonies that bloomed from their vases.

We walked towards Kai, who was already seated at our table. He couldn't come with me since he had to pick up Faith's engagement gift from Pacific Place before heading over. He grinned and waved at us, fixing his tie as we approached him.

He looks gorgeous in that blue suit.

"Nice scarf," Kai said, gazing at the horse's head on my right shoulder.

"It's Grace's," I said. "But if it looks *that* good on me, maybe I should keep it."

"You can for a thousand dollars," Grace said.

"Seriously?"

I shivered under the horses, whose eyes were probably already judging me for disrespecting their four-figure price tag.

"How uncultured are you, Cynthia?" a voice said.

I turned around. Standing behind me was Christie, dressed head to toe in white like a lost bride, with her signature high bun pinned into place by a tiara.

"Hey, you made it," Grace said.

"Of course!" Christie said. "Faith's engaged to the richest family in Jakarta. Of course I'll be here."

I rolled my eyes.

"Hey, new girl, can you save me a seat? I'm going to touch up my makeup in the bathroom. Kenny's coming."

"Kenny's coming?" Grace asked.

"I know, right?" Christie said. "I have to look pretty for him."

Christie pranced towards the bathroom, but her hair didn't move an inch.

"Wow," Grace said. "I can't imagine being her boyfriend, let alone her boy toy."

"My cousin told me that Kenny likes bossy girls," Kai said. "I heard his wife, Lisa, is very mild and sweet. Maybe that's why he's having an affair with Christie."

"But why would anyone be attracted to Christie?" I said.

"You said it, girl, not me," Grace said, trying to cover up her laugh.

A couple moments later, I saw all eyes move towards the door. A man showed up in a clearly tailored white suit. I heard some whispers around me of girls asking if he was "Faith's famous friend" and what they should do to "get his autograph."

It wasn't long until I realized that the tall frame, broad shoulders, and slightly crooked nose could only point to one person.

Ray. Adorned from head to toe in expensive things. Smiling like he had nothing in the world to be sorry for.

A wolf in sheep's clothing.

My breaths quickened into staccatos that sent a sharp pang to my chest. *You're a lot stronger than you think you are, CeCe.* Faith's voice echoed. *I saw it all happen. It's not your fault.*

But seeing him again, in person, made me think otherwise.

"CeCe," Grace said, squeezing my hand. "Just ignore him. It's okay. We'll make sure he won't come near you."

"If he touches you, he will never see the light of day," Kai said.

I smiled, but the reality was more grim. All I was thinking was that Ray was here, and that he would hurt me again.

I looked the other way, seeing Faith greet her guests near our table. She looked busy, but she was going to come to our table eventually anyway.

Perhaps having Faith here would help me clear my head.

"Faith!" I called out, waving. "Over here."

When Faith saw me, she smiled, pinching the ends of her dress up. The pink dress bounced at her shins as she ran over swiftly with her five-inch heels.

"Hello, hello," she said.

"Wow, future Mrs. Budiono," Christie said, coming back from the bathroom.

"You look so beautiful," I said, getting up to hug her.

"Thank you for coming, you guys," Faith said. "Let's take a photo."

The photographer told us to huddle in together. Faith instructed Kai and I to sit close together while the three girls stood up behind us. I let my hand hide under the tablecloth to warm it up and Kai's fingers met me there. He stroked my thumb with his and I reciprocated.

The photographer started counting.

"*Satu.*"

I held my breath and sucked in my stomach.

"*Dua.*"

I smiled for the first time that week.

"*Tiga.*"

Kai let my fingers go.

"Faith!"

I could recognize that voice from anywhere.

"Hey, Ray," Faith said.

Trembling, I looked down at my feet. My body wanted to either run out of the room or burst into tears, but I stayed, even though I couldn't breathe, even though I could feel my back beading with sweat. Being afraid of Ray was the last thing I expected of this whole ordeal, yet here he was, hugging Faith in front of me as if he had the privilege to live life as if nothing had happened.

I fisted my hands. It was all I could do.

"Congratulations, sis," Ray said. "Let's all take a picture."

"Okay, yes," Faith said.

I thought Faith wasn't going to be his friend anymore.

Ray huddled with the girls behind me. His fingers grazed the back of my shoulder. Panic started to eat at my heart. *Why are you so nonchalant, Cecilia? Why are you so timid, Cecilia? How will you face him at work on Monday, Cecilia? Cover your neck, Cecilia. You're going to lose everything you've built here, Cecilia.*

No one likes you, Cecilia.

You're not good enough, Cecilia.

I wanted to scream.

"*Satu.*"

I inhaled. Pursed my lips. The world around me silenced into white noise.

"*Dua.*"

My feet were solemnly planted on the carpet. I embraced the darkness that engulfed my being. I exhaled. The darkness molded into a gradient of gray.

"*Tiga.*"

The camera's flash shocked me back into reality. I saw Ray give a bottle of Dom Perignon to Faith, who thanked him and left. Christie followed closely behind her. Then he said hello to Grace, Kai, and me.

"Hey CeCe," Ray said. "Can I talk to you?"

"Get away from me," I growled.

"But CeCe," Ray said. "I'm sorry."

"Ray," Grace said. "She said no."

"Yeah, but I was drunk, and going through a lot, and—"

"I said no."

I felt my eyes swell with tears. I hid behind my veil of hair, which I fortunately hadn't pinned in a bun like every other woman in this room did.

"Cecilia, please," Ray said. "We have to work together, so can't we just move on, I—"

"Hey, man," Kai shouted, standing up. "She said no today, she said no the other week. Don't you understand that?"

"KP, don't do this bro."

"Stop calling me KP!" Kai shoved him. "Get out."

"But—"

"Get out!"

Shooting me a side eye, Ray walked away.

"Are you okay?" Kai asked, sitting back down.

I curled into him as I let the tears fall, ruining the little makeup I had on.

"I think so," I said, sniffling.

"Good," Kai smiled, tucking the hair in front of my face behind my ears. "I got you, CeCe."

As women's curls and men's ties loosened throughout the night, so did Ray's sobriety. Grace and Kai watched him closely on my behalf as he guzzled several glasses of whisky in a fifteen-minute time frame. Faith put him on a corner table with Mike that was far out enough from our reach, but close enough that I could overhear their conversations.

"Bro," Ray said, sloppily dropping his arm on Mike. "I thought she liked me, bro."

"Who? Cecilia?" Mike said.

"Yeah. She's so hot. I just wanted to kiss her so, *so* bad."

My stomach churned. I tried to focus on my *mie babat*, a delicious distraction, but their voices were so overpowering that even food couldn't pull my focus away from them.

"But she didn't want to."

"Exactly!"

Ray slammed the table.

"Ray, shut up," Mike said.

"She's the first girl, really, the first girl *ever*, to turn me down," Ray's words started to slur. "How dare she? All I did was be nice to her."

"I know you're having a hard time, bro, but this is not okay."

"Cecilia!" Ray shouted.

My shoulders tensed up. I whimpered and curled into my stomach. I fisted my hands, but the harder I squeezed, the more I pierced into the scabs from his nails.

"Hey," Mike growled, pinning Ray to his chair. "Keep it together, asshole. It's my sister's engagement party. You better not screw this up."

"Or what?" Ray said. He downed another glass of whisky. "Or what, huh? You know what you're going to do, big boy?"

"What?" Mike scoffed.

"Your sister's best friend," Ray sneered. "Gracelyn. You want to do her, right? I know you do."

"Ray."

"Just say the word and I'll make it happen. Tonight. Right in the middle of the party."

"Shut up!"

"No, you shut up," Ray said, slapping the side of Mike's head.

Mike got up and threw a punch at Ray. Just as Ray lifted his fist, Christie walked in with a handsome young man on her arm. He wore a black tuxedo that was way too fancy, even for the cocktail dress code, but at this point it looked more like everyone dressed the part but me.

"Is this drama I see?" Christie asked, her eyes wide.

Ray drank another glass of whisky and let out a nervous laugh. He slammed the glass on the table, sending vibrations so strong that one of Faith and Jonathan's framed sepia photographs collapsed.

"Oh!" Ray exclaimed. "It's the slut."

The man on Christie's arm pulled away from her and stormed towards Ray. His stocky figure towered over Ray. Even from a distance, I shivered.

"What the fuck did you just say?" the man said. A half-shaven beard clung onto his face like hooks.

"Bryan!" Ray clapped.

So that's who Bryan is. He looked a lot less muscular in my mind. This Bryan didn't look like someone Christie could mess with. I watched as Christie's face turned pale. I couldn't predict what could happen next, but it didn't look pretty.

"The famous Bryan," Ray continued. "I've heard so much about you."

"What do you want?" Bryan asked.

Ray proceeded to walk in circles around Bryan and Christie, like a vulture cornering his prey.

"I want..." Ray spoke, slurring his words. "Kenny Prasetyo."

Oh no.

The mask of makeup that Christie wore wasn't enough to hide her fear. She started twirling around with the huge emerald ring on her finger, perhaps to try and avoid the time bomb that was going to explode.

"Kenny, as in, Christie's business partner?" Bryan said. Completely oblivious to the situation, he turned to Christie. "What is he talking about, babe?"

Christie was clenching her fists this time. Kai and I looked at each other. She was treading on dangerous territory. I felt slightly bad for her, but she should've known that she couldn't keep up the charade for very long.

"Well," Ray said, pointing at a couple who were eating quietly at the next table. "Mr. Nice Guy Kenny over there, you know, the one with the wife next to him, has been sleeping with your slut."

"What is he talking about?" Bryan turned to Christie, raising his eyebrows.

"Oh, you don't know? Why don't you ask him?" Ray chugged a new glass of whisky. "Hey, Oom Kenny! Come over here!"

Armed with a maroon suit, Kenny approached us. Most of his skin was too smooth to look almost fifty, but the wrinkles around his eyes said otherwise. His wife, Lisa, holding his hand, was a petite woman with sweet lips and a beaded satin dress that trailed behind her. As the couple inched closer, Christie trembled. She squeezed her fists tightly like I did, but her faux acrylic claws couldn't pierce through her palms like mine could.

"I can't believe this is happening," I whispered to Kai. "I can't believe Kenny showed up."

"He's close to Jonathan's dad," Kai said. "Of course he'd come."

"This is going to be bad."

"I know."

Mike grabbed Grace's hand and walked towards our table, towards Kai and me. Kai gripped my hand under the table. *Don't clench your fists again, CeCe*, his grip said. *I'm here to hold you so you won't break.* I thanked him by stroking his hands with my thumb.

"Oom Kenny!" Ray opened his arms. "How are you? And Tante Lisa, you look womanly as always. Do you want some whisky?"

"Aren't you Tommy Kurniawan's son?" Kenny asked.

"Why yes." Ray took another swig of whisky. "And you're the beautiful man with the beautiful wife."

Mike got back up, squeezed past Christie, and marched toward Ray. His face was flushed with anger, perhaps because of how much hell Ray was about to unleash on his sister's engagement party.

"Ray," Mike leaned into Ray, mumbling through his teeth. "Let's go."

"No!" Ray snapped. "I have…I have to let them know."

"Know what?" Lisa said, looking at Kenny, who was sweating through his suit jacket.

I held my breath. Lisa's cluelessness was unsettling. She definitely would've known something, right?

"This is fantastic, isn't it?" Ray chuckled. "Why don't you tell them, Christie? I'm sure you've slept with enough men in your lifetime to tell at least one of them the truth."

The corner of Christie's lips twitched uncontrollably. All eyes were on her, which I guessed was what she wanted, but for all the wrong reasons. She mouthed a "sorry" to Lisa as her ghastly white face burst into tears.

But Christie's apology acted as the final piece of the puzzle that clicked in Lisa's mind.

"It's true?" Lisa said, her nostrils flaring. She inched further away from Kenny. "And yet, after all this time, I still believed you."

"Honey," Kenny said, reaching for Lisa's hand.

But Lisa jerked her hand away, threw her wedding ring on the floor, and left the room. All that remained was a stillness that almost felt suffocating.

"You bastard," Bryan shouted, charging into Kenny.

Kenny watched helplessly as Bryan prepared to throw a punch at him. Perhaps he felt guilty. Perhaps he hated himself enough. I could relate, to an extent.

When Bryan's fist was inches away from Kenny's face, Christie stepped in. Her mascara was melted, and her dress was wrinkled. Usually Christie would care, but today, she had other priorities.

"Stop!" Christie cried. "Babe, stop, please. I'll explain everything. It's not what it looks like."

"Get out of my way, you whore," Bryan said.

"Hey! Don't call her that," Kenny said.

"Are you being serious right now?" Bryan said, raising his fist again.

"I know this is a lot," Christie said. "I just, I'm sorry, Bry. Please. Let him go."

"You're defending him, Chris?" Bryan said. "Really? You're really going to humiliate me in front of all these people?"

In a fit of anger, Bryan grabbed Christie by her hair and tossed her to the side. Dark, untamed locks collapsed from the top of her head. Her tiara toppled onto the hard floor, fragmenting into unsalvageable pieces. I gasped. Grace and Kai did too. Without her hair up, Christie looked naïve and vulnerable, like a helpless kitten.

Gripping onto her scalp, Christie let out a high-pitched scream. At that moment, the harpist stopped playing. The air conditioner roared. All the guests stared, including Faith's family, who had previously been unbothered by all the commotion, now perhaps confused about why a woman with long hair had anything to worry about. Crouching down, Christie's terrified eyes bounced around the room.

"Babe." Bryan reached out to hold her. But Christie pulled away. Refusing to look at anywhere but at the floor, Christie darted out of the ballroom, sobbing into the curtain of hair that masked her humiliation.

I smirked, a little glad that Christie finally got what she deserved, but still feeling a little bad for her. Bryan and Kenny both ran after her. I looked at Grace, who was staring at a drunk Ray howling with laughter.

"This is ridiculous," Grace said, dashing over to Ray's table.

Kai held my hand under the table to stop me from hurting myself further. Having him by my side made everything slightly better.

"Ray," Grace shouted. "I think you should leave. You've caused way too much damage already. I can't let you stay here and ruin my best friend's engagement."

"Mikey," Ray sneered. "It's your girl."

"He's drunk," Mike said to Grace. "He needs to go."

"Let's go," Grace grabbed Ray's arm.

"What do you want, bitch?" Ray said, jerking her arm away.

"Excuse me?" Grace said.

"I want your friend over there. Cecilia. That's who I want."

Grace's face morphed in front of my eyes. She threw a hard slap across Ray's face, causing him to reel backwards and lose his balance. Ray held his face, stinging from the impact, and snarled at Grace. Fortunately, Faith and her family were again too engaged in party festivities to notice.

"Motherfucker," Grace said. "You do one thing one more time and I swear to you I will—"

"You will what?" Ray chuckled. "Sue me? Report me? You need me, Gracie. You know that you could only rebuild your precious doggy salon with Awan Fajar's endorsements."

Ray had been endorsing Oscar & Vinny's? Was that Grace's miraculous solution to her PR problems?

Maybe everyone's friendships in Jakarta truly were based on favors.

Grace clenched her jaw.

"I told you not to tell anyone," Grace said.

"After your recent PR scandal, I could give you another one, this time about you," Ray whipped out his phone and started tapping away. "Gracelyn Michelle, the oldest granddaughter of oligarch Awi Kusuma…oh, she slapped Awan Fajar? And abuses dogs too?"

"Ray," Mike said. "Stop it."

"Or what?"

Grace twitched her eyes, angry to the verge of tears. Tension loomed like an ominous fog. But I couldn't sit there and mope any longer. I had to do something. I couldn't just stand and watch my friend be obliterated by a manipulative animal.

I unlaced my fingers from Kai's and stood up.

"CeCe, what are you doing?" Kai asked.

"I have to stop this," I said.

"Don't," Kai said. "He'll hurt you."

"I can't let him do this to Grace."

"Will you be alright?"

"I don't know."

Kai paused.

"Then I'll go with you," Kai said.

I marched towards Ray, scared to the bone, with Kai trailing behind me like a bodyguard. He took out his phone and held it in front of him, filming in case anything went wrong.

"Ray!" I shouted.

Grace and Mike stared at me in horror.

"My dear," Ray smirked, turning his attention towards me. "Are you here to finish what we started?"

"You need to leave Grace alone."

My hands were trembling, but I stood rooted to the ground.

"Calm down, baby," Ray said, getting up from his chair. "You need me to kiss you again?"

"You didn't kiss me, you bastard," I screamed. "You call *this* a kiss?"

I lifted my dress, revealing the blue-black laceration on my waist. Grace cupped her mouth. Mike looked away. I didn't care that I was exposed. I didn't care if people judged.

This was my body. My story. My battle.

"This," I said, pointing at my wounds, "is sexual assault."

Ray scanned my body with his eyes. I expected him to erupt with laughter, but all he did was just stand still. I didn't know where I got all this courage from, but it felt so empowering.

I glanced at Faith, who was busy shaking her guests' hands.

"It's just a kiss, my dear," Ray said. "You liked it, so stop making it such a big deal."

"Are you serious?" I erupted. "I trusted you, you bastard! You were my friend. My boss. You introduced me to this world and these friends, and yet you were the asshole who took everything away from me."

Ray kept quiet, keeping his gaze on his glass of whisky.

"You are a control freak who preys on those weaker than you," I said. "But get this, Ray. You don't own me. You can't break me. You can have your power, but you can't take away my dignity."

I looked back at Kai, who was smiling at me. The color drained from Ray's face. I couldn't tell if it was from defeat or sorrow.

"You can't do anything," Ray said. "You don't have proof."

"Yes, she does," Kai said, holding up his iPhone.

"KP, you wouldn't dare!"

Ray stormed towards Kai, ready to throw a fist at him.

"You need to leave," Mike said. "Or you can say goodbye to me, your friends, and to your precious Awan Fajar."

"Mikey," Ray said.

"For the last time, it's Mike."

With one gesture, Mike called the security guards, who picked Ray up and escorted him out of the ballroom.

Kai rushed over to me, dropping his phone along the way. I leaned into his arms as he wrapped them around me, shielding me from the darkness.

"I'm so proud of you," he said, kissing my forehead.

I looked at Grace, who was still crying from the words that Ray scarred her with. I walked over towards her and draped the horse shawl over her shoulders.

"CeCe," Grace said, sniffling.

"Hey," I said. "Are you okay?"

"I should be the one asking you that."

"I'm fine," I said, leaning on her shoulder. "Better than before, actually."

We settled back down on our table. Kai left us to get drinks. I caught a glimpse of Mike, who was now standing awkwardly in the corner of the room, talking to Faith. Grace mouthed a quick "thank you" to Mike, who looked terribly exhausted after having to deal with his drunk friend all night. He locked eyes with her briefly, blushing as he walked with Faith towards the photo wall. Perhaps he was relieved that he still had a chance to fall in love with Grace, little by little.

+

The harpist played a more uplifting tune as the rhythm of the night returned to normal. Ray was escorted home. Christie and her men were nowhere to be found. Faith finally spent some time at our table, chatting with Kai, Grace, and me, where we updated her on what she had missed.

"That's…a lot," she said, taking a bite from her *kue putu*. "Jeez. I can't believe I missed all of that. At least you're all okay."

"CeCe is a superhero," Grace said.

"Indeed," Faith said, squeezing my shoulder.

We got up to go to the buffet section to get more of the delicious *kue putu*. I tapped Faith's shoulder.

"Faith, actually," I said, forking over some of Tante Lam's homemade *nastar* on my plate. "If you have some time, can I talk to you?"

"Of course," Faith said.

I followed Faith into a corner right outside the ballroom, quiet and far enough away from the festivities.

"Is everything okay?" Faith asked.

"Totally," I said, holding her hands. "I just wanted to say thank you for everything. The late-night calls, listening, and just...I don't think you understand how much you..."

My voice became shaky. I didn't know how I'd turn out without Faith. She leaned in for a hug.

"Oh gosh, girl, of course," Faith said. "I'm always here to help."

"I just...thank you."

"I know what difference it makes for one person to believe you. I can't disappoint my fifteen-year-old self by not helping another survivor."

She leaned in for another hug. I sobbed again, but this time, my tears broke my chains away.

24

I held the cup of hot green tea to my lips and exhaled, feeling steam heat up my eyes. Its comfort permeated through my skin like electricity.

I glanced at my phone. 7:30 p.m. on a lazy November evening. It had been half an hour since I'd first sat in David's office alone. Kai said it was rude to eat before your guests arrived, even if I didn't like them very much. So I just sipped on my green tea, feeling the sensation of diluted tea leaves burn down my throat.

The office felt a little chilly after hours. Jackets draped over empty chairs. The buzz from the electric sockets were more prominent. Ray hadn't been at work since Faith's party a month prior, which sounded relieving on paper, but I'd been filling in for him while he was gone.

Imagine having to pick up the slack for your boss who assaulted you. How humiliating.

I walked out of David's office to refill my hot tea at the water dispenser, counting the empty minutes as I waited for the mug to fill. *Wasn't it a little strange that the CEO wanted to meet me, a junior employee, personally for dinner?* The anticipation was slowly eating me up with each passing minute. He was definitely going to fire me; I could feel it.

Was he going to fire me for being rude to him about the partnerships?

Or worse, did he find out about Ray? What he did to me? What I went through?

I shivered.

But I couldn't let David fire me. I couldn't be jobless after only six months of being in Jakarta. What would my friends think? What would Oma and Opa think?

That I'm incompetent, dumb, and useless.

At 7:42 p.m., David burst into the room. He brought a Louis Vuitton shopping bag with him and sat on his ergonomic Herman Miller chair, right across from me.

"Sorry I'm late," David said. "I had to buy a birthday gift for my girlfriend."

"It's alright."

"Have you been waiting long?"

"No," I lied.

"Great," he said. "You brought something to eat like I asked?"

He could've paid for my dinner, at the very least, if he is going to fire me.

"Yeah," I said, opening the food container filled with the *gado-gado* that Bu Ratih had made for me.

David opened his own box of food, a medium-rare steak with a mountain of rice and boiled vegetables. He took a ravenous bite, steak juices spilling onto his stubble.

"Anyway, how are you?" David said. "How was your, how should I call it…two-week sabbatical last month?"

Maybe he doesn't know about Ray after all.

"It was good," I said. "Well-deserved."

"Well-deserved break for a long six-months' worth of work, huh?"

I carved a smile on my face. My gut churned, but I wasn't sure why.

"I'm just kidding," David said, slapping his fork on the steak. "Don't be so sensitive, Cecilia."

I sipped on my green tea again, burning my tastebuds to hide my flushed cheeks.

"You must be wondering why I called you to dinner on a random Wednesday, right?" David said. "I wanted to apologize."

"For what?"

"For how I raised my voice at you about the Artika Jaya a while back. You're honestly right about the whole thing. We would be so much better off with Artika Jaya."

David took me off the project after my leave, assigning me with tasks that Ray would have otherwise done. Amidst the hustle, I had no time to wallow over the stupid pitch.

Either way, it was a long overdue apology. I wondered why he picked tonight to apologize.

"Thank you," I said.

"I just...the CEO of Artika is a dick, you know?" David said. "What's his name...Haryanto Tjandra, I think? Right?"

"With all due respect," I said, sipping my green tea. "I don't think that changes the fact that Artika Jaya is still a better option for us, especially compared to Wahana Salim."

"Oh, we're still going with Wahana Salim."

"Wait, what?"

My green tea almost went down the wrong pipe. With all the filling in for Ray, I had actually forgotten about the Artika Jaya deal from months ago.

"I discussed it with Ray over a call yesterday and he agreed," David said. "It's not optimal, but I mean, Arjun is having a hard time. I want to help him out."

"You're the CEO," I said through my teeth. "You can do whatever you want."

"Sorry. You understand, right? I really hope you don't make a big deal out of this."

David's words rang familiar. I was tired of nodding, but I did it anyway. I munched on my greens to distract myself from the awkwardness that loomed over us.

"Cecilia," David said. "I can't believe we've never chatted. I should've been more attentive to you, but as you know, these past six months have been hectic for me. But I really appreciate you. You've exceeded my expectations as my first hire."

"I'm your first hire?"

"Our first *team* hire," David said, swallowing his food. "The last person I hired was KP about two years ago. Kopi Sedap is small enough to not afford teams. You're expensive, you know."

I smirked. Kopi Sedap *did* give generous salaries and benefits.

"When Ray said he needed help on the marketing side, and your grandpa approached me to hire you, I was pretty hesitant, you know? I didn't have a big enough budget to hire another person."

"Wait, what?"

"Don't take it the wrong way. I'm glad I hired you, but at the time I just…I couldn't turn down the President Commissioner of Mandala Group! They supply our coffee, for God's sake, so it wasn't like I had much choice."

Opa Robby supplies coffee for Kopi Sedap?

"You…you…you know my grandpa?" I stammered.

"What do you mean? Of course I know Oom Robby. Ask your grandpa if he knows Jeff Kwok. Jeff Kwok is my father. When I was starting Kopi Sedap, my dad was the one who connected me to Oom Robby so I could get him on board as our supplier. You know, since Mandala Land owns the largest coffee plantation in Kalimantan."

All the neurons in my mind started to buckle together like a zipper. Everything made sense now. The interview I screwed up. Getting picked up by the CEO on my first day. Being the only junior employee at the office. David's wrath at Ray, and not me, when it was I who made the mistake.

I thought David's special treatment towards me was because he liked my work ethic, not my last name.

"Are you shocked? I was too. I didn't know that Oom Robby had a granddaughter that was old enough to work! And then when you mentioned in the interview that your dad had died…I was shocked, like, oh my goodness, I completely forgot about James Wongso."

I clenched my teeth.

"And then I remembered the gossip when I was in high school about the exiled Wongso family! The whole scandal between James Wongso and the waitress, them eloping in LA, and them having a daughter instead of a son…I remembered everything. Who knew that his daughter would work in *my* company twenty-three years later? Isn't it crazy how destiny works? So, obviously, when Oom Robby called me and told me to hire you, I just *had* to accept."

In that moment, the world moved in slow motion. My lungs sank. Each heartbeat echoed throughout my body. Each bone dissipated to white noise. I was numb, numbed in a way that made it hard to think, hard to feel, hard to breathe.

Was this what the world thought of Dad? A thoughtless, rebellious son who eloped in LA for a scandalous rendezvous? And I, his only daughter, was just a byproduct of his neglect towards the Wongso name?

"You're the talk of the town, Cecilia Wongso," David said.

"The town?"

"Oh yes. 'The prodigal Wongso returns home.' It's a story that sells, you know. And, guess what, you made Kopi Sedap famous. I have you to thank for that."

In other words, this entire time, the world knew that I was naked.

What else did the world think of Dad? Did they think that he was shameless for borrowing money from Oma and Opa? That he was a failure because he couldn't secure seed funding for his startup? That he was an idiot for leaving his multibillion-dollar inheritance for a waitress?

That his clueless, middle-class daughter must be so naïve to move to Jakarta and think that she could fit right in like a glove?

I traveled all 8,973 miles to Indonesia for Dad. I listened to Oma's nagging for Dad. I survived through Christie and Ray for Dad.

Yet it was Dad's invisible legacy that now broke me.

"I'm sorry," I muttered. "I have to go."

I scrambled for my things, hugging loose items close to my chest, and darted out of the office. I folded myself in the corner of the huge elevator that took me thirty levels down and ran towards the main entrance. A couple coins fell out of my wallet, but I let them go, pushing the heavy glass door open as people stared.

Keep yourself together, Nonik, Oma's voice bellowed. *You're Robby Wongso's granddaughter.*

Disoriented, I rushed to the streets, illuminated by car lights and single bulbs dangling by a pole. Anxiety rang in my ears. *You're so nonchalant, Cecilia. You're so timid, Cecilia. You've lost everything you've built, Cecilia.*

No one likes you, Cecilia.

You will never be good enough, Cecilia.

I held my head and screamed at the darkness, running aimlessly while suffocating from pollutants. I tripped on a pothole and broke my stiletto heel—the new ones from Jimmy Choo that Oma had just gifted to me. I took them off, held them in my hands, and kept running.

I ran barefoot past the toothless man. I ran past his toothless family. I ran through the dark alley that I was afraid of months ago. *I'm not timid,* I told myself. *I stood up to Ray. I'm not timid.*

But you still have nothing here, Cecilia.

I ran and wailed and screamed until I saw a flicker of light that illuminated the *warung* across the street from the house. The woman who owned the place stared as I ran past her without extending a warm greeting. And finally, I arrived at the old black gate with gold flakes. I banged on the dense iron until my knuckles throbbed.

Pak Sutikno rushed out. The poor man was probably trying to relax, but here I was again causing an inconvenience. "I'm sorry," I muttered, but he didn't hear me. He briskly unlocked the gate, squinting at me to make sure that my melted mascara was nothing more but a delusion.

"Non." He grabbed my arm. "Are you okay?"

I jerked away, muttering "I'm sorry" again. Pak Sutikno chased after me but gave up, everyone would. Everyone did.

You will never be good enough, Cecilia.

Wailing, I used my sleeve to wipe away my snot, catching my breath while I ran up the steps to the big door that used to welcome me. I shoved the door open. A scorching light shone on the dirt all over my body. The stray pebbles and plastic wrappers that pricked my feet. Unknown grey matter that soiled my heels. The musty smell of cigarette smoke that hooked onto my navy blue blazer.

Leader growled, showed his teeth, and almost bit my ankle. I wasn't welcome, but I came in regardless. I didn't take off my shoes. I didn't announce my arrival. Instead, I stormed into the living room with my snot, tears, and sweat merging into one heavy layer of moistness on my face, deciding to confront Oma and Opa off-guard and unarmed.

"Nonik," Oma said, her eyebrows furrowed. "What happened to you?"

"Is it true?" I demanded, panting.

"What?"

"Kopi Sedap. Jeff Kwok. Everything."

"Jeff Kwok?" Opa said, pausing. "Why?"

I held my breath.

"Jeff owns the parent company of Kopi Sedap. And the CEO is his son David, right?"

I curled my fingers into a fist.

"Why? Did you meet him?" Opa batted his eyes at me.

"So it was you, Opa?" I said. "I got the job because you... Jeff Kwok owed you a favor?"

"What do you mean?" Oma snapped. "Of course we helped you. Did you think you could get a low level job in a Jakarta-based startup with a foreign passport and no help?"

"Oh my god!" I yelled. "Oh my god, it's true, isn't it?"

"It is true, yes," Oma said. "And what's wrong with that?"

Anger fumed within me and burst into words.

"I didn't come to Indonesia as a basket case," I cried. "I didn't come to be helped. I'm not a puppet. Don't you get it?

I'm Cecilia Poetry. That's it. That's who I am. Not the grand-daughter of Robby Wongso."

"But you *are* my granddaughter, Nonik," Opa said.

"Oh! Oh, okay," I sneered. "So all the shit I've faced here, all the condescending things you and Oma made me endure over family brunch, over a stupid job form, over my friend-ship with a fucking sexual predator…it was all because I'm your granddaughter?"

"Don't raise your voice with me, Nonik," Oma said.

"What do I have left, Oma? What's mine here? I moved to *your* country, live in *your* house, have *your* name, and now you're telling me that the job I work for is also *yours*? And you expect me…you expect me to be okay with that?"

"Of course, Nonik," Opa said. "You're our granddaughter. Of course we'll take care of you."

Buckets of tears overflowed to the edge of my lips. Oma Shaan opened her mouth, but no words came out.

"You said you wanted me to come to Indonesia to spend time with you," I continued. "You said you didn't want to lose both Dad and me, Opa. And I came, okay? I came. I tried. I tried so hard to be what you wanted me to be."

"Nonik, you are everything we wanted you to be," Opa said.

"But you never really loved me, did you? You just wanted to stop the rumors. You think I don't know about the 'exiled Wongso family,' huh? The youngest Wongso son who eloped with a wait-ress to have a bastard daughter? The butt of the country's jokes?"

"Cecilia," Oma said.

I walked up to the grand piano behind Opa that had all the family's photos, except for mine.

"He's your son!" I cried, slamming my fist on the keys that exhaled a thwarted melody. "Did you even love him? Look! Where is he? He doesn't even exist here!"

"Cecilia, you've misunderstood. Let's talk about this," Opa said.

"You...you rejected every aspect of me. My name. My clothes. My own mother. *Don't wear that, Nonik. Don't eat that, Nonik. Kamu kurang ajar, Nonik.* I'm not...I'm not even...I was never a part of this family, was I?"

"Cecilia," Oma said, more sternly this time.

I grabbed a photograph of Oma and Opa with Uncle Richard, Aunt Isabella, and their families. In a fit of anger, I shattered it on the floor. Glass splinters dotted the carpet. One pricked the sole of my left foot that already hurt from the asphalt.

"Cecilia, please," Opa stood up. "Please calm down, and let's talk about this."

"Where were you on Dad's wedding day?" I bellowed. "When he got his promotion? When he broke his leg on the hiking trip to Colorado? When he lost his best friend Uncle Keith in a car accident? Where were you?"

"Enough," Oma said.

"I'm done," I yelled. "I'm done with you, I'm done with Jakarta, I'm done with this family. I can't take it anymore."

Oma and Opa tried to call me back down, but I was able to outrun their old legs. Leader chased after me, barking as I dashed up the stairs. I quickly burst into my bedroom and slammed the door, holding it shut with my back.

I came here for you, Dad. But you were never even here.

Tears stained the carpet and wood floors as Leader's barks faded into the distance. I slid to the ground, holding my knees, as my chin trembled like a child's.

Never in my life had I felt so alone.

As I buried my head in my arms, creating a void for myself to crawl into, I thought about Dad: the day he taught me to ride my bike, how bad his cakes tasted when he attempted baking, and his smile. And yet, in spite of all these brilliant qualities, he was rejected by his own people. Forgotten. His legacy rebuked by those who barely knew him.

Maybe this was just fate telling me that my family would always live in a cage. Maybe Mbak Ani was right that fate played a part in my misery. Maybe that's why Dad had left Indonesia all those years ago. People were always going to look, but we were never going to be seen.

I understand now, Dad. I understand why you left this shitty place, this shitty family, for a much better life. You didn't have to care about family. You didn't have to care about your reputation. You didn't care about anything but yourself, Mom, and me. To you, we were all that mattered, and that was perfectly okay.

I was perfectly okay.

You talked about Indonesia like she was your first love, but she never loved me. I tried. I really tried. I made friends. I got a job, or attempted to. I appeased Oma and Opa so much that I lost a part of myself in the process. And I really tried my best, but in Jakarta, my best wasn't good enough.

I'm sorry, Dad. I don't belong here. I will never belong here.

V

Sunset

Two hearts walked the steps of a broken
ballad. Toes caught between
shards from a toppled vase.

Cracked china in coarse skin, she used
hard blinks to ease the pain. He punctured her as she
leaked. Wet tongue glues the inside of her lips.

Winter kept her insides warm when he did
not. He threw away her mittens. He saw
fire in her eyes—when there was nothing

but a silent scream like nightfall,
a screech that fills from the stomach
and spills from spaces behind the eyes

turning her whimpering mouth
into foam. She was a slave
in a courtyard of rubies;

a woman living in a world of walls
woeful of the smog that shades her sky

To lost girls enslaved by Love:
look up. Orange smears often
tint blackened clouds.

25

Rumbling clouds outside my window woke me from a deep slumber. I cried again, maybe a little harder than the night before. It was hard to distinguish between dreams and reality when waking up felt like a nightmare. Yet I brushed my teeth, slipped into a t-shirt that was large enough to hide in, and buried my hair in a bun.

I sat at my vanity and stared into the mirror. I traced the edges of my jaw with my fingers, feeling all the bumps from whiteheads that I had never noticed before. There were plenty more under my lips, too.

As I lingered on the image of myself, I started noticing more acne and more mistakes. One eyelid was droopier than another. My nose had no bridge. The center of my cupid's bow wasn't aligned with the line between my two front teeth.

In a fit of anger, I swept my arms across the table and knocked down the mirror, but the mirror didn't shatter like I wanted it to. Instead, it sustained a crack that meandered across its surface like a serpent, destroying its aesthetic but not its function.

The mirror lay on the floor at an angle, returning a disfigured reflection of me with multiple noses and a jaw that was separated from the rest of my face. I fisted my hands, so eager to punch the shit out of the hideousness in that portrait. But I couldn't find the energy within me to get up and assault the mirror, to let it break all over Oma's precious carpet.

I banged my head against the table, clawing at the wood as if it was going to give me comfort, and sobbed into the void.

Since I had arrived in Jakarta, I hadn't broken anything. I was good. I treated everyone with respect and kindness to the best of my abilities and expected the same. And if that expectation was lost, I fought. I fought until I was heard. I fought until things were made right, which also meant that I would concede if I made mistakes. That was the system I stuck with for most of my life. It was the system that got me into college, attached me to friends, and taught me to have a relationship with my parents.

But everything started to collapse after I came to Jakarta. Oma scolding me for things I still didn't understand. Christie reminding me that I wasn't good enough for doing nothing. Ray trying to steal the only autonomy I had over my body. In a span of six months, the framework I had trusted for all of my life shattered beyond repair.

If I hate it so much here, maybe I should just leave.

My stare pivoted from the cracked mirror to the closet. I missed Mom. I missed Macy. It wouldn't be such a bad idea to move back to LA. I could just find a teaching job at Westwood and be done with Indonesia for good. Why stay at a place that rejected me over and over again?

I dragged Mom's suitcase out from behind the closet and started tossing clothes in it. Mom's blazer, my USC hoodie, and the dress I wore to Faith's party. As I added more clothes into the suitcase, the pinstripe suit glared at me, mocking me from its plastic garment bag.

The suit made me feel so powerful, but was I really going to bring it back to LA? Oma bought it for me. Ray complimented it at work. I couldn't possibly bring this, right? It was stained with too much blood.

My thoughts were interrupted by knocks on the door.

"Nonik," Opa's voice called out. "Open the door, please. I want to talk to you."

I said nothing and kicked the suitcase into the closet. After all, this was Opa's house. It wasn't like I could restrict him from coming into the room.

"Hi, Nonik," Opa said, creaking the door open.

I looked away.

"I brought you some *es teh manis* and Marie Regal cookies," he said, putting a tray down on my vanity. "Can I sit?"

As if bringing tea and cookies gives you permission to sit in my space.

But again, this was his house, and I couldn't do anything to prevent him from sitting anyway.

Opa sat on my bed. "Come sit here."

I approached him slowly. The softness in his gray eyes amplified his laughter lines. He was trying to smile empathetically, and because I understood his warmth, I looked away.

"I've never told you how much you look like your father."

My eyes watered, but I refused to speak.

"Okay, I know you don't want to talk, but is it okay if I do?"

No, but you're going to do it anyway.

"I want you to understand that I got you the job at Kopi Sedap to help you. How do you think I'll feel if I can't provide for you as your opa? I can't withhold food from you if I have it just because you want to harvest the grain yourself. Of course I'll help you."

"I didn't want help," I snapped.

"But you needed friends, right?"

I kept quiet.

"And something to do besides babysit Oma and me?"

I still refused to open my mouth.

"Nonik, you don't need a job. You're a Wongso," Opa cleared his throat. "Look at this house. Look at the places we go to, the clothes we wear. I have worked all my life to make more than enough money for you and your children to spend. In fact, you don't ever need to work for the rest of your life."

Well, if you put it that way—

"But I knew that after spending all your life abroad, the last thing you wanted was to live like a Wongso. And I know how hard it is to get a job without an Indonesian passport. Your mom told me that you had a hard time looking for jobs, too. So I called my friends and pulled some strings. You think it was easy, Nonik? No one wants to hire foreign, fresh college graduates because they're expensive. And inexperienced."

I bit my lip. Memories of Mom and me sifting through job listings and crying through sleepless nights flashed before my eyes.

"But your job gave you a place to learn, make new friends, and get acquainted to live in Jakarta beyond me and your oma. You met your friends through Kopi Sedap, right? Lam Ing's daughter, Awi's granddaughter?"

Opa gave me what I needed when I didn't even know that I needed it.

I fidgeted with my fingers in that realization.

"You wouldn't have met them if it weren't for Kopi Sedap."

I nodded.

"Can I ask you something, Nonik?" Opa said, shifting closer to me. "Why did you decide to come here?"

"You told me to come," I said.

"I did," Opa said. "But I never forced you to get on the plane. You did that by yourself. Why?"

I wet my lips.

"Dad talked about Indonesia a lot, so I just wanted to experience what his life was like. That's all."

I would've said more, but my apathy held me back.

"I miss him, your father," Opa said.

"No, you don't," I scoffed. "If you did, you'd at least have pictures of him."

Opa reached into his pocket and pulled out his wallet. I expected someone with Opa's wealth to be using the latest Bottega wallet, but his was an old slab of leather in a disgusting brown color, a marriage of apricot and mahogany. A black pen's scratch marked its age.

He flipped the wallet open. A faded photograph was taped on the inside. It was a photo of a skinny boy with ruffled hair sitting on the beach, surrounded by water and sunshine.

Dad.

"This was our trip to Bali," he said. "1983."

I reached out to touch the picture. Through the photo's matte surface, I felt the ocean breeze against Dad's hair.

"James loved the ocean," Opa continued, eyes fixed on the photograph. "After that trip, he always begged me to go to the Thousand Islands. You've gone, right? With your friend Gracelyn?"

I nodded.

"I didn't have enough money to buy a boat back then, so we borrowed a friend's until Mandala was stable enough that we could get our own. After we got it, James went on most weekends with his friends, or even just alone. He was so happy out there. I figured he chose to go to university and move to LA to be near the ocean, too."

A tear trickled down my cheek. I couldn't help it. I remembered the weekly trips we made to Santa Barbara to visit the beaches and indulge in fresh seafood. It was a routine thing until life caught up to us, when I got busy and Dad got sick.

"Did he ever get his diving license?" Opa asked.

"He got it in Maui," I said. "Dad was a rescue diver."

"Really?"

Opa's voice turned shaky.

"Sorry, Nonik," he said, dabbing a handkerchief under his eyes. "I'm just…it was his dream for so long. I'm so glad he did it."

I sniffled.

"I am sorry for not telling you more about your dad," Opa said. "I wish you had said something. It hurt a lot when you said that your oma and I didn't care. It's easier to say that we were over the grief, but the truth is that we still miss him so much. Oma hugs his pictures and cries every night."

Oma does what?

"Your dad's pictures aren't in the living room because she moved them all to our room."

Images of a frail Oma cradling Dad flashed before me. She hugged the photographs to her bosom as she rocked back and forth in a dark room, wailing for her son to return to her. The moment pierced my heart just as it did when Dad's EKG stopped pulsating, when he was wheeled to the morgue with a white sheet over his head.

Dad died in front of me all over again. And this time, my grandparents felt the pain with me.

"Your oma and I were scared to get close to you because we didn't know if you were going to stay or go back to LA again," Opa said, wiping his eyes. "We don't want to lose you like we lost our son. You're our granddaughter. James' little girl."

Opa came in for a hug. Without hesitation, I leaned into his broad shoulders.

"I love you, my dear Cecilia," he said. "I hope you remember that forever."

It was the first time I had ever heard those words from Opa's lips. A dam of tears finally burst open. I could feel again. I felt alive. I sobbed, feeling his pocket square rubbing against my cheeks.

Opa walked towards the vanity to get some tissues and the tea he brought for me.

"Drink some tea," he said. "It'll make you feel better."

I took the tea out of his shaky hands and took a sip. I wiped my eyes and looked into his, ones that told a story of war, triumph, and love. Each exhale from his wrinkled lips melted my iced-over heart.

"Thank you, Opa," I said.

The ash skies parted to a warm shower. Rainwater slushed on the rooftops. Birds chirped, hopped into shelters. I cozied under my blanket with my iced tea. Opa blew his nose into the tissues he'd grabbed for me and tossed them into the bin by my bed. He opened his calloused palms and invited me to place my hands in them.

"Can I ask you something?" Opa asked.

"Sure," I said.

"Why are you so ashamed of being a part of this family?"

The question stunned me like a taser. Electricity entered and left my body all at once.

"Um…"

"It's okay," Opa said, putting his hand on my back. "You can tell me. I won't get angry."

I took a sip from my tea. The cup almost slipped from my sweaty fingers. What could I say? I wasn't ashamed, I was just afraid, I wanted to belong, I—

I took a deep breath.

"I don't belong here, Opa," I said, my voice shaking again.

"Of course you do," he said.

"I don't," I said. "We live a good life in LA, but it's nothing compared to how you live here. I mean, you guys have drivers. You live in this beautiful home. You got me a job with one phone call."

"Is there anything wrong with that?"

"No, but it's just…it's not me."

"But it is you."

I squinted my eyes. How could he insist that something that wasn't mine, was?

"Nonik," Opa said. "Whether you choose to include it in your job forms or your public persona, your name is Cecilia Putri Wongso. You are James Wongso's daughter. My granddaughter. All of this will be yours one day when Oma and I are gone. It's yours already."

"But I didn't grow up here," I said. "I never knew Uncle Richard and Aunt Isabella. I didn't know that Mandala was worth billions until four months ago. I…I don't deserve all this."

"You deserved all of this from the moment you were born, Cecilia," Opa said.

"I didn't work for any of it, Opa."

"Of course you didn't," Opa said. "I did."

I chewed on the flaky skin on my lip.

"Nonik, why do you think I work so hard?" Opa asked. "Hm? Why do you think that, at seventy-six, I'm still going to the office, still involved in the business? I told you we have more than enough money to live."

"To earn money?"

This is definitely a trick question.

"To provide," Opa said. "To add value to people's lives."

I stared at the space between Opa's eyes.

"I work because I'm in the position to help other people, Nonik. It's so selfish of me to not give, to not provide, if I have the means to, right?"

"I guess."

"If I have food and don't share it with the hungry, wouldn't I be selfish?"

"Of course," I said. My mind felt like an incomplete puzzle. "What are you trying to say?"

"You have all of these things, Nonik. You grew up in a comfortable home with food and water. You went to university in America. You come from a wealthy family. Not everyone is as lucky."

Opa paused.

"Don't run away," Opa said. "Do something about what you have. You don't have to give away all your material possessions to the poor. But you should love. Love other people. Give them a piece of you, Cecilia. Give them wisdom, kindness, compassion. Give them your life, and they will give you something to live for."

I stared at Opa, repeating his words in my head. I noticed the lines under his eyes, the height of his forehead. The details looked like Dad's. They were all Dad's.

And suddenly, a fire ignited in my soul.

This is why Dad wanted me to come to Indonesia.

Opa's words felt like the final piece of the puzzle that I needed. Neurons in my brain fired together and clicked like clockwork. I felt my soul glow into a phoenix. My wings spread.

Every inch of me fell into Opa's arms. He didn't say anything; he didn't have to. I lay in his warm embrace, listening to the serene pitter-patter of rain as the thunder roared and the lightning struck.

I trusted Opa with my life at this very moment. For the first time since I arrived in this strange place, I finally felt safe.

26

Mom woke me up with a phone call at 7:00 a.m. She had just come home from work to rake the leaves that fell from our now-barren trees.

"CeCe, darling," she said, the cool November wind echoing through the speakers, "I miss you."

"I miss you too, Mom," I said, rubbing the sleep out of my eyes.

"When are you coming home?"

"Home?"

"Aunt Krista is going back to Cupertino for Thanksgiving next week, and I would really love for you to come home."

I glanced over at my suitcase, half-piled with rage and clothes that weren't tainted by the likes of this strange place.

"When?" I asked.

"Can you be here for Christmas?"

"I guess I can make a trip home."

"Really?" Mom squealed. "You can take leave from work?"

Right. Mom doesn't know.

With Opa's help, I had resigned from Kopi Sedap the day before. Because it was Opa who called, the resignation was effective immediately, and Pak Sutikno returned the company laptop on my behalf. I never had to set foot in that office ever again. I never had to see Ray or David again. And I didn't feel guilty about it.

"I...quit my job, Mom," I said.

"You quit?" Mom gasped. "What did your grandparents say?"

"Actually, Opa helped me quit."

"So you're unemployed now?"

"I...I got another job offer."

I lied. I was nowhere near another job offer.

Alicia and I had another conversation over the phone after Faith's party a month ago, while I was still running around in Kopi Sedap, making calls and filling in for Ray. Even though she had offered me a job at Alpha-Omega, I told her that I couldn't leave Kopi Sedap so soon. That was, of course, before all havoc broke loose with David, and before I stopped caring about breaking my contract.

I emailed Alicia on the Friday after talking to Opa and asked if the job position she offered was still open. But she still hadn't responded.

"That's amazing, CeCe," Mom said. "Congratulations. I'm so proud of you."

"Thanks," I said, feeling the bitter sensation down my throat.

"Did you not like Kopi Sedap? I expected you to stay a little longer."

I shivered, picturing Ray's sinister smile and David's guffaw in the background.

"Um," I said. "It's not where I'm meant to be."

"Okay, darling. As long as you're happy."

When Mom hung up the phone, I walked towards my suitcase in the closet. I was planning to go back to LA at some point, but the question was how long I wanted to be away from Jakarta.

Even though I knew that Opa was my ally, I missed Mom. I missed running in parks and long drives along Sunset Boulevard. I missed the scorching sun that didn't bathe my body in sweat.

Most of all, I missed being just Cecilia Poetry.

I knew from experience that declining Alpha-Omega's job offer a month ago meant that it was almost impossible for the position to still be open now. Sighing, I cracked my fingers and opened my iPad, scrolling through Google to look for cheap plane tickets and job openings in LA.

As I was about to apply to a tutoring job near an elementary school in Santa Monica, I received a text from Oma.

Nonik, meet me at Grand Hyatt Fountain Lounge at 9 after my morning meeting. Sutikno can take you.—07:47

I clenched my jaw.

Oma and I hadn't spoken since we fought five days past. It was easy to avoid people in such a big house, with the exception of awkward lunches and dinners.

Maybe it was a good thing that she finally wanted to talk. But I also knew that nothing good could come out of Oma, who always had a sly trick up her sleeve. The least I could do was hear her out since she was my grandmother. It was comforting to know that I had the upper hand; if anything happened, Opa would definitely defend me.

I locked my iPad with my browser tabs still open, got out of bed, and got ready to meet Oma.

After showering, I made sure not to wear anything that Oma had given me. Instead of the blue Dior blouse that I was eyeing, I slipped into a white t-shirt and jeans that I bought from H&M years ago and slung an old purse over my shoulder. I scurried downstairs, bidding goodbye to Leader, Mbak Ani, and Bu Ratih, and got into the Mercedes with Pak Sutikno.

It was 8:57 a.m. by the time I arrived at the Grand Hyatt and walked to the Fountain Lounge. An open space sitting underneath a glorious chandelier, the Fountain Lounge was decorated with fake trees and couches scattered throughout the space. Behind me was a large window that opened up the space to a breathtaking view of Bundaran HI.

Oma sat alone by the window. She was wearing a tweed Chanel jacket over a red dress. How radiant she looked in contrast to my t-shirt and jeans. How small I felt next to her.

Shame flooded over me like a tsunami.

"Nonik," Oma said.

Why was Oma acting like nothing had happened in the past few days?

"Hi, Oma," I said.

My fingers grew cold from the anxiety and air conditioning.

"Sit," Oma said. "I just ordered *pisang goreng* and apple crumble. You like that, right?"

I nodded.

Oma and I stared at each other and then at the floor for a couple minutes. An unnerving silence settled over us. I sipped on a free glass of water, tracing the outlines of the table while listening to the piano playing in the background. Classical piano was a great companion to the dwelling awkwardness in the room.

A waiter brought a plate of *pisang goreng*, setting it on my table. "*Terima kasih,*" I said, while Oma said nothing.

"I still remember the last time you came to Jakarta, Nonik," Oma said.

"That was a very long time ago," I said.

"I remember you came for Karina's grandma's funeral," Oma continued. "You were so small. You kept playing with the stuffed bear I gave you. Do you remember?"

I nodded.

"Something happened that week," Oma said. "But you probably don't remember. You were too young."

Dad would always shut down whenever I asked him why we weren't in Jakarta like the rest of his family. Mom refused to talk about it, especially after Dad passed away. Eventually, I stopped asking and swallowed the hard truth that nothing I did could give me the answers I wanted.

I held my breath. At last, someone was going to tell me what happened eighteen years ago.

"What happened?" I said, feeling adrenaline pumping through my arteries.

"Your parents weren't supposed to move back to LA," Oma said.

I squeezed the seat cushion under me.

"What do you mean?"

"After your parents got engaged in LA, your opa and I had been trying to get them to move back to Jakarta. After long nights and a lot of convincing, they finally decided to come after the honeymoon, but then James found out that Karina was pregnant with you. So we postponed it. And when you were five, we finally convinced them to move. At around that same time, Karina's grandma passed away, so they decided that they'd just move all together."

Makco's funeral. No wonder we packed big suitcases for that trip.

"I'm sure you know that Opa and I never agreed to James' marriage to Karina," Oma continued. "She was a nice girl, but she didn't come from our society. I've always thought that your father could do better."

Yes, you've made that very clear for twenty-three years.

"At some point during a family dinner one night, I got angry and yelled at Karina. Honestly, Nonik, I don't know what she did to make me yell at her like that. And that obviously tells you that whatever we fought about wasn't anything worth getting angry about."

Oma's eyes watered as she gripped her purse tightly. I took a bite of the *pisang goreng* and sucked on the banana's sweetness while Oma continued her story.

"That night, your dad and I had a huge fight," Oma said. "Karina was crying. I remember she told James to stop, but he was just so angry at how Opa and me treated Karina. He broke a couple plates and photo frames. He said that we didn't love him if we didn't love Karina, and that you, Nonik, didn't deserve to live in Jakarta with unlovable people like us. And my biggest regret was that I was so stubborn. I didn't apologize. I just kept pushing that Karina wasn't good for him. Then, the next morning, all three of you were gone. And that was the last time I saw James."

Oma's tears smeared her eyeliner. The *pisang goreng* I had just swallowed felt like ash in my throat.

"We barely kept in touch after that day," Oma continued. "We got birthday and Christmas emails, but even those were very short and cold. Those years were so rough, Nonik. Robby and I thought about James every day. I cried most nights. But I thought that if I had said something, things would be worse. Then, about six years ago, your dad told us that he needed money to start up a business with some friends. Of course we gave it to him. He said that, as his thanks, he would come to Jakarta soon and bring you, but with the new business and you being in high school, it was difficult to find time."

I did remember the day when Dad started calling Oma and Opa more often. But he never told me why. He always shut down whenever I asked him.

"And after slowly rebuilding our relationship, James called to tell us about the cancer. We sent over some more money to cover the costs for chemo and other treatments. He promised that he'd let us come visit him when he was ready. But the next phone call was a month later, when Karina told us that he had passed away."

My heart sunk, and within her words my mind fell back to Dad's final days. Mom's screams. The buzz from a rogue light bulb. His deafening peace.

"The first few months after we came back from his funeral in LA were so difficult, Nonik," Oma said. "I stopped eating. I couldn't leave my room. The only thing I could do was hug him, through his pictures that were more than twenty years old. I had so many regrets. I failed as a mother. I was so depressed that Opa bought Leader to try and take my mind off things. It helped, but I'm still in pain."

I gulped, remembering the image in my head of Oma cradling Dad's photographs.

Oma's grief and my own bore a striking similarity. Guilt pricked at my insides. She loved Dad more than any of her other children, and yet here I was thinking that she didn't care.

"Talking about him still hurts, Nonik. So when you said that we hated James, that we never loved him, it was the most…" Oma's voice turned shaky. She held her mouth. "I felt like I lost him all over again."

Oma sobbed in the middle of the Fountain Lounge. People dining at neighboring tables stared. Not knowing how to comfort her, I offered Oma some tissue.

"Thank you," Oma said, dabbing the tissue on her eyes.

I've never seen Oma so depressed. She was an iron titan, the woman of the house, who constantly kept things in order and held her head high. In the midst of all that she reigned over, I had forgotten that Oma was human, too, that she could break just as much as I could.

I took another bite from my *pisang goreng*.

"I'm sorry, Oma." It was all I could say.

"I'm in the same state as I was last year," Oma continued. "When you got angry at us that night, you reminded me of James. So, before I lose you like I lost him, I want to fix things, Cecilia. I know I've made mistakes, but I want us to fix this."

I wet my lips. I traced the outline of the table with my fingers again. I understood where Oma was coming from, but I couldn't erase months of mistreatment just because Oma wanted to change. It wasn't fair.

"Oma," I said, tears at the edge of my eyes. "I was very angry at a lot of things, and I've been bottling a lot of it up until I exploded that night. I'm sorry for taking that anger out on you. I hope you understand that I didn't mean most of the things that I said."

"I know," Oma blushed, taking a forkful of apple crumble. "I told you all of this not because I wanted you to apologize, Nonik. I thought you deserved to know what I did to your family."

"I appreciate you saying all of this, but I…"

How can I say this to a seventy-year-old woman who has just poured out her heart and soul to me?

"I'm leaving Jakarta."

Oma's face turned pale.

"You're…leaving?" Oma's voice was tense and frigid, like an elastic band about to break.

"I've just applied for a job in Westwood this morning. And I booked a flight to LA that leaves in two weeks."

Oma dropped her fork.

"I…I thought you liked it here."

"I don't."

"You don't?"

"Oma, I don't belong here. And Mom needs me."

"I need you."

"But you never acted like you did."

I looked down. I finally had Oma in my grasp, but I thought it would feel a lot better than it did now.

"I can't…I can't lose you like I lost James, Cecilia."

"I'm not the person you want, Oma," I said, a tear falling down my cheek. "I'm not Dad. I'm Cecilia Poetry. I went to a public high school. I owned two pieces of branded clothing before I came here. I eat Chipotle for lunch, not some fancy *nasi tumpeng* made by a private chef. I lived the average, upper-middle class Asian-American life, and frankly speaking I don't know anything about this world that you expect me to be a master of."

Oma wiped a tear from her face.

"I'm not the Wongso princess you expected."

I sighed. A burden lifted itself from my chest after all those months of pain.

Oma took a bite from her apple crumble, but I couldn't eat anything anymore. Instead, I stared out the window, at the cars that circulated Bundaran HI, hoping that the chaos of traffic would stop me from crying.

"I know," Oma said, breaking the silence. "I know I've been harsh, Nonik. But, to be fair, I don't know you."

"You never gave me a chance to tell you who I was," I said. "You just kept criticizing me, Oma. For how I dress, how I eat, and even who my friends are."

Oma picked at the chipped red polish on her fingernails. Had I said something wrong? Was I going to screw this up even further?

"Don't leave, Nonik." Oma avoided eye contact with me.

"I have to," I continued, tears spilling out of my eyes. "There's just…too much has happened. I can't…I can't stay here anymore."

I couldn't control my tears anymore. I sobbed. Oma leaned on the table, her drawn-on eyebrows raised.

"Did something happen Nonik?" Oma said. "You can tell me. I promise I won't be angry."

The hardest part was asking for help. Being vulnerable. What Ray did to me was always going to leave a scar, but if I didn't talk about what happened, I knew that I could break. And to be strong, to get better, to be completely healed, I had to face my demons headfirst.

"I was…assaulted."

The rogue words tasted sour against my tongue.

"What?" Oma raised her voice.

"Tommy Kurniawan's son," I said. "Raynard. He assaulted me."

Oma gasped. She slumped on the chair, her face a compound of shock, frustration, and sympathy. Just like that, I shattered Oma's perfect image of the Kurniawan family. And it felt pretty damn good.

"Cecilia," Oma said, her eyes scanning my body. "How… how did this happen?"

I shook my head.

"Are you alright?"

"No."

"Come here, Nonik."

Oma leaned in for a hug. She cradled me in her arms, stroking my forehead as I sobbed into her shirt. People stared, but I didn't care about what they thought. At that moment, only Oma and I mattered.

"I can't believe I let this happen," Oma said.

"It's not your fault, Oma."

"I promise you this, Cecilia. For as long as I live, I won't let anyone hurt you ever again."

And with those words, Ray's hold over my body slightly lifted.

"I love you, Cecilia *sayang*," Oma said.

"I love you too."

I got up and hugged her harder. Oma jerked a little, but later leaned into my arms. I held her tighter, feeling her clothes rub against mine. I'd wanted to hug my grandma since I was a little girl, but I never found the right time to do it.

"Don't leave Jakarta, Nonik," Oma said. "I want to do this with you more often."

I gave Oma a sheepish smile.

"There's nothing for me here, Oma," I said. "Dad is gone. He hasn't been Indonesian for the past twenty years."

"Yes, but—"

"I'll visit. I'll visit as often as I can."

While Oma silently picked at her apple crumble, my eyes wandered out the window. The 10:00 a.m. traffic slowed around Bundaran HI, with cars jammed up against one another. I imagined myself in one of the vehicles, indulging in the beauty of serene stillness that allowed me time to relax and reflect.

Perhaps I had grown to like Jakarta's traffic.

But the thought of moving back to LA brought relief and excitement. I couldn't wait to see Mom again. To be near nature again. To frolic at overpriced farmer's markets again.

What about your friends?

They'll live without me.

Faith has been so good to you.

She has Grace.

But Grace needs you.

She has Faith.

And Kai?

Kai has…

No one.

No. He has Faith and Grace, who I'm sure will take care of him on my behalf. And he will understand. He loves me enough to let me do what was best for me.

But the thought of leaving Faith, Grace, and Kai still tugged at my heart. They'd done so much for me. I'd invested so much in these friendships. I couldn't possibly leave them behind. But they'd understand why I had to leave, right?

I'd bought my plane ticket already. My suitcase was half-packed. There was no looking back. I was done with Jakarta, and it was done with me.

With these thoughts, I bit into Oma's apple crumble, disappointed that it didn't taste as sweet as the ones Mom used to make at home.

27

Against Oma's wishes, I went for a walk outside alone, though I was fully clothed this time. I couldn't stay in the house for too long. I had to think.

Since becoming unemployed, I didn't know what to do with so much spare time. Faith, Grace, and Kai still worked nine-to-five jobs. Opa and Oma had back-to-back meetings with Mandala's shareholders. So for a week, during the day, I had a choice to stare at Netflix or get some exercise. I chose the latter.

I missed people-watching with Mom in LA. When I went to USC, I imparted this love for people-watching to Macy, who would get out her sketchpad and draw strangers doing strange things. Then we'd usually get Chipotle or Chick-fil-A, which were right around the block from our apartment near campus. Jakarta had none of these things. My walks were a circle around a neighborhood, watching people in vehicles and beautiful homes hiding behind tall gates. The closest thing to a Chipotle or

Chick-fil-A here was Bu Ratih's cooking, which was back at the house.

The morning was refreshing. Several bikers biked past me. Sparrows convened with their families. Trees coexisted peacefully with the rest of the world. Flies and mosquitoes buzzed around. The neighborhood was nice and quiet. Still, the morning breeze felt a little stale, smelling like grass and sewer water.

After forty-five minutes of going in circles, listening to a podcast that Kai recommended, my nose caught whiff of an overpowering earthy scent. It was sultry and soulful, yet young and inviting.

Curious, I followed the smell to the *warung* right near our house. It was the landmark I used to know that I was close to home, but it never caught my attention otherwise. I only knew that an old woman owned it, and that there were always people over whenever I drove by to go to work.

I inched a little closer. The smell grew sharper, stronger, more piquant, granting a visit to Mom's stove in LA where she attempted to cook *nasi tumpeng* with an Indonesian spice that her friend smuggled in for her. Its name was at the tip of my tongue, but I couldn't recall it.

The sign on the *warung* read "Soto Ayam Bu Cumi," or Bu Cumi's *soto ayam*. A woman cooked behind a table full of goodies for sale. Cups of instant noodles were stacked on top of one another. Tea cartons were squeezed between bags of *Indomie* and my favorite coffee candy, *Kopiko*. Packets of instant tea, coffee, and milk draped across a pole, dangling above the *Indomie* like fairy lights.

The woman looked like she was in her fifties. A warm breeze billowed the ends of her hijab, revealing a joyful face and laughter lines that were visible from a distance. She tossed ingredients into the pot, swirling its contents furiously and simultaneously, then taking a whiff of the aroma and smiling to herself. Then, she punched a fist in the air, swaying to nothing but an arrhythmic rustling of leaves and child's laughter around the block. I was mesmerized.

It was neither breakfast nor lunch at the awkward time of 10:30 a.m., so the woman was just cooking with no customers to serve. I'd never seen anyone cook with such grace, waving the ladle eloquently like it was a magic wand. She had great command, perhaps because she was confident that her food tasted good enough to sell.

After hanging the ladle on the side of the giant pot, the woman lifted her hand and waved at my direction. I was knocked back into reality. I looked behind to only find a tree stump and a skinny stray cat licking its paws.

Is it so obvious that I've been staring at her?

Cheeks flushing red, I sent a sheepish smile her way. As I tiptoed backwards, her waves turned into elaborate gestures, signaling for me to come over. A sweet grin nestled in her hijab.

Her cooking does smell really nice.

It's not like I have anything better to do.

I walked over, hugging my arms as the breeze roared. I thought I must have grown accustomed to the smell at this point, but the smell only grew sharper and earthier, even though I still couldn't figure out what it was.

"Hello, Ibu," I said, waving at her.

"Hello, *dek*," the woman said.

"Oh, my Bahasa Indonesia is very bad...*jelek sekali*," I said, hopefully correctly.

The woman chuckled, her wrinkles more prominent up close. I sat on one of the benches in the dining area, adjacent to where her stove was. The woman gestured for me to come closer, to stand by her side.

I took a proper look at her face. The sun had dried up her skin, but not its color, which was a warm sienna, sun-kissed to a tan that sparkled under her hijab's sequined rims. Her eyes, deep and dark, brought such a joy that radiated youth. Age drooped her eyelids and cheeks. She had aged poorly yet was beautiful in spite of it.

I sat on one of the benches in the dining area, adjacent to where her stove was. She gestured for me to come closer.

"Are you sure?" I asked, and then remembered that she couldn't understand me anyway.

She came over and pulled me towards the stove, grinning from ear to ear. Humidity engulfed my entire being. The smell was stronger now, more soulful. She took out a spice and started to peel it to reveal a watery orange flesh.

Turmeric.

My mind immediately flashed to the week before my departure from LA, when I took those daily trips to Urth Caffé with Mom. I licked my lips, tasting the Rumi Latté that shared strong turmeric and cinnamon notes. Turmeric brought out a mature taste in the coffee blend to make a vibrant and vivid impression.

I looked at the woman, who had just tossed her cut-up piece of turmeric into the broth and stirred it before turning the stove off. Her hijab and chopping board looked like someone had splattered yellow paint on it. The stains on her fingers looked several days old, looking almost jaundiced.

The woman poured the broth into a ceramic bowl, stamped with yellow fingerprints. She dropped a clean spoon into the bowl and handed it to me. Chicken, bean sprouts, and sliced eggs floated on the broth. Steam from the soup carried the beautiful aromas, enticing me to try just a spoonful.

"Try, *dek*," the woman exclaimed, tossing a spoon into the bowl. "*Enak.*"

"Oh, um, *terima kasih*, but I'm not hungry…um, no *lapar*," I said, even though my mouth watered.

It was so hard to form sentences, but at least my Indonesian was getting better.

"*Sedikit*," the woman smiled, pinching the air with her fingers.

The woman pushed the bowl closer to me. She watched, starry-eyed and eager, as I raised the spoon to my lips. A burst of flavor erupted in my mouth. Salt and citrus and herbs tickled my taste buds all at once that I had to beg for more.

"*Enak?*" the woman said, following with a chuckle.

"Wow," I exclaimed, giving her two thumbs up. "*Enak!*"

The woman followed with a hearty laugh, reaching over the table to give me a pat on the shoulder.

"How much?" I asked, reaching into my pocket to grab my wallet.

Smiling, the woman shook her head.

"What, no, I can't," I said. "Here, please take this. You've been too kind to me today."

I whipped out a Rp20.000 note from my wallet, but she pushed my hands back. The more I tried to insist that she take the money, the more she laughed and shook her head, insisting that I didn't owe her anything.

We ended that back and forth with her closing the note in my palms. She said something to me that I couldn't understand, nor did I have the language capacity to insist any further. All I could do was accept her kindness and say, "*terima kasih*."

The woman watched as I slurped up the soup, delighting in the textures present in the bowl. The soup felt greasy, but I didn't care. Unlike the other dishes I'd tried in Jakarta, I couldn't taste the soup's ingredients. The broth was clearly yellow from the turmeric, but its taste wasn't as strong as it was in the Rumi Latté. How oblivious I was to this goodness. How blind I was to its components. The woman could've used rat stock to enhance the broth's flavors, and I would still eat it. It was beyond delicious.

I gazed at the woman, who was wiping down her stovetop. She caught my gaze, grinning as she saw me inhale another mouthful of soup. I'd never seen someone so joyful in Jakarta.

My seat was in view of the entire *warung*. Behind her stove was a door to a little room, perhaps the size of my bathroom across the street, that was slightly opened. It housed a single mattress and three pillows, with a blanket that was tousled to the side. A line of laundry hung next to the room. Three pairs of sandals, one large-, one medium-, and one small-sized, were lined up just below the clothes.

The warung is also her family home.

Guilt swept over me. She probably only made two pots of soup a day to serve fifty bowls to fifty customers, which meant that she probably made a little over Rp600.000 a day to spend on rent, electricity, and a child—more than I spent in one sitting at a restaurant with my friends. All day, the woman chopped up vegetables and poultry, staining her hands and clothes in the process, washed her clothes and dishes, and raised a young kid, for just Rp600.000.

Forty dollars.

And yet, the woman still refused my money.

Tears started to glaze my eyes. I took another slurp of soup that somehow tasted even better. The little she gave me was much greater than anything that I had ever received during my half a year in Jakarta.

Love other people. Give them a piece of you, Cecilia. Give them your life, and they will give you something to live for.

Opa's words echoed in my ear. How selfish would I be if I had so much, yet gave nothing? I had to give the woman and others like her a much better life than Rp600.000.

Before I knew it, my spoon scraped the bottom of the bowl. I clinked it on the side and grabbed my wallet again.

"Here, Ibu," I said, giving her six Rp100.000 bills. "Please, this soup was really good."

The woman's jaw dropped. She waved her hands in front of me, pointing at a sign that said a bowl of *soto ayam* only cost Rp12.500. Tears started collecting in her eyes.

"I know," I said, folding the Rp600.000 in her yellowed hands. "But I want you to take this, Ibu. *Terima kasih* for the *soto ayam*."

"*Alhamdulilah*," the woman said, pressing my hands to her forehead. "*Terima kasih, dek*. Thank you, thank you."

The woman wept. I hugged her tightly, saying "*terima kasih*" to her for much more than just the soup. She stayed in my arms until she felt comfortable enough to let go. I wiped the sweat off my forehead with my sleeve, gathered my things, and prepared to leave.

"*Nama kamu siapa, dek?*" the woman asked.

I paused. I understood that she was asking for my name, but I wasn't sure if the name she asked for was the name I wanted to give her.

I knew now that I couldn't run away from being a Wongso. But Cecilia Putri Wongso didn't sound right either. I couldn't be a *putri*. I was James Wongso's daughter, but I was no princess. I desperately had to find a middle ground, a way to marry the person I was and the person I had become.

I took a deep breath, gathering the courage and confidence to say the name that I had made up in my head aloud for the first time in my life.

"Cecilia Poetry Wongso," I said. "That's my *nama*. Cecilia Poetry Wongso."

"*Terima kasih*, Cecilia," the woman said, bowing her head.

"*Terima kasih,* Ibu," I said. "I will come back again."

The woman beamed, waving, as I walked briskly across the empty street and into my gated home. The smell of turmeric faded in the distance.

"Non run, good?" Pak Sutikno asked as he unlocked the gate.

"It was...beyond anything I could ever imagine," I said.

Leader jumped on me with a wagging tail as I cradled him in my arms. Mbak Ani came rushing out from the kitchen.

"Hello, Non," she said with a half-smile.

Our relationship had been awkward since I yelled at her a couple weeks ago.

"Mbak Ani," I said, putting Leader down.

I walked over to hug her. I understood now that Mbak Ani was only trying to help and hated myself for not seeing this earlier.

"I know this is long delayed, but I'm sorry for yelling at you," I said.

"It's okay, Nonik," Mbak Ani said, beaming genuinely this time.

I walked into the kitchen with her, where Bu Ratih was cooking. She looked up and said hi.

"Non," Mbak Ani said. "Ani have to say something to Non."

"What is it?"

"Ani leave next month."

"That's nice that you're taking a break," I said. "It's been a while, right?"

Mbak Ani looked at Bu Ratih, who raised her eyebrows.

"Ani no leave," Mbak Ani said. "Quit. Ani quit."

"You're quitting?" I said.

My eyes drooped like a wilting flower.

"*Iya*, Non," Mbak Ani said. "Ani want go home."

"Home?" I gasped. "What about your uncle? What if he hurts you again?"

Mbak Ani sighed. She pursed her lips and beamed from ear to ear.

"Ani run away five years. Is time for Ani to help Papa Mama *warung* in Tegal."

"That's amazing," I said. "I'm so happy for you."

I hugged her again. Bittersweet tears trickled down my face.

I'm going to miss Mbak Ani so much.

"Non say Ani not wrong?"

"Yeah," I said, happy that she actually took something away from the confrontation. "It's not your fault."

Afterwards, I went back to my room and went to the balcony. I breathed in, inhaling all the stale air in its glory. A skinny cat hissed at a skinny dog. Flies hovered above a pile of trash across the street. Indonesia was flawed, but it was also beautiful.

Maybe I was too blinded by the likes of Christie and Ray to see what Indonesia truly held for me. I had to see if there was more for me out there, to wrap my own brain around the different ways that Indonesian people lived, the different values they had, the way they saw things.

The woman who smelled of turmeric gave me so much when she had so little, whereas Christie and Ray only stole from me when they had so much. Perhaps I was too closed-off by my privileged biases to see the bigger picture. Perhaps

I was too judgmental of a society that was hesitant to accept me but did anyway. Not many people were as lucky.

I need to stay here. I had to. This was my legacy, my calling. It was what I was born to do. After all, my name was Cecilia Poetry Wongso.

Eve's Portraiture

If you tell me that she
is sweet like honey
from Willy Wonka's lips,

My tongue will disagree.

It believes that she is a
fragment from antique chinaware
that reeks of rose gold
womanhood:

A bitterness that has dispersed
since a serpent's corrupted touch,
her rogue acidity like dwindling leaves
from a willow tree that caresses
doves in the gentle night.

28

Six a.m. felt brighter than it did on typical mornings. My eyes were small from having to wake up two hours earlier than I normally did. I felt jittery and cold from the awkward morning, but LA's December was going to be colder. I slipped into a sweater and leggings, comfortable clothing that would last me eighteen hours on a plane.

Mbak Ani came to my room to help me with my things.

"Nonik only bring this?" Mbak Ani asked, surprised at the small suitcase I had packed when she was used to Oma Shaan's fat suitcases on trips.

"Yes," I said. "Well, this and the box filled with the stuff that my mom wanted me to bring back. But I don't need that much. The rest of my clothes are in LA."

Mbak Ani sat by my bed as I ran around to grab some last-minute items. By the time I came back to Jakarta in January, she would already have left.

"Ready?" Mbak Ani asked.

"I'm ready," I said.

Mbak Ani teared up. I went in to hug her; it was the last time I could.

"I'll miss you," I said. "But I'm so proud of you. *Terima kasih* for everything."

"*Terima kasih,* Non," she said. "Non change Ani's life. Ani never forget."

I grabbed my backpack as Mbak Ani took my carry-on. We walked downstairs together.

The house glowed under the warm sunlight, which overflowed onto the wood railing and shone on the intricate carvings. It made our home feel soft and warm.

Oma Shaan and Opa Robby waited for me at a sofa by the stairs, holding hands. They were still dressed in their pajamas.

"I know you're only going to be gone for a month, but I'm still going to miss you," Opa said.

"I'll miss you too, Opa." I hugged him.

"Sorry that we can't take you to the airport. We have an important call today that we cannot miss."

"Don't worry about it," I said. "I'm not leaving forever, Opa."

"I know."

I turned to Oma, whose face was puffy. She wasn't wearing any makeup for a change, so she looked a lot like Dad.

"Thank you for giving our family another chance, Nonik," she said as I came in for a hug.

"Of course."

"Don't forget to buy my Brookside chocolate. And my Tate's chocolate chip cookies."

"Yes ma'am," I chuckled.

"And tell Karina we say hi, Nonik."

Oma and Opa walked me to the S-Class, waving as Pak Sutikno whizzed me off to the airport.

The roads were surprisingly crowded on this sunny morning, but I still arrived earlier than I had expected. Pak Sutikno helped me with my bags.

"*Selamat jalan*, Non," he said. "Safe trip to you."

"*Terima kasih*, Pak Sutikno," I said. "See you in January."

Pulling my carry-on, I popped my AirPods in to blast Lauv and walked into the terminal. His music somehow always reminded me of LA. As I walked towards the check-in counter, I heard someone call my name. I turned around.

"Faith! Grace!"

I ran towards them. They looked a little different today. Faith wore a t-shirt and jeans, while Grace wore a sweater and yoga pants. It felt good to see them in their own element, removed from the fancy clothes and expensive makeup.

And behind them was a tall, slim man with shaggy hair, holding a single rose in his hand.

"Kai?"

I dropped my bags and jumped into Kai's arms, wrapping my body around him.

I beamed. No one had ever thrown a surprise gathering for me before. Little did I know that the first time would be at an airport, leaving the place that I never expected to call home.

Maybe Dad really had a reason why he wanted to send me halfway across the world.

"I can't believe you guys came all the way here for me," I said, scratching my head. "At 6:30 a.m."

"We wanted to see you before you left," Faith said.

"I'm sorry I wasn't able to hang out before today," I said, squeezing her hands.

In between packing and running around Jakarta to buy the spices, snacks, and souvenirs that Mom wanted me to bring for her, I couldn't find time to see Faith and Grace. I only saw Kai once when he came over to help me pack my clothes.

"Oh girl, don't worry about it," Grace said. "You'll be back in no time."

Just as I was about to walk with them to a cafe, the airline announced that check-ins for my flight were about to close soon.

"Go," Grace said, looking at her watch. "You're going to be late."

"But you guys came all the way here, I—"

"Of course we did, babe," Kai said, planting a soft kiss on my forehead. "We wouldn't miss this for the world."

The four of us came in for a group hug. I snuggled into the warmth of my friends' company, leaning my head against Kai's shoulder. Even though I would only be gone for a month, the goodbyes felt slightly permanent. Perhaps, in that moment, I was also saying goodbye to a part of myself that would always remain in Jakarta.

"I'll see you guys soon," I said.

"Say hi to your mom!" Faith said.

"We'll miss you!" Grace said.

I waved goodbye to Kai, Faith, and Grace as I headed towards the check-in counter. The lady behind the desk taped and labeled the box full of Mom's things while I fidgeted with my fingers. I looked back one last time to my friends who were waiting outside the terminal, grateful that I had made such thoughtful friends in the short months while I was here.

But my walk towards the security gate was interrupted by a familiar voice.

"Cecilia!"

I jerked my head back, popping my AirPods back into their case.

Kai ran towards me like a puppy fetching a stick. I wondered how a man as perfect as he was could look so clumsy in a crowded room, filled with strangers and kids who looked with judgmental eyes.

For all he knew, someone could recognize him. But he didn't look like he cared.

With each step, Kai's leather necklace bounced on his collarbones. His shirt was unbuttoned way too low. His belt was way too loose. Yet, he scooped me up into his arms and kissed me in the middle of the airport. People stared, some whispered, but I leaned into him and firmly pressed my lips against his, my palm resting on his chest.

"Safe flight, babe," Kai said.

A tear rolled down my cheek. I loved this man. I loved him a lot.

"I'm so pathetic," I chuckled, rubbing the tears out of my eyes. "It's just a month. I'm literally going to see you after the new year."

"It'll fly by," Kai said. "Plus, you'll be with your mom and you'll have a good time. And you can always FaceTime me."

"I know. But I'll still miss you."

"I'm going to miss you, too," Kai said. "Go. Don't miss your flight because of me."

"Okay."

I pulled the handle on my carry-on and gave Kai another goodbye kiss.

"Text me when you arrive," Kai said.

"I will."

Kai walked me to the security checkpoint, waving as he disappeared behind the walls. Grinning to myself, I ran my thumb on the surface of my lips to savor Kai's kiss.

The airport terminal was quiet in the mornings. Duty-free shops were just opening to reveal red and green Christmas decorations, illuminated by the sun that meandered into the space through the ceiling-height windows. In Jakarta, December was sunny enough to not feel like Christmas.

I didn't have much time to browse through shops, so I boarded the plane instead. The plane was crowded but empty. Longing smelled like jasmine essence and musty towels. If I was finally going home, why wasn't I happy?

As I kicked my shoes off and tucked my legs into the seat, a text from Oma came in.

Nonik sayang, how was the surprise with your friends? Hope you had fun. Safe flight ya. Call me when you transit in Tokyo. Miss you dear…—07:16

I beamed. I couldn't believe Oma was in on the surprise too. No wonder she and Opa Robby didn't come with me to the airport.

I popped my AirPods in, texted Oma back, and enjoyed the music as the plane disembarked from the terminal and took off. The city's skyscrapers shrunk, looking toy-like, as we flew above the haze. I saw blue sky and clouds again. I was happy to see Mom and spend Christmas with her, but I missed Kai already. I missed Mbak Ani. I missed walking around my neighborhood, drinking with Faith, and shopping with Grace.

Leaving the city that made and broke me all at once made me feel nostalgic. I had never experienced so much uncertainty about different aspects of my identity until I came to this place. Jakarta taught me how to practice love and care, even when the demons caught up to me, creeping in slowly through cracks in my self-esteem.

But I knew beyond reasonable doubt that deciding to stay was the wisest decision I made. Jakarta was my destiny. It was my life. It was where I was meant to be.

I placed a hand on the window that separated me from my home. Dad loved Jakarta so much that he made me come back on his behalf. I wondered if the Jakarta I fell in love with was the same one that he did. I wondered how things would be different if he was still alive.

Amongst the clear sky, the musky airplane smell, and Lauv's beautiful voice, I leaned into my thoughts and slipped into a deep slumber.

+

Mom picked me up at the airport in Dad's jet-black BMW. She waited by the pick-up point with a hand full of balloons and a small bouquet of flowers.

"Mommy!" I cried, running towards her.

Mom looked a little different. She cut her hair inches shorter, now fashioning a blonde bob instead of her usual long, dark locks. Her dress was a lot brighter than the monochrome wardrobe she had after Dad's funeral.

"CeCe, darling!" Mom hugged me, pulling the veil of hair away from my face. "You look so much more grown up."

"I was only gone for six months, Mom."

"I know, but you're glowing, my dear."

I helped Mom stuff her box and my carry-on into the trunk and we drove off.

The Californian winter was chillier than I had remembered. Heat felt distant. I warmed myself up with the old car's faulty heater, longing for the Jakarta heat that I always complained about.

"So how was the trip?" Mom asked, fixing her eyes on the road. "You look a lot more pale than I expected you to be."

"I know," I chuckled. "I didn't get a lot of time outdoors in Jakarta."

"You must be hungry," Mom said. "Do you want to grab lunch?"

"Yes, please."

"Okay good, because I booked a table at the Cheesecake Factory near our house."

"No way," I squealed in joy. "You're the best, Mom. You know me so well."

We parked the car at the valet and walked towards the Cheesecake Factory, packed with people. It was a little strange seeing white people in a crowd when I was used to only seeing Asians for six months.

Mom told me to get seated first as she had to rush to the bathroom, so I used that extra time to browse through the menu. I ate very little for lunch to make space for their Oreo Cheesecake. I'd been craving it since I went to Jakarta, and I was ravenous. While drooling over their menu, I heard a familiar voice.

"Did you miss me?"

I turned around.

"Macy!" I gasped.

"Surprise, bitch," Macy said, coming in for a hug.

"Oh my gosh," I said, squeezing her in my arms. "What… what are you doing here? You told me that you're still wrapping up work in Seattle."

"I took the weekend off to come see you, silly! Your mom told me that you were coming back, so we arranged this little surprise for you. Did you really think that Karina was in the bathroom for this long?"

I paused. Macy's words didn't sit right with me.

Right. Macy won't know to call Mom Tante Karina.

I unlocked my phone. 3:10 p.m., which meant that Mom had been in the "bathroom" for ten minutes.

"You both are too much." I smiled.

"Don't worry," Macy said. "She's out shopping now. Apparently, there are amazing Christmas sales at Nordstrom or something."

We put our orders in, a slice each of Oreo and Fresh Strawberry Cheesecake. It felt like college again. Macy and I used to come to the Cheesecake Factory at The Grove almost twice a week. It was how we gained the Freshman 15, or rather the Freshman 25.

"So," Macy said, playing around with the ice cubes in her water glass. "Tell me about Indonesia. What's it like? How's the food? I imagine the *sate ayam* to be spectacular."

"My friend's mom is a celebrity chef," I said. "So I've been treated well."

"A celebrity chef?" Macy gasped. "That's insane."

"And the people are just...wow. I mean, I thought people at USC were talented and gorgeous, but Indonesian people are on a whole new level, Mace."

Macy took a bite of the Fresh Strawberry Cheesecake.

"How so?" Macy said.

"Literally all of my friends are rich, smart, beautiful, and so damn accomplished."

"No way," Macy said. "Those people exist? That's so unfair."

"I know, right?" I said.

I whipped out my phone and showed Macy a photo of Faith, Grace, and Kai from the yacht trip to the Thousand Islands.

"That's Faith," I said, pointing at her signature smile. "She's a UI/UX designer at Gojek, which is the equivalent of Uber here. And she's marrying into one of the richest families in Jakarta."

"Oh my god," Macy chuckled. "Well, with those looks, I don't think I'm surprised."

"Actually, she went to USC too. She's a year older."

"Wow," Macy said. "Who's that next to her?"

"This is Grace, Faith's best friend. This girl is such a go-getter. Her family owns the largest tobacco company and TV station in Indonesia, but she branched out and started her own company two years ago. She now owns and runs the best dog groomer in Jakarta called Oscar & Vinny's."

"Holy shit," Macy pointed at her black bikini. "Is she a model? Her body is stunning. Talk about a full package, brains and beauty."

"Exactly. It's probably why Faith's brother is after her."

"Scandalous," Macy cheekily grinned. "And who's this cute guy?"

My fingers lingered on Kai's face, feeling his kiss on my lips again. It had only been a little over twenty-four hours, but I missed him dearly.

"That's...my boyfriend."

"Your *what*?" Macy's jaw dropped. "Oh my gosh, CeCe! You leave for six months and come back with a hot boyfriend?"

I shoved Macy.

"His name is Kai," I said. "We worked together at Kopi Sedap. He's the Chief Tech Officer."

"You work with him?" Macy said. "That's so sexy."

"No," I said. "Not anymore."

Alicia from Alpha-Omega Capital had responded to my email while I was on the plane, offering me the general analyst position with a January start date. I had yet to reply back to her, but I was so excited to take the job.

"I just got an offer to work at an all-women venture capital firm."

"That's awesome," Macy said. "Wasn't that what you wanted to do since sophomore year?"

"Actually, it's better than what I wanted. I get to work with multiple startups now instead of just one."

"I'm so proud of you." Macy squeezed my hand.

I gobbled up the slice of Oreo Cheesecake. Macy talked about her time at Microsoft, telling me about a project that she had to work on, but it got too technical for me to understand.

"The team I work with in Seattle is extremely talented, but they're not the *best* looking, if you know what I mean," Macy rolled her eyes. "If I were you, I'd definitely feel so, I don't know, small and insignificant among them...cool kids."

I picked at my cuticles.

"Exactly," I chuckled. "And then you have me, ugly, stupid, and mediocre."

But Macy's face remained solemn. She clinked her fork on her plate, right next to her half-eaten cheesecake.

"CeCe," Macy said, shifting in her seat. "You are not ugly, stupid, or mediocre. No one has the balls to travel thousands of miles away to a family that used to hate you. Seriously. I even moved out of my apartment in Seattle just to stop my grandma from bothering me. And here you are, confidently moving all the way to a new country, a new job, to a place that may or may not accept you. Not many people would do that, let alone survive it. You're kick-ass, girl."

I took a sip from my water. I guess she was right. In hindsight, moving to Indonesia was a pretty gutsy move.

"Why are you looking at me like that?" Macy said. "It's true."

"Thank you, Macy."

"Maybe you think you're small because you're surrounded by the greats. But you forget that you're just as smart, kind, confident, and beautiful as all the people around you. I'm sure your boyfriend Kyle can attest to that."

"Kai," I giggled.

"What?"

"His name is Kai."

"Okay, whatever," Macy said. "You get the point."

"I do," I giggled again. "Thank you, Macy. It means a lot coming from you."

We chatted until the sun set and our cheesecake slices depleted into dirty plates. I was so used to Jakarta's day-long sunshine that I had almost forgotten that darkness dawned upon us at 4:00 p.m. in the winter. My body started to ache from all the travel, but I endured it for Macy.

Just as I was about to get up and use the bathroom, Mom walked in with multiple Christmas-themed shopping bags in her hands.

"Hi, girls," she said. "Did you have a good time?"

"Thanks for organizing this, Mom." I got up to hug her.

"Hi, Karina," Macy said, licking her fork clean. "You look like you had some eventful Christmas shopping."

"Indeed," Mom grinned. "Thank you, Macy, for coming all the way here to surprise my CeCe."

"Of course," Macy said. "It's the least I could do for my best friend."

I beamed, holding Macy's hand. The distance hadn't erased my friendship with Macy after all.

"Are you sure you don't want to stay with us?" Mom asked.

"Oh no, don't worry about it," Macy said. "One of my uncles just moved down here from Portland, so I'm staying with his family. And to pay my rent, I promised to fix him dinner right after sundown."

"You better not be late then," I said.

"I'll see you tomorrow, girl," Macy said. "I want to go to K-town with you again."

I embraced Macy in my arms, our bulging bellies rubbing against each other.

Mom let me drive the BMW home. Sitting behind the wheel was as nerve-wracking as one may imagine after not touching a car in six months. The freeway was dark, with the exception of the car's headlights and street lamps. Yet the city lights always seemed to safely guide us home.

I pulled into the driveway of our humble home, tucking Dad's car into the snug spot in our garage, and helped Mom get the bags out.

It feels good to be home.

"Finally," I sighed, dropping the car keys into the pot near our front door, just as I always did.

"I'm going to fix up a quick dinner," Mom said, dropping her shopping bags by the door. "Any special requests?"

I was stuffed to the brim with cheesecake, but I'd always make room for Mom's food.

"Anything's good."

I wiped my shoes on the welcome rug and slipped them off.

"You take your shoes off now?" Mom said, approaching me from behind.

"Oh," I giggled. "Oma made it a habit."

"It's nasty, huh? Bringing all that dirt and grime from outside into the house?"

"Yeah."

I placed my shoes right by the door and went to take a cold shower. There were a couple watts left to sustain my entire being since it was 2:00 a.m. in Jakarta, or two hours past my regular bedtime. Cold water splashed on my face. Yawning, I rubbed the cold into my eyes to jerk them awake.

Wrapping my hair in a towel, I waddled into the kitchen.

"Help me set the table, please, darling," Mom said as she sauteed pasta and garlic.

"Okay," I said.

I took the placemats and silverware and placed them carefully on the table. I arranged it the way Mbak Ani did. Forks on the left, spoons and a glass of water on the right. Mom placed the dishes on the table.

"I made your favorite today," Mom said. "Spaghetti marinara and grilled fish. You told me you were craving this in Jakarta, right?"

Guilt churned my stomach. After tasting Indonesian food, spaghetti marinara seemed so bland.

I only craved it because I missed you, Mom.

"Looks delicious," I said, smiling through my teeth. I hated lying to her.

I scooped up some pasta and dumped it on my plate. Mom's cooking couldn't compare to Bu Ratih's, but it would always be my favorite.

"CeCe," Mom said. "I wanted to ask you something."

"Yes?" I said.

"Did Oma talk about your dad at all?"

"She did."

"What did she say?"

I sighed. *So when you said that we hated James, that we never loved him*, Oma's voice replayed in my memory. *I felt like I lost him all over again.*

"She misses him," I said. "A lot. She said she's still crying everyday about it."

Mom chewed on her fish silently. She stared at anywhere but the plate of food in front of her.

"I miss your dad," Mom said. "I thought it would get easier after almost two years but changing the color of our bedroom walls didn't end up making much of a difference."

"Of course not," I smiled. "I still miss him every day. And I learned from Oma that the emptiness is never going to go away."

"Your dad would've been so proud of you. You've grown so much. You're becoming more and more like him."

I clenched my teeth. I glanced at the empty chair where Dad used to sit. I watched as his ghost dumped a spoonful of pasta on his plate and smiled at me before disappearing again.

"So how was Jakarta?" Mom said. "Have you started working for that new company you just joined?"

"I start in January," I said. "But I'm really excited for it."

"What happened to Kopi Sedap? Didn't you say that you liked it there?"

"A lot of things," I said. "Mainly because it was a really toxic environment for me. I wasn't respected there. The CEO constantly disregarded me and my work and made horribly destructive choices for the company. I had basically zero say and could only watch the company drown. It was so frustrating."

"Yeah, your dad used to complain about that a lot when he was working in Jakarta. That's partially why we moved here."

I pursed my lips, twirling the spaghetti on my fork. I wondered if I should tell her about Ray. He was out of my life for good. Telling her changed nothing about him. But not telling her meant that I had to pretend for the rest of my life.

Mom was the kindest soul in the world. But if I withheld the truth from her, she would treat me as if I was the same person as I was before the assault when I wasn't. She'd treat me like I was being my authentic self when in reality, I was hiding behind layers of pride like a coward.

"Is there something else, sweetie?" Mom asked. "You look a little distraught."

She looked at me with a glimmer of concern in her eyes, the same eyes she used whenever I grieved over Dad's loss, even when she didn't want to hear about it anymore. She endured the pain, so I didn't have to.

After all that Mom had been through in the past few years, the last thing she deserved was to be lied to.

"I..."

Mom put her fork down.

"I was sexually assaulted by my friend."

Mom gasped. Without a moment's hesitation, she rushed to my side and embraced me, letting me weep in her arms.

There's one thing about trauma that people don't tell you about. When you talk about it, when you think about it, the trauma eats you up again. From the bruises on my neck to the screeching strobe lights and my bleeding waist, the night replayed vividly in my mind. I folded into myself. I wasn't completely okay; I didn't think I would ever be, but the scars that tamed me could only make me stronger.

"Are you okay, darling?" Mom asked, stroking my forehead.

I held my neck and brought out all the confidence within me to croak out, "No, Mom, I'm not okay." What started off as glazed eyes turned into a torrential downpour of tears.

"It was so hard, Mom," I sobbed into her chest. "There's so much I haven't told you yet."

"I know, CeCe, I know," Mom said, patting my back like she would a baby's. "I understand."

Being in Mom's arms reminded me of all the pain I had endured in Jakarta. Oma's wrath. Christie's condescension. David's blatant disrespect. The support I neglected to ask for all the times I had felt so alone. Being in Indonesia was the first time I had seen the world as both broken and whole, all at once. Loving myself became difficult, especially when demons started to creep in slowly through cracks in my self-esteem.

"Cecilia," Mom said. "Do you know about *kintsugi*?"

I shook my head.

"It's a Japanese art form of mending broken pottery with gold lacquer."

I wiped my tears away with Mom's sleeve.

"There's beauty in the broken, Cecilia," Mom said, stroking my forehead. "Life isn't easy. Moving across the world isn't easy. It was never going to be. But you did it anyway. You are the gold that glued our family back together. You did something that even your dad couldn't. And I cannot be prouder of you, darling."

Eyes red and swollen, I looked up at Mom. I felt like I was looking in a mirror. All the scars from Oma Shaan and Opa Robby's cruelty, Dad's passing, and other aspects of her life sparkled like gold flecks on her skin.

"Thank you, Mom," I said.

After dinner, I helped Mom with the dishes and went back to my room. I sat on the window seat, which was decked out with blankets and pillows, just as I had left it in May. I ran my fingers against the pillows' fringes, remembering how distant but close Jakarta was to my memory.

I was broken and whole, all at once. And that was okay.

I opened the window, looking out into a pitch-black sky dotted with brilliant stars, dancing around the moon's silver glow. I never knew how much I'd miss the stars until

Jakarta hid them from me. Each star twinkled beside the other, reminding me that only together could they create stunning constellations.

In the middle of the cosmos, I saw Dad beaming from the heavens. The subtle Californian breeze brushed against my skin. In the silence, an earthly fragrance filled the air.

GALLERY

———

This is typical weekday traffic on Jalan Sudirman that Cecilia
was struck by when she arrived in Jakarta (Chapter 3).

Photo by Summertime Studios

This is Alto, the restaurant at the Four Seasons Hotel in Jakarta,
where Cecilia met Faith, Grace, and Mike (Chapter 7).

Photo by Summertime Studios

This is SCBD, the area where Cecilia works and lives (Chapter 8).

Photo by Summertime Studios

This is Jalan Senopati, the road that Cecilia passes by on her jog (Chapter 8).

Photo by Summertime Studios

This is Taste Paradise, the restaurant where Cecilia's family celebrated Opa's seventy-sixth birthday (Chapter 13).

Photo by Summertime Studios

This is Pison Coffee, where Christie told Faith and
Grace that Cecilia was a Wongso (Chapter 15).

Photo by Summertime Studios

This is La Vue Rooftop Bar at The Hermitage, where Cecilia and
Ray had drinks and admired Jakarta's skyline (Chapter 16).

Photo by Summertime Studios

This is a private yacht dock in Ancol, where Cecilia, Faith, Kai, and Grace alight on the Kusuma family yacht (Chapter 19).

Photo by Summertime Studios

This is Bakmi Orpa, the restaurant where Cecilia, Faith, Grace, and Kai spotted Oom Tommy Kurniawan with his mistress (Chapter 19).

Photo by Summertime Studios

This is Jalan Muara Baru, the road in North Jakarta that Cecilia
and Kai drive by on their way to their date (Chapter 20).

Photo by Summertime Studios

This is Bundaran HI, the monument that Cecilia admires
from the window of the Grand Hyatt hotel's Fountain
Lounge while talking to Oma Shaan (Chapter 26).

Photo by Summertime Studios

This is a *warung* in Jakarta. Cecilia visits one across her house (Chapter 27).

Photo by Summertime Studios

GLOSSARY

Adik (Dek): /ah-dik/ Little sibling.

Aduh: /ah-dooh/ An expression to show hurt, annoyance, disappointment, or curiosity.

Aiya: /ay-ya/ A speech expression, used to express dismay or surprise (Mandarin: 哎呀).

Anjing: /ahn-jing/ Directly translates to dog but is also used as a curse word.

Awas: /ah-wahs/ Watch out.

Babi guling: /bah-bee goo-ling/ Roast pork.

Bakmie (Mie): /bahk-mee/ Noodles.

Bapak (Pak): /bah-pahk/ Mister; an older gentleman.

Batik: /bah-tihk/ Traditional Indonesian textile art.

Betul: /buh-tool/ Correct.

Bicara: /bee-cha-ra/ Speak.

Bubur ayam: /boo-boor ah-yum/ Chicken porridge.

Bundaran HI: /boon-de-rahn ha ie/ The Hotel Indonesia (HI) Roundabout. Jakarta's monument located in the heart of the city.

Cengkeh Bunda: /cheng-keh boon-dah/ Name of a fake restaurant (Chapter 9) but translates to Mother's Cloves.

Coba: /cho-bah/ Try.

Changshan: /jang-shan/ Chinese traditional men's shirt, also called *changpao* (Mandarin: 长袍).

Cheongsam: /jong-sum/ Chinese traditional women's dress for women, also called *qipao* (Mandarin: 旗袍). Derived from Cantonese pronunciation.

Cucu: /chu-chu/ Grandchild.

Dua: /doo-wah/ Two.

Enak: /eh-nahk/ Delicious.

Es Cendol: /es chen-dol/ A Southeast Asian dessert with coconut milk, brown sugar, and rice flour jelly (*cendol*).

Es Podeng: /es poh-dng/ An Indonesian dessert with coconut milk, ice cream, bread pieces, chocolate sprinkles, and peanuts.

Es teh manis: /es teh mah-niss/ Sweet iced tea.

Feng shui: /feng shuay/ Chinese geomancy (Mandarin: 风水).

Plumeria: A white & yellow (sometimes pink & yellow) subtropical flower that grows on trees. They are also commonly known as frangipanis.

Gado-gado: /ga-doe ga-doe/ Indonesian salad with vegetables, boiled potatoes, tofu, *tempeh,* hard-boiled egg, and peanut sauce.

Gamelan: /ga-muh-lan/ Traditional Indonesian percussion instrument.

GBK: Gelora Bung Karno, a stadium in Senayan that also houses athletic facilities. Many go to GBK to exercise & walk or bike around its complex.

Gojek: An Indonesian ride-hailing and food delivery app.

Gulai ikan: /goo-lay ee-kahn/ Indonesian fish curry.

Ibu (Bu): /ee-boo/ Miss/Missus; Mom; an older woman.

Indomie: /in-do-mee/An Indonesian brand of instant noodles.

Iya (Ya): /ee-yah/ Yes.

Jaga image (jaim): /ja-ga image/ Guarding one's image to present in a certain way.

Jayus: /ja-yoos/ Someone who tries to be funny but fails to do so.

Jelek: /juh-leck/ Ugly; bad.

Jiejie (Jie): /chiye-chiye/ Older sister (Mandarin: 姐姐).

Kamu: /ka-moo/ You, used casually towards people you are close to or younger than you.

Kangkung belacan: /kahng-koong beh-lah-chan/ Water spinach (*kangkung*) with spicy, shrimp chili paste (*belacan*).

Kebaya: /kuh-bah-yah/ Traditional Indonesian formal outfit with batik.

Keluwak: /keh-loo-wak/ A Southeast Asian fruit that, once fermented, is harvested for its seed to use as a spice.

Kijang Innova (Kijang): /kee-jahng ee-noh-va/ A popular Toyota car model in Indonesia.

Koko (Ko): /ko-ko/ Older brother, derived from Hokkien (Mandarin: 哥哥).

Kopi Sedap: /ko-pee suh-dahp/ The company that Cecilia works for. Directly translates to "delicious coffee."

Kopiko: /ko-pee-ko/ An Indonesian brand of coffee candy.

Kue putu: /koo-ay poo-too/ Indonesian steamed cake.

Kurang ajar: /koo-rung ah-jar/ Extremely disrespectful or rude.

Lah: A speech expression used at the end of a sentence that emphasizes a myriad of emotions, depending on the tone in which it is spoken (Mandarin: 啦).

Lapar: /la-par/ Hungry.

Makco: /mak-choh/ Maternal great-grandmother, derived from Hokkien (Mandarin: 祖母).

Mangga: /mang-ga/ Mango.

Marie Regal: /ma-ree reh-gahl/ A local Indonesian brand of biscuits.

Masuk angin: /ma-sook ahng-in/ Indonesians believe that when wind (*angin*) enters (*masuk*) the body, people fall sick with cold-like symptoms.

Mbak: /ehm-bahk/ A way to address a woman in Indonesia.

Meimei: /may-may/ Little sister (Mandarin: 妹妹).

Mie babat: /mee bah-baht/ Noodles with beef tripes.

Mie goreng: /mee go-rang/ Fried noodles.

Nama: /na-ma/ Name.

Nasi tumpeng: /na-si toom-peng/ Indonesian yellow rice with vegetable and meat condiments.

Nastar: /nahs-tar/ Indonesian pineapple tart.

Nonik (Non): /no-nik/ Little girl, also could be used as a term of endearment.

Oma: /o-ma/ Grandmother.

Oom: /ohm/ Uncle; a way to address an older man, usually in parents' generation.

Opa: /o-pa/ Grandfather.

Pagi: /pah-gee/ Morning.

Pisang goreng: /pee-sahng go-rang/ Fried banana.

Putri: /poo-tree/ Princess or daughter; a common woman's name in Indonesia. Old Indonesian spelling changes the "u" to "oe."

Rawon: /rah-won/ Indonesian black beef soup.

Rendang: /rehn-dahng/ Curried Indonesian beef from West Sumatra.

Sambal: /sahm-bahl/ Indonesian chili sauce or paste.

Sate ayam: /sah-tay ah-yum/ Chicken skewers on a stick, charred over a flame. Usually served with peanut sauce.

Satu: /sa-too/ One.

Sayang: /sa-yahng/ A term of endearment; dear, darling.

SCBD: Sudirman Central Business District.

Sekali: /suh-kah-li/ Very; once.

Selamat jalan: /suh-la-maht ja-lahn/ Have a safe trip; goodbye.

Selamat siang: /suh-la-maht see-yahng/ Good afternoon.

Senopati: /suh-no-pa-tee/ A district in South Jakarta.

Siapa: /si-ya-pa/ Who.

Sop buntut: /sop boon-toot/ Oxtail soup.

Soto ayam: /so-toe ah-yum/ Indonesian yellow turmeric soup served with chicken, bean sprouts, vermicelli noodles, and boiled egg.

Suster (Sus): /soos-ter/ Nurse; also refers to a child's nanny.

Tante: /tahn-tuh/ Auntie; a way to address an older woman, usually in parents' generation.

Terima kasih: /te-ree-ma ka-see/ Thank you.

Tiga: /tee-ga/ Three.

Tempeh: /tehm-peh/ Indonesian fermented soybean.

Tukang parkir: /too-kahng par-keer/ Parking attendant.

Tukang: /too-kahng/ A blue-collared worker.

Udah: /oo-dah/ Already.

Warung: /wa-roong/ A small family-owned business or a modest street food stall.

Wayang: /wa-young/ Traditional Indonesian puppet.

Xiao: /siao/ Small, little (Mandarin: 小).

Xiaolongbao: /siao-lohng-bao/ Broth-filled pork dumplings (Mandarin: 小笼包).

Yi-yi: /ee-ee/ Auntie; a way to address mother's sister.

ACKNOWLEDGMENTS

───

When I was six, I wrote my first "book" on three stapled pieces of paper. Titled *The Three Superstars* (I know, how creative), the "book" told a tale of my dogs, Cleo, Archie, and Lammy, who tried to find their way home. To have a real novel in my hands in 2021, fourteen years later, is truly an unexplainable feeling. Creating *She Smells of Turmeric* during the COVID-19 pandemic was not an easy feat, but I am extremely humbled to have the people I did to hold my hand along the way.

Firstly, I would like to thank my parents, Peter & Evy Sondakh, who have loved me through my grammar mistakes and excessive book shopping sprees, as well as supported my writing journey throughout the past fourteen years. Thank you for allowing me to grow into the woman who can bring Cecilia's story to life.

A special thanks to Bagaskara Linanda, who helped me ground Cecilia's Jakarta in reality, drove me around Jakarta to document different parts of our home, and allowed me to vent my frustrations and joys about the book.

This book wouldn't be possible without my editors, Anne Kelley, Casey Mahalik, Stephanie McKibben, and Michelle Felich, who helped to meticulously create and shape Cecilia's journey. Thank you for reading and loving this story as much as I do.

I have a village and a half to thank for their generous contributions, support, and love for *She Smells of Turmeric*. I am eternally grateful to you to who have supported me through my writing and publishing journey.

Thank you to my interviewees, who shared their passions, lives, and opinions with me to aid in the creation of this book:

Annissa Ramadhanti	Jocelyn Leison
Beth Enterkin, LCPC	Nadya Soetedja
Eric Setiadi	Nathan Gunawan
Evy Sondakh	Peter Sondakh
Faye Simanjuntak	Sam Budiartho
Jeffrey A. Winters	Sarah Jade Hakim

Thank you to my beta readers, who volunteered their time to contribute their perspectives to early drafts of the book:

Aldwin Li	Gabriella Suman
Alexandra Sipahutar	Jocelyn Leison
Bagaskara Linanda	Joyce Lu
Catherine Chen	Nadya Soetedja
Dhiraj Narula	Sabrina Hartono
Elizabeth Kelly	Sarah Jade Hakim
Evy Sondakh	Susan Chenxuan Li

Thank you to my Indonesian friends and family, who looked over definitions and pronunciations in the glossary:

Angeline Lim	Jasmine Herawan
Arel Triyono	Jason Bharwani
Bagaskara Linanda	Madeleine Setiono
Denessa Bismarka	Moses H. Siregar
Eric Setiadi	Nadya Soetedja
Evy Sondakh	P. G. Otto Noordraven
Georg Gaidoschik	Sarah Jade Hakim

Thank you to the many friends and family who pre-ordered the book and followed along with my writing and publishing journey:

Abed Nego	Ananda Linanda
Abel Tan	Andrea Reyes
Alan Chao	Andrew Haryono
Aldwin Li	Andrew Moeljohartono
Alex He	Andrias Boga
Alexandra Chang	Anggara Linanda
Alexandra Sipahutar	Annabelle Utama
Alyssa Kangsadjaja	Annissa Ramadhanti
Amanda Tedjawinata	Arel Triyono
Amit Sharma	Aryan Jain

Ashley Grace Witarsa

Astri Melati Rahardja

Ay Tjhing Phan

Bagaskara Linanda

Benson Widjaja

Bryan Allen

Catherine Chen

Chloe Rekso

Chng Huan Qi

Christopher Andersen
Muliadi

Christina Nursalim

Clara Brigitta

Clara Linanda

Claudia Sondakh

Coonoor Kripalani-Thadani

Damordaran Gopaulen

Daniel Sim Kuan Yi

Denessa Bismarka

Dhiraj Narula

Eileen Yap

Elizabeth Sirapandji

Elya Samsuddin

Eric Koester

Eric Setiadi

Evy Sondakh

Fi Fang Lim

Fredric Lie

Gabriella Gwen

Gabriella Suman

Georg Gaidoschik

Gianna Chan

Grace Lau

Grace Teeple

Gratia Anadena

Hana Ananda

Hans Koes

Hubert Leo

Indah Gunawan

Irene Otthay

Iris Lin

Isaac Winoto

Ishaan Narain

Iwan Lee

Ja Hyun Koo

Jap Johanes

Jasmine Herawan

Jason Bharwani

Jason Hambali

Jeffrey Jahja

Jen Kit Ker

Jeni Thanos

Jeremy Angsono

Jerry Zhang

Jessica H. Tan

Jiakai Chang

Joanna Tasmin

Joceleen Hardjadinata

Jocelyn Leison

John Harkin

Jonathan Hanitio

Jonathan Moeljohartono

Jonathan Tejakusuma

Joseph Ian Tanuri

Josephine Sitorus

Joshua Bloom

Joyce Giboom Park

Joyce Lu

Juanda Lee

Justin Pejman

Karen Winoto

Karthik Vempati

Katherine Wardhana

Kenneth Setiadi

Keyla Athalia

Kristian Andre Budiman

Larry Lim

Leah Broger

Lilian Setiawati Prasetio

Liliek Moeljohartono

Marcelo Hilário De Santana

Marcolius Angjaya

Matthew Ong

Matthew Thomas Ong

Melanie Deshayes

Merry Mulyati

Michael Kosasih

Michael Lukito

Michelle Burlock

Mieke Kolonas

Mindy Douthit

Nadia Tendian

Nadya Soetedja

Nathan Gunawan

Nicholas Taniadi

Nicholas Tjandra

Nicole Hong

Olivia Catherina

Olivier Gabison

Parama Suteja

Patrice Haryanto

Patricia Tang

Patrick Mandiraatmadja

Patrick Pynadath

Peter Sondakh

Ploenta Voraprukpisut

Rachel Darmawangsa

Rachel Tanuwidjaja

Raina Mak

Rany Fetrix

Renata Halim

Rizal Gozali

Rizki Indra Kusuma

Rongzhen Zhou

Rudy Suhendra

Ryan Jusuf

Sabrina Hartono

Sam Budiartho

Santhi Budiartho

Sarah Jade Hakim

Sarah Yoon

Serap Kaya

Serena William

Shania Tanuwidjaja

Shirley Tan

Si An Tan

Stefan Tomov

Ted C. Fishman

Tiffany Priscilla

Timothy Lin

Trung The Ha

Valerie Fong

Valerie Setiawan

Verinder Syal

Xena Danella

Yvonne G. Van der Kloor

Yvonne Yuen

My final thanks goes to New Degree Press, especially Eric Koester, Brian Bies, Zoran Maksimovic, Liana Moisescu, and Matt Phillips, for helping me turn a pipe dream into a physical book.

APPENDIX

Epigraph
Ephesians 2:7 (The Passion Translation) is a sermon on God's kindness.

Foreword

Statistik Indonesia. *Badan Pusat Statistik*. Jakarta, Indonesia: Badan Pusat
Statistik, 2020.
https://www.bps.go.id/publication/2020/04/29/e9011b3155d45d70823c141f/statistik-
indonesia-2020.html.

Na'im, Akhsan, and Hendry Syaputra. *Kewarganegaraan, Suku Bangsa, Agama,
Dan Bahasa Sehari-Hari Penduduk Indonesia: Hasil Sensus Penduduk 2010*. Edited
by Sumarwanto and Tono Iriantono. *Badan Pusat Statistik*. Jakarta, Indonesia:
Badan Pusat Statistik, 2010.
https://www.bps.go.id/publication/2012/05/23/55eca38b7fe0830834605b35/
kewarganegaraan-suku-bangsa-agama-dan-bahasa-sehari-hari-penduduk-
indonesia.html.

Setiawan, Hayyan. "Keanekaragaman Hewan Berdasarkan Jenisnya Di
Indonesia." *Ilmu Hutan* (blog).
http://ilmuhutan.com/keanekaragaman-hewan-berdasarkan-jenisnya-di-indonesia/.

ABOUT THE AUTHOR

—

Natasha Sondakh is an award-winning Indonesian writer whose works have been published in literary magazines, as well as recognized by the University of Iowa, Columbia University, and the Alliance for Young Artists & Writers. Her poem *Lantern* was displayed at the Art.Write.Now exhibition in New York City.

Natasha has served on editorial boards of various publications, in addition to being featured on TEDxJIS and Nine Lives Podcast for her work in translating Indonesian short fiction. When she isn't writing, you can find Natasha exploring local shops and restaurants with her friends. Otherwise, she will likely be on her couch, surfing shows on Netflix with her dogs Ollie, Harvey, and Hoshi.

For more information, you can find Natasha on her website at www.tashasondakh.com and on Instagram @natasha.sondakh.

Made in the USA
Las Vegas, NV
30 April 2021